Eternus

Kimberli Reynolds

Borderline Publishing LLC
406 S 3rd Street
Boise, ID 83702
www.borderlinepublishing.com

Library of Congress Number: 2001012345

ISBN 978-1936408481 (Paperback)
ISBN 978-1936408627 (eBook)

I. Title
2012
This novel is a work of fiction. Any resemblance to real people,
events, establishments, organizations or locales is coincidental.
Names, characters and incidents are the product of the author's
imagination.

Printed in the United States of America on post-consumer recycled paper

To my children, from whom my inspiration for the characters derived, I love you deeply.

To my husband, for believing in me and supporting me in all my crazy endeavors.

For my sisters, both blood and kindred, I am so blessed to be surrounded with greatness and love!

My adoring parents and those that have been my mentors and mentees, I have learned great lessons that I hope to pass on to my readers, I thank you all and cherish every chance I get to be in your shadow to learn.

Humbled before you I go, it is not myself that is great, it is all of you through me that makes it so.

...unknown

1

New Beginning

Curiosity got the best of me. Curiosity is usually to blame for most of my dilemmas. Staying put would mean another round of orders from my mom, but taking a hike in the beautiful mountains down the road would give me some freedom. I had to hurry before my parents woke up. I didn't have a cell phone, so they would have to wait until I returned to yell at me for leaving. "Best to ask for forgiveness than permission," my grandfather would joke as he stole cookies for me from the cookie jar as a kid. I knew this situation remained different than the cookie robbery.

I walked from our new house in the country down the almost deserted dirt road and stood mesmerized by the towering mass in front of me.

I, of course, looked at the mountain and the tree line as a whole at that moment. Not taking into account all the creatures I might encounter nor the haphazard walking conditions I would face. The day appeared so lovely—the orange-red glow reflecting on the top of the mountain signaled the sun rising behind me. The mountains surrounding me were breathtaking as they began to wake beneath the veil of deep green shadows. Stillness enveloped me. I could feel the crisp mountain air, untainted by the city, and the warmth of the sun stirring the cool morning shadows that bathed the valley. It promised to be a great morning to hike.

I glanced over my shoulder. Our house stood on a small, rolling hill down the road I had just walked. The stream bed cut into the ground and ran silently away from the house toward the bridge.

I looked down at my feet, aware that I had on my old pair of sneakers and not hiking boots. I stood at the intersection of my road and the one that paralleled the base of the mountain in front of me. No trails were discernable along the hillside from this distance. Determined to make a go of it anyway, I crossed the road and started to cut across the field of waist high grasses that swayed in the slight breeze.

Although most of the land behind me had crops or cows, the areas along the base of the mountain were untamed. It marked the transition from my real, unsettled world to what I imagined to be a tranquil oasis.

I watched and listened carefully as my pants brushed the grass with each step. Rattlesnake country. I had never seen a rattlesnake, but I had heard when you hear the sound of the rattle, you instinctively know. I spread my hands wide, enjoying the feel of the grass brushing softly on the palms of my hands as I walked.

My shoes squished into the damp soil.

I looked up and headed toward the base of the trees. The pines were a deep green and smelled fresh. I noticed rocks with yellow moss, dead fall, old pine cones, pine needles, and plants littering the ground everywhere in the undercover of the trees. I picked a path carefully as I entered the woods.

I climbed up through the thicket until I saw the thick grassy meadow below. I paused to listen. I could hear my breath and feel my heart pumping from the slight climb. Alive and alone, just what I wanted.

The shadow of the trees made goose bumps form on my arms, but my body warmed from the scant incline of the hill. The breeze stilled. I took a deep breath of the fresh air and enjoyed the coolness plunging into my lungs.

A faint smile played across my lips. Peace.

I scanned the area. Birds chirped and fluttered about their morning routine. Bugs crawled across the rocks and on the leaves of plants, the smell of pine, thick in the air. This felt like home more than the new house. Back along the ocean there were forests, although much thicker vegetation covered the ground due to the amazing amount of rainfall the Oregon coast received. A dull ache spread through me. At least I could steal myself back to that place when I needed to by coming here.

I spied an indentation in the ground floor above me. It seemed to run at an upward angle along the hillside. I climbed the last ten paces. I scanned the game trail heading up or down, depending on which way the deer, elk, coyote, mountain lion, or whatever else lived in these forests were going. I wanted to follow it up. The real world needed to wait until I felt ready to return. The trail ran upward until it crested a ridge, where the mountain gave way to a small recess, thick with underbrush. On the other side of the brush, the mountain rose again. This is where the trails split. The upper, steeper section ran up toward a rocky outcrop big enough to sit on.

My feet didn't skip a beat.

The rock loomed bigger than it appeared. When I rounded the top, I noticed cracks that had been created over time, from rain-water freezing and thawing, acting like a chisel. The yellow moss ran in lines around the rock. I looked around and noticed another set of rocks even higher up the mountain. They were the same light and dark grey speckled color. The peak jutted clear of the tree tops. I imagined a spectacular view from there and decided to conquer the precipice. It took half an hour before I crested the rocks and climbed to the top.

Blood pounded through me, the sensation rhythmic in my throat. I inhaled the crisp morning air in fast unison with the beat of my heart. When I reached the top of the mountain all of my efforts paid off. I picked a place to rest, awed over the expanse of beauty before me.

The valley spread out in yellows and greens. It appeared obvious that the land here had rich soil. On the right side of the valley, a thick tree line rimmed the northern shoreline of the long reservoir. To the left, the mountains clung to the edge of the valley and seemed never to end, disappearing out of sight. Straight ahead I could see the fields, the road, and my house. Beyond the house were more trees, roads, and fields. Houses dotted the land here and there. Beyond all of that, another huge mountain loomed. The sun's rays draped it all like a warm, orange blanket. White, soft clouds layered themselves around the mountain in sheets.

I could feel the breeze on my skin now that I had broken free from the shelter of the trees.

I closed my eyes. I let my hair wisp in the air and tickle my cheek.

I knew I had found the peace I was looking for. We had been here only a few short days, but moving from a town that had more people, it would be hard to get used to. I missed my few friends that I had collected over the years. Although not overwhelmingly popular, I had a few close ones. I tried not to draw attention to myself. I never dated a boyfriend. I only acquired friends that were boys—some that I had secret crushes on remained secret. I liked my studies though—learning clicked for me in high school. I seemed to be one of the few students that actually tried to get good grades. I opened my eyes again, wondering if this place even had a school. I scanned past our new house and over to the left. There seemed to be a very small collection of businesses close to the highway on the other side of the valley. Donnelly, our new home town, I couldn't see a building large enough to be a school.

A few months ago, I had been at school when the emergency call arrived. They had pulled me from my class to explain that Dad had been in a serious accident, and I needed to go to the hospital. Dad suffered severe internal injuries in the roll over. The doctors felt it necessary to ask for the hospital chaplain to sit with us. Nerve-racking. I cannot remember a time I felt so helpless. Wait and see, hope and pray, and rip your heart out were all motions of the day. When he pulled through we cried and laughed. Then came the troubling recovery. Confined to a hospital bed in the house, after his one month visit in the hospital, Mom and I doted on him. His job, forced to relieve him of his position, prompted Mom to find a better job, and that job led us here. I believe it is called... nowhere. Nothing normal could exist here.

It has been said that beginnings are scary, endings are sad, and it's what lies in the middle that counts. I could not discover the happy story in the middle of ending everything where we came from and the scary beginnings in Po-dunk-la-la-land.

I stood up and absorbed the view for a few more minutes. As I walked off the rocks, I affirmed in my mind the reason for my walk this morning. I don't mind a little change, but all of it came at an overwhelming speed and I needed to get away.

I hadn't really had much time to take it all in—although more thankful than words could say that my dad's health improved. I think the stress of the move, Dad's health, and Mom's new job, had her wound up like a top. My calm and collected mom, she starts her new work next week and she's acting nervous—pacing and ringing her hands. Even though I understood, she was getting on my nerves. Orders were being thrown at me left and right, hence my need for seclusion today. To make matters worse, since pulling in the driveway, I hadn't seen a single person. Mom, of course, went to the small "town

store-slash-gas station" for some limited variety food. That
proved there must be people around here that needed food, but
I had hardly seen a car pass by.

The rock seemed easier to climb down. I noticed an area
above me covered in pine needles that would allow me to
continue my walk up to the top of the mountain.

I walked with my head down, watching my step.
Occasionally my footing would slip on pine needles and I'd
catch myself. I decided to not push my speed, as no one knew
my whereabouts, and I didn't want to be 'found' later with a
broken leg, starving to death. But, that sounds like something I
would do. Grace is not my middle name. I abhor drawing
attention. I figure my ability to wreak havoc upon myself at
my expense is a curse intended to draw attention from the rest
of the world. Who said God doesn't have a sense of humor?

Ground squirrels crossed my path and ran to hide. Birds
continued their songs as I climbed higher. I don't know how
long it took. The sun peeked overhead as I reached a ridge half
way up the mountain.

Thirsty! My tongue had gone dry from the exertion. I
hadn't thought to pack a drink. Not good! I'm usually
prepared.

The sun beat down now. I noticed a clearing ahead with a
small, sloping meadow. I walked forward to the shade of a tree
along the edge.

I tied my maroon hoodie sweater around my waist, taking
it off felt liberating and helped to stop the nagging thirst a
little. My pale purple tee shirt made of thin material seemed
refreshing.

As I walked to the edge of the meadow, I saw a deer and
her fawn, heads down, tails flicking in the air, seeming to enjoy
the sun and the freedom. I had to agree with them.

They were downhill from me, on the other side of the
meadow. I slowly sat down on a bed of pine needles to watch
them.

Movement swift and fierce exploded from the trees right next to the doe. The fawn jumped to the side, avoiding the blur. In an instant, the doe hit the ground in one fluid movement, with something large attached to her throat. I struggled to see details. My mind reeled for certainty. An image of my own human vulnerability flashed before me. The thing appeared deadly, something I would never survive. What had I seen? Light brown fur obstructed my view of it. As the two thrashed on the ground, the fawn bleated in confusion. It could hear squeaking sounds coming from its mom's throat. The deer lay kicking and struggling. Finally, as the strength drained from the victim, the fawn fled into the forest.

In that moment, I realized only I and whatever clung to the neck of the now deceased deer, remained at the meadow. It had happened so quickly I had forgotten to breathe. My body lit up with a fire that tried to make me run. My brain, trying to help me understand, willed me to move.

I gasped as I gulped in, starved for air. Too loud. The being's keen ears heard. The head jolted above the body of the deer. Fear washed over me. It seemed to have human features, but menacing overall with blood smeared across its strong jaw. The man in the meadow straightened. He stood slowly, seeming to grow in front of me. Eyes closed, he took a deep, long breath. A smile formed across his lips. He opened his eyes, and they bore into me through the shadows.

His dark hair, his tan skin, he stood shirtless, muscles etched on his form, dripping in small amounts of blood. He almost floated, like his feet never found a dip or uneven footing. He stepped around the deer with grace. His eyes, never faltering or blinking, he walked slowly toward me.

I rose to my feet, my hand steadying me on a tree. Wrong place at the wrong time. *Why me?*

My heart stopped. I couldn't see color in the eyes. They were white.

I willed my left foot to step to the side, from where I had come. My movement appeared to stop his advance. His hand motioned quickly to me, although a blur, it seemed to ask me to wait. I didn't acquiesce to see what the hand motion meant. I ran. I ran hard, my fear completely consuming every attempt at rational thought. My ears burned. My heart pounded. My footing fell uneven upon the ground. I knew I had to proceed to the left of the hill and then drop straight down to find the game trail from earlier. Coronary thumping grew so loud in my ears that I could not hear what followed me. It kept a beat to my own rendition of a requiem that I hoped would not be my own. I suspected at any second a pain would shoot through me as I hit the ground, something large and fatal ripping at me.

Tears streamed down my face in pure terror, cool against my hot skin. They blurred my vision making it difficult to pick a smooth path. The effort required to keep myself upright, infuriating. I had to fly. A large thicket lay ahead, directly in my path. Below it to the right, I saw an area clear of rocks and plants but covered in pine needles. It led straight downhill to a flat, slight plateau that would allow me to run to the left again. I didn't think, I just charged for it. My footing slipped on the needles and I slid down the side of the hill on the heels of my feet and my hands. As soon as I hit the bottom, I jumped up and began running again, pine needles sticking out of my palms.

Dying to take a breath, to fill my lungs, a burning started in my chest. My body expended too much of my air. I became afraid I would faint as trees blurred and the ground swayed beneath me. I collapsed into a ball as the inferno engulfed my upper body. I trembled as I gulped the fresh air. Nothing had reached me yet.

I stood, legs wobbling. I looked around. The thicket behind me shielded anything that might be tracking me.

Soft laughter caught my ear, followed by growling, deep and foreboding. It reached me from across the mountain. I gasped and turned in the direction of the sound. It seemed distant, it had just started its pursuit. The hair on my neck began to stand on end. With new found strength, I forced my legs to move. I ignored their burning and willed them into speed. I knew the chase had just begun.

I had a head start, although I didn't know how. That male thing must have desired a game of cat and mouse.

My heart lodged in my throat, and moans escaped my lips as I exerted overpowering force. I knew blood still flowed in my veins. Death had a fight on its hands.

My feet were flying downhill with no idea where they were going to land. As I slipped and stumbled, I prayed they would not betray me. My body screamed at the pain in my lungs, but I paid no attention. I believed the creature pursuing me able to deal torturous agony beyond anything my body could muster. In that conclusion, I resolved myself to push until I died.

It had taken all day to climb that mountain, but coming down like this had to be much faster. I just had to make it. I needed to be free, flowing as a current, rushing to the bottom, unabated by trivial twigs and pebbles. I saw the path just ahead. I anticipated teeth in my back at any moment. I could almost feel the air charged around me, as though lightening might strike. The air hung thick like mud, still and weighted. My right foot landed on a thin stick, snapping it. The weight of my body pushed my foot down under a root, locking it in place, as my body continued moving. Although my foot dislodged itself as I tumbled, I could not correct myself. I hit hard, landing on my arm and hip. The wind completely evacuated my lungs. Powerful burning grew in the middle of my chest and spread outward like wisps of heavy mist until my entire body hurt. Helpless, I rolled to my back longing for release from the ache and for my lungs to fill. I looked around as greens, browns, and yellows blurred around me.

When I landed, my hip hit a rock and my head hit the ground, adding to my discomfort. I could see my feet up hill from my torso. I noticed the cool, grainy dirt under my arm extended on the path. My body missed the flat ground there, haphazardly resting on fallen branches, pine needles and rocks. Paralyzed and dormant I lay. The burning in my lungs like a million knives. My breath hard to find, my mind grew fuzzy from the lack of air.

I felt like a tiny mouse, nestled in a layer of vegetation. I needed to stay coherent, but felt the edge of darkness closing in. I believed the predator had closed the distance by now. I had laid there too long.

Movement to my left. I wanted to scream, but my lungs seemed broken.

White. So white, staring down at me. Blood, dripping from his mouth, he smiled. He held a curious look in his eyes, tilting his head back and forth. Crouching... peering down from above me... fading... blackness...

I'm not sure how long I had lain there. I was not even aware of my surroundings. As the cold from the ground and the pain in my body seeped into my brain, realization followed. Horror. I forced my eyes open. My head throbbed, pulsing with every beat. My hand involuntarily went to my head. No blood. My hands were scraped and aching. I noticed the whole mountain in shadow and my skin grew chilly. Most of the day must have slipped by, but I appeared to be alive.

I looked around. Nothing.

Maybe I had dreamed it. I tried to sit up. My back hurt. I forgot about that. I imagined my body covered in nasty bruises. I pushed myself to sit upright. From somewhere deep inside, the pain, the anxiety, and the fear surfaced. It flooded into my thoughts and I had to fight tears. How could I have survived?

I stumbled to my feet. Sure enough, my right ankle hurt to put weight on. I glanced at where I thought the person had been looking down at me. Although my vision remained blurry, my body chilled when I tried to recall what he had looked like. I gazed up the hillside. My feet had cut a path down through the pine needles as I'd slid. Other than that, there were no noticeable indentations or scrape marks to prove my visitor had followed me.

I shuddered.

Glancing at a long stick on the ground, I used it to raise myself. It would be the perfect size for a walking stick.

I picked my way down the trail. No birds sang. I willed myself to believe it had to be the sun disappearing for the day. To entertain the thought of the creature watching me from somewhere close, causing the birds to be silent, would mean my last nerve and what remained of my level head would disintegrate. Feeling as banged up as I did, another fall might leave me on the forest floor for the night.

I chose not to think about it. I just kept on the path and tried to go faster. I counted my steps. As the edge of the forest came into view below me, I estimated how many steps until I broke free from the darkening shadows.

As I neared the bottom, I wanted to run from the hill to safety. The knowledge that my back faced whatever lurked in the forest sent chills down my spine.

I found the road, a little farther from the tree line than where I had entered. I started to walk back toward the intersection of the dirt road that would lead me to my house. I kept a vigilant eye on the forest to my right. My senses piqued, making it hard for me to relax, my breath punctuated and unsteady. I had to get home. My parents must be worried. I hadn't told them I planned to hike nor how long I would be gone. I heard every noise above the sound of my shoes on the pebbles.

Nothing sounded out of place, and yet everything did.

By the time I could see the road where I needed to turn, dark shadows arose to reach me from the mountain as the sun began its rapid decent. I wanted desperately to get home before it completely disappeared. My thirst did not bother me as it had. My muscles shivered in the chilly air.

Dark enveloped me by the time I made the turn off to my house. The last of my reserves were fraying away. I knew safety was within reach. If I needed to scream for protection now, someone would hear me.

I could see the yard light on at the house as I approached. An overwhelming desire to cry welled in my throat. I choked the tears of relief back. A county squad car sat in the drive way. As I rounded the last curve to the top of the dirt driveway, I saw my mom at the door, walking out behind an officer who still had his note pad in hand.

"Ok, if that's all the information you have, then I will make sure everyone is aware." The officer nodded to Mom. "I'll call it in right now."

As he turned to walk away, they both spied me walking from the shadows.

My mom yelled and ran toward me. The officer followed. Dad ambled from the house soon after.

Mom wrapped me in her strong embrace and cried in my hair. "Are you okay? Where have you been? I've been terrified!"

She kissed my forehead and then looked into my eyes. Dad grabbed me, too, and hugged me tight.

The officer asked me the same questions. Mom would not let me get much out except, "Yeah, Mom, I'm okay."

She gushed all of her anxiety over the commotion of the day, how she had come into my room to wake me and I had already gone. As the time stretched on, she'd thought the worst.

She continued on and I thought my head would explode. I reached for my temples, and the officer noticed the wooden stick I dropped as I reached up.

Dad cut in. "Sharlene, I think we should get Rhiannon inside the house. She looks like she needs to sit."

"Oh, yes. I am sorry, dear! Please forgive me, what did you do to yourself? Look at your clothes honey! Dried mud, you tore your pants. Honey, are you okay?"

"Ma'am," the officer said, "I'm not going to radio this into dispatch. But I would like to ask a few questions."

"Of course, thank you!" Mom walked me to the house. She kept thankfully silent.

She settled me at the dinner table, I groaned as I sat. The pain in my hip made the chair as uncomfortable as a jagged rock.

"Do you need anything?" Mom referred to my obvious discomfort.

"Can I please have some water? And maybe some food?" The shaking in my hands told me I needed some form of sustenance, although my appetite seemed suppressed by the event on the hill.

She went into the kitchen and started rummaging around in the cupboards before bringing me a glass of water and some pain reliever. I shared the more mundane aspects of my walk with the officer and my dad. I didn't go into details. I imagined the looks on their faces as I told them about a poacher that didn't have weapons, just teeth that he used to kill deer. I imagined how much they would believe me. It actually sounded lunatic to me as I thought about it.

It seemed like an innocent walk turned into a typical Rhiannon 'oops' story. Dad and Mom were used to those.

Mom brought me a warmed up plate of spaghetti. The red lumpy sauce made me stare. An image of the deer and the beast-man drenched in blood emerged from the frayed fabric of my mind. I pushed the food away and gazed out the window, drained. Pitch black, not even a moon to light the meadow and field. I could just barely see the silhouetted outline of the few trees that grew in the yard.

I imagined the water flowing in the creek below the house to the left of the meadow. It must have been a powerful stream

13

at one time. It had dug a c-curve into the hill where the house sits, causing the back yard to drop 50 feet right out from the back of the patio.

I thought about the events and wondered if I should tell the officer. If someone else happened to run into the thing in the woods and something happened, I would feel responsible.

I stammered, "I just wanted to say..." then my voice faltered as I gained the attention of the officer and Dad whom had been discussing things.

"What is it?" the officer quizzed, as he turned his full attention to me.

My mouth opened and a small noise, of no consequence, emitted itself—only to be forgotten as the words "it was a man with teeth that ripped a doe's neck out" trapped themselves in my brain, saved from being spoken.

Instead, "I twisted my ankle" flew from my lips. *Great, what a coward.* The officer nodded at me and continued talking with Dad. I put my face in my hands.

The officer talked for a moment longer before he told me to be sure to tell my parents before I hiked next time, then he stood and Dad escorted him out the front door.

Mom was beside herself with concern that I hadn't eaten. I excused myself from eating due to an upset stomach.

Dad kept checking on me throughout the evening, no matter what.

I finally decided to go to bed. I felt tired from the hike, in spite of the nap I had unwittingly taken on the hill.

Thankfully, the painkiller helped me to sleep until morning.

I didn't feel like going to the store the next day. Terrible images kept playing over in my head. But I had to agree, I needed to get out. The aches in my body caused limited movements, so I shifted about like a grandma. My ankle wobbled loosely, but the pain didn't hinder me. I figured a little walking would be good for it.

Mom and I drove the dirt road in our old red car. It smelled of dirt and stale air, making me want to spray air freshener in it. But nothing ever seemed to help, except time to allow the annoying scent to numb my nose, so that I would no longer notice.

I wished time would hurry and do the same in my soul. I needed it numb. I didn't want to put together and make sense of the horrific images of yesterday. I would then have to deal with them. I started to believe I imagined the entire thing.

We lived about three country miles from the gas station. It had very limited options as far as food. If we needed to stock up on real food and have any variety, we would need to drive into the nearest town, McCall, situated fifteen miles north on the highway. We only needed milk and eggs today to bake some cookies. Still anxious over my well-being, my mom wanted to pamper some life into me.

Mom and I chatted about the new town and the farming community and Dad. We both agreed his recovery seemed rapid.

Rounding the final corner before the gas station I could see cars parked in the lot—several more sat at the gas pumps. I imagined most were tourists passing through on the highway needing to gas up on their way to the bigger city two hours south of here.

The store, a log cabin design made from dark, thick timbers, sat at the intersection of the only highway and the main road to the reservoir. It even had an old sort of horse post resembling ones seen in old western movies, although I could not entertain the idea of seeing a real horse tied to one of the posts. I believed the intent was to stop cars from ramming the front patio of the store, also made of wood. Teenage boys had arranged themselves atop the poles to the left of the front door.

My mom pushed through the door and held it for me. I walked through. A group of teenagers and kids stood at the checkout counter, giving the cashier a hard time. The one closest to me didn't pay attention to the others. He faced me with his head down, staring at nothing on the floor. He was a little taller than I, with light blonde hair brushed toward his face, styled in a way that separated chunks of hair, making it look sculpted.

I followed the path my mother had taken down the aisle to his right. As I moved closer to him, he looked up. Our eyes met.

His expression became tense. A shock had instantly jolted through him. He held my gaze. I could not tear my eyes away. I had never seen color so blue before. Like an ocean in the summer, churning with a wild, crashing tide against the rocks. In that brief instant, I recognized passion and pain between us, deep inside me. I shook my head in confusion over the uncontrollable emotions I felt.

I had to pass close to him as the aisles were small. A hot breeze blew through the closing door behind me mixing with cold air inside, further adding to the shock my body felt. I turned my body to enable me to slide past him in the small walkway. Our arms touched in passing. An accidental bump that I normally would have politely apologized for, shot a surge of electricity through my arm. I grabbed it, my eyes widened with the shock, the static sensation lingering. He closed his eyes, seemingly reacting to the feeling as much as I had. I staggered to the back of the store, heart fluttering, my face felt hot. I knew it must have grown red.

An intense fragrance had imprinted itself on my memory. Woodsy, with a hint of lavender—he smelled clean and expensive. More than the smell, something undefined lingered in my soul. I felt strangely calmer than I had ever been in my life. What had just transpired? I had no idea what had happened or how, though my body reacted. His eyes held so much in them, I felt I should know them. How odd that I would know those eyes, yet I swore to myself that I had seen them before—somewhere. His scent was peace. His eyes were comfort.

I shuddered as my mom opened the door to the cooler. She reached for the milk and asked if I felt cold.

Her question didn't register. I chanced a look back up the aisle at the counter. His gaze still intense, face tilted toward the floor, he looked at his open palms. His body reminded me of an athlete, strong and carved. I could see the muscles bulging under his tee shirt. He seemed apprehensive, lips pursed, sucking in a breath though his nose, his chest expanding, then he let out his breath slowly. I equated it to someone trying to regain composure after an uncomfortable incident.

The rowdy teens and kids behind him messed around and pushed each other. The clerk laughed with one of the females. His lips parted and said something. He slowly looked up at me, hands still in front of him. His eyes wide, he peered at me. Everything slowed down. Everyone seemed to move in slow motion. I could only hear my own breathing. One of the girls from the group pushed around him to get to the door, seeming not to notice him.

As the door opened again, his hair fluttered, but his eyes did not move from mine.

He mouthed something, seemingly to me, and then he walked out. The liaison between us cut short, and noise filtered back in.

Mom turned around to ask me again if I felt cold.

Shaking my head a little, I said, "No? Oh, no. I am not. I'm ok." I think.

My head felt dizzy. My heart pounded. Bumps rose on my arms and shivered down my back and legs. What on earth had just happened?

I stepped back so my view of the door became unobstructed. I could see all of the teenagers jumping into the back of two trucks we parked next to.

Blue-eyes that I had just spent time staring at stopped by the door of our car—on the side I sat—and surreptitiously touched the door handle. I shook my head, trying to understand. I stepped toward the door. Abruptly, letting me know I had been discovered, a taller, thinner, darker-complexioned male stepped in front of the door. His darkness contrasted starkly with his white shirt. His arms crossed, and his face expressed unpleasantness. His eyes burned into me, dark, maybe even black. I stared at him. I knew him. His eyes flashed white.

My breath caught and I stepped backward, bumping into a food rack. I wanted to scream. I covered my mouth with my hand. White eyes, red blood. I connected his face to the image on the hill involuntarily. My legs instantly threatened to buckle. I reached out to steady myself on the shelf. Chip bags fell to the floor.

He seemed amused at that and chuckled to himself as he turned.

The trucks had already backed up and began to leave. He nimbly bounced from the step to the ground, made a one handed grab onto the tailgate, and settled himself on it, never looking back.

There I stood rooted, watching. My mom checked out and walked by before I realized we were ready to leave.

I bent down on wobbling legs and fumbled for the snack bags. When I finally had them haphazardly back on the racks, I followed Mom to the car.

We left the gas station and started to head down the road toward home.

How could I have possibly recognized that face if I hadn't seen it before? The incident on the mountain had to be real. But killing a deer with your teeth? *Really?* "Come on, Rhi,

18

your imagination has got to stop," I quietly scolded myself. But my thoughts fought each other: Maybe I should err on the side of caution and not divulge my fear right now. But what if he tried to kill me? If I didn't say anything to anyone, no one would know who to look for. But then again, he had already had a great opportunity. This was too much. I decided to stay close to people and not go into the forest.

I could not get the queasy, uneasy feeling to leave the pit of my stomach. I had trouble focusing on the things my mom had decided to talk about. "Breath in and out, Rhi. Focus. Nothing is wrong...remember?" I tried to reassure myself.

The road on the way home bordered the north edge of the reservoir. A bridge spanned the channel that fed the lake. It stretched a quarter of a mile through marsh on both sides of the slow moving water.

Our plan was to drive home, drop off the few groceries, get Dad, then head toward McCall for a look around the resort town and eat some dinner.

Our car had to stop on the two lane quarter of a mile land bridge because of two trucks that had pulled to the side and were parked in our lane. I immediately recognized the trucks from the store. I started to shrink into my seat.

I wanted to cry out. I, again, silently debated about what or if to tell my mom? She would probably laugh at my joke, and then take me to a psychiatrist after I started to go mental on her for not believing me. I didn't believe my own mind at this point; how could anyone else?

Too much. I must have hit my head on a rock when I fell. I could not possibly be remembering things correctly.

When the car in front of us decided the oncoming traffic lane was clear enough to go, it started to pull into the left lane, passing around the parked trucks. I looked down the edge of the guardrail next to the trucks. My eyes caught him.

That electric emotion from the store shot through me again as his sunglass-shaded eyes seared right back at me. He sat perched on the rail, water flowing below him. He hadn't even searched our car for my face. He knew right where my eyes would be when the car in front moved.

He gazed at me from under his sunglasses—I could imagine the deep blue. The breeze fingered his blonde hair. His lips moved to say something. He seemed to say to me whatever he had said at the store. No one else seemed to be around him, the tall dark one not visible. The others must have been swimming below him in the water.

Our car passed behind him, moving past the trucks. Mom mumbled something about the road not being a parking lot and the danger of it. I could see him straighten and then look over his left shoulder as we passed. I didn't dare turn and look. It might look too obvious. I could see in the side mirror that he hadn't moved. He watched the car until we disappeared into the trees.

We left our new home and headed north to McCall, a small town happily situated at the end of the long valley north of Donnelly. As we drove the main street and breached the top of a rise, a beautiful lake mirrored the sun. Tops of houses and businesses lined the road leading to the lake. So blue. Boats played out on the water. Some were towing water skiers, some were fishing, and others just bobbed lazily.

We drove down to the end of the main street which seemed to dead end into the lake, but instead made an abrupt left turn. More shops and an old theater edged the sidewalks along this road. A large, indoor skating rink flanked one of the corners to the left. Shops and tourist stops promised good browsing. We passed the grocery store and crossed over an old, stone, gothic-looking bridge. I noted a park on the right—bright green grass edged up to narrow, sandy beaches and docks. Then we were out of town. Wow, not very big. Still larger than the small town we now called home.

We turned around and parked along the street next to the ice skating rink. We meandered up town; our destination dinner. Mom had not decided what she wanted to eat. I felt dazed by the crazy couple of days and did not contemplate eating. I tried to be enthusiastic as we looked through the windows of some of the shops. Most housed specialty items and souvenirs to attract tourists. We stopped to comment on intricate scarves in colorful patterns on display in one window, and then in another display, Mom oohed and awed at some art created out of the knotted pattern of an old tree.

Shoppers passed the windows, talking and pointing. Kids skateboarded down the sidewalks in groups. A group of teens chatted seriously, walking slowly, as if no one else existed. Summer seemed good and alive.

Mom led us down to the water. We hadn't really any time to talk with all of the unpacking and organizing of the house. Me, I had been the ever-silent partner on the long drive over here from the coast.

"How are you feeling?" Mom asked Dad.

"Honey, I'm feeling great." He patted his chest like an ape. It made Mom and I laugh. We knew he still experienced aches. We would catch him grimacing at times, but would always play it off, doting on him.

"I mean to say, how is my ape of a man feeling hunger-wise? Does he need a banana split or a thick steak for dinner?" She smiled adoration at Dad.

"Oh," he answered sheepishly, "burger and fries, the redneck delight. If we are going to fit in around here, we might as well start eating like it." He smiled back.

"Grease and salt it is, dear."

"How about you, Rhi?" Mom looked at me.

"Anything," I answered, staring at the way the sun shone off the tops of all the waves, the huge mountains in the background. It looked painted.

She put her arm around my shoulder and gave me a squeeze.

"School is going to be starting soon. I hear the school is right here in McCall." She turned to walk back toward town.

"Really?" I followed behind the two of them. "I wonder which of these one-room school buildings will educate grades K-12 at the same time."

She laughed at my reference to an era generations removed.

"It won't be that bad," Dad promised, punching my arm.

"I know." I looked down, feeling bad that my emotion over starting school here showed. I didn't want my parents to feel guilty, in any way, for uprooting me in my senior year, the year of my 18th birthday. Although I had moments of wanting to scream and cry over how unfair the situation ended up, my dad was still with us and that mattered a great deal more. I understood they made sacrifices after he nearly died. They had lost a lot. I heard them talk one night about this being a "starting over". It seemed to me they were trying to pep each other up for the promise of a better future, one where we started off with less than we had.

I looked up and smiled the best smile I could muster to my parents. "Come on. Let's get some dinner. I'm famished." As I pulled ahead of both of them, I took Dad's hand, dragging him with me.

Mom tried to connect back with the conversation that had almost started, as she followed close behind. "I know this is a smaller place, and it does not seem like there is much to do, but just wait, honey."

Dad continued her thought, "Small towns are great places." It sounded like a repeat of his speech about growing up in a small town and how great life was and how he and his friends still kept in touch.

"Dad," I presented my warning frown. He squeezed my hand, letting the conversation drop. I smiled knowing he would start it up at a later time.

We ended up eating hamburgers from a local, fast food restaurant, then headed home. Our headlights illuminated the house when we arrived. Our bedrooms were on the second floor, mine down the hall from my parents. An additional bedroom on that floor and mine shared an adjoined bathroom.

Boxes still needed unpacking, but I pushed them to the edges of the room. My clothes were put away in their drawers, but none of my personal things were unpacked. I could not bring myself to do that yet.

A breeze picked up and I noticed that the curtain billowed because of the open window. I hadn't remembered opening it. However, my mind had been a bit fuzzy as of late. I got myself ready for sleep.

2

The Journey Begins

I had an odd sensation being alone in my room. It would take me time to get used to the creaks and groans of the new house without my breaking into goose bumps. I could hear my mom coming up the stairs. I glanced around the room toward the closet. I had left the doors open, and I could see inside. The space sat empty, dark space. Over-stimulation the last couple of days had my mind on pins and needles. I grabbed my PJs and walked into the hall.

"Good night, Rhi," Mom said in a quiet voice as she reached up and ran fingers through her hair, trying to stifle her yawn. "Do you like your room?"

"Ya, it's great. I love you, Mom. See you in the morning. Is Dad looking for a job tomorrow?"

"I think so. He is very experienced. He will find something." She smiled at me.

My question had been more selfish than that. I really wanted to know if I would have to be alone in the house, but didn't want to mention it.

"I know." I smiled back at her. "Good night, Mom. Love you." I yelled into their room, "Night, Dad."

Eternus

"Good night, Rhi. Love you, Sis." he called back. Mom winked as she turned to her room, shutting her door behind her.

I turned my face to look over the balcony at the dark downstairs living room. Boxes, couch, end table. We had only brought the bare minimum in furniture with us on our move. My eyes trailed through the edge of the dining room where I had sat the previous night with dad and the officer. My mind traced the path through the kitchen and into the family room with the fireplace. No furniture sat in that room yet. It was decorated with more boxes that needed unpacking.

My mind turned left and walked toward what would normally be the garage door, except the previous occupants had changed it into a game room. A bar stood on one side, and I could imagine a pool table joining it in the center of the floor.

Before the garage door an additional bedroom could be accessed on the right, on the left, a bathroom, and before the bathroom, a small hallway that led back into the living room and the front entrance.

Too much space. I normally relished being alone. I felt nervous in this strange home. Would we even hear if someone did try to break in?

I walked to the bedroom door next to my bedroom. Turning on the light, I glanced around. This room had no furniture in it. I walked in. The window remained shut. No one hid in the closet or on the ceiling. *My gosh, the ceiling? Really?* I definitely needed to chill. "Come on, Rhi," I calmed myself, as I knew I had a case of the jitters.

I opened the door to the shared bathroom between the rooms. I turned the light off in the room as I walked into the bathroom. I shut both doors and instantly felt calmer. My unease melted away. Just me in the bathroom. I changed into my PJ's, brushed my teeth, combed out my long, dishwater blonde strands, washed my face, and then looked intently in the mirror. My blue eyes were not striking against my blonde lashes. It bugged me that I needed to wear mascara in order for my lashes not to look singed. I liked to wear as little make up as possible.

My oval face had a light pinkish tone, my cheek bones an average height on my face. I definitely had some German decent somewhere in my history. Mostly my ancestors came from different backgrounds like most people. I even had some Cherokee Indian. I guessed that contributed to the tan I so easily acquired during the summer months. I could definitely use some sun now. I had dark circles under my eyes. Great, the zombie look is such a popular fad. I definitely would not be the belle of the ball.

I opened the door to my room. That 'not alone' sensation washed over me again and made the hair on the base of my neck stand. Considering what I had seen on the mountain, I felt sure I would not be able to make my mind relax enough to sleep. I looked around again and even looked under my bed. *Nothing, silly.* But still, if I could not relax after lying in my bed, I would sneak in to my parents' room and sleep there.

I stretched. I thought about closing my window, but with it being on the second story, and the house having nothing to climb on, I felt confident no one could get in. The cool air tingled on my skin. A storm is capable of causing unease. I had seen horses anxious about a pending cloudburst race and buck, harboring a pent up need to flee from it. Maybe I had picked up on the nuance of a storm coming, and my mind simply reacted like the horse's.

I turned off my light.

I sank into the cool sheets and pulled my blankets on top, knowing I would grow cold in the night.

I really hadn't analyzed the events on the mountain much. I tried to keep it from my mind. I think that I knew what I saw. I think.

My body started to tremble as I ran the thoughts around in my mind. I needed not to freak my mom out. If she knew my thoughts, she would never let me walk the woods. This house would feel like a prison.

The guy that blocked the door at the gas station, I suspected him to be the same one from the woods—yet he seemed different. Different did not even fit. On the mountain he appeared commanding, terrifying. I hoped I would not find him in my nightmares as I slept. I didn't think I could handle it. Officially he hadn't done anything to me. His intention— obviously not to kill me. I knew that for sure. Why else would I still be alive?

I remembered that the blackness had wrapped around me. Passing out had been my best defense, ugh. He had looked down at me with his dark eyes. They seemed amused. A smile had teased at his lip, his head tilted in a curious fashion. Yes, definitely losing my mind. I promised myself that I would not go back into the woods for a while, if ever.

My heart thumped in my chest as I recalled the incident. I tried to close my eyes.

His blue eyes met me there. The look in the gas station, bewildered and staring into me, it captivated me. Then, by the water on the bridge, my insides stirred. Fluttering. Strange and inviting. What had he said to me?

And then the tall one had appeared again. The face seemed to match the one that loomed over me on the hillside. Could it be? A chill trickled down my back. I gasped.

I ran to my parents' room. They already slept. I sneaked a blanket and curled up on their floor. I knew there had to be a logical explanation for the events. Had it not been for my nerves and my tired brain, I would be able to figure it out. But tonight I needed to have comfort.

My eyes closed. I pushed the images away from me. It took too long for me to find sleep.

That began the start to my series of dreams.

Red silk surrounded the room on the curtains and the couch. The walls consisted of large slabs of grey stone. Burning candles on candelabras lit the room and also lined the mantle. They remained the only source of light. A few tables around the room held lanterns and candles. No electric lamps occupied the space. The furniture looked old, yet new—Victorian style and very tasteful.

My dress of deep red extended to the floor. The collar had a high cut, which plunged to a V in front. I wore a huge black necklace. The gem rested in the V.

Happiness enveloped me. Complete rapture. I threw my head up, laughing. The white ceiling stretched so high that the faint etching around the panels became indiscernible. Lights from the burning candles flickered in the darkened shadows up so high. The curtains ran from ceiling to floor. Long pendants in different colors hung on all of the walls. The fireplace on my right burned, inviting warmth into the room.

I stepped lightly toward the settee and sat down, closing my eyes. I propped my feet onto the couch. I leaned my weight onto my right shoulder and back, extending my hand over the arm of the couch.

I kept my eyes closed, and I could feel anticipation and excitement with a premonition of something great about to take place. The air I breathed cooled my throat and felt crisp on my tongue. I smelled the most wonderful, earthy scent of oak and lavender. It filled my soul with caring and peace. Like nothing I could remember—it so touched and moved me, I doubted I would forget it.

A soft finger traced my outstretched hand. My chin rose up and a deeper smile formed on my lips.

The finger felt warm against my cool skin. It ran up my arm. It traced my sleeve at my elbow, and then moved to my chin.

I didn't open my eyes.

Soft, dewy lips brushed mine. It sent unexpected shivers down my body. My head reeled. I tilted my head back a little as the tingling sensation slid down my body to my legs.

A cool cheek brushed up against mine. Then lips brushed my neck. Kissing me, those lips sweetly and slowly touched and moved down one side of my neck and up the other.

As my smile faded, my lips parted. Something familiar—completely invited and desired—enveloped me. My fingers were being kissed. Slowly, his mouth drew one of my fingers in. My senses reeled. My body writhed with eagerness. Desire mounted in me like I had never known.

His warm hand held mine, and he pressed his lips back on mine, passionately taking my breath away. I felt him move slightly away while he still held my fingers.

Then something unexpected nestled in my hand.

I brought my chin down and opened my dreamy eyes to look at the large, engraved, wooden box with a dark blue ribbon. A gasp escaped my lips. Joy filled me. Then I looked up into his eyes.

Those eyes. Blue like the water. Desire and happiness overflowed them and crashed into me, holding me peacefully and entirely.

His mouth moved and delicate words flowed from them, "Memor meus diligo Eternus..."

Those eyes. I gasped and sat bolt upright on the floor. My stomach still tingled, my heart still pounded, and my breath came uneven. Tears in my eyes threatened to overrun.

The words. I could not understand them.

Shocking eyes. My dream held so much love and adoration. Where did that come from?

My dream felt like home. My dream felt alive. Real.

I lay back, my body willing, my heart pounding, my face flushed. What a dream. I wanted to fall back into that feeling. I struggled to relax. I do not know when I fell back asleep.

Mom woke early the next morning, showered and readied herself for work. I grew faintly aware of her bending to kiss my forehead before she left. My night of sleep had been entirely ruined. I had been in and out of sleep so much. My mind replayed the dream over and over.

How had my mind conceived such an elaborate setting? My heart still fluttered as I stood. Hope and longing etched into my soul, as though I were heartsick. I found it unnerving. Something had touched me deep in my core. Silly that a dream caused me to be a puddle of goo inside.

Wake up.

I went into my room, grabbed some clean clothes and showered. I noticed the unease from the night before had gone.

I went downstairs and found Dad in the kitchen mapping out his day. He had a coffee cup in hand and looked over the ads in the small valley paper.

"Do you have a game plan?" I asked.

"Ya, although not a very good one." He smiled at me and tousled my hair, just like he did a long time ago. I secretly loved it.

I smiled back at him. "You'll get something today, Dad. Something you have always wanted."

"I hope so," he said, as he left the kitchen. I could hear his footsteps as he ascended the stairs to his room.

Breakfast from a box, we really hadn't stocked up on any groceries yet. I thought fresh fruit would be nice.

I finished my cereal as Dad came down, looking great and ready to tackle the world.

"You look outstanding," I told him, even though he looked like a cat in a dog kennel.

"I feel like a kid on the first day of school," he admitted. He kissed me on the cheek and headed toward the front door.

"Love you, Dad."

"Love you, Sis."

There I stood, alone in the house for the first time. I checked all the doors and windows to make sure they were locked.

I decided to make myself useful and started unpacking more items.

I put an ear bud in one ear. I wanted to listen to music, but didn't feel comfortable enough to block out the sounds from the house.

I started singing. My voice not one to share out in public, I love belting it out when alone.

I danced a little and closed my eyes for the chorus as the tempo sped up. "Ohhh, beautiful flash of light."

I unpacked the rest of the kitchen, hoping I put things where they needed to go. Mom and I had a rhythm in the kitchen. We would take turns cooking for each other. Dad was never really allowed in the kitchen, as a general rule. He tended to cook pizzas with wrappers on them or microwave potatoes until a hard ball of potato, the size of a pea surrounded with a crunchy shell, remained.

I looked out the window past the back patio and decided fresh air sounded good—staying close to the door, of course. I moved to the glass door that led to the patio. Grabbing a sweater, I let myself out into the morning air, which still felt very brisk, quite a contrast to the expected 90 degrees for the day. I leaned against the railing for a time, breathing in the fresh air. I could see the far side of the stream below me. The beach appeared rocky and gave way to bushes and then trees. Trails led up to the road that passed through the area.

My eyes looked up to the mountain looming in the distance. The very one I had been on just two days ago. The momentary reflection of the day's events left me weary, as I constantly scanned our yard for any unexpected guests.

The yard under the patio made a natural slope from the left to the right. The patio accessed the ground level around the front of the house, making a walkway. By the time it reached the back yard, it elevated enough to walk under due to the slope of the grass. It just happened to be wide enough for patio furniture (none of which we had), BBQs, and fun stuff (again, short in that department). Stairs stepped down to the sloping yard.

I hadn't had time to really explore yet. Would I be safe? Should I stay inside all day? My mind tried to argue the danger. Logically, I overrode the argument by using the memories I had of my dark room as a child. Always afraid in the dark, I knew I saw things, movements. Time and time again, they proved to be nothing. I concluded that my silly notion and feelings of uncertainty resembled similar occasions as a child. Determined that I had grown past that, I decided to take a break from my work and saunter down to the water.

The rocky stairway led to an opening that appeared to have a fire pit about halfway down the side of the fifty foot embankment. I reached the fire pit area that stretched out wide and long, then continued down the next section of rock steps opposite the fire pit at the far end of the natural patio. The water ran calmly.

Vegetation edged both the water and a small stretch of sand wide enough to sit and take off one's shoes and dip one's feet into the water. I sat down to do just that. I rolled up my pant legs while I tried to judge the depth and then stepped in carefully.

The water shocked me. I hadn't expected the temperature difference between it and my warm socks to be so great. The slimy rocks made for uneven wading. I didn't want to fall, so I intently watched where I placed each foot. A small pang of ache started seeping into my skin from the chilly water numbing me. I reached the creek's far side and stood looking back. The house loomed above me to the right. I could see the patio, the dining room and living room doors, as well as the big window in the kitchen right in between them. Repainted in recent history, the dark wood house seemed to have stood the test of time. Home. I guess I could grow to like it. Nature surrounded it. We seemed to have privacy, a lot of it.

I turned to scan the area around me. Downstream, about sixty yards away, the water lumbered under the bridge that had led me to the escapade that had turned terrifying, or so I'd imagined.

I picked up a stick and started to walk. I traced lines in the rocky sand. Not like the sand at the beach, it seemed much coarser and unrefined. It massaged the bottoms of my feet. The bushes were thick where they grew under the trees and out toward the water's edge. I kept close to the water and away from the trees.

The water started to rush as it curved below the house at a seventy degree angle, flowing toward the bridge. I came to stop at the bend. I noticed a log had wedged itself into the angle of the curve. It had stayed there long enough that a sandy spot had built up on the other side of it. Plants with small yellow flowers grew in the shallows.

I waded into the water to see how deep it became running toward the log. I noticed to my right, where the water slowly moved opposite the log, that the beach seemed larger than the others. I could easily spread out on a towel to sunbathe when it became warmer.

I took a step onto the slick, larger rocks prevalent in the fast moving water. Looking forward into the depth of the pool, I decided it might be over my head.

I peered over at the log area, certain that I could see the bottom. It might be fun to swim here when the water warmed.

"Good morning." A deep voice boomed from behind me.

I startled and turned quickly. Too quickly. My foot slid, my knee buckled, and I tipped backward into the cool, rushing water. My typical, clumsy self. I noted a blue shirt before I landed on the rocks and rolled backward into the water. I closed my eyes anticipating water engulfing my face. Just as soon as I submerged, the current carried me. Although not a fierce current, it moved enough to pull me along and I noticed that it swallowed again under the bridge. I knew I needed to find my feet to stand because this stranger might be a much bigger threat than drowning. It could be the one from the mountain.

Not enough time had passed to enable me to get my feet under me before strong arms reached out and cradled me, pulling me out.

My head broke the water and my hand flew up quickly to wipe the water from my face. I hurried to get my eyes opened. I had to know who grabbed me and assess my danger.

When they opened, the world stopped.

Although he wore dark glasses, I knew him in that instant. I could imagine those blue eyes looking at me.

I smelled the same warm, lavender and earthy scent from the day before. Inviting. Crisp and clean. It stirred something in me. My mind blanked out, like a power surge wiping my hard drive clean.

I didn't hear a thing, immediately deaf to sounds surrounding me. The breeze wrapped around us and caught his short hair—loose strands danced around the ends that haphazardly poked up.

He stepped to the beach and chuckled with me in his arms.

"Still amazingly agile, I see," his melodic voice chimed.

Amazingly agile? How could he know me enough to reference my clumsy behavior? I pushed off him to stand. He let me go and steadied me while my feet felt for the ground. I became aware of this being the first time we had ever spoken to each other, the first time I had heard that thrilling voice.

My ankle throbbed, and I pulled my knee up to protect it—in doing so my balance left me. As I started to topple, he grabbed me and helped me to sit down. I must have rolled it on the rocks before I fell in. Of course, the same ankle I twisted on the hill.

"That bad, huh?" He stepped over to a fishing pole and tackle box and returned with a jacket.

When had he been fishing? I didn't notice him at all when I looked over to the beach. I believed myself to be completely alone. He wrapped the jacket around me. Soaked in cold water, I shivered in the chill morning. He dripped water from his waist down.

"I...um..." I tried to take in everything, yet wanted to run and longed to stay all at once. "Thank you. I thought I was alone here. You startled me."

"That seemed kind of obvious. I immediately felt bad that you had to take a cold bath because of it."

His head bowed and his face seemed haggard.

Surreal. Inside I had such peace. A perfect stranger, alone on the beach below my house. I should be on guard and trying to leave. I remained rooted to my spot, consumed by tranquility. I could not be sure if his voice, his body, or his scent had been more alluring, but as a whole, something felt right about him.

My heart raced, and I could sense the skin on my face heat up. I knew that meant I turned red. I could not stop staring at his face—smooth and perfect. Not one flaw. His jaw tightened and released. He had closed his eyes, obviously struggling for some kind of control.

His biceps flexed as his hands clenched and released.

He jumped toward me, his movement so quick I lurched backward. The distance between us that had been about three feet—in a fraction of a second shrank to a few inches. We were close enough our breath mingled. He perched on his clenched fists and his toes, ready to pounce. He looked like a linebacker ready to hit his opponent as soon as the whistle blew. His lips thin and tight, his body rigid. It seemed the tension in the air would explode at any moment. The anger that seemed to emanate from him sent warning thoughts racing through my mind. *Flee, Rhi.* I brought my arm up to protect me so rapidly that I knocked his glasses from his face. In a split second I saw ghost white eyes, then he sprang to his feet and turned.

My breath stopped. I saw him at his gear, his back to me, taking deep breaths.

I didn't wait. I stood as best I could, dropped his jacket and rushed toward the shallow creek bed that I had crossed to get here.

I hobbled. My ankle had obviously been hurt, even though my heart heaved in my chest. I had no luck picking up speed. The brush next to the stream impeding me even more.

A rapid swoosh came from behind me and gentle hands wrapped my waist and legs, lifting me from the ground. He cradled me there in his arms, like a fragile child.

I pushed away, frightened.

"Sorry," came his polite and authentic response. He wore his glasses again. "I injured you. Please let me help you get to your patio."

My mouth opened in horror—I couldn't force my words out. I didn't want to be imprisoned by his arms. His face pleaded to me.

"No," I said forcefully, struggling against his strength. "I can do it."

I tried to squirm from his hands to no avail. The fear around my heart tightened. I didn't know what to expect next.

"I would never hurt you," he lamented. The crystal tone of his melodic voice and the utter sincerity were not lost on the moment. His demeanor seemed to humble in front of me.

"I will leave as soon as I make sure you get to your house."

The sincerity in his countenance and the seemingly humbled attitude helped me to relax enough to stop fighting. I remained leery and leaned away from him as he carried me. In response, he held me slightly away from himself, as though he carried a platter of food. I took this to mean he understood how disarming the situation had become. He avoided eye contact and kept his head lowered, appearing disappointed somehow. Gingerly he carried me across the water, scooped up my things in one hand, and jogged up the side of the hill. No effort.

In fact, in comparison to me, he didn't breathe as hard at all. He gently placed me next to the door leading into the living room.

He walked to the edge of the patio. He paused and turned his head to the side, looking at the ground. I thought he would say something, then his muscles tensed and he turned and ran down the steps. I hobbled to the edge of the balcony to watch him retrieve his items. He had already reached the beach below. It took only a second for him to collect them and he rushed into the undergrowth of the trees.

I waited to see if a car would leave on the road headed toward the mountains or passing my house, but nothing appeared.

I went inside, locked the door, and took a pain reliever. I raced to change out of my cold clothes. I then propped my foot up while lying on the couch with an ice pack. I covered myself with blankets for warmth.

The situation by the water rolled in my mind. My whole body went from freezing cold in the water, to elated and warm in his arms, to a reaction that I had felt two days before—to flee. Then as he took me up the path, a calmness came over me. It seemed I had always known comfort from him, a type of peace I felt from the protection of my parents.

My head swam. Am I losing it? Had my mind finally lost itself in the deep fear and resigned itself to a fate of death? I thought back to the dark man on the mountain. The blood dripping and the white eyes, in my mind, easily became the one that had just carried me. My peaceful image melted and reality sank in. I could not avoid the fear. And more, I no longer trusted my instincts.

White eyes, Rhi, for heaven's sake. It's not normal, not earthly. For the first time since the hill, I let the hot tears race down my face.

White eyes. For the third time I had seen white eyes, of that, I became positive.

I dialed my mom's cell. She didn't answer, and I didn't leave a message.

I listened in the house for any sound. Alone, my mind created scenarios that I didn't want. Yet, even through the fear and my overactive mind, a hunger gained power deep inside me. A soft happiness insisted upon conquering the dark thoughts. I found myself daydreaming about his respectful demeanor.

I stayed downstairs the rest of the day, isolated to the couch and living room. I knew this area to be safe and secure. I had the phone ready beside me, as well as a baseball bat, just in case.

3

Discoveries

I seemed to grow acclimated to the feel of the house. The sounds no longer bugged me with Dad and Mom home. I still froze and stopped breathing in order to listen better if a noise did make itself heard while I stayed alone. I never believed in ghost stories, but if there were apparitions in this house, they had done nothing physical. Kind of warming under the circumstances.

But ghosts of a sort did affect me. I dreamed, repeatedly, about those crystal blue eyes looking at me with adoration . The places in the dreams were all different; sometimes in public, sometimes in private, but they all seemed familiar—like home. They were always far in the past, so removed from the present day.

I could not understand how my dreams captured such vivid detail in the buildings and the people surrounding me. Maybe I had seen too many DVDs, but I had come to love sleeping, with my own little movie playing in my head. I always woke up with my heart pounding and a desire to sneak back into my dreams and find him there.

I saw those eyes everywhere during the day, sometimes with sunglasses and other times unfettered, just the gorgeous blue showing. In public I saw them, in the grocery store, on a walk down by the water, everywhere. Sometimes far away from me, sometimes close, his eyes drew me in. During those times I realized I must have been staring. I always averted my gaze.

I knew I must be lonely. My hypnotic dreams were leaving me in a haze during the day. Maybe I needed to get some friends and get out of the house. I decided today would be a good day to sunbathe down by the water. I showered, straightened my room, and put on my swimming suit and shorts. I threw a beach towel and sunscreen in my bag and drove to Cascade Reservoir, only ten minutes from my house. I parked next to a row of other cars.

Nervous about meeting new people, I needed to find a secluded, sandy spot and not draw attention to myself.

I took a big breath and stepped from the car. Down by the water's edge I noted two long docks stretching out into the water, separated by a boat ramp.

Beaches flanked each side of the docks. Teenagers grouped near the water on both sides. A football game was raging to the left. I noticed a great deal of sand flying as players dove for the ball.

I walked to the right. The beach gave way to a three foot, dirt cliff topped by enormous trees. Their roots intertwined into the dirt.

I sauntered across the sand, glancing at the faces turned in my direction, avoiding the long looks, yet taking it all in. The water reminded me of home. I loved the water. Here it appeared glassy, unlike the ocean, and reflected the few clouds above.

Thick, dark, wooden posts jetted up from the water as if once an old dock sat there, high enough to let the tide come in and go out. That would prove impossible, however—tides do not happen on lakes. Even though the posts seemed out of place, for a moment they transported me back to the coast, if only in my mind, comforting me.

I could hear murmurs all around me. Were they talking as they noticed me, the newcomer?

I chose a place somewhat sheltered by the small cliff and an old tree root ball that stood as tall as me. I spread my towel out and sat.

I heard an ecstatic "Hi" come from beside me.

I looked up to see a shadowed face leaning down. She smiled, extending her hand in greeting.

"Hi," I said, feeling a little out of place.

"You must be new here."

"Yeah, we just moved here a few weeks ago." A few weeks of torture thanks to white eyes that haunted my nightmares, I thought to myself. As I looked up into the smiling face I noted that there was at least one friendly person here.

"Great, I'm Carlee."

"My name's Rhi." I reached up and shook her extended hand.

"It's great to meet you, Rhi. Are you going to school here, too?"

"That's the plan."

"Well, we all go to school in McCall. There are not very many students."

I wondered what a school would be like with hardly any students.

"I can't wait," I said, not trying to hide my lack of enthusiasm.

"Where did you come from?" she seemed genuinely curious.

"We just moved here from Oregon. We always went to the coast at Florence and played. I miss the rain."

She laughed. "It is kind of dry here. I've never been to the Oregon Coast. Hey! Let me introduce you to the gang."

I stood, taking my time, hoping that courage would join me soon. We walked towards the group of both guys and girls, about fifteen of them. Dark hair, light hair, short and tall. They were all having fun. Some were chasing each other, throwing sand. Some were talking to each other. You could tell the couples by how closely they sat. They all noticed us walk up.

Carlee introduced me in a booming voice, "Hey, everyone. This is Rhi!"

I cringed and silently cursed my luck at having the first person I met be the rare and gifted one that didn't need a megaphone for announcing.

People flooded in, surrounding me. I couldn't take it all in.

They were grabbing my hand and shaking it. I heard comments like, "Rhi, nice to meet you."

"Where did you come from?"

"How long have you been here?"

"Did you move here permanently or just for the summer?"

My ears were inundated with voices, and so many people surrounded me. I wanted to go hide in my car and avoid the overwhelming feeling. I tried not to make eye contact. My hands were being involuntarily shaken. And just as quickly as the barrage began, everybody dispersed. Thankfully, Carlee answered most of the questions they asked.

Carlee retrieved my towel from the safety of the cliff and spread it out to sit beside her towel.

As I sat down, more towels moved around mine, quickly covered by their owners—all guys, all talking. I picked up names: Bob, John, Heath, and Kyle. A cold soda suddenly cooled my hand. Bob's dad owned the convenience store in town. I guessed that the soda came from him. John and Heath both helped their families run their farms. I missed what Kyle said about his family. They were all talking over each other to get my attention.

Carlee rolled her eyes. "Come on, guys," her voice inflected. "Give her some room. Geeze!"

Bob smiled at that. He seemed a little more interested in me than the others, flirting with dark eyes. He had light skin, the kind that would pick up a little tan in the summer. He had rounded facial features. His body appeared husky even though he had a fit physique. He wore his dark hair in a trendy style, and his swim trunks looked expensive.

"Hey, Rhi," he said, "I talked my dad into letting me take his boat to Payette Lake next weekend. Would you like to come out with us? We are going to be waterskiing and wakeboarding. It would be fun to have you there." I remembered the lake. It had been the one my parents and I had walked along.

Bob passed me food—cheese sticks and chips. I nibbled on them as everyone talked. He kept me well supplied, no danger of starving.

The sun peeked out of the clouds. I realized I hadn't applied sun screen.

I pulled it out of my bag and started swabbing it on my legs. I decided not to take off my shorts. It felt too strange having all the guys around me. I applied lotion to my belly quickly, self-conscious of this new-found attention. I wished I could find a bathroom to escape to. I lathered my arms, then thought about my back. Well, I could just leave it. I didn't want to mention that I needed help. I froze as I thought about that. It would be a little obvious not finishing with my back.

Carlee saved me. "Do you want me to do your back for you?"

I looked at her and said thank you. I handed her my bottle and she rubbed lotion on my back. I heard all the guys give exaggerated sighs. I ignored it. I realized my awkward, clumsy body drew attention for some weird reason to those of the opposite sex. I didn't understand it, and I didn't welcome it. I just wanted to be me and not stand out.

"Hey, where are you living?" Bob asked.

"I'm on Wildcat Road," I said. "You know where the power lines are?" I referred to the power lines that crossed Wildcat Road two miles from the main highway.

"Ya," said Kyle.

"My driveway is the second drive past the power line." I found it funny that I now lived in the country and had to give directions according to power lines and cow pastures.

John blinked. "You mean the dark house overlooking the stream?"

I nodded.

Heath's eyes twinkled. "That's the old Carston place. They just left one day. Rumor has it that he up and killed his old lady. Buried her body under the house."

I didn't like this new twist. It gave me cause to worry. I already had heebie-jeebies in the house. I shuddered and stared at him.

John agreed. "Yeppers. That old geezer went berserk. They pretty much kept to themselves before that anyway."

Bob smiled a devious grin. "Have you noticed anything odd?"

Carlee stepped in. "Cut it out guys. Even if you're not giving her the creeps, you sure are giving them to me!"

They all laughed.

John explained. "We are just having fun!"

The story still made me sick to my stomach even if they were just having fun.

As the day turned to afternoon, I discovered Bob, Carlee, and Heath were seniors just like me. John and Kyle were both juniors. Some graduates from the previous year also amused themselves at the beach that day. Of course, because they were older now, they didn't mingle with the high schoolers that much.

Heath's big brother Ryan happened to be one of those new adults. He had an arrogant air about him. Tall and muscular, I imagined that he had been one of the football stars.

I saw him glance at me as he walked towards our group. He smiled back over his shoulder to his friends. They stood around the edge of the water with sodas in their hands, laughing.

Ryan turned and curved in a wide arc around our group. It looked like an offensive strategy. Heath didn't realize he had been marked as prey. He sat behind Carlee and me, talking in whispers with her. Their conversation was timid. They were interested in each other, but neither one had said anything yet.

All of the sudden, sand showered everywhere around Carlee and me. Heath yelled, "Hey!" and the fight began. Heath struggled with Ryan, two times his size. Ryan held Heath around the throat and one leg, struggling to get to the water's edge. All the spectators laughed except Carlee and me. We tried to brush off the sand, which clung to our freshly applied lotion.

I watched, mildly amused, as Ryan maneuvered deeper into the water with Heath. Heath finally gave up and they both disappeared. Heath surfaced first, ringing his dripping hair, gasping for air, watching the depths for Ryan to appear. The water resembled dark onion soup.

Heath's eyes widened, his lips gaped with horror. He looked up in shock, as his body jerked back under the surface. In a few seconds, Ryan came up choking and laughing, water pouring off his body. He triumphantly held up Heath's shorts for everyone to see.

Raucous laughter erupted from the beach. I felt sorry for Heath, even though there was comedy in the escapade.

Heath surfaced quickly. Beet red and angry, he scanned the area for Ryan. He stood in water chest deep. Thankfully he didn't move into the shallow.

He slapped the top of the water with his fist and yelled, "Come on, Ryan! Grow up!"

Ryan retreated to his friends. I didn't think he even heard Heath over their loud laughter.

I got up and shook out my towel. Carlee did the same.

It became obvious we would not be getting the sand off of our bodies or out of our hair without help. I knew it meant I needed to get into the water. I didn't want to go in so close to the "newly christened" Heath.

I looked at Carlee. "Hey, I'm going to go jump off the dock and get this sand off."

She glanced at poor Heath with sympathy.

"I will come with you. I think I have sand in my suit bottom."

We walked with our towels toward the dock.

No one seemed to notice us as they paid attention to the words exchanged between Ryan and Heath. Ryan's friends were even joining in the banter. Kyle, John, Bob, and the rest of the group were just laughing. I wondered how long they were going to torture Heath before one of them stepped in to help. Glancing at Ryan and his burly friends, I thought it might be a while.

I strode with my head down, watching my footing in the sand, talking to Carlee.

"Does that happen much?"

"Yeah. Ryan is such a jerk to Heath. He is always pulling stuff. Heath really hates it, but he also adores his brother. Ryan is the football hero," she added dryly. "He scored the winning touchdown that put our high school in the playoffs last year. The game rocked. He is talented, but I hate how he treats his brother."

"Why does Heath still like him so much then?"

"They became very close a few years ago. Inseparable, actually," she said. "Their mom passed away suddenly. It devastated both of them. Heath worshiped his mom."

I instantly felt bad for them. I tried to imagine how losing my mom would be. It helped me understand their complex relationship.

"I guess their dad didn't take it well, though. He started drinking and spends most of his time drunk. I noticed Heath coming to school this past year with bruises and black eyes. He will never talk about it. He's always quiet and withdrawn for a few days afterward. Then he snaps out of it."

"How does Ryan deal with it?"

"Well, calling him hovering wouldn't overstate it," she paused. "It's almost like the things, whatever they were, that happened at home might as well have happened to him. He would go out of his way to check on his little brother between classes, making himself late to his own. He always stayed with him at lunchtime instead of going off with his buddies. Then after a few days, things would go back to the way they were. Just like today."

She continued. "There were a couple of times that Ryan came to school with his face messed up as well. The same day Heath's new bruises would not be bad at all. Makes me wonder if Ryan did not step in to help Heath."

I began to think that I could like Heath and his quieter nature. I understood why Carlee seemed drawn to him and felt protective of him. If they ever figured it out, they would make a cute couple. Her bubbly personality and curly, brown hair, his tall, stocky build, black hair and brown eyes. I could easily see it.

I looked up as we approached the dock to see where to step. I checked the boat ramp so as not to interfere with anyone launching their boat.

I saw someone starting to back his boat down to the water's edge. Back home, people launched their boats from the right and took out on the left of the ramp. The direction the boat made as it backed down to the water indicated the same regulations applied here.

I stepped onto the dock and focused on the boat. I wanted to get out of the way as the owners started the process of off loading it. It loomed in the air, much larger than a normal boat. The windows below deck indicated it had a cabin.

A woman came around from the front of the vehicle quickly and jumped onto the dock. She held up her hand so the driver knew to stop. He had the boat close enough to the dock that she reached out and untied the mooring lines from the front and the back.

I kept walking, hoping to arrive at the end of the dock before they reached it with the boat.

I noted the details of the boat and the people already sitting in it. Kids, coolers, lifejackets, a wakeboard tower with wakeboards bungeed in their carriers, and smiles on the kids' faces. I glanced at the massive motor mounted to the transom, but my focus jerked to what lay in the background. Then I heard a creak as the brakes on the truck let loose to bring the boat further into the water and instantly blocked my view.

Had I seen him? My heart stopped. My feet stopped. My view now hindered by the boat. Blonde hair, firm muscles, white tee shirt, but his eyes were covered with dark glasses. I had only seen temporarily.

Carlee looked at my face.

My body believed what I saw. That familiar feeling of locking eyes sent a thrill through me that I didn't want, but had curiously begun to long for.

I proceeded forward, willing my feet to move. I could make an excuse to get myself out of here.

The boat slid from the trailer easily and rested lower in the water. The woman put her weight into guiding it farther off the trailer so it would not catch as the driver pulled out.

And there they were.

Maybe twenty people on the far beach. Children and teenagers mixed in the group. The one that I had briefly made eye contact with had his back to me now. That made it easier.

They were tossing around a football in the sand. Some of them were graceful, sinuous, their movements fluid, rapid and punctuated. They stood out against the slower, gyrating gate of some of the other guys. I found it hard to turn away.

I saw the black-haired one from the store and the hill. Fear squeezed my heart like a vice. I took a step back. I had decided that it had been a dream, but my body reacted. It knew better. My breath caught in my lungs. He did not notice me. I moved forward with Carlee. My desire to leave grew.

At the end of the dock, she shook her towel out again.

I just dropped mine—my head still down.

She looked at me.

"Are you okay?"

Noticing where my eyes had focused, Carlee looked to the far beach as well.

"Those are some of the people we will go to school with this year." She offered. "I heard one of them quit the football team about three weeks ago. Too bad. He was one of the star players last season. I'm sure he would be in the spotlight this year. He just walked off the team after practicing most of the summer with them." She shook her head in dismay as she readied herself to swim.

She looked at me one more time. "Are you sure you are okay?"

"I'm not sure I'm feeling all that well," I lied.

"It is probably all that food Bob's been feeding you!" she laughed. "Well, lets swim and then you can leave if you need to, but I want to get your phone number so I can call you. My cell is in my car, so I will walk you to yours."

"Ok, that would be fine." I did need to get the sand off me before I sat in my car. With the hot days, I could only imagine what the vinyl seat would feel like with sand and sweat.

We stood there. Carlee seemed impatient with her hands on her hips as the boat launched. The motor groaned to life as it backed out and then kicked into gear. The driver spun it around in no time. Waves rocked the dock. Carlee laughed and flung herself into the oncoming melee. She broke the water after the shallow dive and exhaled rapidly.

"Cold?" I asked.

She smiled. "No, it feels good, really!"

I giggled at that. I could tell she had just spoken one of those statements everyone makes when they don't want to be the only one dumb enough to plunge into the cold water.

I thought about how I needed to take my shorts off. Instantly self-conscious, I glanced to the beach where Ryan finally started to cave in to Heath's demands to return his shorts. He held onto the trunk of the tree, and using a stick, placed the shorts on a branch that overhung the cliff and the beach. After he successfully placed the shorts on the branch, up high and out of reach, he apologized mockingly to Heath and told him, "There you go, Bro!"

Everyone laughed again, except Heath and his friends.

"Come on, Ryan!" Heath yelled. Then he turned to Bob and said, "Bring me my towel please..."

Bob did not skip a beat. It seemed he felt it time to end Heath's torture.

Heath wrapped himself in his now drenched towel and sauntered defeated out of the water.

I scanned the surface assessing the direction of my dive. I noted to the left, past the dock area, a large tree had toppled into the water. The trunk had been the only part visible and it appeared large in circumference. The giant must have stood as a beacon over the water. The tree seemed far enough away from the dock that I had little worry of danger from it.

No one paid attention to Carlee and me. I slipped my shorts off quickly and headed to the end of the dock. I glanced over to the other beach and caught his eyes on me. Too much. His eyes looked at me, even through his glasses my body responded with a yearning deep inside—a connection existed that I had to have. I needed to wash it away.

I dove deep into the water. I wanted the pit of my gut to return to normal.

The water felt cool, not unbearable. I could hear muffled screaming and laughing, faint clicks from deep in the water, and motors from boats. It felt good to be in the water. I loved the water. I always felt whole around it. Many times at the ocean I would sit and let the water wash my mind blank. I would stare for hours, mesmerized by the ebb and flow.

I swam underwater, letting the feel of the current work against my skin. I enjoyed the feeling of weightlessness. I caught glimpses of my hair wisping forward into view when I pulled my arms ahead, getting ready to propel forward. I loved the liquid feel of the underwater world. This lake trapped darkness better than the ocean. The lack of light felt a little eerie, but the two seemed similar enough that I relished the peace in it.

I knew I would need to surface soon to breathe. With one last push with my arms and legs, I flipped over, expecting to drift slowly to the top. I closed my eyes, enjoying the ripples of water coursing across my face.

In a second, my forward movement halted. I could feel sharp pokes down my back and on my stomach. I opened my eyes. I could see the sunlight attempting to filter down through the murky water. I realized I had been seized by branches of the fallen tree. I had swum farther than I had anticipated. I attempted to grab the large limb that loomed above me. Larger and smaller branches protruded down, poking my abdomen. I pushed with my left hand against the larger wood and pulled with my right on a smaller branch to break it. The branch only moved in the direction of my arm. The tree must have still been green, fallen only a short time ago, the fibers were not brittle enough to snap.

I let go and the branch scratched my side as it flung back into place.

I began to wiggle. I chided myself. This was the very thing I thought to avoid when I had surveyed the area. I knew I needed to free myself and breathe. I felt above my head with my hands. I could not escape that way. More branches and thick pine needles were there.

A small bubble escaped my lips. I didn't watch it ascend to the top where I desperately wanted to be. A moan emitted from my throat, the familiar underwater talking that I had done in the bathtub as a child.

I pushed against the smaller, pine needle-rich branches and rocked my body, using a kicking motion with my legs to try and free myself.

Chest pain. I needed to get air.

I had success pulling myself through most of the mass of tree.

Then my hair stuck. My stupid long flowing hair betrayed me in the last moment. It twisted itself around twigs that I had been unable to see.

A cry escaped me in the form of a large bubble. *Dumb move, Rhi.* Immediate panic. I began to kick and flail. I knew I had no choice but to fight to survive. My lungs blazed like fire refreshed with gasoline.

Still sandwiched between the top and bottom logs, I started to grab chunks of my hair and pull against what trapped it there. I began to feel fuzzy. I kept trying to pull. My eyes seemed to grow blurry. I struggled to discern between the shimmering sunlight and the darkened shadows. I tugged again on masses of hair and some of it broke free, but not enough to allow me to move.

My throat spasmed, trying to suck a breath. I forced my lips to stay closed.

Oh no. Oh no.

Stuck. The thought weighted itself on my chest like rocks. This would be my death.

I kicked frantically. I hit the tree, cursing it silently. I tried to spin around but the branch gashed my throat. My last moments. I could not move. *Not my choice—I do not want to die. So stupid of me to swim out this far.* I kept fighting until I grew too tired. My motions seemed to slow. I found myself fatigued and staring down the long straight trunk. A fish, agile and free, swam into view over the top of the pile of massive tree, from the opposite direction I had swum. It changed directions a couple of times, then darted back, away from me.

My body felt limp.

Something grabbed me from the darker depths below. It startled me and my legs began kicking weakly. It felt like fingers and hands. I could not see.

I heard branches breaking behind me though the sounds were muffled underwater. Then my body descended downward, through the branches that had stabbed me in the back. My hair forcefully ripped from the branches, and some of it from my scalp, leaving a fresh sting where cool water hit. For a split second I floated free. Then the hand on my back pushed me toward the top of the water.

My throat spasmed again. I needed only to open my mouth and my body would do the rest.

With rapid motion I launched rocket-like, up with such force that I had to close my eyes. Head up, my arms were pushed behind me by the force of the water.

Water shot into my nose. It burned. My throat contracted again and again, letting me know I would lose the battle soon. I wanted to scream. Just as the top of my head pushed through the water, I involuntarily inhaled. Water and air filled my lungs. I knew drowning in that moment. My eyes bulged.

I tried to cough, water shot out. I tried another breath as I re-submerged in a bobbing motion. More water, I think air came in too, but I could not be sure, the feeling thick, cold and heavy.

The deprivation of air had left me exhausted, my limbs like strings. The surroundings faded. My chest hurt. My eyes watered. I could make no sound. I could not take another gulp of air. My body would not let me.

Every part of my body convulsed. With all the force they could muster, my muscles launched me on my side, and I threw up water. The first inhale seemed like minutes long. I managed to get on my knees, grabbing my throat and chest. I crouched there with my head down. Breath moved through me, though barely. I could feel the sensation of water trickling up my throat from my lungs. It dripped from my mouth onto the wood of the dock. I kept breathing, raspy. I didn't want to move. I didn't care what I looked like. I so welcomed the vital ability to breathe.

I felt a trembling hand on my back. I grew faintly aware of someone sitting in front of me. The energy in the air seemed tense. No sounds.

Then all of the sudden, someone spoke.

"She is breathing!"

"Wow, her color's returning. I never saw anyone so purple before."

"Rhi, are you OK?" Carlee kneeled in front of me, leaning forward to talk into my ear softly. I struggled to shake my head yes. My throat and lungs burned so badly.

The hand on my back patted me and then released. It belonged to someone on my right. That person stood and I could see out the corner of my eye as his bare feet walked away down the dock. As he left, I looked up. I could see him. Mr. Blue Eyes without a name. He seemed so gorgeous and peaceful as he walked away, his white tee shirt glued to his skin. My irritated eyes played tricks and I thought it funny that he seemed to radiate a halo of light as he walked into the shadows cast by the trees. His hypnotic-patterned swim trunks still sucked tight to his frame. He did not turn around, but his head turned to the side, still listening.

No one said anything for a moment.

"Wow, he saved her! Leone saved her!"

Leone. Were they talking about him? I focused on living, but my mind replayed the name in my head.

"I know, that was horrifying. I could not believe she did not surface—then she shot straight out of the water, followed by Leone!"

I remembered the feel of air breaking through the fluid that had encased me. Propelling me back into the world I knew and took for granted every day.

"Thank goodness Leone remained calm. I'm not sure if I would have known what to do if I had been required to perform CPR."

CPR. The thought rushed through my mind. *Oh my gosh. I did drown--or almost.* Tears came to my eyes as I accepted all this new information.

"Young lady!" I heard feet running down the dock toward us.

"Young lady!" Someone knelt where my life-saver had been.

"Are you alright? Oh my god. I cannot believe what happened! I watched the whole thing. When you did not surface, I ran to the park ranger and told him to call 911. Thank goodness. The ambulance should be here shortly."

I trembled, tears coursing down my nose and streaming onto the wood. My lungs felt like the scorching embers in the bottom of a campfire. My throat felt it had been ripped to shreds, and my lips burned and tingled.

"Her coloring looks much better." Someone said from in front of me.

People began to mumble to each other, retelling the incident.

The rest of it blurred. Obviously stress and anxiety were high. Nervous laughs incongruently punctuated concerned comments.

Heath still stood in his towel. His shorts still hung in the tree.

Then I heard the siren. I just wanted to leave.

The ambulance and police car pulled close to the dock, and a paramedic raced toward the group quickly with her black bag in her hand.

"Rhiannon!" my mother's voice boomed with shock. "My God, Rhi, what happened? Are you okay?" *Of course, Mom has to be the responding EMT... Fabulous.* I had probably been the very reason she decided to take the courses to begin with. I have always had a talent for seeking out danger.

People all started talking at once, trying to answer her questions. She held up a hand to silence them. Then she pointed to Carlee. "You tell me what happened."

As she retold the story, my mom checked my vitals and listened to my breathing. She left me with my face down to make sure fluid did not pool in my lungs.

When Carlee explained who saved me, she then pointed in the direction of where Leone stood. Mom nodded to the group, not sure who saved me.

"Do you think you can sit up?"

"Yes," came my croak of a response. She helped me turn and sit.

She looked into my eyes and touched my throat. She looked into my mouth and my ears. She felt my arms and ankles. This seemed much more of a work-over than most people received.

"Mom..."

She just looked at me. "I am worried about those lungs. Fluid in there is never good."

She scooped me up in her arms and helped me walk down the dock. Carlee brought the paramedic bag. I sat in the back of the ambulance on a gurney.

Carlee smiled at me from the door.

"Nothing like making a first impression," I squeaked to her.

"I will meet you at the hospital," Carlee asserted. The door closed.

I laid back on the gurney and watched the ceiling. My insides were aching. I wiggled around trying to avoid the discomfort in my body, but it only grew worse. At least it helped me to know I was truly alive. I could not escape the pain in my throat. He had saved my life. I didn't even know what that meant. Had I really died or had I just been close to it?

I remembered having to breathe, the necessity unbearable. Even though I tried to remain breathless long enough to make it out of the water, my body had overridden my logic and I had inhaled water. I remembered the feeling of the cool water surging down into my lungs—so heavy, not soft and light like air. My body had felt so fatigued and water surrounded me everywhere. I had tried to breathe again after sucking in water, but my body could not do it. Then, the next thing I knew, the dock was under me.

The ride took about thirty minutes. The lights were flashing, but the siren did not blare. I felt thankful for some peace. I knew Mom had called Dad already on his cell phone to let him know what happened. Of course, he would be anxious, but not shocked.

I closed my eyes trying to focus on breathing through the ache.

I must have drifted into a sleep. I woke up when the engine turned off.

Mom rushed me, bed and all, into the hospital. Dad waited in the triage area. He must have been close to the hospital in order to have beaten us.

The doctor explained to my parents the issues with partial drownings, mostly for my dad's sake.

"On the other hand, when people take huge amounts of water into their lungs, such as a drowning, or even inhale a teacup worth of water at once, it may effectively cut off oxygen supply and cause unconsciousness or death. We are very lucky someone was there quickly." The doctor motioned toward my obviously non-dead body. "When a person has taken water into their lungs and has stopped breathing, CPR is required. She should be able to breathe normally with some residual coughing. But I think we need to evaluate her over the next few weeks to be sure that no infection sets into her lungs. Also, something to consider, the longer the person has not been able to breathe, the more chance they have of brain damage, because of the brain being deprived of oxygen."

Dad looked like he could pass out. He grabbed Mom to steady himself.

"Geeze!" I screeched. "I am not brain dead. I'm fine really, except for my scratchy throat and achy lungs!"

The doctor looked at me. "I'm sure you're just fine. I want to examine you and get a thorough diagnostic. I'll order an x-ray of your lungs to make sure the fluid is gone."

"Rhi, you really know how to scare me." Mom sighed, sitting on the bed next to me.

My hand kept touching my lips and tracing them. "Sorry, Mom, I really don't know what happened. I was being safe."

"You're turning into one of those 'extreme sports' kind of people aren't you, kid-o?" Dad winked.

"The cops were there talking to everyone and obtaining statements. I know there is really no one to blame, Rhi." Mom suggested. "But, my gosh! You seem to always be the one that ends up in the situation. A tree? Amazing. Who would have thought?"

"You keep messing with your lips." Dad noticed. "Do they hurt? Are you doing well?"

"Yeah. They just have an intense tingle to them." I announced.

"Is that normal?" Dad asked the doctor.

"I have not heard of that being a side effect. But, if your tissues lost blood flow for a little bit, they might be tingling as the oxygen is reaching the tissue again." He walked toward the door. "Keep an eye on them, color and feel."

Dad tousled my hair again. "I'm just glad you are okay." Then he kissed my head.

I winced from where my scalp stung, reminding me about the patches of hair I lost. I tried to gently pull my hair straight around the areas without making him feel bad.

"Did I hurt you?" he asked. "I'm alright. I pulled a bit of my hair out when I tried to free myself from the log."

"Let me see." Mom stepped to me. "I can't believe I missed it."

The doctor also began to examine me.

"Really, Mom, I didn't mention it. I had actually forgotten about it until now." I hated that she felt responsible for any of this.

"It looks a bit raw, but I think it will be okay. I will put some ointment on it for now." The doctor assured us.

Mom rubbed my back. I looked up at her and knew that look. She was blaming herself for my discomfort. I shook my head.

We were in the hospital for three hours by the time they discharged me. Mom had gone back to work to finish her shift.

Carlee had been in the waiting room with a ton of other people wanting to hear updates. When the nurse told me my groupies were outside, I asked if Carlee could come back and see me.

I wrote down our house number on a tablet sitting on the hospital tray and told her to call me. I explained we were going to be there until the x-ray came back, but everything else checked out fine. I pleaded with her to tell everyone to go on home.

Dad and I grew bored while we waited for the discharge papers. He began to grab cotton swabs, making antennas stick out of his head and playing with the instruments in the room. He, in effect, tried to make me laugh, which proved to hurt more than anything so he stopped.

When the x-ray finally came back, the doctor studied it and said, "A lucky set of events that took place. By turning you over and keeping your head down, it appears that most of the fluid left your lungs by itself." He smiled at me. "I'm going to take a precaution and give you a prescription for antibiotics, just to be on the safe side. I want you to go to your doctor or come back here once each week for the next few weeks so we can check and make sure those lungs are staying clear."

"I will make sure she gets the medication and the checkups," Dad said, doing his stern face and wagging a finger at me. I smiled at him.

Then we left. Dad stopped to get something to eat. I just ordered a milk shake. I thought it might make my throat feel better.

4

Waking Up

The phone rang the next morning.

"Hey girl!" Carlee's voice lilted on the other end. "How are you doing?"

"Pretty good. My lungs aren't burning like they were. My throat still hurts. I've been spraying some numbing stuff into it."

"Do you feel like going to the movies tonight? Do you think your parents will trust us?"

Although my body felt better, my mind still reeled from the near death experience. I laughed. "So, who is 'us'?"

"Oh, well, mostly everyone. Me and the guys."

Well, that completed the list of everyone I met at the reservoir. "I'm sure my parents will be fine." I stated that, even though I knew Mom might object, saying my body needed to recover. "They understand no one made a careless mistake. Really, no one is to blame. It's just my luck. I will ask them and let you know."

Carlee's voice seemed light and cheery as she trilled, "Sounds great! We will be leaving here about five. We want to get something to eat before the movie. It starts at nine—the late showing."

I snickered thinking nine o'clock could be considered the late showing. "Sounds good, I'll let you know. Oh hey, what are we seeing?"

"I'm not really sure yet. We just want to hang out. We'll see whatever is playing."

"Okay, talk with you soon."

We hung up and I dialed my mom's cell.

"Hey, Rhi,"

"Hi, Mom."

"How are you feeling? Any better?"

"Yeah. I had a nightmare about it last night, but I'm okay. I think most of my freak out is over." I didn't divulge the still nagging ache in my chest and throat, worried that she might not let me go out.

She paused on the other line, probably thinking about what I had just said.

"Mom, Carlee just called. Everyone is going to dinner and the movies tonight. Can I go?"

"Hon, I think it would be a good thing for you to go out, but is it wise after last night? Don't you think you need some rest?"

"Mom, I'm fine. Really."

She paused. "Fine. What time will you be leaving and what time will you be back? Also, who is driving you?"

Standard protocol for my parents. They seem to thrive on details, but I am glad they care.

I filled her in on the details of the evening.

"I want you to make sure it's okay with your dad. But if it is fine with him, then you can go. Please call if you need me."

"Thanks, Mom. Love you."

"Love you, too."

I always wanted to let Mom know that I did care, even when I seemed "possessed by my evil, meaner twin" as she would say. It continually seemed to pay off for me.

I found Dad in the game room tinkering around with a TV and stereo system. His back to me, he was engrossed in his work and up to his ears in cables and wires. He looked like Dr. Jekyll's experimental robot. After telling him my plans, he managed to tell me that he hoped I would have fun. I took that as a "yes" from the dad corner.

I decided to watch television that afternoon. A program came on that I normally would not watch, but I grew interested none the less.

The screen-shot blipped off in the middle of the narrator explaining the meanderings of meerkats and pounding music started.

The tempo gripped me. Perhaps the most ominous of events would unfold before my very eyes. I rolled them instead. The addiction to the drama in society is annoying. So, on those occasions when I am tuned into it, the melodramatic music gets to me.

"So what is it today? Did someone lose their cat in a tree again?" That would make big news around here, where nothing ever happened. The news reports in the morning have five minutes of things to talk about. And then the rest of the hour, they repeat it all. I guessed it could be worse.

A female voice announced, "This just in. A truck has been found on the back roads around Arrowrock Reservoir, north east of Boise. No bodies have been found. A solitary golden retriever stood guard at the vehicle, waiting for her owner. We'll take you now to Alyse, live on scene."

The scene separated into two camera shots, one from the news room and one to an average woman standing with her back to the water.

"Thank you, Bridget. We are live on scene right below Arrowrock Dam, where investigators are struggling to make sense of the situation."

The news anchor looked down into a monitor as the new imaged appeared. A man in a sheriff's uniform talked about the findings. His rotund belly hung over his dark belt. Sweat glistened in the sunlight on his forehead.

"A passerby found the rig, just like it is."

He pointed behind him. The camera angle did not follow.

"It's resting right under where the driver's door frame is, with the front wheels completely off the road. It's just lucky it didn't go over, the drop off there is almost straight down to the water."

"What is so unusual about the find?" the reporter prodded.

He reached up and scratched his head.

"Well, that's the hummer of it." He paused. "The driver's door has been completely ripped off its hinges. We found it below in the water, like something just took it off."

The news anchor didn't respond, she continued to hold the microphone in front of the officer.

"Oh, Yeah, and the dog. Nice dog really. She has been sitting next to the truck, whimpering. She must truly love her owner. We have boats looking through the water here trying to find a body."

The camera panned to the left and I could see the yellow, two-door compact pickup sitting precariously with the body of the truck resting on the edge of the precipice right behind the tires.

I tried to imagine what it had been like to be the driver looking down the front of the hood into the blue far below. How lucky they had been to have the truck stop where it had. Only an inch farther and all would have been lost over the edge.

I could see the poor dog being petted. The handler held her by a leash.

>"Bridget, the investigation is still ongoing and the road is temporarily closed. So, if you are headed to the reservoir today, expect delays."

"Thank you, Alyse."

Bridget, in the newsroom, once again took over the entire screen. She recounted the breaking news and added:

>"The identity of the person possibly driving has not been divulged at this time. We will keep you updated as we find out more."

Weird. How scary would that be? This truly was the biggest news story since we had arrived.

When I finally looked at my clock, I realized I had fifteen minutes to get ready. I changed into pants and a black tee shirt. I brushed through the tangled mess of my hair and decided to put it in a ponytail and wear my favorite baseball hat.

As I walked down the stairs, the doorbell rang.

I rushed to the door and opened it. Carlee stood there bouncing and smiling. I checked my pocket to make sure I had stashed my cash.

I yelled to my dad and let him know my ride had arrived. A muffled "have fun" came from the depths of the house.

I closed and locked the door on my way out.

As I walked around the front of the house, I could see into the game room area through the long panes of glass. Dad had cords hanging out of his mouth, a TV box of some kind in one hand, and more cords running into different entertainment components in the other. The sight made me laugh. I waved to him. His eyes smiled back at me more than his lips, and he nodded in my direction for added acknowledgment.

I stuffed myself into the only available seat in back of Carlee's car. Heath sat in the front seat. Bob and Kyle hunched in the back with me.

"Hi." Heath leaned around to see me.

"Hey, Heath."

Bob nudged me in the ribs. "How are you doing?" he asked.

"I'm doing well. Just quite a scare, really."

"I think you scared us all. We didn't even have enough time to get to know you and you were trying to leave already." Kyle joked.

A new song announced itself with a strong beat and familiar back up vocals. Carlee turned it up. I felt grateful to her for the distraction. She started singing the lyrics loudly and gave me a wink in the rear view mirror. She understood my need to change the subject.

Bob leaned closer to me. "Are you going to go anywhere before school starts up?" School loomed too closely on the horizon now. I didn't want to think about it, but it became apparent he wanted to start some conversation.

"I think we are going to see my Grandpa." Thinking of him made me smile. He has always been a great man. Even though we were not really making plans to go, I felt the need to set up some scapegoats, just in case.

"That will be cool. Where does he live?"

"He's up in Northern Idaho, a little town called Viola." I looked at Bob's blank face. "Don't worry," I chuckled, "not many people know about that town. It's fifteen minutes north of Moscow."

"Oh, okay. I know where Moscow is."

The idle chitchat continued until we pulled up to a restaurant on the other side of McCall. The wooden structure had been lacquered into a honey tone.

We filed in. It seemed to be an older establishment. The diner smelled of deep fat fried foods, cooking sugars, and breads. Forks scraping plates, dishes bumping each other, and milling voices proclaimed dinner time.

The waitress led us to a large table she had made out of two smaller tables. "What can I get you kids to drink?"

We all placed our beverage orders while looking over the menu and talking.

"Are these going to be all together or are we doing separate checks?" she asked.

Heath blurted out, "I will get mine and Carlee's," while pointing toward Carlee sitting close to him.

The waitress glanced at Bob and then Kyle.

At almost the same time they said, "I will get hers," pointing to me.

I could not help rolling my eyes. "Thanks, I will be getting my own."

Both guys deflated. I didn't want to ruin the evening. "I eat way too much for the average pocketbook," I joked, trying to relieve their rejection.

They let the issue die.

Carlee piped up, "Hey, did you guys see the news report this afternoon?"

She scanned the faces at the table. Bob, Heath, and Kyle all shook their heads. I said nothing. I wanted to see if she had seen the same report I had.

"Some poor person almost went head first into Arrowrock Reservoir." Her eyebrows up, she reminded me of a teacher surprising her class of jug-headed boys with a story. They sat at attention.

"They showed the truck on the news. It seemed barely to be on the road. Pure luck kept it from going over the side. But the weird thing is, the door to the driver's side had been ripped off and thrown into the water. At least that's where they found it, a distance from the truck. That's what the radio's report said."

"Strange," Heath said, still looking at Carlee.

"Is that all they know?" Bob pressed.

"That's all they talked about."

"The owner had a dog." I added.

"Oh, Yeah, that golden retriever." Carlee's mouth pouted. "She sat next to the truck, whining for her owner to come back."

"That one," I smiled at her. "I wonder if he had tried to step out of the truck, maybe after hitting his head or something, and fell into the water. How far away is Arrowrock Reservoir anyway?"

"It's out of Boise, about an hour north of there," Bob answered.

"But what about the door? Any idea what it takes to rip off a truck door?" Kyle asked.

We were all silent for a moment. The image I drew in my head had a man in red tights and a cape. I thought I would keep it to myself.

"Maybe the truck door already had problems and if the truck had come to an abrupt stop, then maybe it flung itself into the water." I offered a weak explanation.

Kyle's eyebrows went up and he exhaled. "I guess anything is possible. It's just not something you hear about every day."

They continued talking as I watched the waitress with a tray of drinks.

As she made her way back to our table, and hopefully to take our orders, a new group walked in the door. With a word to the newcomers, she changed directions and led them toward a table.

I noticed a beautiful, tall redhead in the group. Something about her caught my attention. Her honey skin reminded me of an old-fashioned cameo portrait, perfect and flawless. It might have been the way she held her head high, so sure of herself, that made me take note. I secretly wished for that kind of confidence and felt a pang of jealousy at how mysterious it made her appear.

She pulled her dark sunglasses from her eyes and dropped them into the handbag she had draped across her arm. She was

70

simply divine. She wore a fitted shirt that flattered her thin waist. Her blue jeans were rolled in the latest fashion, showing off her perfect ankles. She wore heeled flip-flops with shining stones embedded in them. She radiated class and style. I believed she could put anything on and make it look right.

Her smile, though, drew me in. It lit up her face, and it seemed, her entire being. I felt a desire to learn about her and ask her the secrets she knew, the ones that allowed her to float so gracefully and seem open to the entire world around her.

I had been so completely amazed at her that, when the next person walked around the corner, I sucked in a breath. Tall, dark, and brooding. The face was unmistakable. The one I had nightmares about from the mountain and the gas station, though I noted his eyes were a golden brown in color. I sank into my seat a little and pulled the menu up higher. I tipped my chin to let the brim of my hat conceal more of my eyes. I peaked past the edge of my menu and watched. As they walked to seat themselves, another person rounded the corner of the wall.

I sat up and looked straight at him, dropping the menu down to the table. *Leone.* He looked immediately at me as he pulled his sunglasses from his eyes. I swam with giddiness in their depths. More than anything I focused on his eyes. They ensnared me. My heartbeat rose. I could not turn away. He seemed to will it, not wanting to break the contact either. I could hear my own heartbeat swishing though my ears, and my face began to warm.

His lips arched into a beautiful smile at me, and I realized my attention to him had been overly obvious. I dropped my head back down to my menu. Even though I had withdrawn my gaze, I could still feel his on me. I had to concentrate not to look back at him.

Carlee's voice caught me as I regained focus on what was being said at our table.

The beautiful female of their group caught the attention of the guys at our table. No one had noticed me gaping at Leone. To Bob's, Kyle's, and Heath's favor, they regained their composure and withdrew their stares.

"Lauriel," Kyle said under his breath, acting like he had been staring at his menu. "What I wouldn't give to have her realize I existed."

"I know what you mean." Bob chanced a look.

They both glanced side long at me before becoming engrossed in their menus again.

The waitress focused her attention on Leone. Though obviously much older than he, she acted like a school girl in his gaze. I lowered my eyes as she maneuvered to our table with the drinks.

So this is Leone, to whom I owed my life. The one I felt deathly afraid of and entranced with all at the same time. My hand touched my lips. The feel of him forever burned there. The sensation had lasted hours. As Leone took a seat, I chanced looking at him again under the brim of my hat.

"...so what do you think?" Bob asked.

"Oh, uh... about what?" I pulled my eyes away from Leone to my menu.

"The special of the day? Rocky Mountain oysters!" Kyle laughed.

I missed the joke.

Heath and Carlee snickered as well. Heath added, "They come with a side of fries or a baked potato." His smile widened.

The confusion on my face must have been too much. They all started laughing.

I grabbed my drink and drew in through the straw.

"They are bull testicles," Kyle exclaimed rather loudly.

I almost spewed my soda on the table. As it was, the overwhelming pressure in my throat fizzed, burned, and shot out my nostrils. I grabbed the napkins in front of me and shoved it under my nose. I might as well have stuffed two fists full of straws up my nose. The intensity of my carbonated nostrils made my eyes water.

My friends laughed. The commotion had everyone in our section of the restaurant twisting in their seats to get a better view.

"Ya, haha!" I grumbled. "I'll gargle peanut butter for my encore."

I knew my face had turned beet red, as hot as it felt. I had the sinking feeling that even if I tried to leave, the door would not be close enough. *As if yesterday hadn't been bad enough. My lungs ached, my throat hurt, and now my nostrils feel like they have been packed with muscle rub, not to mention the slamming of my pride.* As close as they were to our table, I suspected Leone's group saw the whole thing. I didn't look in their direction—based on the movement I caught out of the corner of my eye, I was confident Leone's tall, dark friend laughed right along with the friends at my table. I could now put the sound of his laughter right alongside his white eyes in my nightmares.

Dinner took too long.

My appetite died by the time my chicken salad arrived.

I noticed our friends at the other table ordered meat with everything else on the side. Picky eaters. I knew some people that couldn't let anything touch on their plates. When Leone cut into his steak, it must have been rare, almost raw. I could see the steak bleeding from a distance. By the end of their meal, plates full of french fries, salads, coleslaw, and other unrecognizable sides remained piled in the center of their table. I assumed untouched. Protein diets must be all the rage. I knew a person was called vegan if they ate only vegetables. I couldn't think of the term for a person that ate only meat. I thought of carnivore, but the picture in my mind resembled a bear or a dinosaur. The closest I could come was cannibal. Honestly, the thought of it just creeped me out. Sometimes my mind went a bit overboard.

I had a brief image of Leone's friend with blood on his mouth and white eyes. I shivered and looked back at my plate.

Bob decided to talk about the incident at the beach again. "We're really glad you are feeling better."

"Well, I did until your oyster talk," I reminded him.

"You're not kidding," Kyle said. "You are the talk of the town. Man! Thank goodness for Leone. He truly deserves all the credit for pulling you through that."

Bob growled, "Ya, but did you see his face as he gave her mouth to mouth?"

I really did not want to be talking about this. Could I find a rock to crawl under? I looked around. Maybe I could just get under the table.

"I couldn't tell whether he got his kicks from it or if he tried to save your life," he continued, his eyes in Leone's direction. "His face seemed almost anguished while he leaned back, and then he appeared to be in bliss when his lips were on yours."

Leone's face angled down and tipped to the side. Bob had spoken loud enough that he could have heard every word of it.

"Come on guys, I've been having enough trouble keeping my thoughts away from that. Could we please not talk about it the rest of the night?"

They agreed.

Leone stood from his table and walked to the waitress at the cash register. He spoke with her for a moment. She glanced at our table then nodded to him.

I wondered what plan he had concocted. I figured the new recipients of his bill were probably Kyle and Bob. I smiled thinking of the secret pleasure I would have after the torture they gave me during dinner. I could only imagine the names people would come up with for the soda-nose incident.

He produced money from his wallet and walked out. I assumed wrong. Dang. I would have to figure out another way to get Kyle and Bob back.

When the waitress came and delivered the checks, she passed one out to everyone, then looked at me and said, "Yours is on the house." She walked away before I could ask any questions. Bob and Kyle looked like someone had just socked them in the gut.

We took the car into town, parked, and passed the shops my parents and I had meandered through weeks before. The lake to our left appeared to have blue crystals dancing off its waves in the setting sun.

"Hey, when we go boating tomorrow, meet me over there." Bob pointed to a road that angled to the right of the strip mall where Mom and I had walked. On our previous trip, I hadn't realized the main street into town divided either to the left or straight to disappear around the edge of the building. Bob pointed to the marina.

"You'll park in the lot and then walk out to the third dock. You'll see me. Bring lots of sunscreen, CDs, and anything else you need. I have the food," he winked at me, "and life jackets."

My decision to go had not yet been made. Being out on the water did not make my list of top ten things Rhi-needed-to-do so soon after my... experience.

We turned the corner to head up the main street away from the marina. The theater sat at the end of the side walk, past a coffee shop, a clothing shop, and an outdoor sportsmen's store.

I hadn't heard of the movie we were about to see which didn't surprise me. I didn't follow movies much. I caught them when they were shown on TV, but normally I didn't go out of my way to watch them.

I paid for my ticket, but Bob beat me to the punch with popcorn and soda. Kyle, obviously on the same brain wave, did the same.

I tried my best to be happy about that. I smiled and thanked them kindly.

They looked at each other and laughed. At least they can be civil during the rut. I didn't want to be "in season" despite their efforts.

We picked seats toward the back. Carlee and Heath sat glued to each other's side. I figured, as close as they had been since dinner, they would probably not pay attention to the movie, which sort of left me on a date with two guys that I do not want to be on a date with. Great. They sandwiched me between them.

As they were talking about a "great action flick" with blood and gore one of them had recently seen, a chill ran up and down my spine.

Movement from behind me caused a breeze to flow across my neck as people filtered into the aisle. Sweet smells, floral and fruity, pleasant and calming. Then a distinct one seemed to settle around me.

I closed my eyes. Familiar. One that I had been introduced to time and time again. Wood infused with lavender—old to my senses, older it seemed than my mind could remember. A peace settled inside that filled me with love and caring; the feeling so incongruent in the theater with my friends that I could not help but shake my head in confusion.

"Oh, sorry," Bob said to me. He must have thought my eyes were closed because he leaned in front of me to talk with Kyle. He had given up on getting Heath's attention.

"I think it must be a really exciting movie," Kyle said. "I haven't seen it yet."

"I won't spoil the ending for you," Bob carried on. "But you are going to love the scene where..." I tuned him out.

I drifted back into my mind. I knew where that smell resided in my memory—the dreams. It existed as the aroma of safety and overwhelming love that left me gasping for air as I woke from those visions. I leaned forward slightly, making it hard for Bob to ramble on. He simply moved his body to talk around my back.

I turned around and looked at the row behind us. Leone had seated himself directly in back of me. His friends flanked him on both sides. They were looking at me. When I met his eyes, he smiled. My heart rate sky rocketed and threatened to pound out of my chest. I could hear it thumping loudly inside myself. I assumed my cheeks flushed red.

His dark-haired friend did a "huh". He must have thought my response seemed funny. I quickly corrected myself in my seat.

The movie started.

The rest of my group became entranced in what they were watching. As I watched, my eyes became dreamy, my head sleepy. My spine tingled. I tried to focus on the screen, but my vision began to blur. I felt a light-headed sensation, like spinning too fast on a merry-go-round. The characters changed, the scene changed, and the setting changed. What everyone else in the theater saw became another movie entirely to me.

The hair on my neck prickled, thousands of needles tapped against my skin. I identified the sound of breathing close to my ear and felt the movement of air along my neck and earlobe. Although, logically, I could not understand why or how someone could get close enough to me without anyone in my group noticing, I felt positive someone was there. As entranced as I had become in that dream-like fog, I could not turn around and confirm my suspicions. I sat firmly rooted and relaxed in my seat.

The screen changed to a sepia color for me. The movie seemed to go back in time to World War II. Leone stood there with me. We were enjoying the closeness, kissing in the choreographed spots, walking hand in hand, enjoying our lives. The setting must have been Hawaii. The sun, the palm trees, the American warships in the harbor, and the clothing all denoted the place and time.

All the while the story played out on the screen, my body came alive with an electric sensation. Prickling began to course down my back and legs. My arms tingled. My fingers pulsed and twitched. When I had fully succumbed to the emotions on the screen, I became her. I felt as her legs worked tirelessly, rushing her forward in the dusk of the evening. I could feel her beating heart picking up speed as she began to run toward the pier. I experienced her ache as she broke the heel on her shoe and twisted her ankle. I understood the panic as she knew something stalked her in the shadows.

She grabbed her other shoe and flung it aside. I smelled the acrid, black smoke that clung to the harbor all day from the attacks. The thick air coated my lungs as I inhaled. I knew it to be the smell of thousands of deaths in the harbor. My mind numbed from the day's events, helping the wounded where I could until they were taken to the hospital. But now, fear of another sort coursed through me. I screamed for Leone. I understood him to be on one of the rescue boats still combing the harbor.

I reached the end of the pier and fresh cries rang out from me. I screamed for Leone again. I screamed with every ounce of my being from the top of my lungs. I could not see any boats.

Cold, sharp pain gripped the back of my neck. In seconds, I realized someone or something had inflicted the searing sensation and held me. I could not turn around. It lifted me from the ground. My hands were attempting to hit and knock the grip loose. My feet were kicking.

Whatever had seized me now spoke to me in a low, grumbling voice. "I told you not to run. Now look what you did. You spoiled my fun." A terrible growl came from behind me...

The intense pain in the back of my neck from the daydream shocked me into blinking. My breath came rapidly and I sat up straight. My hand flew to the back of my neck.

The screen came back into true color and the sounds of the theater again surrounded me.

The woman on the screen did not move voluntarily. The camera angle, a shot from the depths below, showed her silhouette drifting downward into the deeper water. Her hair floated all around, her arms wide, and legs wrapped in her skirt, she danced with the ocean tide creating a beautiful motion in the fading rays of sunlight surrounding her.

I lost my breath. I lost control. I knew firsthand what it felt like to see the sun fading away from me as I slipped deeper into the depths of the water. I understood how the woman felt as she drifted, weightless. I needed out of the theater. I struggled to stand, spilling one bucket of popcorn onto the other one at my foot.

I jumped over Bob and four other people on my way to the aisle and escape.

I ran from the room. Death, drowning, deep water, pain, body tingling, I feared I would snap. Tears began to sting my eyes.

I pushed open the door to the bathroom and rushed in holding my stomach. I made it to the end stall, locked it, and leaned against the wall. Tears fell hot, wet, and unabated. I sank to the floor, clutching my gut. I must have sounded horrible—great sobs escaped my mouth. At least no one else needed the bathroom at that time. I had it to myself. *I picked a great time to have to deal with these emotions—Dad's near death accident, moving from my home, white eyes and blood on the mountain, almost drowning, being rescued, dreaming every night of my rescuer, yearning to be near him, being teased by my friends, and now, reliving my drowning in a distorted dream*. I cried until my tears ran dry. I felt purged and drained. I sat on the floor, staring at the blue stall door, numbly noting the scratched-in words from previous users.

Someone came in and went into the other stall. I grabbed a handful of tissue, dabbed my eyes, and wiped my nose. I knew without having to look that my eyes were probably beet red and bulging out of my head. I do not look pretty when I cry. I went to the sink and splashed cold water on my face and held palms full of it to my eyes. It felt good. It didn't help, however. I looked as if I had lost a fight with a salt shaker.

I pulled my sunglasses out of my purse and slid them on.

I snuck out of the bathroom and waited to hear if any of my friends were in the lobby.

As I hid behind the bathroom partition, I heard Bob tell Kyle to go back in and he would check on me. That way Kyle didn't miss the last half of the movie.

I snuck back into the bathroom.

The older lady stood at the counter washing her hands, looking at me.

"Could you please tell the gentleman in the lobby that I'm in the bathroom, I am okay, and that I will be in here for a while? I'll meet them in the lobby when the movie is over," I pleaded.

She paused for a moment. I wondered if she could tell I had been sobbing.

She just nodded and left.

I listened from my hiding spot.

I heard Bob say, "Okay" and "Thank you" and the theater door opened and closed. I chanced another look. I slid out the front door. I needed to breathe. The air felt good. It seemed to be in the high 60's with the sun down, enjoyable and crisp, a welcomed sensation after the heat in my skin from crying.

I felt so dumb walking down the sidewalk in dark glasses. I did not make fashion statements, but there I found myself.

I decided to go to the coffee shop and ordered a chai latte.

I perched on a tall stool facing the window so I could see my friends as they left the theater. I took my glasses off, hoping people could not see my swollen eyes as I faced the darkness outside.

My mind wandered back to the sensations in my body in the theater and the movie on the screen. *Me, in the movie... and Leone?* My mind had twisted. It seemed I could no longer discern between reality and dreams. Everything affected me so deeply. The passion and feelings in the movie were just as strong as the dreams I had been having, but my dreams were set, as far as I could tell, in a stone castle of some kind in the middle ages. Maybe I should see a shrink.

I have never been obsessed before. I could not even explain why I would be obsessing over Leone. We hadn't even shared a conversation, though he had saved my life.

A familiar tune started to play in the shop. "...beautiful, beautiful flash of light. Ohhh, beautiful flash of light." I found myself singing along quietly, "Distance between us is nothing new." I hummed some of the words and sang some under my breath. "Dreaming, dreaming, ohhh, you're a world away."

I heard a soft laugh beside me. I startled.

Leone settled down on the stool next to me. He kept his eyes on the table in front of him.

"Very meaningful lyrics," his voice sounded harmonic to my ears.

"Leone, right?"

His eyes met mine and he nodded with a wide smile—a smile that almost knocked me out of my chair. To say he was charming would have been an understatement—he was simply glorious. I noticed that distinctive smell again. How could a fragrance create such a peace inside of me? Maybe it had to do with pheromones or something, although I never really believed in that stuff.

"And you are Rhiannon, correct?"

I shook my head, pondering how he knew that. I hadn't introduced myself as anything but Rhi to my new friends.

A new choke caught in my throat. "I have to thank you so much for saving my life."

"You don't have to thank me." He paused. "My destiny is to be there for you." It should have been a joke, but he seemed dead serious.

"I really don't understand." I studied him closer, looking for answers. Just more questions came to mind. "I have turned this over and over in my mind. I swear I saw you on the beach just before I dove in. In a matter of minutes you found me. The branches had me thoroughly caught. Then suddenly , I was clear of them and launched out of the water. I could never... I don't know of anyone who could swim that fast and that strong while dragging another person." I lifted an eyebrow and squinted my eyes, interrogating.

"I do believe you must have the timing of the events off. I assure you, I only assumed where you were and am thankful I was correct." He shrugged, as if I were making a big deal out of nothing.

"And your eyes, on the sand at my house—when you scooped me out of the water—your eyes were white!"

"I cannot explain what you thought you saw then. Maybe the sun shined off the water into your eyes."

"No, I know better. I've tried to talk myself out of what I saw, but I also saw your friend's eyes a week ago...at the gas station." I didn't want to go into the mountain incident. "His were white then!" My voice grew louder, perhaps a little frantic, not necessarily in anger, but more dreading that I'd begun to lose my mind.

"I cannot help you with what you think you saw. Only that the eyes you see are the eyes I have." And those eyes connecting with mine made my thoughts stumble.

I stared into them. Longing crept in. Yearning, like an age-old fire that cannot be extinguished, reflected there.

"How do you do it?" I narrowed my eyes as I looked at him, my brows furrowed. My pulse rose. I felt as if I needed to defend myself in case he knew my mind had started slipping the day I met him. "How do you end up everywhere I am? When I'm out... catching me when I fall... saving my life... vividly haunting my dreams?"

I blinked as I realized in my exasperation that I had divulged something secret. Now that was out. I needed more water to splash on my face. I could feel the temperature rise on my skin, scalded like the milk in my tea. I shook my head, knowing I turned crimson from my error. I could not look at him. I didn't want him to have that power over me. To his credit, he remained unmoving and quiet.

I smelled that warm scent of him again, and my insides turned to goo. A sensation washed over me. My entire body relaxed, and there were no cares or worries left in the world— someone had shut a door to everything, and only Leone and I remained.

I decided to breathe through my mouth instead of my nose. It made it easier to avoid thoughts of having him closer.

After a long moment, he broke the silence. "Have you ever sat with someone you desperately loved with all your heart and soul and watched them slip from your hands?"

My head turned to him. I watched him through narrowed eyes. I had no idea what to say. I had never experienced anything like that.

He continued on, "What would you do to see them again?"

"I, uhh," I tried to say something, anything, but just shut my mouth and turned back to my tea. I shook my head at that experience that we had not had in common. It had probably been a private matter.

For several moments we sat wordless. I waited for him to explain. *Why would he bring it up with me if he didn't want to talk about it? Do I want to know? I hardly know him. And after all, I'm not a psychiatrist, for heaven's sake.* No, I considered it a moot conversation. There were other things I needed to know, though.

After the long pause hung in the air between us, I braved getting some answers. "Did you buy my dinner tonight?"

"After the teasing you were getting from your friends, I thought it the least I could do. After all, I helped get you into the spotlight yesterday." He didn't poke fun at me. His eyes looked away in what appeared to be guilt, his shoulders slumped, and his frame seemed to wilt. He continued, "I am drawn to you. Not in an 'I'm merely interested' sort of way. I hear..." He trailed off.

I studied him. Trying to figure him out left me perplexed. He did not act like the common, everyday guy. He didn't seem to be caught in the awkward, "not a man yet still a kid, but I am acting like I'm mature enough to take on any serious issue" phase of life. No, as I studied his movements, mannerisms, and humbled gestures, I knew machismo had been lost on him. He tipped his face to look at the floor, eyes wide, focused on something unseen, his forehead pinched, his lips slightly down at the corner. While lost in his thought, I glimpsed a sincere, soft sorrow that held him. It seemed to indicate he, too, had hinted at a secret. I felt a compassion growing for him.

"I will never hurt you," he began again, his lips pursed and brows furrowed. He made a fist and stabbed it into his open hand for emphasis. "I will do all I can to make sure no one else hurts you either."

My mind reeled. *Hurt me? Wow. This guy's deep. Didn't he just tell me in a matter of minutes that he lost someone terribly close and now he's worried about me? I am by no means someone who tries to fix others, but there is something weird about him.* There was also something comforting, and peaceful, and strange.

I continued to look at him.

He moved to get down from his chair, his back to me.

"No," I thought to myself, "don't leave now." I became mesmerized by his complexity. I could truly not figure him out.

"Somehow I feel like I have known you forever, but I have only learned of your name today," I uttered to his back wanting the conversation to continue. I wanted to know more. Where did his strong sense of protection come from?

Without turning his head, he asked me, "How long is forever?"

I stumbled to reply. I shook my head. I tried to form words with my mouth. I searched for a response, anything to keep him here in conversation. I simply didn't know what kind of an answer he looked for.

Then he walked gracefully and quietly out the door. His silhouette disappeared into the night.

In no time, my friends walked past the glass in front of me. Carlee spied me first. She waved and then rushed for the front door.

"Rhi, oh my gosh, are you okay? I searched the bathroom for you and everything!"

"I'm sorry, Carlee. I needed to get some air. Then I just found myself here ordering something to drink."

She gave me a big hug. "I didn't realize that part was in the movie. I am so sorry!"

"I'm fine, really," I said.

Carlee bought herself a coffee and then we walked back to the car. The others hovered close to me and talked about the movie. Everyone avoided reference to the drowning scene.

My brain churned as we drove home. I remained quiet and no one forced me to talk. I think they all felt guilty for the movie. I welcomed the solitude. I concentrated on my discussion with Leone so much that I did not help to ease their tensions.

"Hey, Carlee. Can you pick me up in the morning on your way to the marina?" I asked, stepping out of the car onto my driveway.

When I looked back in the car, I noted to my amusement, their eyes bulged and mouths gaped. They might catch flies! I stifled a chuckle. They had obviously given up on me going.

"Ya, of course! Are you sure?" her expression still sounded shocked, however, her tone indicated that she wanted a true answer.

"Yes. I am fine, really."

As everyone exhaled, they seemed to melt into their seats, sounding like deflating balloons. The guys all looked at each other.

Smiling, I turned and waved. "Good friends," I told myself.

5

Lost My Heart in Atlanta

Dad and Mom lounged on the couch, focused on the TV when I entered the front door.

"What are you watching?" I asked as they looked up.

"Oh, I wanted to watch one of my oldies," Mom said.

I came around the side of the television to see. An oldie but a goodie, I knew the movie *Gone with the Wind,* a classic. Clark Gable charmed the screen in this rendition of a Civil War-swept America. I had watched it a million times with Mom. Dad even enjoyed it once in a while. I guessed this would be his once—for a while. Mom snuggled into his arm as they lay back into the couch.

It made me feel whole to have my parents still mushy over each other. I would never let them know that, though.

I lay on the floor and watched as Terra burned and people fled from Atlanta. I grew sleepy, and my eyes glazed over. I slowly became the movie. It grew so real. I could see the burning all around. People screaming. Shots ringing out in the distance. The sounds grew louder.

I could smell dry hay and straw burning as stables blazed. Horses from the livery stables in town were running wild, changing direction to escape the chaos, their whinnies piercing.

I searched for something missing. Someone or something. Yearning swelled to desperation, but I could not place its cause. I dashed toward the dark boxcars ahead of me.

My yellow dress, so heavy and cumbersome, had a low cut in the front stating the fashion of a southern belle. Ruffles flowed in curving arches, twirling around the skirt. I held it in a tight grip as I turned down the roadway to the left, and then circled to the right again crossing the tracks. My breathing raced to keep up.

The street steeped in an eerie, red glow, reflected the flames shooting out of second story windows. Dark smoke billowed from the mercantile store. Hardly anyone remained, fleeing the onset of the madness. Alone, I ran headlong into town.

A name escaped my lips, "Leone!" I ran down the alleys. Searching. Something more than the fires caused me panic.

I desperately needed to find him. Life itself depended on it.

I stopped short and cinched up the ends of my skirt and yanked off the under slip that made my skirt billow. It swung like a pendulum as I ran, causing me to slow and trip. I ripped the yellow, floral hat from my hair and tossed it with the slip. Closer to the burning businesses now, my naked arms stung from the flames, the hair singed by the heat.

I saw another alley on the left around the burnt out corner bar. I headed for it looking for Leone. It seemed that I knew I would find him here. Perhaps we had just been separated from each other on this road.

Premonition ran through my body in the form of my heart skipping a beat. I stopped mid-step.

Something deadly lay ahead in the dark shadows. A deep laugh echoed toward me. So close, it seemed only ten paces from me.

My hands were spread in front of me. I could see them as I watched the ground, where the light turned to the dark shadow of the night. My spine tingled and the hair on the base of my neck began to stand on end. My thoughts raced. Where do I go? I shook my head and stepped backward to the middle of the burning street. I had expected to find Leone. I scanned up and down the street for anyone.

"Leone...please...where are you?" I choked out as the billowing, black form rounded the corner.

It didn't seem like his feet touched the ground. He floated, one hand reaching toward me, a seemingly innocent gesture. Instinctively I knew better.

My breath caught in my throat. I looked around and made a dash for the alley across from me.

Faster and nimbler than I, he blocked me from retreat in an instant. His robes swayed in front of him as he stopped. A gold, filigree crown on a bald head reflected the fire.

"What do you want from me?" I choked out.

"Tsk, tsk." His head shook from side to side and he looked down at his folded hands in mock despair. "I'm always so sad when he leads you on like this."

"What are you talking about?"

"I timed this rather well, actually. I thought for a minute I would have to give up and try another tactic. But you, the vulnerable, simple creature you are, have such a knack for getting yourself into trouble. It could not be more perfect."

My knees threatened to buckle.

His arms reached out toward me. "He is coming. I would guess about five minutes." With amusement in his eyes, he added, "Or six hundred of your lovely heart beats... My-my, you are rushing a bit. There might be a few less, because it will slow as blood drains from your beautiful neck."

My hands went to my throat. His bald head reflected the still-burning city with a red glow, accented by the crown. His eyes matched the city in an eerie crimson. His round face, white and pale, was pure terror to behold.

He extended his hand, enshrouded with rings. He floated toward me again.

I leaned back, trying to step my feet backward, but they would not move.

His dark robe came into focus. It shined like the stars in the night sky. There were blood red ribbons extending from his shoulders and racing in circular patterns to end in big drip-like circles.

I stared up at him. The crown on his head, I could now see, resembled a crown of thorns, making a mockery of Jesus. His arrogance disgusted me.

He chuckled, following my gaze. "Ah, yes. I would have you as my queen. Here, even if for a minute, I will dance with you as royalty." He took his crown off and gently placed it on my head. I flinched, not wanting his corruption to touch me. Before he removed his hand, he stabbed the golden spires into my scalp. An instant ring of fire burned where each of the needle sharp points broke the skin, digging deep. My body buckled in an attempt to escape the pressure. The sound from my own throat seemed foreign as blood began to pool and trickle from my head.

As my hands reached up in reflex to pull the crown from my head, his hands caught them and he forced me to stand straight.

"Let's not forget our dance." He smiled, his teeth white and shining. He drew me to him. My body became his unwilling partner, no longer under my control.

He leaned into me and lifted one of my hands to his cold cheek. He began his sickening song.

"Lub dub dub. Lub dub dub. Lub dub dub. Doesn't it keep such perfect time?" His movements pulsated with his song, pulling our bodies in a triangular motion, forward and backward. Blood dripped down my forehead into my eye.

"No!" I wanted to fight. I pled to my frozen body to move and fight back. Our bodies began swirling to his maniac song. He paused every few seconds and licked at the blood droplets.

He pushed me back at arm's length and looked into my eyes. "Lovely smell, a little young, not perfectly aged yet, but sweet and flavorful none the less." Fear beyond anything I could have imagined wretched through my soul. How could this be the end? This must have been the evil Leone had tried to tell me about. I hadn't listened. I thought he'd been a bit odd when he suggested anything about danger. Now, as I faced my end, I quivered and shook. I wanted to live. Tears, hot and fresh, mixed with drops of blood slowing their decent down my cheeks. He drew closer. He seemed to enjoy the terror on my face and the magnified beats of my heart.

His breath smelled sickly rotten. It was stale and old, but worst of all, I could smell *my* blood there.

"Dinner must have been spectacular, darling queen." He pulled me close. "I taste faint red wine and roasted meats. Quite an elaborate party you enjoyed at your celebration tonight. Too bad he did not have the will power to consummate your fate as soon as your lips touched his. That is the beacon that lets me know every time that he has found your aged and antique soul. Over the years his yearning for you has grown so powerful, you make him shine brighter than any other. You know?" He looked down at me again. "No, I imagine you don't."

He pondered his assessment. "He would not have explained that yet. You see, Caliga Leone—that would be Master Leone to you, is too pure in his current form. Never taken the blood. Silly of him really. He always decided to be good. Now, that goodness is your undoing, dear girl." He smiled down at me. I continued to struggle against him. "Whenever you are near, his little, trapped, pure soul shines. When you touch him he grows brighter, and when you kiss, your souls mingle again. Because I created him, I have a special

attachment, you see, sweetness? When he shines, I see. When I
see, I know it is time to hunt. He ages like fine wine. Each time
you leave and again return, his brightness is stronger." We
suddenly stopped spinning and he peered down the street into
the shadows. His expression changed from interest to a
boding, evil smile that showed his obscenely white, uneven
teeth.

He looked back at me and began to spin again. "I do hate
to waste you. I would love to stay and chat... to find out what
it's like to wander the earth, eternally searching for the end."
As we spun faster and faster, I could no longer make out the
distinction of the buildings surrounding us, a red blur. "If I
didn't detest him so badly, I would allow you to live. But I am
addicted to the search and demise of you—truly the funnest
form of sport, one that I have enjoyed for centuries. And alas, I
must say 'bona nectaris pulchritude'... good-bye, sweet
beauty."

He bent his head to my neck. I could feel his teeth as they
pierced the skin under my left ear. Unfathomable pain
threatened to wipe out my consciousness, lancing into my skin.
Unable to move, I tried to endure the agony. With each beat in
my chest a blazing pain spread down and burned a path to my
heart. I gained some small control of my body and began
hitting him, trying to get free. I gasped as my body succumbed
to his feasting. I grew light-headed. My vision slid from me.
Sounds swished together. The pain in my chest started to
recede the way it had come, taking with it my ability to move.

"Rhinata!" I recognized the voice that I longed for. I heard
feet on the cobblestone coming toward me, reaching my ears
through my fog.

I felt my body falling. The robe fled. I limply hit the
ground and lay where I fell. Colors blended. The crown tinkled
to the ground, bounced and rolled away. The sound seemed
magnified in the hallowed space once occupied by thoughts.

He came into view, so handsome. He screamed, although I could no longer hear it as the haze began to wash over me. He scooped me up in his strong arms.

His blue eyes were torn with despair. He clutched me to him. His lips moved and the words, "memor meus diligo eternus" softly touched my ear.

I sat straight up in the living room. The TV showed Scarlett descending the stairs in her dress made from the green curtains of Terra.

I blinked and looked around. Dad and Mom looked curiously at me. I knew sleep etched the contours of my face, explaining why they were amused. It had definitely been an earth-shattering dream.

Even so soon after it though, tendrils of the dream worked their way to the surface and became bombarded with logic. I sucked in and let out a breath. I became focused on the dream. The image of the man blocked out my consciousness of the living room. I clutched my chest and reached for the area below my left ear. The pain in my dream might as well have been in my own flesh and blood, the same as the daydream in the theater.

"Rhi," Mom's voice filtered to me, "are you okay? You're ghost white."

I nodded.

"Another bad dream?" she asked.

I looked at her and nodded again.

"Honey, why don't you go relax in a bath? I will make you a cup of tea." Her eyebrows slightly arched and her head tilted. I could see her concern and knew Mom needed to have the comfort of my being alright.

"I think I will," I said.

Mom got up from the couch and I heard her put a cup in the microwave to warm.

Dad, always good at changing the topic, asked how the night with the friends went. He paused the movie as I explained my exploding nose trick during dinner and our walk through town. I felt myself relax a bit.

"Wow, Rhi," he cackled, "I would have paid to see that nose trick." He reached over and rubbed my shoulder.

"Thanks for your support, Dad." I smiled weakly at him.

Mom came around the corner of the kitchen with a cup, a tea string hanging over the side. She smiled and handed it to me. Before she sat back down, she rested her hand on my head.

"I'm glad you had fun," Mom said to me.

"Yes." I nodded. I remembered my invitation to go boating the next day and hadn't yet received permission.

"Dad, Mom, Bob invited me to go out on his dad's boat tomorrow?" I watched Mom's face become horrorstruck. "Bob's dad owns the convenience store. They have life jackets and, *yes,* I will be wearing one. All of my friends are going to make me. And Carlee will be there…" I hoped I didn't sound too eager.

Dad spoke up before Mom's concerns could be voiced. "I think so. Don't you, honey?" He looked at Mom.

"I guess," she sighed, obviously she had planned a rebuttal. "I want some chores done when you get home tomorrow though, okay?" Her tone firm.

"Sure, absolutely," I chirped, as I stood.

I kissed them both, thankful for the way things worked out, especially for the fact that they had not asked me questions about my dream.

The bath warmed me, and the tea calmed me.

As I lay there wrapped in fluid tranquility, my mind attempted to recall the details of the dream.

The ghoul-like man had been so ugly. I recalled his taunting and teasing. His obvious intention had been to kill me from the moment he entered the dream. I had screamed for Leone.

Leone in this dream, too?

I splashed water onto my face and took another sip of tea.

Leone and the creature knew each other. The strange events unraveled in my mind. He had said they had a long history. Indeed, the creature said something about 'creating' him, something about his soul glowing. I would have laughed at that implausible idea except for the strong deep-down feeling that something had been affirmed inside me.

The more I thought about it, the stranger the dream seemed, and the more everything defied logic.

It became clear that I needed to forget the dream and stop analyzing it.

When I stepped out of the bath, I definitely felt better.

I just hoped I would get a complete night of sleep.

6

Boating

I picked out my one-piece swimming suit and my stretchy shorts with a matching top. I didn't want to expose anything in the close quarters on the boat. I double checked my bag. I even stuck a book in—just in case.

I walked downstairs to the game room that overlooks the driveway as Carlee's car reached the top of the rise next to our yard. I walked through the door as she turned a circle in our huge, dirt driveway. I hopped into the car the minute it stopped.

"Feeling better this morning?" She asked.

"Much."

We talked about school. She gave me the run down on who to avoid and who to talk with. I mentally noted that I would make up my own mind about that, especially considering Carlee never talked with Leone and his friends and they made her list of avoids. Bob and Heath played football and basketball with him, but said they never really hung out. They said he was an exceptional athlete that could do anything and do it well. I grew to think no one really had anything bad to say about him. People tend to make different assumptions. I saw myself leaning more to the wanting-to-get-to-know-him-better category. It could also be that hero-who-saved-your-life-now-you-can't-live-without-me complex talking.

I wondered if we were going to have classes together.

I jumped back into the conversation. "Any teachers I need to avoid?"

"Mr. Crowley. He is a grump. I had him last year for English. I'm not sure what he teaches for seniors, though. Just keep that name in your head." She smiled.

We chatted all the way to the marina. I decided that I really liked Carlee. She was genuine.

We parked and walk down to the docks. There were more people than just us planning to take a boat out today. I glanced at the lake. It spread wide and ran long, situated in a valley with large mountains at the other end.

The docks were definitely the eye sore, so modern they contrasted with the beauty of the backdrop. It looked to me as if God had painted the scene just to take our breath away.

The first dock did not have very many boats moored to it, but those deeper in the water had boats of every kind. My eyes flitted around and landed on a newer, red and shiny boat that had people loading. Wakeboards lined the tower. Then I spied Leone.

Mr. Tall and Dark reached out and grabbed the tower with one hand and swung himself into the boat without so much as a jump.

The beautiful lady the guys called Lauriel was there, too. Drop-dead exotic. Her suit, of course, a bikini, and she had the body for it. The kind that left the rest of us ladies cleaning up the drool from our guys. I felt completely fine with it, though. I had no expectation that I would ever be more than average. I kept glancing over at Leone as we searched for Bob.

Finally we spotted him on the far dock, lifting bags into the boat. We walked up in time to help him lift the cooler aboard.

He threw a black and blue life jacket at me.

We waited for a little while longer. Heath and Kyle came bounding down the dock.

"Let's go!"

Heath took the first turn at wakeboarding. He showed off his skill as he bombed the wake of the boat, tugging against the forward motion and launching himself into the air. Every few attempts he would flip, water spraying from the board, to land on the other side of the wake and continue on.

Carlee followed his maneuvers, whistling and hollering. He had probably sealed his affections now. She could obviously not have been more proud.

"Amazing," I told him as he boarded the boat again.

"Thanks," he beamed.

Carlee's grin never faded as she handed him a towel.

Bob, hand still on the steering wheel, looked at me. "Are you ready, Rhi?"

I gulped. "Uh, no… no thank you. I have no desire to get in the water today."

He laughed, already knowing the answer.

Kyle pulled another board from the tower. He jumped into the water. Heath passed him the board and organized the rope so he could better throw it to Kyle.

We were drifting slowly away from Kyle as he wiggled into the boots.

I noticed a boat making a wide circle around us and trailing a slalom skier back and forth across the wake like lightening. The skier caught air that seemed taller than the tower on the boat. He rolled three times in the air before landing perfectly, digging his weight into the oncoming water, forcing an arch of spray out toward our boat.

Even with that amazing feat, no one on his the boat cheered.

I recognized the group, then I recognized the skier. Leone caused another rooster tail from under his ski as he pushed back to the other side of the wake. He wore a black, half wetsuit that completely covered his torso. It formed to his body and left me gawking.

Then our motor slowly pulled us farther away from Kyle and Heath threw the rope.

Kyle seemed good at boarding, though he didn't do any real stunts.

"Rhi, there is tons of food in the cooler and bags full of stuff over there. Help yourself whenever you get hungry." Bob winked at me.

I smiled. I looked across the water to where Leone's boat rested. They were a great distance away from any other boats. I could barely discern Leone climbing out of the water. I watched until he disappeared into one of the seats of the boat.

"I have a tube we could blow up, and I could tow you around. In fact, it would fit both you and Carlee," Bob broke through my obsessing.

"I'm not sure." I paused. "I might feel like it later."

"Oh, Rhi. It's so fun. And Bob will go slow." Carlee tried to assure me.

"Okay, but only if you don't try and kill me. I have had enough of that."

Bob laughed. "I would be happy to help you have fun today," he said with a twinkle in his eye.

Kyle rode the board for a while and Bob started talking to Heath about taking over at the wheel so he could have a turn. They were in agreement.

Kyle let go of the rope and slowly lowered into the water. Carlee flipped the orange, man-in-the-water, caution flag so other boaters would look for the head sticking out of the water as we came about.

Bob killed the motor and began putting his lifejacket on. He grabbed Kyle's board.

Boating

The shiny, red boat pulled alongside ours.

"Excuse me," a voice called from the other boat, "I wondered if Miss Rhiannon would accept an offer to come aboard and take some spins with us." Leone stood close to the side of his boat, while the two others on board seemed to watch something in the distance.

My face flushed. He wanted me to come on board. The guy with the scary eyes sat at the wheel. I looked at Carlee. She scrunched her face around. "Get real."

My mind said no. *White eyes, bad experience.* My heart, however, fluttered in my chest. *Time with Leone.*

Bob looked as shocked as Carlee. He obviously did not think it made the good idea list either.

"Sure," I said, smiling at Bob, trying to affirm the right to make the decision for myself, but I added, "just for a little while."

Bob seemed to struggle to understand what just happened to his day of boating. Even Kyle, Heath, and Carlee all looked shocked. Heath had his mouth open, a bite from his sandwich still showing. Kyle just shook his head at me.

"Rhi," Carlee whispered, "are you nuts? Do you really think that is safe? We promised to keep you safe today."

"I'll be fine. I have some questions to ask him. Besides, he saved my life remember?" Carlee raised an eyebrow and nodded her agreement, shrugging her shoulders.

"As long as we can get you back for your tube ride," Bob grunted.

"I promise."

I took Leone's hand as I jumped from one wooden deck to the other.

He pulled me quickly, so much so that the force caused me to end up close to him. I looked into his face. For a moment my heart forgot to beat. His hand felt cool against me. The touch sent shocks through my skin.

Everyone remained quiet. I looked back at my friends. Bob stared. I waved and told them I would be back soon. Leone guided me to sit by him.

The motor kicked and we slowly slid away from the other boat. When we were a safe distance from them, the tall, dark one opened the throttle.

"Rhi, I would love to introduce you to my step-brother and sister."

I nodded. I had thought they were just friends. I felt a little relief knowing Lauriel would not be competition.

"This is Lauriel."

"Pleased to meet you." She nodded her head. I nodded back. She wore dark glasses, just like Leone.

Leone skipped to the driver. "I believe you have met Dante," his voice curious, as his hand flitted toward the driver.

Dante let go of the wheel, turned, and walked toward me. He took my hand in both of his and bowed low. He kissed my hand.

"It is a pleasure to make your acquaintance." His unexpected chivalry made me pull away from him, not wholly trusting this new version. The thoughts in my head conflicted. My checks flushed. The white eyes I had seen on occasion were now covered with dark glasses. His smile seemed warm and I could find absolutely nothing threatening about him.

In the next second he jumped back to the wheel, the boat still going full bore across the water.

"Dante has been willing me to introduce you," Leone explained. Dante presented me with his smile of agreement.

"Stop the boat," Lauriel shouted. I looked around to see what had happened.

She stood up, unaffected as the boat's speed lurched me forward. I had to brace my feet on the floor to keep steady. No one else moved. They seemed made of stone.

She took off her shorts, danced to the stern of the boat, hopped up, jumped, and spun into the water.

"It is time to cool off," Dante said jokingly and bounded to the back, diving gracefully off. I waited expecting a splash. It never came.

Leone grabbed me by the hand. I felt my body swoon as we were alone on the boat. How did his scent always calm me? I felt so relaxed with him, a stranger still, that I might as well have been enjoying a warm bubble bath by candlelight with a glass of wine in my hand. Not that I drank, but it had been the image of peace that I felt connected to. *Drunk? Maybe.* This emotion he managed to evoke in me had to be coming from some mind-altering chemical. Someone would've had to slip it to me each time I found myself close to him, though.

"I really have to speak with you." His tone softened, and his eyes seemed sorrowful. "We have all talked at great length about the correct way to do this."

My mind wondered. *Do? Do what?* I did not feel threatened by Leone, but my gut tightened none the less.

"I believe I have put you in danger."

"That's silly. You saved my life. How on earth could you have that backwards?" I retorted, pleased at my light-hearted response to his worried tone.

His face became firm and serious. "No, I know I put you in danger."

I stammered, trying to find a way to explain to him that my health had been cleared. I checked out okay. I would not end up with pneumonia, and I felt great.

He stopped me short by saying, "You must understand that I spent... time trying to find... you." He struggled to find the right words. I wondered why I could not understand what he attempted to say to me. He was adamant he get his point across.

I just looked at him. Whatever he'd to explained had me perplexed, so I didn't want to interrupt.

His voice grew soft again, not unlike teaching a child. "For now, let me tell you how drawn to you I am."

Okay. He is drawn to me. My heart rate raced. As if in response to my heart, he placed his hand on my neck. He seemed to enjoy the pulse. A gorgeous smile played across his face.

His eyes opened and he realized where his hand lay and quickly withdrew it. My skin burned where his fingers had been. My own flesh yearned to consume him. I gently rubbed the area trying not to make a big deal.

"I'm an old soul." He paused. Figurative speaking I assumed. I tried to grasp every word of what he explained. "You are my beacon, guiding me through each day. When you are not there for long periods, I begin to get frantic that I will not find you again. I struggle and second guess myself as to where you are. It is my curse. I have missed you before. It makes the anguish harder. I want nothing more than to have your smell encircle me at all times for the rest of eternity, have your heartbeat lulling me to my own heaven, and your body, so warm next to me." He averted his eyes, not wanting to see my reaction.

My mind tried to recapture what he had said. *Cursed, long periods apart, finding me.* My face must have looked like a comic strip as I went from furrowed brows to a relaxed expression and back again, as I tried to grasp it all. We sat in silence for a time. I ultimately did not understand a thing he told me. It seemed to be a poetic explanation of strong feelings. A very hungry part of me grew excited by this implication. Yet another part of me wanted to yell at him for thinking I could be silly enough to fall for the mushy babble he spat.

The two arguments in my mind battled. I finally resolved to follow what my natural being told me. While sitting with him my body reacted, tingling and turning to noodles. Something deep inside me filled with a calm I had never experienced before. This new found feeling in my body won over the logic in my thoughts that told me danger existed in falling in love with his words.

I could tell I had begun to feel strongly for him—*what bad could happen? A heart break?* So he missed me. I needed to rebuke his statement. "I see you everywhere I am. I'm guessing you didn't miss me *that* many times."

"That is not exactly what I meant," he explained. "I wonder during those times if you've found love or if you lived with emptiness inside you as I do."

Found love? Emptiness? It had only been last night that I first spoke with him. "I'm not so sure I understand," I stammered.

"Rhiannon. I fear that when I saved your life, I put it more gravely in danger than you could ever imagine."

My eyes widened, and my head pushed back in disbelief. The conversation made no sense. I battled with myself again. It was outrageous for him to keep insisting danger lurked around every corner. And now, it became grave danger. *Really?*

"I see the confusion. I will make this clearer to you, I promise. I'm not sure if doing it so quickly would be in your best interest." He seemed passionate about his beliefs. "I am severely worried about your safety." He turned and looked into my eyes taking both of my hands in his. I silently wished to see the blue there instead of his dark glasses.

"I know I can be a klutz. But I believe when it's time, it's time. I figure my headstone will read, 'What can we say? Rhiannon died because she was Rhiannon,'" I joked.

"Please, Rhi." His voice cracked. "I don't think I could lose you... again," he said the again quietly. Before I could question it, he continued. "I don't want to seem controlling, but I have a code that I follow in my existence. I must require that I am close to you all the time."

Is this some ploy to get me to date him? This is getting weird. I looked at the intensity in his body, chin high, shoulders back. He let go of my hands, studying me. I knew he believed in what he said.

Sensing my thoughts, he said, "I would not want you to act like my girlfriend. I just need to be close to you so I can respond if there is danger." I couldn't tell if he was desperate or persuasive.

"Close to me?" *Like stalking close? Not sure I want that.* "Okay," I reluctantly conceded, not knowing what all I had signed on for.

"I will need you to introduce me to your parents, so they can learn to trust me. I will be taking you to meet my mom, as well. You will know how to get to my place and how to find hiding places."

"Hiding places?" My voice strengthened. I looked toward the shore, it seemed too far of a swim for me. I couldn't see Bob's boat.

"Yes, I promise you." His shoulders slouched as he opened his hands, palms up, focused into them. "I will help you to understand. I feel it would be too overwhelming to have you learn about this all at once."

I sat there for a minute, absorbed in this talk. "I am not saying yes to your staying close to me. I will say yes to you letting me ask questions and understand what you are talking about." He reached for my hands again. The pins and needles feeling that I'd noticed earlier returned. How could his touch do this to me each time, then remain for so long after he let go?

I gazed at the mountains around me. Their beauty amazed me. Off in the distance, snow still topped the peaks.

In that moment I realized that the only sounds were the waves lapping against the side of the boat. There were no voices and splashing. Panic swept through me. I jumped up and looked out the back where everyone had disappeared to swim. I saw no one.

"Leone, they're gone!" I jumped over the back of the boat and landed on the deck.

I scanned the water frantically, ready to jump in, but not sure what direction to start looking. How could I not have paid attention to people in the water? How careless of me. It was not my boat, but it only took one person to notice when someone had gotten in trouble.

Leone grabbed me from behind before I could make a dive.

"Whoa there," he whispered into my ear and pulled me into him, as he leaned into the transom of the boat.

"I promise they're fine." His breath wisped against my neck. My heart skipped, and my body became gelatin. My knees threatened to buckle as he held me tenderly in his embrace. My eyes closed. I could feel my entire body light up with volts of passion.

I could not respond at first. I do know how long we stood like that. It felt so right. I didn't want it to end. My entire body needed this. I suddenly felt a passion burning in the pit of my stomach that I never knew existed.

I spun to face him. His desire seemed etched in his face. I put my hands on his cheeks and started to move toward him with my lips. It felt like an entirely different person had completely taken me over. My one and only thought became Leone. I had to touch him. I had to feel him burning my skin. I needed nothing but his kiss.

He turned. His face strained. The movement appeared to cause him pain.

"I had better return you to your friends before they think I kidnapped you." He grabbed my hips and pushed me away. He led me by my hand inside the boat again.

I sat, wrapped in the memory of the electricity pulsing through my body and my animal-like uncontrollable response to him. I wondered if that offended him and caused him to react. I felt sickened about my response as well. I'd never been so unabashed with a guy. My parents would have been horrified, but not as much as I was. I turned and looked out the side of the boat, my back to him, ashamed and embarrassed by my behavior.

I had obviously misread everything. He did not desire to be close to me. My abrupt advancement must have really turned him off. It had become as urgent as my own breathing, just to touch his lips to mine. I desired that burning sensation he had given me at the dock. Chalk this up to another Rhi screw up. I hoped no one would hear about it, definitely not the kind of thing I wanted to live down in a new school.

We found the other boat flying across the water.

Our boat stayed a safe distance away until Bob let go of the rope.

We pulled up slowly.

When we were close enough, I stood and jumped off the edge of the boat toward Bob's without looking back.

As I surfaced and started to swim, I could hear Bob asking where everyone else on Leone's boat had gone. Leone explained they were at the shore waiting.

The small explanation left him staring at Leone, then at me.

I climbed into Bob's boat and wrapped my towel around me. The others adjusted their things, finding their seats and not really paying much attention to me or Leone anymore. I noticed Leone standing in his boat, staring in my direction. He flashed his glorious smile and turned toward the steering wheel. Then his boat left us.

I felt a yearning to cry, but managed to stay composed.

As I promised Bob, I let him take me on a spin on the tube. Carlee gleefully and excitedly bounced in the waves next to me.

I held on tight for my life, as well as my sanity. If the day's events had been different, I might be having the time of my life.

We spent the rest of the day out on the water.

Everyone knew something changed while I'd been away from them, though I tried to act normal. Bob became extra attentive. He had decided his new job would be to protect me.

By the time I returned home, the sun set low in the sky.

Dad and Mom were in the yard working. I waved to them as I went inside.

A shower sounded good. The sun had my skin feeling tight and tired, so I chose a cold one. I covered myself with aloe to help with the healing from the sun. I brushed my hair and put it in a pony tail. I dressed in comfy shorts and baggy tee in my bedroom.

I walked into the hallway. Below me on the couch, Mom talked intently to Leone. My heart fluttered at first sight. Leone looked up immediately in what seemed like a response, before Mom noticed I even stood there. Then a realization hit me. Mom sat talking with the guy that told me weird things and that I tried to accost earlier. I imagined her disgust at me. I still wondered myself, about the conversation between Leone and I. Would he try and talk with Mom about those weird things?

"Look who is here, Rhi. Leone..." She checked with him, making sure she had his name right. "Came to see you. We were just talking about how he spent his summer. He practiced with the football team most of the summer." She seemed excited by the last bit of knowledge and a little too eager to have someone call on me at the house.

"Thanks, Mom," I said.

"Leone." She turned her attention back to him. "Can you stay for dinner?"

My heart skipped at her unexpected invitation.

He and turned toward her. "Thank you for the invitation, but I cannot stay for long. I came to return Rhi's sunglasses to her. She left them boating today."

I calmed a bit. Then he smiled a brilliant smile to Mom. I think she was just as shocked at his allure as I had been.

"Thank you," I said. I walked down the stairs and extended my hand for the glasses.

He bowed slightly as he handed them to me. He put his own sunglasses back on then and excused himself.

I walked him out. I didn't want Mom to think I suffered emotional, self-inflicted torture over him.

I, of course, tripped off the last step. So much for my stoic appearance.

He reached out and caught me before I fell. He helped me stand.

"I want to take you to my home tomorrow," he said.

"Okay," I muttered, curiosity rimming my tone.

"Meet my mom." His brows were up.

"Right." I felt just an unsure about the whole thing as I had after my stupid move on his boat.

"Don't worry.' He smiled. "She will love you."

I looked down. That hadn't been my concern. "I'm more concerned with me being myself." I referred to my inability to control myself in his arms. A point I don't think he picked up on.

"I expect nothing less," he said quietly, more to himself, then added in a louder voice, "It's settled. I will pick you up at nine." He disappeared to his car.

7

Leone

My dream made me so happy. For the first time since we moved here, I dreamed of present day. Not as royalty in the middle ages, not running through the deserted, burning streets of Atlanta, not as a woman in World War II, just me, in my own skin. And my skin felt more alive than ever before. And Leone had been there, burning my skin with his touch, churning my insides, yearning to be consumed by the feelings.

I woke early, but after attempting to fall back asleep for some time, I decided at 5:30 a.m. to begin my day. I grabbed my robe and quietly walked down the stairs to the kitchen. I started a fresh pot of coffee. While I waited for it to finish, I unloaded the dishwasher and reloaded it. Mom would appreciate the gesture.

I grabbed a cup of freshly brewed coffee and went to stand on the back patio and watch the sun lighten the sky. The valley that stretched to the mountain in front of me lay still and blanketed in darkness. I heard coyotes calling to each other. I could hear the creek trickling along below me.

By the time my parents awakened, I had pancakes and eggs ready for them. The morning had been so peaceful. Having the family share that calm seemed perfect.

Leone showed up at nine, just as promised.

He had a nice truck. Not overstated, but obvious. The windows had a dark tint to them. The compact extended cab had a short bed and a standard engine. It required him shifting gears using the clutch—I noted how fluid the motion had been. The truck did not buck or jump. It had been my experience to give whiplash to anyone in my vehicle as I shifted. A truth I chose to remain quiet about.

Silver-beige paint on the exterior set off the black pin-striping down the side. Plush, leather seating, soft and warm, matched the darker interior, and I noticed the seats were heated. The display on the dash had more buttons than I could figure out.

He noticed me sneaking a look at the stereo.

"It's yours to change."

"Oh, really...I'm good." The radio played one of the oldies my parents listened to from time to time. A classic I knew the words to, but chose not to make my debut in his truck. I felt content to just to be there with him. My own calm seemed out of place to me with the strange statements and behaviors from the day before. The questions that had been racing around in my mind had stopped. A meditative drunkenness and serenity overpowered me. I decided to just enjoy the feeling for the moment.

We drove down the back side of the reservoir for a distance, then turned onto a dirt road on the right. A solitary mailbox stood as the only indicator this road could possibly lead to a residence. The forest grew thick. There were places that the sun could not penetrate, and it cast a darker shade over the road. So secluded. It seemed like forever before the trees gave way to a huge meadow and a large black wrought iron gate and fence. Every thirty feet a stone pillar separated the sections of fence. The fence, at least nine feet tall, towered above us as we drove through the open gate. I stared in awe.

We had to travel another five minutes before the house came into view.

It loomed, a dark Victorian against the monstrous mountain behind it. I instantly loved it. It had two turret rooms, one on each side. The front patio stretched from the left side around to the right, then disappeared at the back of the house. Behind the left side of the patio a large, tall garage stood. The shingles of the house and garage were black, adding to the majesty. The taller turret on the left had second and third story floors that held the same circular shape as the patio below.

The right, smaller turret had only one additional level to it. The patio, again following the shape of the room above it, decorated with antique looking furniture. Tables, chairs, rugs, and vases all matched the theme completely.

The yard in front had a beautiful stone statue of a mostly naked woman holding a vase from which she watered the flowers at her feet. The figure stood easily taller than me. The only clothes she wore wrapped around her waist and hung down to her upper thigh, covering her groin area.

Leone chuckled when he read the expression on my face.

His everyday clothes, vehicle, and mannerisms hadn't prepared me for the grandiose house that loomed before me.

"This is our peace. Away from the rest of the world," he tried to explain. "We do not invite many people here and your reaction would be the reason why." He paused. "We are trying to fit in."

That caught me off guard.

"Why wouldn't you fit in?" I questioned.

"Years of experience." He did not offer any other explanation. It seemed to be the only answer I would get.

He stopped the truck in the front along the grass.

I stepped out and he came to stand beside me. He appeared at my side so quickly it caused me to step back toward the truck.

He took my hand and walked me toward the house slowly. His eyes scanned all the windows and doors. I began to feel apprehensive.

"We can leave," I said. Not sure what the issue could be.

"No, we just need to go slow." His eyes did not move from the house.

We quietly edged around the stone statue. Standing next to her, a good head smaller than her, I felt very small. Her body, though in proportion to her height, made up about two of me. Her carved face captured serenity as she gazed at the growth on the ground around her. Her breasts were uncovered. Cloth hung elegantly in stone from her arm that stretched upward, holding her vase. It amazed me to know that water flowed from the vase into a small pond wrapping through the plants. Around the garden were plants that I recognized and some that I didn't. They excited the senses to smell them on the breeze.

We walked up the stairs. Leone reached the top step as the front door flew open. I hid slightly behind him.

A beautiful woman slid through, just enough to rest inside the frame. Her smile invited and her voice welcomed. "Leone! I'm so glad you made it!"

"Thank you, Mom."

"I just finished baking some cookies. Please come in. *Everything* is just *fine*." The way she enunciated the last part made me take note.

Leone relaxed. "Great! Thank you." He gave her a kiss on the cheek and they both turned to me. I stepped up into the doorway.

Then she said, "You must be Rhi. You can call me, Nohi."

She took both of my hands in hers. Her light, olive skin felt cool to the touch. Her eyes, a beautiful amber, were glowing with excitement. She stood taller than me and had a toned

114

physique, though she covered herself in respectable, casual clothing. She had brown hair cut to lay in short strands surrounding her face. Enthusiasm radiated from her.

She hugged me, like a long lost acquaintances. I hadn't expected the rapid motion let alone such a warm welcome.

"Please come in!" She hustled along. "I have been waiting to meet you."

I looked at Leone. He did not seem to notice that remark.

My eyes took in the enormous house. The dark, freshly polished woodwork shined. A large, circular table stood in the middle of the entry room with a large centerpiece of flowers. Smaller items surrounded the arrangement including an old, wooden box. The top and bottom edges were inlaid with bone. There were light and dark brown diamond patterns surrounding the box and the lid. Delicate, white accent touched the top and bottom of each diamond in etched bone.

"That is called a Certosina Casket," his mom offered, seeing where my gaze was drawn.

My eyes grew wide. She chuckled.

"It's really a box that held the important belongings of those deceased. An old ritual, really. In fact, the belief dates back to Egypt." Her brows raised. "This one is from the Renaissance, somewhere around Greece." Her eyes met Leone's. He smiled sweetly at her.

I looked at another item on display. A long, leather tube, beautifully engraved with intricate detail, lay to the other side of the flower arrangement. It had darkened with time. Antique-looking silk ropes hung from the lid. Leone picked it up and opened the lid. He handed it to me. I could not take my eyes from it. The inside, divided into thirds, was lined with red silk. Three documents remained rolled tightly, one in each compartment, all aged and brittle. The leather had hardened and it felt cool in my hand.

"This is a Cuir Bouilli," he said. "It dates back to the 1400's, more specifically to 1403. It held important documents for the Roman Pope as he gained strength in his community."

"1403!" I blurted out. Suddenly conscious of my hands holding something they should not be. I shoved it back to him—sure I had already destroyed the precious piece of history.

Leone laughed at me. "Yes, that old. We love to collect pieces of our history."

"Our history?" I asked so quickly I didn't have time to delete my curiosity before I made it public.

He looked down and stepped around me while saying, "What I mean to say is, we only know where we are by looking into the past."

I think I had heard that answer before, from my history teacher.

The buzzer from the kitchen broke the awkward silence. "I have to go check the last batch of cookies." Nohi fled from the room.

I looked around and really absorbed the surroundings. To the left a doorway entered into another room that would be the ground level of the larger turret. The furniture there looked expensive and stately. The sunlight filtered in and highlighted the crisp, rich colors.

To the right were double doors that entered into the smaller turret room. I guessed it to be a bedroom.

Leone started to walk around the table to the left. I followed.

I noticed a series of shelves on the wall past the doorway. A copper container the shape of a tuna-fish can with a copper, cone-shaped lid caught my eye. The latch seemed simple. The tooth that jutted out from the lid lined up with the two teeth on the bottom and a pin ran through them to keep it closed. The container was very pretty. White had been painted into circles on four edges of the box itself and on two sides of the

116

lid. The circles were painted in such a way that the letters left unpainted read 'IHS' in copper. A flag reached from the top of the H and waved, caught in a permanent wind. Turquoise paint filled in the rest of the item, leaving an intricate weave in the copper pattern.

A matching one sat on the shelf below, except that light blue and dark blue replaced the turquoise color. The copper details were in arching patterns and fleur-de-lis.

"What are these?"

He walked back to me. "That is called a pyxide. Most of them are found in graves, but they were used as a container during life for small objects, such as jewelry or toiletries. They could have a string put through them so they could hang, either on the person or on a wall." He seemed pleased that I asked. "Did you ever stop to think that the attached pocket hadn't been used regularly in the early 1800's? It made things like the pyxide important before then."

"I guess I never thought about anything like that." We do tend to take things for granted.

"Come with me." He motioned toward another room a few feet from where we were standing. "I need to show you some things."

Considering I had just seen things I would not expect to see in America, I became eager find out what could be next.

We walked into the long corridor. When my eyes adjusted to the dark, I noticed the lamp in the far corner remained off. We were in the back part of the large, turret room. The end wall curved following the form. Wooden tables bordered one side. There were no chairs. Along the opposite side from the tables a large bookshelf had been built into the wall. I could make out the shape of dozens of books in the dark. At the end of the hall next to the lamp a set of spiral, wrought-iron stairs disappeared into the ceiling. Leone stepped aside to let me pass in front of him. I paused for a moment and looked toward him. In the dark, he seemed to glow. I could see every detail in his face. I stepped back and tried to understand what I saw. The glow had been so faint that I wondered if light filtered in from the front foyer, playing tricks on my eyes. Behind him, I could not see any objects. The darkness enveloped everything in the corner. Curiosity overcame me. I reached up to touch his face. I had to know if I really saw the difference in his skin.

His smooth skin felt cool. The moment I touched him my eyes were stabbed with a brightness that seemed to emanate from him. I blinked and narrowed them to slits to protect them. At the same moment he flipped the light on in the corner. He closed his eyes as mine adjusted to the light. He touched my hand with his, then removed it from his face.

I stood there, eyes adjusted to the light, my mouth open, and my hand tingling from his touch. I wanted to ask what had happened. As I heard the questions firing away in my head—*Did you just glow? Are my eyes going bad?*—I decided they sounded ridiculous and chose to keep quiet.

"Please." He motioned with his other hand toward the stairs. "I do need to talk with you."

I turned and started climbing. My hand slid along the cold rail. It seemed to be twisted metal, the pattern rippling under my fingers as they slid over. I climbed until I reached the faint light from above. I glanced into the room. Wall-length curtains were drawn across windows and allowed only faint light into this room. It seemed to be a lounging area. A long ottoman-like sofa sat beneath the window. The light blue reminded me of the powder blue skies in spring. It had a white blanket draped over the back. A stack of books sat on the end table next to the lounger—all open to different pages, one resting on top of the other.

He wrapped his arm around my middle and pulled me to the next set of stairs. I felt self-conscious having him grab me in that way. It thrilled me and at the same moment caused me to worry. I felt unprotected, my heart open to falling, and us alone in his room. He let go as the stairs were within reach,

next to the other set, they extended up to another floor. He
went first this time.

On the third floor the circular room resembled a bedroom,
more modern than the rest of the house thus far. The overall
colors were blue with salmon accents. A huge stereo system
filled most of the shelves, seated among myriads of CDs. A
large, flatscreen hung from the ceiling. Movies lined the shelves
below it, alongside the DVD player. A deep couch hunched
across the floor in front of the window. Wider and much
deeper than a normal couch, it looked comfortable.

"That is an interesting bed." I motioned toward the huge
couch.

He smiled. A hidden secret tucked behind his eye.

"Is that what you use to sleep?"

He just winked at me in response.

I turned to look behind me. An armoire, massive in size,
stood along the wall. It had spikes at the top that nearly
reached the crease between the wall and the vaulted ceiling of
the turret. Carved, wooden spirals swirled down the front of it.
They protruded from the armoire, not engraved into it. It had
two large compartments on top, drawers in the middle, and
two large drawers on the bottom.

"This is a French piece from the 1600's. And interestingly
enough, it's made from American walnut."

"I am beginning to not be surprised by your knowledge of
far off times." I stepped toward the armoire, turning again to
look through the room. "So, this is your bedroom, right?"

"Yes."

"Why does it seem so different?" I pushed him for more
information. "Wow, you don't have an actual bed with
blankets. I mean, ya, the big couch, but don't you worry about
changing the sheets?"

Amused at my questioning, he answered, "Actually I do."

He walked to a carved, wooden slab that stood close to the
armoire. I'd passed it off as a structure that had been built into

the house. It didn't seem to have shelves or a door knob, but ran floor to ceiling. Leon pushed on it and an average-sized bed folded out into the room. I nodded in acquiescence.

"A hidden bed, clever." I asked.

"He motioned me to the couch.

I walked over, observing him as I sat down. The cushions were so soft. I sank into them. I didn't feel comfortable enough to slide into the back cushions yet.

He spun around to the television and turned it on. He hit play on the DVD. The blue picture flickered into color. Leone sat onscreen in a strange room, looking beyond the camera at someone else. His head nodded, 'okay?' to someone seemingly behind the camera. Then he seemed to focus into the camera and started talking.

"My name is Leone. I am currently from Donnelly, Idaho. I am creating this documentary to help assist you with all the information that I need to share with you. I broke it into chapters. In order for you to use this, I have codes that I will give you for each chapter that will allow you to view them when you are ready."

On video, he looked down at his hands and then back into the camera.

"You need to understand that if this video and its codes get into the wrong hands, I and my family will be done. I am giving you power over me and those that I love by giving this to you. But most importantly, I am giving you power over you. You are either in danger or you are destined to spend your life in solitude."

Leone paused the video.

He looked at me. My raised eyebrow and pivoted head expressed my desire to say, "What is this, more crazy talk?" I needed to stay centered in my mind because this DVD thing, coupled with what he talked about yesterday, had me thinking insane thoughts about Leone.

"What do you mean?" I spat.

"I must know that no matter how crazy you think this is or how crazy you think I am, that you say nothing of it to anyone."

"But why?"

"Just promise," he said with fierce conviction.

He caught me off guard. He'd never spoken forcefully to me. I had a moment of deciding I didn't have to put up with this psycho-forceful talk. However, my thoughts eased into a desire to see what other weird things were going to be said.

"Of course, I would never do anything to hurt anyone. To hurt you."

He relaxed.

The video continued.

"I do not know your name yet, but I can sense that you are coming close. I cannot wait to see what you look like."

My hand went to my chest.

"I am tied to you by the most impossible connection ever. I would never do anything to endanger you. I would never do anything against your will. I have made a pact to defend and protect the weak and defenseless, to respect the honor of women, and to never turn my back upon a foe, among other things. In this, I am bound through my history and yours to my obligation.

"There are unanswered and strange things that I know you have seen about me, because you are watching this now. I have chosen not to explain any details in the intro to this video. I want to understand how you react to the past."

Leone shifted in the room and looked at me. He kept his distance, just in case, but moved from the center of the room to stand at the other side of the couch. I noticed that I could easily run to the stairs to escape. I inched closer to the edge of the couch opposite him.

"I have known you before," the TV intoned. "It is the concept of returning souls. You do not have to believe it. But I have been in your life, in some form, most every time."

My eyes flew wide open. I grabbed the edge of the couch and slid the rest of the way until perched on the edge.

My thoughts went wild. *What? This is crazy! Does he really expect me to sit and listen and believe this? Maybe this is a little too creepy.* I jumped to my feet. I thought now would be a good time to go. I gaped at him.

His face seemed etched in sadness. He didn't look ready to pounce on me. Instead, the look in his eyes reminded me of my vivid dream in the castle when I had been given a ring in a wooden box wrapped in dark blue, silk ribbon. Such love passed between us in the dream. That very love appeared reflected in his eyes at that moment. I slowly lowered myself back to the couch.

He paused the video. "We do not have to watch anymore." Obvious heartbreak cracked his voice.

Looking at him with his shoulders slumped in defeat gave me pause, and even though my mind urged me to leave, my heart willed me to stay. "I think I'm okay."

He paused for a moment. "You are a horrible liar." He smiled weakly as he started it again.

"The reason for me breaking this information to you is... a being is always after you. My fault in the matter is my burden. I must do all I can to keep you safe. My heart would desire nothing more than to sacrifice my existence to make sure you live in complete peace the rest of yours. It never seems to work that way. You can think of me as your protector. I would not ask for anything more. As time allows, and as you are able to accept the details, I will unlock more information for you. I finally have to say, I apologize whole-heartedly

for your agony and desperate feelings. In this life, I am
determined to change your fate."

The screen went blue again. I glanced away. I didn't want
to make eye contact with Leone. I tried to replay what had
been said in the video. *Incredulous. How on earth can anyone
expect me to swallow this? It might make a clever book, but it
does not come close to reality.* My mind flipped from blaming
myself for trusting my wishy-washy heart to flashes of the
intense dreams I had been having.

"I'm sorry," he interjected. "Perhaps this is too soon to
start the video with you. I just felt the familiar pattern starting
in your life. It always seems to pick up when our lives cross."

"What pattern?" I twisted the last word, my voice
sounding disbelieving.

"Accidents, ones that you only survive because I'm there."

My mind recalled, too clearly, the water and the tree. Yes,
he saved me. That had to be the real issue with me. I have the
damsel in distress scenario going. Funny how stories always
left off with happily ever after, dot, dot, dot—expecting you to
believe their lives together were all diamonds, roses, and
champagne. They forgot to tell you where their lives
transformed from that familiar rated 'G' movie to the 'R'-
rated, serious, psycho story. And look, the handsome, prince
psycho is your husband.

He continued, "I have no way of knowing if you would
make it through those incidents. I have never paused a second
long enough to challenge it. When I move to action, it is as a
reflex."

"Accidents," I blurted out. "Come on. Maybe things are
supposed to happen that way? Did you ever stop to think that
I'm just being a klutz? My entire life I have had mishaps.
Maybe fate called and now I'm just tempting it. I'm really not
desperate. I can take care of myself."

I felt a sense of defensiveness about this specific fault. I didn't like the feeling of being so out of control that I might actually need a protector to protect me from myself.

"I assure you I meant no offense in my words." He walked over to me and bowed in front of me. One knee touched the ground. The other bent at a perfect ninety-degree angle. His right arm crossed his chest. His head bowed. His left arm extended toward me, holding a package.

I had an awkward feeling that I'd time-jumped to another era, another world completely. I didn't think I could fathom much more of his craziness.

I really didn't want to take the package from him. I didn't want to be obligated in any way to remain, if I chose to leave.

"It is not so much a gift," he said forcefully, reading my mind.

I was shocked and a little embarrassed that his assessment of me was so accurate.

I reached out toward the package, paused, and grabbed it quickly.

Leone stood and walked toward the stairs. He kept his back to me. I knew I had hurt him. His fists were clenched by his side. I fumbled the wrapping open. There, in my hand, lay a red, shiny cell phone.

A phone? Why did he give me a gift? And why was it a phone?

"I will take you home now," he spoke at me over his shoulder. With one final glance toward me he disappeared down the spiral stairs. I noticed his slackened face and somber eyes. I felt a pang of remorse for the pain I caused him—it quickly became replaced with the indignation that I felt. How could he expect me to fall for his story?

I sat there motionless in his room, struggling to gain control of all the confusing thoughts in my mind. I gazed at the blue screen and glanced around once more. Things were different than when I walked in the front door only thirty minutes ago.

I wonder if his mother knew of this diabolical scheme. I decided to go to the kitchen, at least to say goodbye before I left.

As I descended the first flight of stairs, I stopped to review his second floor room. The surroundings were very comfortable. I meandered across the floor to the lounge chair and glanced at the open books I'd noticed earlier. They were on specific times in history. It appeared the main topic focused on Medieval Rome and Europe around the late 700's, early colonial America, and the Black Death in the 1400's.

Black Death? I glanced at a phrase highlighted in yellow and underlined with pen.

Ravenna, Italy had been one of the last towns hit with the plague. Among those hit the hardest, it had been almost completely wiped out from the deadly disease. The population declined to an estimated twenty survivors, not enough to clean up the disaster.

The section went on to talk about the time it took for outsiders to come and wipe the streets, houses, and businesses clean. Ravenna, baked in the sun, ended up a cesspool and took years before it had a substantial economy again. I shivered to think about hundreds of dead lying unburied for months. Gross. And Leone seemed fascinated with it. A little scary.

Notes were scribbled into the columns in pen and pencil in all of the books. It had been read more than once. I wondered about the time periods. More books stacked under those that were opened. Among those books, I glanced at an odd one. The title on the top of the page read Knight Stalkers. It seemed to be off topic from the rest. I turned the cover closed enough to read the author, Leonous Givante.

"Leonous Givante," I whispered. I studied a moment longer before deciding it to be a mere coincidence that the name resembled Leone's. I also made a mental note to search the topic on knight stalkers.

When I made it to the front entryway of the house, I turned opposite the front door and followed the smell of cookies to the kitchen.

Nohi stood at the sink cleaning dishes. Her eyes were sad.

"Hello again, dear," she said to me. "Please sit. I would love to give you a sample of the cookies."

The kitchen lived up to the gorgeous standards of the rest of the house. The floor appeared to be large slabs of quarried stone. It reminded me of something you might see in an Italian kitchen. Indeed, the entire kitchen reminded me of such a setting. It would not have surprised me to look outside and see a valley of grape vines.

I noticed the living room off the kitchen had more rich colored furniture and a large television turned to a local station. Local being Boise, of course.

Nohi set a plate of cookies on the breakfast bar across the counter from where she worked, indicating, I assumed, where she wanted me to sit.

The TV news changed to an update that drew Nohi's and my attention.

"No word yet on the whereabouts of the driver of the truck found at Arrowrock. Investigators have not yet released the name due to an ongoing investigation. Police Chief Maston says the vehicle found two days ago is registered to a Boise man and his body has not yet been recovered. Maston also stated the forensic specialist reviewed the door hinges and confirmed it had been forcefully removed. The dog has been returned to the family who said she awaits her master's return."

Nohi looked at me then went back to her work. The news anchor continued into the next story.

"Another murder in Boise overnight. That makes three in the past two nights. The two from the night before were believed to be related to animal attacks. Last night's findings said the bite marks seemed more like a human's. Mark reports on the story."

As the screen flashed to a man standing in an alleyway, Nohi picked up the remote and turned off the television.

I shook my head at the report, stepped up onto the high stool, and situated myself, placing the phone on the counter next to the plate as I reached for a cookie.

"Weird reports. It's sad about the accident." I opened the conversation.

"It is. I feel sorry for the man and..." Nohi paused, her back to me still. "...the victims."

"This is a beautiful house," I commented, holding on to the cookie. I tried to gauge the right moment to talk about the phone.

"Thank you. It is a bit of all of us. Of course, the kitchen fits me the best." She smiled as she turned back around to me.

"Oh." Her shoulders relaxed and a smile played across her face as she looked at the phone. "So, that's it." She made eye contact with me. "He decided on the phone then."

I sat in shock at her full knowledge of it. I had hoped that she would know nothing, and in doing so would release my mind from any concern, other than that of being played a fool. Now, that assumption evaporated, my mind wanted an explanation.

"He means well, dear," she offered. "It is a thing of faith really. And trust. I imagine if I were in your shoes right now, without any recollection or reasoning before you, this would all seem like insanity. I can only ask that you see Leone through my memories and to at least carry that phone with you. Everywhere. Can you promise me that? Just carry the phone?"

"Oh, uh...yes," I stuttered, still holding my cookie.

"Let me tell you about Leone. He is kind and caring. There is not a vicious bone in his body." She pulled out a large zip-lock bag from a drawer and began putting cookies in. "He is the most sincere person and very trustworthy." Her voice became soft and she picked up a small Mediterranean accent as she relaxed with her thoughts. "He will not lead you astray. I swear this to you, my dear. Just allow him to be a friend."

She had filled one bag and now started on a second. Dozens of cookies still cooled on the counter.

"I don't understand any of this."

"Perhaps it is better if there is no understanding. Perhaps there is never going to be a need for any concern. Those are things for the ages." Her eyes were focused on something long ago.

"Ages?"

Her eyes came back to the present and looked down at the counter. She busied her hands filling a third bag.

"Love and hearts, dear." She sighed. "You should never wager on a human heart. They love fiercely and can change suddenly." She zipped the third bag closed.

"Now, here are some cookies for you to take home to your mom and dad from us. I believe Leone is waiting to take you home."

"Three bags? That's a lot of cookies. We could never eat that many. Why don't you keep some here?"

"Oh," she sighed, "we don't really eat cookies. Watching our figures, you know. It is an old familiar smell. I wondered if I correctly assumed you had a favorite." She smiled quizzically at me.

I looked at the cookie in my hand. Two more oatmeal raisin cookies sat on the plate ready for me to indulge. I hadn't noticed before what kind they were. "Yes. These are my favorite. How did you know?" I sat the cookie back on the plate, not so hungry anymore.

Leone

"A lucky guess." She smiled a beautiful, knowing smile. Turning, she grabbed a smaller baggie and stuffed my remaining cookies in it.

She accompanied me to Leone's truck with the four bags of cookies and my phone. My new phone. An unwanted phone. Not even a needed phone. *What will my parents ask, and what will I tell them?* I didn't think I could answer those questions for myself.

As I reached for the truck door it opened. I looked in to see Leone retreating to the other side of the truck, behind the wheel.

"Thank you," I said. He nodded.

I placed my load in the middle of the long bench, then grabbed what Nohi had in her hands and set them with the rest.

Turning back, I thanked her for all her kindness. She grabbed me quickly and gave me a tight, strong hug.

"Take care of you," she ordered. "And come back."

I nodded and climbed in.

"Do not forget our agreement," she reminded me.

"Please buckle up." Leone's voice sounded strained. I did as he requested. He slowly pulled away from the grass and turned around in the driveway. Nohi and I waved to each other.

"I really love your mom." I tried to start some semblance of a normal conversation. He smiled and nodded his head in agreement.

"She is making me keep this weird phone on me at all times."

"You do not *have* to do anything. Although, I wish that you would."

"I made a promise to her, even without understanding. She is the kind of person I would never break a promise to."

"Then to her, I am eternally grateful." His voice lightened. "It's a satellite phone. No matter where you are you can call.

129

There are phone numbers to all of my family members in it already," he noted in a satisfied tone.

I looked down at it. I knew it didn't look like an ordinary phone. It had a huge antenna on it.

"It's just a precaution," he reminded me, sensing my apprehension.

"I could never figure it out. How do you answer it anyway? What on earth am I going to tell my parents?"

His laugh appeared to be genuine. I thought I could really love that laugh, airy and light. In that moment my heart skipped. I could see the shine in his light blue eyes as he looked at me. His deep dimples—I hadn't noticed them. This had truly been the first time I'd seen him this way.

"I realized this would be a complication for you. I will teach you everything you need to know. It's a fascinating piece of technology—an amazing evolution. It is perfect for traveling families. It looks similar enough to a cell phone that we can just explain to your parents that it's an old one for you to use." Amusement rimmed his face. "I believe your parents will be happy to know you'll take it with you next time you decide to go on one of your hiking trips."

I gasped. "Who told you about my hike?" I instinctively crossed my chest with my arms, as if to protect myself from the truth. As the ramifications of Dante being on the hill with a bloody mouth and white eyes—and Leone's knowledge of it sank in, I clenched my fists and gritted my teeth. My eyes narrowed as I glared at him.

"I'm sorry," he conceded and looked away. "That was private."

"Private? *Private*!" My voice squealed. "I'm still not even sure it happened." Tears threatened to pour over my face. "You did not answer my question!"

He seemed to flatten. "It's best I say as little as possible. Just know you are never in danger with him. Never!" He emphasized that by boring his gorgeous eyes into me. They were shimmering again.

"And how do you do that with your eyes? They look like water churning in the rocks." I wanted to have all the information out. I wasn't sure I could take anymore. The dam was about to break and all of the pent-up confusion would gush out.

"Just stop the truck," I ordered, trying to control the overwhelming feeling that my world existed as a lie. He just looked at me.

"Stop the truck!" I needed some fresh air before I got sick. He pulled the truck over. I jumped out, staggered, and grabbed the tree closest to me. I hated being weak. I let my knees buckle under me. I started to shake. I could not control it, so many fears and so much psychotic self-analyzing. What had happened to me? My world turned upside down.

In no time he crouched beside me.

He tried to cradle me in his arms. I pushed his chest away from me. He must have understood my weakened attempt at distancing myself because he backed away. I scowled at him. He had not slipped his glasses on, and his eyes were black in the sunlight. I froze. His eyes like coal.

"Leone. What is happening? Your eyes are changed again!" My voice betrayed me, quivering in fear.

He touched his temple, trying to remember if he'd left his glasses in the truck. He exhaled his frustration at being caught in a lie.

"Yes, Rhi. My eyes change. That's why I wear glasses most everywhere. They are not able to cry either, even though my soul may scream out in agony for my loss."

Freak of nature. I turned then and started to run down the road. *The white eyes on the mountain. They scared me to death. They challenged my dreams.* I ran faster. They bent my reality around until I didn't believe myself. Then Leone's eyes were white on the beach. Then they are blue. Now black—*not possible!* I wanted to run away from this whole unbelievable place. I wanted to go back to the coast.

Not able to cry. What a crock of garbage he kept feeding me.

I heard the truck roar to life again behind me. *What are my options? Will he hurt me now that I got an answer from him that he hadn't been willing to give me before? Some secret so profound, so unnatural, that I put myself in danger of being silenced for good? Or were they just a pile of lies that he tried to use to manipulate me?* My fear bubbled into my throat with gasping moans. *The eyes, though. I would gladly give back this knowledge. I didn't ask for it in the first place.*

In my normal world I complained about being bored. I hated chores, and laundry, and curfew. Why couldn't it be that simple again?

The engine grew closer. *Push it, Rhi.*

I could feel the closeness of the truck. I jumped off the road and rolled into the brush. I kicked to get up and run. Flipping over onto my knees, I sprang to my feet and pushed through shrubs. I knew the road surrounded the reservoir and stretched below me somewhere. I dodged trees and finally broke out onto the road. I scanned up and down it. There were no cars. I listened through my heavy breathing and did not hear his truck. I started walking the road toward my house. As I passed the turn off that lead to Leone's house, I stopped and listened. I couldn't hear his engine on the hill. I searched the dirt road and could not discern whether a fresh set of tracks came from the driveway.

A few vehicles passed as I walked. I looked at each to make sure no one followed. The sun shone bright and hot. I had no idea of the time.

I didn't want to have anything more to do with Leone. He couldn't be real. I could not see how I had possibly remained safe from all the things that my eyes had seen. Things that did not happen in everyday life. For an average, boring person, this was all too much excitement. I felt like I watched a new mini-series named "X-files Goes Rhi". The best thing would be for me to ignore Leone's existence.

By the time I reached home, my throat was dry and sweat dripped from my forehead. I stepped up to the front door. On the patio were the cookies and the phone. Attached to the phone, a note read, "Use it just as you would a normal cell phone." Normal cell phone. Just like everything with Leone, normal did not describe it. I put the phone in my pocket.

I entered the front door with all the cookies. I heard Mom in the kitchen. I decided to give them to her.

She appeared surprised to see me home so early. I decided to avoid the complicated and unbelievable truth.

Mom told me to thank the Ghiovanies for the cookies as she put most of them in the freezer. She mentioned that Dad would eat all of them at once if she gave him the chance. I chuckled in agreement. We called him "the cookie monster" for good reason.

"Mom, do you think we could go to Boise for my birthday instead of a party? Then we could shop before school starts?" More than anything I wanted to leave here—even if just for a day.

"Sure." Her voice seemed to come alive. "That would be fun. We haven't done anything like that in a while. Are you sure you don't want to invite someone to go with us? How about Carlee?"

"Oh, I could invite her? Are you sure?" I asked.

"Honey, you're turning eighteen. I want you to have as many friends around as you can."

"I think Carlee will be just fine."

When I had asked Carlee, she rattled on about all the stores we were going to visit.

I spent some time later that day online, and among other things, remembered to search for knight stalkers. I found it comical. The first thing I found explained vampires of noble birth. It didn't even sound interesting to me. I tried to visualize Leone reading something like that. As I chortled, my eyes took in a passage on the page. *They can hear rather well, indeed, they can even hear the faintest of heartbeats from across a room.*

I canceled out of the page. Some people would believe anything.

8

Girls Night

I grew sick of dreaming of Leone. Even though I hadn't seen him around or talked with anyone about him, he inundated my mind almost every minute.

I just wanted my ordinary life back and to have no knowledge that things existed that did not fit into my normal paradigm. I wanted peace in my thoughts. I wanted to be understated and unnoticed. Most of all, I didn't want to dwell on the most beautiful and breathtaking being who had ever entered my life. I did not want to think about him, need to be around him, or crave to know what he did at any given moment.

I just had to quit him. I didn't think myself strong enough to be anything different from the low-key person that I had grown up being. I no longer wanted to endure the fear or speculate the meanings of what Leone hinted at. I had to stop dreaming. I needed to disconnect from victim scenarios. I would have to accept that he saved me, close the whole chapter on my life, and move on.

I made up my mind. The start of my senior year at school sped toward me. I needed to focus on getting through the first day. Then the second day, then the first month, the first quarter, and then finally, graduation and I would be ready to leave to go back to the coast.

So my plan took shape. I would just sneak glances at him through school. He would soon find someone else to shower his attention on. Maybe eventually, when the weirdness of the situation we shared together wore off, we could be friends. He did save my life. I shouldn't seem ungrateful.

A girls' day did sound fun in the "big" city with Mom and Carlee for my birthday. I couldn't wait to see what Idaho did to make a big city. If it resembled the country at all, then downtown would have barns filled with fashion clothing that would closely resemble overalls, all the rage with the cows. My hopes left no room for anything grandiose. Most of my excitement came from getting away.

Carlee explained she'd never been part of a day dedicated to female spending and looked forward to sharing it with us. Not knowing anyone made the necessity for a large party null.

"Happy birthday, Rhi," she chimed as she jumped into the car with us. She handed me a card.

"Thank you." I opened it. A $20 bill fell out. I read the card and laughed at the joke on the inside.

The road from Donnelly cut through beautiful country, although still much drier than I liked. We traveled along a river that cascaded across large boulders and shot spray into the air. I imagined that these were unclassified rapids here. I could not imagine anyone trying to navigate these waters. The road twisted around sharp cliffs. I grabbed the dashboard from being unaccustomed to the roads—even though Mom drove it well.

About forty minutes from home, the rapids calmed into rolling water with occasional obstacles. We passed a restaurant at the intersection of two highways. It seemed funny to put such a place in the middle of nowhere, until I realized there were tons of rafters on the water at the other side of the restaurant. Small kayaks and large multi-person rafts were launching out into the water.

"Oh, that looks like fun," I blurted out to really no one in particular.

Carlee saw the same group. "It's a blast! Have you never been rafting?"

"No, never," I said.

"This year we are supposed to go with our lifetime sports class in school. The senior class got to go with Mr. Hoslin last year. They had so much fun."

"They took a class down that water?" my mom asked incredulously.

"Well, from here on down it's much calmer than the stuff we just passed by. It really is a nice raft trip. The guides are professionals."

We kept watching the water every chance we had between the trees. Everyone wore life jackets. It looked safe enough.

"I think I might have fun with that." I could visualize myself sitting on the edge of the raft, playing in the water.

"Hopefully we get some classes together," Carlee crooned.

"I hope so. I won't know anyone and would love the company."

I had filled Carlee in on Leone and me just being friends. It seemed only logical. She didn't know I'd been to his house nor, that I went ga-ga looking into his eyes.

By the time we reached Boise, the arid desert climate claimed the hills. Trees and shrubs gave way to sagebrush and grasses.

Mom drove toward the freeway and took us to the mall. I must confess I underestimated the size of the city. It actually had some tall buildings and theaters and people everywhere.

The mall was average-sized, but had some of the good stores in it. We were looking for bargains.

Mom led us to a store that hosted home décor. She wanted to help pick some items that would create a more pleasing bedroom for me.

The problem with me? I had tastes that spanned different eras. None of it flowed when put together. I asked the sales clerk to assist us. She became flustered with my unbreakable code of likes and dislikes. We just meandered around and looked. I grew aggravated with myself.

My eyes finally spied a Victorian-looking lamp, classic and understated. I studied the details to be sure I liked it. Mom agreed it seemed perfect. I thanked her and kissed her when we walked out of the store with it.

In one of the stores, Mom and Carlee found a birthday hat, which to my dismay, they made me wear. I left it on for only a short time before I snuck it into my bag.

By midday Carlee had bags, I had bags, and Mom had bags draped off our arms. We decided to rest in the middle of the common area on a bench. We were not really paying attention to anyone milling around us. The conversation focused on Carlee's incredible find, versatile, dark brown boots that could dress up her indoors outfit or go rugged in the snow. Extremely fashionable and fifty percent off. Of course, I couldn't find any in my size.

I looked up to see a man staring at me. He wore dark glasses, but I could feel his gaze. His hair as red as fire, shocked me into staring. He wore two necklaces. One was strung with black, long beads, etched with silver, that alternated with small round and metallic beads. The details on the second were harder to discern. It appeared to be a lumped metal design with a red stone in the middle. It sat lower on his collar bone than the first. It struck me as unusual and hung from a silver chain necklace. I glanced back at his face, then turned my eyes away. When I glimpsed back, he had not moved from his spot. He stared me down, brazen and without consideration. With arms folded on his chest, he leaned against a pillar, one leg crossed over the other.

I suggested we get moving again. We planned to go to one more store and right then would be a perfect time to leave.

When I stood up to walk, a bubbly, amber blur rushed up to hug me. In a stunned moment, I staggered back and looked to see who accosted me.

"Lauriel!" my voice trilled. "I didn't expect to see you here!"

"Hi, Rhi. It is so good to see you." She scanned my face.

Mom and Carlee gaped at both of us. I turned to Mom to introduce Lauriel. When I turned back, I saw Lauriel stare at the man who had been looking at me. In that split second, I glanced at him and glimpsed a smile on his lips right before he disappeared in the crowd.

I looked back at Lauriel. Her face held no information for me.

"Lauriel, this is my mom, Sharlene." I motioned toward my Mom.

"It is so nice to meet you!" Lauriel hugged her.

"And this is Carlee. I'm not sure if you two know each other."

Lauriel hugged Carlee, too, much to Carlee's surprise. "I have seen you around," Lauriel asserted.

I explained to Mom, "This is Leone's sister."

"Oh, okay. I briefly met him. He seems to be a very nice young man."

Lauriel smiled at that. "He is."

"We're here shopping for Rhiannon's birthday," Mom mentioned.

"It's your birthday?" she intoned, hands on hips, her body cocked sideways, pretending to be mad for not telling her. "Happy birthday." She gave me another hug.

"Thank you," I said, taken aback at the sudden enthusiasm over me.

139

"I hope we get to have classes together this year, Rhi," Lauriel said. "It would be fun!"

"Ya. I'm hoping to know someone in my classes," I agreed.

We all started to walk again.

Lauriel seemed to know a ton about getting through a day in school. She shared some funny view points, and she had us laughing in no time. While we walked, she nonchalantly scanned the crowd, searching for something—or someone.

"I hope you don't mind me tagging along for a little while," she said. "I lost my group. I think they do it on purpose." She winked.

"Of course not." My mom assured her. "You make the day even more enjoyable."

Lauriel smiled. "I love you already."

We laughed.

We spent another hour or so trying on clothes.

Lauriel picked out clothes that we all tried on. Her taste ran a lot more expensive than mine.

"Really, that?" I pointed to a silk, little number that she held up. It looked like it might cover one of my thighs.

"Oh, of course!" she mused. "I bet you would look absolutely amazing in this. Perfect for a birthday dress!"

"Really, the only things I bought today were pants, sweats, and sweaters. I'm not a girlie girl."

She frowned at my explanation.

"Put this on. You have no idea how beautiful you are. Wouldn't you agree, Carlee?"

Carlee beamed. Lauriel dressed us both and Carlee seemed enchanted by her choices.

"Come on, Rhi! You will look knock out in it!"

My mom enjoyed it as well. She had always wanted me to dress more like a girl instead of the tom-boy I loved to be.

My shoulders dropped in defeat. I grabbed the dress from Lauriel and trudged into the dressing room again. The last items had been shirt on shirt combinations that I kind of liked, but would have never thought to put together. She jokingly told me that she would be my personal advisor. Wonderful.

I pulled off my clothes and slipped on the black silk dress. It slanted at an angle above the knee, showing off more hip on the right than on the left. Low cut in back, I assumed they used the missing fabric for the front, because it fell in soft ripples down to my waist.

I turned and looked in the mirror at myself. I hadn't known that I could look nice in clothing. Almost like an elegant woman, but I knew better.

I remarked that I didn't want to hear anything when I opened the door.

Lauriel jumped up and down and clapped when I walked out. My face grew red in the mirror from the unwanted display of attention.

"You are sooo beautiful, Rhiannon," she beamed.

"Rhiannon!" Mom gasped. "How lovely you are! Look at you. My baby girl has grown up. You really should dress up sometimes. It's just like it was made for you."

"Awe, come on. I would destroy this thing in ten minutes. I'm surprised it's still on me in one piece."

Carlee said, "You sure do make it look even better than it did on the rack."

I laughed my way back to the dressing room.

"No more dresses," I said.

We were done with the dressing rooms. That made me happy.

"Hey, Lauriel, why don't you stay the night tonight? Carlee is staying for Rhiannon's birthday. Her dad is putting in a pool table today he got from someone at his new job. He wanted the playroom ready to play. TV, stereo, and all. It would be so much fun to break it in." Mom wanted me to start really socializing.

"I would love to!" Lauriel said. "I have plans for that hair!" She motioned to my pony tail.

"Great. I can't wait," I said sarcastically but smiled at her so she didn't feel bad.

"What time should I be there?" she asked.

"Well, I think we are headed out of town now. So, anytime you get back." Mom looked at Carlee and me for confirmation.

"Ya, I'm done."

"Same with me," Carlee agreed.

"Perfect. It has been forever since I had an overnight with girls." Lauriel clapped excitedly.

She kept that excitement going all the way to our car. She even waved at us as we pulled out. Then she ran off through the parking lot.

"She is a lot of fun," Mom said. "You have some great friends here, Rhi."

When we arrived home, we could see Dad finishing up his stereo install in the game room through the long windows. We parked the car right in front of him.

Instead of walking in the front door, we went in the sliding glass door around the side that led into the game room.

"Dad, this looks great." I surveyed the TV that he had installed hanging from the ceiling, the pool table in the middle of the floor, and the stereo he fiddled with behind the bar.

"Thank you, Rhi." He stood up and walked around to hug me.

"The girls are going to have a girl's night and break in our new room for Rhiannon's birthday."

He smiled. "Great! I stocked the small fridge with soda." He pointed to the bar.

I checked inside it. "How cool, Dad!" I said. "This is remarkable."

"Okay, I guess I will let you alone. Just don't break the game room." He smiled.

"Dad, I challenge you to the first game of pool."

His eyes lit up. "You're on!" he said.

I ran my items to my room. Carlee called her parents to let them know we were back and then met me in the game room where Dad and I had already begun the challenge.

"Good shot, Rhi," he congratulated me after my lucky shot. The next one fell short and ended up lining up the queue ball in a perfect combination for him. "Well, not as good as yours is going to be."

"Thanks for being nice to your old man," he laughed. With one easy motion, two balls bounded for two different pockets.

"Bam! I should know better than to try and out do you." I beamed at him and clapped him on the shoulder. He always had been good at this game.

Dad showed me how to run the TV and the stereo.

"I'll start the BBQ," he said, climbing the five stairs into the main house.

"Nice, Dad. You're spoiling us." He smiled big at me.

Lauriel showed up. I felt odd about the situation between her and myself. I did not want to talk about Leone at all. I guessed I would wait and see.

I asked if the girls wanted to swim in the creek below before we decided to hang out in the game room for the evening. They both thought it would be great.

We raced for my room. I threw some swimsuits onto the bed. They grabbed ones that they wanted, and we took turns putting them on in the bathroom.

After grabbing towels and sunglasses, we raced down the stone steps to the water below. We tossed our items onto the grass and jumped in. I walked up the stream this time. There were some larger holes that made the water come to my chest. The water moved slower here with the width and depth. I

143

started swimming upstream at an easy pace. Lauriel soon overtook me. She swam strong into the flow. Carlee kept pace with me. We finally flipped over and floated in the current toward the log beneath my house.

As we passed it I thought about the last time I had been that close and found myself in Leone's arms. I could still feel his strength surround me.

Someone stood on the beach, fishing. I recognized Dante and glanced around him to see if Leone had decided to poke around as well. Dante seemed to be alone. Dante waved at Lauriel and then said hi to me.

"What are you doing here?" she asked with an unwelcome tone. Then she grinned.

She raced up the beach and chased him a bit.

"Oh, my brother!" she chided, hugging him. "Big, big brother."

"You're soaking wet," he complained.

"That's the plan," she laughed.

"Ok, already! You are scaring the fish!" Dante squealed, trying to shake his dripping arms.

She let go and ran back into the water.

"We are having fun tonight. No guys allowed. It's Rhiannon's birthday," she threatened him jokingly.

"Happy birthday, Rhiannon," he said as he bowed to me.

"Thank you, Dante." I tried to ignore his suave mannerisms.

Carlee focused her attention on Dante. He smiled toward her. She looked shy all of the sudden, turning her green eyes away from him. I noticed her cheek color turn a slight shade of pink. I thought Heath might have some competition.

I started walking upstream. "Let's go play some pool."

"That's not fair," Dante called after us.

We ignored him and found our towels. We raced up the stairs. Lauriel scurried as nimble as a cat.

We played pool taking turns each game. Lauriel excelled at that, too. She did not show off. She just seemed to be a natural. She showed us tips, too. I found myself really liking her. It helped that she turned out to be a ton of fun.

Dad and Mom came in and told us we could eat. Dad grilled steaks. It happened to be the only thing he had permission to cook. He cooked mine perfectly. Mom made my favorite salad. Carlee and I ate everything. Lauriel picked enough at the food on her plate that it would not have been considered rude. Is that how she kept her girlish figure? Not good.

When we were done, the birthday song started. Mom made the cake the day before from scratch. My favorite, triple chocolate, caramel with peanuts. I blew out the candles. Dad and Mom pulled out a few packages for me to open. A jewelry box rested on the table after I unwrapped it. When I opened it, I found an old ring, some broaches, and a necklace.

"That was your grandma's wedding ring and some of her favorite jewelry," Mom explained. I looked at some of the items. I recognized a few that she had worn. I held up the ring and examined it. I balked at the thought of being the grandchild allowed to keep it.

"Thank you so much, Mom." I hugged her. "It means a lot."

"Okay," Dad said. "The next one."

I opened the package. Dad obviously picked it out, a pass to the ski resort thirty minutes from town.

"Thank you so much. Now, I can really break a leg," I only half-way kidded.

"You and I." He smiled as he pointed to a badge.

We laughed for a moment. Lauriel put her package in front of me.

"This is from me," she stated.

I opened the small box. A dark blue ribbon had been wrapped around the brown box inside the wrapping paper. I heard Lauriel inhale suddenly as though she'd been shocked by the sight of the ribbon.

When I opened the box, a beautiful bracelet shimmered in the light. It had ruby and diamond-looking stones so beautiful they almost looked real.

"Thank you, Lauriel," I said. "This is gorgeous."

She swallowed and I thought the look in her eyes did not match her teeth exposing smile. "Let me help you put it on."

The bracelet caught the light no matter which way it turned. I could not stop looking at it the rest of the evening.

We ate cake and ice cream. Lauriel passed on the treats, patting her waistline. I hugged and kissed my parents, then Carlee, Lauriel, and I decided to watch movies. Chick flicks, of course. Lauriel started doing my hair, curling it, ratting the underside, pinning it, tying it, and hair spraying it. She started putting make up on me, much more than the mascara I normally wore. When she held up a mirror for me, I didn't recognize myself.

"Wow, Rhi, look at how beautiful you are." Carlee's voice conveyed her surprise.

Lauriel's smile showed and her eyes lit as she appraised her work. "Beyond beautiful," she agreed.

"Thank you," I said sheepishly. "This is just not the 'me' I'm comfortable with. I hope you understand."

"Of course, silly." She tussled my hair very delicately. "But I still get to dress you up every now and then until you 'get' it!"

Carlee, her next victim, adored the look Lauriel created for her. Unsurprisingly, Lauriel did not keep the do we gave her.

We enjoyed our night, playing card games and laughing at the cheesy parts of the movies. It felt so good to have great girlfriends again.

We watched DVDs until two in the morning before I drifted to sleep.

9

Plague of Plagues

My body huddled, doubled over, sobbing. A very faint light filtered into the hazy room. I knelt on a packed solid floor; my hair fell in unkempt strands around my face.

As I opened my eyes, I could see baskets along the wall and a wooden table pushed under the window. A candle burned out long ago, leaving a wax pool running over the sides of its holder, close to the edge. Crudely made glass distorted the view to the outside. Other wooden tables surrounded the area. They all seemed narrow, perhaps to allow for movement in the cramped quarters. One of them held items that seemed to imitate a modern day sink. Large bowls partially submerged into the high table top, held the water needed to clean and cook. Towel-like cloth hung from the edge of one of the bowels and draped down the counter. Metal plates and large utensils were piled neatly to one side. Another cloth hung where it had been thrown, to drape off the side of the table. I noticed blood spattered on it. A basket of vegetables sat on a stool at the end of the table. It, too, had been flecked with red.

The grey light in the room reflected the aching in my heart.

I looked down. The body of my mother lay limp across the floor. Her beautiful features distorted grotesquely with black blotches across her neck and face. Dried blood caked her mouth and chin. Her arms protruded from her body at an odd angle from the swelling that had started in her armpits. She had complained of pain beginning as a dull ache only days ago, just the same as Father, just the same as many others.

It seemed that God had forsaken us. The great loss of life around me could not be explained in any other way.

Rumors had started years ago. The people of Ravenna began to hear of distant family members that had fallen to a mysterious death. Details were always left out. Visitors began fleeing through our town of Ravenna from cities I'd never heard of. They talked about a great evil sweeping the land, leaving few alive to clean up the dead. The disease had been raging, they said, for twenty-two years farther North in Italy. Most everyone laughed at the prospect.

I could not understand. In my six-year-old mind it seemed the stories were of the devil himself. A child's simplicity could never prepare her for something like this.

"The visitors said, in England, France, and north of us people all got sick," I told my mother.

"Evil stories intended to scare people," she insisted.

The people of Ravenna went about their lives, basking in the glory of God's love for them. For centuries before the plague, kings on conquests avoided the town, seeing nothing of importance. No one seemed to want anything to do with it. They even sent their exiled people to live among the commoners.

Perhaps egos played into it, but the people in Ravenna believed themselves to be safe from that evil ravaging through the world elsewhere. But no sooner had the visitors left, the first citizens became ill.

Now my mother lay at my knees. Only hours before, she had been talking to people that were not in the room with us.

She awakened me from my deep sleep, yelling that the dark monster had begun to consume us. She ran around the house pulling at her hair and grabbing at her throat, frantically insisting it feasted on her from the inside out.

She'd scared me so badly I crawled from my bedding and rolled into a ball under my wooden bed frame. I kept my eyes clenched as she wept and raged.

When I opened them, a faint glow emanated from the candle my mom carried. I could tell she ambled toward my bed by the way the light flickered along the bricks and the doorway. It grew brighter as she came closer.

My eyes grew wide in fear. I could see her bare feet, engorged and blackened with dots, walking toward my bed. She paused.

She slammed her fist down onto my bed. I jumped at the unexpected outburst. She cursed God for stealing her child—flinging her energy at the blankets. Each time my bed erupted above me I drew myself into a tighter ball trying not to divulge my location.

As she shuffled from the room, she cried and screamed at the loss of her husband and child.

Did she mean Dad died? He had lain in bed the entire day before. Mom would not let me see him.

Mom wept uncontrollably from the other room. I longed to run to her and have her protect me. I started to move from my spot, intending to do just that, but a horrible sound began to emit itself from her throat. A gurgling cough escaped her. I paused where I lay. I heard her inhale, laboring. The sound grew clearer when she turned back toward my door. Then, as the seconds passed, the sound quieted, replaced with an eerie, heavy silence.

I strained to hear anything. I thought my small ears could discern the sound of the wick hissing as it burned with the candle.

The light did not change and I no longer heard her feet slide along the floor. I crept from my hiding place. As I peered around the corner, I noticed the candle on the table under the window, burning low, casting a glow on my mother's figure leaning forward from her sitting position in the middle of the floor.

She seemed to be struggling. Her muscles twitched down her back. I stepped into my doorway to walk toward her.

She lifted her head when she heard my feet scraping the dirty floor.

When she looked up, I wanted to scream. Blood dripped from her mouth and down her clothes. She reached a hand toward me. Her eyes feverish and squeezed tight through the pain. Her brows furrowed. Sweat pooled in drips on her forehead. Her skin glowed white like my night gown. A small cough racked her body and more blood spat out. Some of it landed in front of her on the table and cloth.

I'd never seen anything like it. It was a common practice not to help others in need unless they were a family member. I wanted this being to be my mom, but as I looked at her, I could not be sure. She looked as possessed as she sounded. I ran back to my bed and hid.

As I raced back to my hiding place, new muffling sounds came from the kitchen. Soon they too, stopped. Utter silence accompanied me through the rest of the night. Even the candle burned itself out.

When the rays of sunlight finally entered my windowless room through the kitchen, I again snuck from my hiding place.

I spotted my mother immediately. She had become a mass of clothing on the floor. I rolled her over—and there I sat. Staring into her lifeless eyes. I knew this was my mom, though swelling had completely distorted her features. I could not cry—everything went dry and barren inside me.

She left me alone. Unless she had been wrong about Dad. I rubbed my eyes and stood, hoping that he lay on his bed just beyond the closed door.

I tip-toed to the door next to my bedroom. If Dad were still alive, how could I explain this to him? When I opened the door and peeked in, I knew my mom had been right. Father lay covered in blood-soaked blankets. His head was turned toward the door. It seemed he still attempted to say something, his face frozen in time. His eyes were wide and hazed over. His mouth lay open, blood-caked and crusty. He, too, had black blotches over his face and arms. Flies already claimed a place at his mouth.

I gasped and backed out of the room into the kitchen.

I turned and looked around our small house. No one remained. I was alone. My grandparents had died years ago. I had no aunts or uncles. Nobody.

I walked to the door and opened it. The sun burned much brighter in the street despite the narrow roadway. I stepped out onto the cobblestone dressed only in my white bedclothes.

The coolness beneath my feet filtered into my blank mind. I checked up and down the street to find someone to help me with my parents.

No one walked the streets. I glanced back over my shoulder. I'd had left the door to the house open. I could see Mom on the floor.

I thought I should leave the door ajar—someone might find my parents and help. I would go looking.

I headed toward the end of the street where it intersected another.

I turned left toward some of the shops. Most days people purchased items that had come from the docks on the other side of town. But today, the streets remained as bare as my heart. Doors to businesses hung from hinges that creaked in the slight breeze from the sea.

I began to tremble. What happened to everyone? A sense of isolation grew inside me. The devil had come while I slept. Maybe I had been lucky to have been asleep. I didn't want to find him on the street. I hoped he had left already.

I looked into the shop windows, walked down other streets. I found no one.

I finally spied movement ahead.

"Hello? Help me!" I yelled in my small, child voice.

A dirty-looking man in a torn, grey coat walking close to the edge of the wall turned to me. He looked more afraid of me than I felt of him.

I ran toward him. It seemed to elicit a deeper fear, for he, too, began to run.

"Please, don't run," I begged. Then, more to myself as I slowed to a stop and the man disappeared around the corner, "Please, don't run."

He ran from me. Afraid? Of me? Mom... dead. I hadn't helped her like a good girl should have, but I'd been so afraid. She didn't seem like my mom. Maybe I could have saved her if I hadn't been such a scaredy-cat. Everyone ran away or died. No one to help me. *Where will I go? Where will I stay? Who can take care of me?* The thought of being alone in the dark streets when night came made my eyes water. I looked up and down the street again, trying to imagine any hiding places.

I sank into the street and cried into my hands.

What happened to the world? Nothing seemed like it was supposed to. I had told Mom that. She did not believe me. I believed. Maybe that is the only reason I still lived. I believed in the evil.

I stood and toddled toward the church. I needed to talk to God, even though He didn't hear children, let alone an insignificant girl.

I saw no one on the three blocks to the church.

I rounded the corner and the Basilica of Sant' Apollinare Nuovo stretched before me and took my breath. With death all around, it stood in the morning light, shining in the rays as God welcomed me from my lonely walk.

The main building, although stories tall itself, cowered under its bell tower, which stretched like a stairway to heaven to the right of the entrance. I wondered who had been blessed enough to climb it in the night and escape the black splotches.

The marble walkway stretched beyond the walls of the church to the left and ended past the bell tower on the right. Magnificent columns towered three times the height of my house and held up the entry.

No one waited in the front of the church. I thought they must all be inside, sheltered from the evil out here.

I scampered to the door and strained with all my weight to pull it open.

The inside was cavernous. Sunlight filtered colors through the tall rows of windows. Dad had told me it would take at least ten of me standing toe to head to reach from bottom to top of the stained glass. It cast the most heavenly beams on the walls surrounding the church. The naïve of the church was surrounded on all sides by repeating arches. Each arch displayed mosaics in Biblical pictures, twelve on each side in the V of the joining arches. More mosaics adorned the upper band above the arches. Thirteen small mosaics decorated the left wall, depicting Christ's miracles and parables. I remembered Dad and Mom each sharing their favorites. The right wall exhibited thirteen more mosaics depicting the Passion and Resurrection. That story scared me.

Blues, reds, and greens swirled through the pictures. They lived more than the town at that moment—but no one moved in the place.

I reverently and slowly crept down the center row between the pews. Although I had been there many times, I could not tear my eyes away from the pictures of Jesus.

I finally slid into the middle pew on the left side, my family's normal place when we attended church. I reached out and ran my hand along the smooth wood. My mom and dad had worshipped here with me. I peeked up and envisioned the angry woman with the brown eyes who always sat in front of us. She always scowled at me. I missed seeing her. I hugged myself. I yearned for my parents to be with me.

The altar glimmered in the colored sunlight. The chalices radiating golden rays, crafted from the sun itself.

Alone here, too, a cry escaped my lips.

Then a movement from the far right front of the church interrupted my self-absorption. I hadn't noticed the figure resting there, close to the arches, just out of the sun's bright rays.

I glanced toward the back along the same row of pews.

Another person sat in the second to the last row. He had been hidden from me behind the arches.

He was dressed in white clothing, just like me. Only his were actual clothes, not intended for sleeping in.

He stood and sidled to the end of the pew, then continued toward me.

As he came closer I could see his face. His eyes seemed kind, although they were a deep black color, the same shade as his hair. He appeared clean, unlike me, and his face resembled the stone statue of Apollo from the town square. His skin color reminded me of Mamma's warm, golden brown bread. He reached out his hand to me as he stopped at the end of my pew.

I had no one. He seemed to invite me. I studied his hand and then his face.

"Please, do not fear me," his voice whispered. "You are safe now."

"But the devil is out there. He took my parents," I flatly told him the only explanation I had.

"I am sorry you had to go through that. There are some that the devil did not take," he said, not believing his own statement.

"Really?" Hope filtered into my mind for the first time since Dad had grown ill.

"Yes," his firm tone assured me.

I took his hand, he led me out of the pew. As I stepped into the aisle, the figure from the front of the church moved, following us from the church.

"What's your name?" I asked, tilting my face up as we entered the shadow of the front entryway.

Before he responded, I noticed his eye color change to a dark brown. The figure that followed us caught up. I peered at the face, concealed by a dark cape and hood.

We made eye contact. His were blue like crystal. And sad. In my child's mind, just another face.

The man in white answered my question. "Dante."

My eyes popped open. *Dante? In my dream?*

The blue eyes. *Oh, how I knew them. They were always there in my dreams. Leone's eyes.*

I just wanted a good night's sleep. *Death and graphic mutilations, a country in devastation. The poor girl.* A tear formed in the corner of one eye, then the other as I remembered the night her mother died. She believed her mom had been evil. I recalled how horrible she felt about herself when she realized that her mother had been dying, not evil. No going back. People were gone. She was alone and isolated.

Disturbed, I lay there on the floor in our living room. *Why would I dream that? Cobblestone under my feet? Her thoughts were as vivid as if it had been me. Dead people. The whole town empty.*

I exhaled and ran a hand through my hair.

"Are you okay?" a sleepy sounding Lauriel asked from somewhere close.

"I had a bad dream. It has me freaked out a little."

"I'm having trouble sleeping as well." I heard the blankets rustling and realized she had rolled over to face me. "Tell me your dream."

I recounted my dead parents, and hiding under the bed, running through the vacant streets, and meeting up with two men in the church. I did not explain that I recognized them both as her brothers.

"I cannot get over it. I remember thinking like a poor, innocent kid and not understanding why people were dying. I believed the mom in my dream had been possessed." I kind of chuckled.

"I'm not sure, but it sounds like it might be the Black Death," Lauriel murmured.

"You think? I don't really remember that much from school," I said.

"I just wrote a paper on it," she explained. "Bubonic Plague. It wiped out half of the population. They say toward the end people were just left in their houses where they died, and the rest fled the towns."

"Gross." I knew exactly what that looked like now. "I don't understand why I had the dream. I remember that a lot of people died. My dream was pretty clear. The bodies looked grotesque."

"Weird, Rhi."

"Thanks." *That's me, 'Weird Rhi'.*

"Go back to sleep—and no dreaming," Lauriel ordered.

I wanted very much to do that. We lay silent for a long time. I kept rolling the dream over and over in my mind. I replayed those sad, blue eyes in my head. It touched me.

Carlee, Lauriel, and I stayed busy together that final week before school started. We did just about everything together. Lauriel did not mention Leone at all. Strange for her, I assumed, but very nice for me. It enabled Lauriel and me to become close.

I never did watch the video that Leone set up for me. It sat in the same spot on my dresser.

I had become the common thread between Lauriel and Carlee. We three drove to McCall and swam off the docks, went to the theater, watched movies at Carlee's or my house, played in my recreation room, had fire pits in my yard, and swam below my house whenever we wanted. We spent hours talking, laughing, and dreading the start of school.

I did not travel to the reservoir where I'd almost drowned. I had no reason. Most importantly, I stopped seeing Leone everywhere I went. Lauriel never invited me to her house. I knew she understood that I didn't want to see her brother.

We decided to travel to school together when it started. When I thought of school my nerves fluttered about in my gut, causing a queasy ache. My palms already sweated. I knew I would have to double up on my deodorant.

Otherwise, I became comfortable in this new place. I dressed daily in one of my new tee shirts with a pair of shorts and flip flops. I wore the ring from my grandmother and the bracelet Lauriel gave me. I left my hair down. I always liked the way I could hide under it when I wanted.

10

Ready or Not

My first stop was the office to register and pick up my class information for what is known as a staggered schedule, some classes each day, some every other. Then I searched for my first day classes. My hands were clammy and my body chilled as I walked the halls of the school. Hopefully there would be people I knew in some of my classes.

It had taken so much time in the office. I anticipated the bell ringing any moment to release first period.

I found my first classroom not far from the office. I looked through the door for a minute and tried to gain my courage. I opened the door and walked in. I didn't look at the class—I just kept my eyes on the teacher. He stopped talking as I approached and looked back at me. I handed him my form; he signed it and gave it back. He motioned to the back of the class to an empty seat. I scanned the back and saw the empty seat. Then I saw Leone. He sat in the opposite corner from the one I moved toward. He looked at me, expressionless.

Heart fluttering, I bumped a few people's shoulders as I ambled my way through the aisle. *Tortured in room 12.* I grunted as I plopped down.

The open window I sat next to let in the early morning chill. I'd brought no jacket with me. I froze the entire period.

History class—not my strong point. It required memorizing dates, times, places, and people's names, the four worst things for me to remember. According to the books Leone kept, history seemed right up his alley. *I bet he aces this one.*

A breeze picked up and brushed across my skin. Goose bumps poked up everywhere and I shuddered. I saw the breeze ripple the papers on the desks next to me before my eye reached Leone. He still ignored me, focusing on the teacher. I surveyed for a moment too long.

He looked toward me. He held my gaze unblinking. I had to look away and break the connection. *How can I make it through this class with butterflies in my stomach for a whole year?*

I begged silently,' *please don't let me have any more classes with him.'*

I grew faintly aware of the teacher talking about the author who wrote one of the text books we would be learning from—Leon Gevonis.

When the bell rang I rushed to the door. Leone made it there at the same time. He held it for me then disappeared.

I tried to get my bearings on class numbers. I spied Carlee in the hall and ran to her.

"Hi, Rhi. How did your first class go?"

"History. Not so good. I can't find room 115. The numbers are leaving me confused." Faint tremblings tickled my stomach as I remembered Leone's and my locked gaze.

"It's down this hall." She pointed. "Turn left at the end. It's right next to the exit. You'll see it. English?" she half questioned, raising an eyebrow and messing up her face while saying, "Good luck!" She must have known more than she wanted to let on about the teacher.

160

I ran to class trying to beat the tardy bell. It won. Dang it! I would have to stand in front of another class now. I walked in. "Rhiannon!" a soft voice whispered to me.

I saw Lauriel sitting in the middle row. Seats behind her were open. I put my stuff behind her and claimed the seat. I noticed Bob a few rows over. We said "hi" to each other. He did an exaggerated sad face at me and pointed to the empty seat in front of him. I just shrugged my shoulders and smiled.

I walked back to the teacher's desk and had her sign the registration paper, then returned to my seat. I patted Lauriel on the shoulder as I passed.

Mrs. Potters began her sermon on handing in assignments on time. Work needed to be immaculate—no spelling errors, or punctuation mistakes, and everything had to be double-spaced to allow her to comment (or nitpick) on the writing. No matter how profound my thoughts were on paper, the spelling always dispelled any notion of my real intelligence, another reason for me to stay humble.

Our first assignment focused on writing about the activity from our summer that stood out most. I knew what the most outstanding thing in my summer was, but I certainly did not feel like focusing on it. She gave us that last half of class to start working on it. It didn't take me that long to write out what I wanted to say. It became the most boring thing that I had ever attempted to write.

That period ended too slowly, a great indication of how the rest of my year would go in this class.

I needed to find my next class. Math. Not my favorite subject, but I generally managed to pass. This math classroom's number suggested it should be close to my first period classroom. I doubled back to my first period, but I could not find it. How frustrating. You would think the people that numbered the classrooms would have been able to count in order.

Frazzled, I asked someone in the hall. He pointed down a hall I didn't recognize. I rolled my eyes to myself as I headed down that way.

The atmosphere felt different over here, if that were at all possible. This hall was exclusively dominated by seniors and felt as if a "membership required" sign hung from the ceiling. Even though I passed the prerequisite of being in 12th grade, my clumsy nature and desire to blend in made me think I actually stuck out like a sore thumb.

I kept my head down as I walked toward the milling crowd. When I looked up at the next door to check the room number, I noticed people looking at me. Curious over the new girl, I assumed. Not the right number so I kept walking, secretly wishing for see-through abilities.

I continued to scan room numbers until I found it.

When I first glanced around, I thought all the desks were taken. They were lab-like desks—long, made-for-two counters with drawers separating the chairs in between. Only one chair remained open along the window in the middle of the row. A kid with brown hair and glasses hunkered at the other end of the desk. Sitting right behind him, sharing a desk with a very beautiful, blue-eyed, dark-brown haired, tanned, skinny girl was Leone. Great, as if swimming my way through my first day in senior-torture had not been frustrating enough.

I acted as if he were a complete stranger and took my seat.

I wanted to ignore his existence as much as possible. I found it hard knowing he sat behind me and me in full view of him, like being in a spot-light. My whole body remained hyper-aware. Even as I struggled to shut off my mind, I found myself curious and wanting to look at him. *Not fair. I have been doing great, ignoring any possibility that I had feelings for Leone anymore. This had to just be a weird infatuation that I needed to get over.*

He passed me a note.

Happy belated birthday. I like the bracelet.

I wadded up the note. I noticed as I crumpled it, the faint woodsy smell of him on the paper. I closed my eyes to let it sink into my core, my own little secret. I did not tell him thank you. I decided I would sit completely opposite this desk next class session. Then I could avoid him.

Mr. Worthen strolled in right as the bell rang.

"Hello, class, and welcome back to the new year. I am going to start by passing around the seating chart. I want you to fill your name in the spot that corresponds to your seat. We will remain in this order until I can see where I need to move people."

My head sank to the desk. Those "how unfair" thoughts played on in my head. An image of shackles binding my feet to the desk while the teacher pointed and laughed at me raced through my mind.

The teacher continued, "As I see who my stronger people and the ones-who-need-help are, I will be partnering you up accordingly." *Ruined. I need to get a lot stronger or change classes.* This close proximity would not work for me, as preoccupied as I continued to be. It felt like a magnetic force stretched between us. I needed to break it for my own sanity.

"Leone," Mr. Worthen walked toward our side of the room, "tell me how it is that you chose to quit football this year after practicing for most of the summer? We could really use you out there. You were one of the best players."

"Sorry, Mr. Worthen," he responded. "I have something far more important to take care of."

"Isn't there a way to do both?" came Mr. Worthen's rebuttal.

"No, really, this one takes all of my time." He chuckled to himself, "And then some."

I chanced a glance back at Leone. His big, radiant smile focused right at me. I turned around, my stomach fluttering like a little schoolgirl. I tried to sink lower into my chair. If only I could disappear.

The rest of class time we worked on problems we should have been able to complete at the end of last year. I couldn't focus enough to remember what numbers even looked like.

Lunch mercifully arrived. I sat with Carlee, Lauriel, and some other girls that Carlee had known forever. They chatted about who had changed over the summer and blah, blah, blah.

I fingered the food on my plate. My eyes kept straying toward Leone. He sat with a few guys that I didn't recognize, but I guessed were sports figures in the school. Hair combed and styled, muscles straining against the shirts they wore, heads held high in confidence. They all snickered at something. Leone looked up and caught me looking at him only once.

When the bell rang to start my next class, I found myself perched on the bleachers in lifetime sports with Carlee. To my surprise Lauriel and Leone also had this class. Lauriel talked with him for a little while, then made her way to me. If Leone hadn't been in the class it would have been nice. Carlee and Lauriel both in one class, and one that allowed us to talk and hang out, very cool. Mr. Lofton walked in—straight and determined, his wiry body stiff like a flag pole. The white papers in his hand fluttered as he walked. He immediately started passing out permission slips.

"These are for the annual raft trip. Get them signed and back to me by weeks end or you will not be going. You will stay in the gym and play badminton." Oh. No good at badminton. I believe the last time I played, I managed to hit myself in the back of the head with the racket and break it on the ground. I guess rafting had to be the choice. I thought back to the rafters we saw on the water and decided it would be fun.

The rest of the day went pretty quickly.

Lauriel and Carlee were waiting next to Carlee's car.

On the ride home Lauriel asked to look at what I had written about my summer.

"This doesn't sound like the excitement I remember from this summer. I remember one hot Rhiannon at the mall. Not to mention a near-death experience." She used a pencil to edit my writing.

She handed it back to me. "Just rewrite it. The spelling and punctuation are perfect now."

"Thank you."

"You are so very welcome." She smiled.

We all decided that tomorrow we were going to wear the same color shirt and pants.

They dropped me off at home. I felt a little tired with the new schedule, so I went upstairs and lay down on my bed. I dozed until Mom came home.

I helped her cook and we ate dinner together after Dad arrived.

I pulled out the permission slip from PE and handed it to my Dad.

I knew letting Mom have it earlier would have meant a definite battle due to my recurring nightmares. She had been doting on my every emotion lately. I figured getting it into Dad's hands first meant a better chance of the conversation going quickly, and I might just have someone on my side.

He read it and raised an eye-brow.

"The water is calm where we will be going. There are very few rapids and we are required to wear very thick lifejackets," I reassured him.

He scrutinized me very carefully as he spoke. "Rhi, are you sure you are up to this? It's not like being in a boat. This will require you to be half in and half out of the water. There is a chance you could fall in. Will you be okay?"

I thought about it. The near-drowning topped the list of the scariest thing I'd ever been through, but I survived. I'd jumped into the water at Payette Lake and it hadn't scared me.

"Ya, I think I'm going to be fine," I told him.

He turned to Mom. "What do you think, Hon? Should we let our daughter try to kill herself again?"

"I don't like you saying it like that," she scolded him. "I think Rhi knows what she feels like. More than that, though, I saw the water as we went to Boise. I know where she's going to be. There weren't very many hard places. I trust her judgment."

I smiled. It had been easier than I suspected. Dad signed my form.

We talked about each other's day then I excused myself for bed.

I dreamed again—they were beginning to be more frequent. The bubonic plague always left me sorrowful. After these dreams, my mind clouded with visions of death for most of the day. The scene did not change, just repeated. Falling asleep started to climb my list of things I most wanted to avoid.

The following day started with my culinary ineptitude, daily living. I had to take the class for credit even though I already knew how to cook. I found it odd that I had Leone in this class, too. I sat away from him again. The teacher said we were going to be cooking at least one thing every week.

I struggled through math, not so much the work, but the who. I tried to focus on the teacher and the lesson he explained. I was so distracted, as if someone was in my head messing with my thoughts. Though I knew that I imagined it, I could feel eyes on me the entire time in class.

In English, I turned in my now polished paper. Then we had lunch.

Drama, I had right after lunch.

I reached it early enough to find a seat in the back. Right before the bell, in walked Leone. He chose a seat in the front.

I slumped down in my chair like a ragdoll and rested my head on the back of my seat. It actually felt nice to let my muscles go limp. If there came a time in class that I needed to play a paper-thin skinned, stuffed, lifeless toy, I knew I could play the part.

I slumped in my chair throughout class and scrutinized Leone's back. I glanced at the teacher from time to time, but I found myself freakishly distracted by Leone's hair. When just glancing at it, I thought it to be blonde. As I studied it closer, I thought I could discern darker and lighter streaks.

Figures. I wonder who he had do his hair. It had to be someone ghoulish and evil. Edward Scissorhands, the bride of young Frankenstein, the Wicked Witch of the West, or maybe even The Joker? None would really surprise me given his flamboyant, psychopathic babblings to me over the summer.

I had been so lost in cruel thoughts, I didn't notice he'd turned around and looked directly at me.

I sucked my lips in and sank my head down on my desk.

No. He really didn't deserve my being that mean to him. *Great, Rhi. You can be so horrible to people sometimes.* I melted lower into my chair, wallowing in my self-loathing for the remainder of the class and heard nothing the teacher said.

When the bell rang, Leone waited at the door to the class. I snuck out next to someone else with my head down pretending I didn't notice him, and headed for the office to turn in my signed registration form.

The next morning I ran late getting ready, so Carlee, Lauriel, and I all were late to school, which accounted for my sliding through the history classroom door as the bell rang. The teacher looked at me through the corner of his eyes and pointed to the last chair. Just like the first day of class, it had been the last one next to the open window.

Why did this teacher love to freeze students?

167

"I suspect the late arrival will not become a habit?" the instructor asked me as I passed.

"No. Not at all," I promised as I continued to walk, not making eye contact with anyone.

I shouldn't have hit snooze so many times on my alarm this morning. I cursed myself when I finally did wake up. I knew I would make everyone late. If I had not been so mad at myself for being mean to Leone in my thoughts yesterday, I might have gotten sleep and this would not have happened.

When I reached the chair in the back, I noticed a nicely folded, jean jacket sitting in it. I looked around. I tapped the guy sitting in front and asked if it belonged to him. He said no, that it had been here when he arrived.

I picked it up, plunked down in the chair, and tucked the jacket on my lap. I thought it would be rude of me to put it on the floor.

Soon the cold breeze got to me and I decided there would be no harm in slipping the blue denim on to keep myself warm.

As soon as I pulled it up around me, I smelled him. The jacket heavy with his scent. *How unfair.*

I looked at him. He faced the front of the room with a large smirk, reveling in his little joke.

Okay, fine. Turn the knife in my back. Apparently, feeling bad about being mean to him hadn't been enough, now he decided to be extremely kind and really dig in.

If my limbs weren't about to shatter frozen to the floor I would have taken it off. My legs still had goose bumps, and my toes felt so frozen they would surely snap off if I tapped them against something. Smart of me to wear flip-flops again. I had to admit, the added warmth did feel good.

I would definitely pack myself a sweater for this class.

When the bell rang, my plan had been to just hand the jacket back to him and walk off, because I was mad at him. Right? I would just push it into his hands and walk away.

He waited off to the side of the door, watching me walk to the front and then toward him. I kept my eyes averted.

When I looked up and made eye contact, his blue, swimming eyes made my legs numb. My feet threatened to stop moving right there. My heart slowed and I instantly felt light-headed.

His eyes were so soft looking at me. Doe-like really. Peaceful. And his grin, wow, knockout and perfect. His lips moist and softened. That perfect face. Was I about to pass out or something? Why did the room spin?

Maybe because I forgot to breath. Yup. Way to be there, Rhi. I gulped in a breath. Not that it was obvious or anything, but due to my throat catching, I coughed. I felt my face grow hot.

He reached out to my arm as I pulled my hand down from my mouth having captured any germs from my cough.

I regained my bearings and reminded myself of the purpose I had in standing face to glorious face with him. I shoved his jacket into his hand before he could touch me, sending that annoying yet addicting sensation through my skin.

His smile faded as he looked down at the jacket, and he nodded his head.

I turned to walk away. *Gosh, Rhi, you're such a jerk. Say something while you're walking away.*

"Thanks." I looked back at him, making a mental note that I really hated listening to the voice in my head. I never could turn it off.

He beamed once again. "My pleasure."

Okay that did not need to be said. Now, I don't feel so bad about almost slighting him in a bigger way. We are even. Or so I thought.

I only had to endure a few more school days before the raft trip. I decided it was a nice gift to have something to look forward to when your day was drudgery and full of trepidation. Leone did that. Even though Lauriel had been the only Ghiovante whom I purposefully spoke with, and she never talked about Leone, just seeing him in my classes kept him fresh on my mind.

The day of the raft trip arrived. My feet felt light and airy. I bounced to my own beat as I walked. Nothing would ruin this day—free from math and Leone's presence in a seat behind me. I had a moment of remembering the sensation of his eyes on me all the time, feeling like he counted my every breath. I noticed the pang of longing seeping in and reminded myself this day would only be fun if I could let it go. I tried not to think about it.

Soon, we were on a bus headed to meet the rafts forty minutes from school. The raft company personnel had us grab life jackets and hop on a raft.

I tightened my jacket and plopped down in a raft in the front, on the left side behind Carlee. Lauriel picked the front right. Kyle filled in right behind her. I engaged in excited chat with the girls, until that too familiar scent fell on me. Butterflies in the pit of my stomach slid down to my legs. I silenced. "Not today," I told myself through gritted teeth.

I turned and saw him out of the corner of my eye. Leone had taken up the position in back of me. It seemed Lauriel thought the situation amusing. I looked around to see where I could change my seat, but the guide of our raft pushed us into the water and began demonstrating the paddles. *Ugh.* I looked up and rolled my eyes to no one but myself. *So much for a calm, Leone-free day.*

The guide demonstrated rowing and asked us to practice rowing in a circle one way and then the other. He told us we were going to get wet and hit some good rapids, but nothing class 4 and up today. There were some groans. I was probably the only one relieved we were not headed for deadly water.

The glossy surface reflected the mountains surrounding us. I could see rocks in the bottom as we glided along. The sun hadn't topped the mountain yet to warm us up. The water felt very cool on my left leg.

I enjoyed the beauty of the area.

The guide brought me to attention. "Okay, around this bend is the first little rapid. We want to pull to the right. It's our first test. I want those on the left side to paddle us harder than the right. Okay? Together now, go and go and..." he kept chanting the rhythm to us.

I managed to keep up for a little while, and then my paddle did not dig as deep into the water, although I pulled back with the same amount of force. The paddle skimmed the top and picked up a large enough amount of water to saturate both of the people sitting behind me. I heard an annoyed yell from the back. Leone just shook to get the water off of him. I turned. I apologized to the kid in the far back and then looked at Leone. His dark glasses were on, but the amusement in his face obvious.

"It's just how Rhiannon works," he teased. I hated the way my body responded to that face.

I decided against an apology to him and turned with a huff, back to paddling. *Why did he always have to do that?*

We rounded the bend in the river and saw the rapids. A little spray shot up in spots. We made it to the far right just as planned, and we bobbed quickly past the rapids. The raft behind us did the same.

We drifted for another short while. The sun peeked over the mountain and the morning air grew hotter.

A paddle fight started on the other side of the raft. Everyone soon had water dripping from their hats or hair, including Lauriel and Kyle. Her eyes bright with excitement. Kyle laughed.

The guide even chuckled. I decided he had seen a lot of this
behavior on his rafts.

We bounced over another smaller set of rapids—the raft
jostled a little as we went. I scanned the bank, trying to keep
my mind occupied with anything other than Leone. I saw a
man standing on the bank in the trees. His arms were crossed.
He wore dark glasses and blue jeans with a button up shirt. He
had red hair and sneered toward our raft as it went by. I knew
that posture from somewhere. I looked toward the other
passengers. No one seemed to notice except Lauriel. Her dark
glasses did not hide the anger in her expression. She glanced
back toward Leone. He too must have been looking. I heard a
small growl from behind me. The hair on my neck stood on
end.

I lurched forward and quickly turned around. Leone glared
toward the bank. My hand came to my throat. Had I heard the
growl or was it my imagination?

Leone did not flinch. His body leaned in toward me, his
hand froze in a motion that told me he had intended to grab
me.

I gazed back at the bank, but the man had vanished.

Chills rippled through me.

I looked at Lauriel, then the bank again. She monitored the
same place on that side of the river.

Goose bumps rose on my flesh. The temperature of the
water was not the culprit.

*What just happened? Who was that man? Did everything
have to end up weird when Leone was around?* I scooted a
little closer to Carlee. So that it didn't seem as if I tried to
escape the growl behind me, I leaned over to her to talk.

"What do you think so far?"

"I love it! What do you think? This is your first time." She
beamed.

"So far, so good."

The next rapid came up quickly. I could actually hear it. A slight panic lanced through me.

"This is a little larger than last time," the instructor cautioned. "Remember what I said about falling off?"

I didn't remember. I'd spaced out, thinking about my frustrations with Leone.

Fortunately, the instructor knew teenagers might not always pay attention. He continued, "Point your feet down stream. And let me catch up to you. Are you ready? We need to start by turning to the right. Go, go, go, good...keep it there. When I yell, we are going to turn quickly back to the left. Ready, set, and go. Left, left, left..."

We had turned from sideways right to sideways left as the rapid hit. The front of the raft seemed destined to head straight down the right side of the rapid, but not before a swell hit right under me and made me lose my balance. In an eye's blink, I toppled into the water. Cool water roiled over the top of me—bubbles all around. Then my face came back up with the raft on top of me.

I tried to push off with my hands. My performance rated life jacket pushed me up high in the water, locking me in place to the bottom of the raft. The sensation like suffocating in saran wrap. I kicked and pulled with my arms. My head turned from side to side, seeking air. None of my actions freed me—my life jacket adhered to the bottom of the raft like Velcro.

The cold underwater meshed intimately with me, surrounding me, tingling my skin. Like a murderous lover it toyed with me and begged for me to take a breath. *No. No. No. Not again. How could this be happening again?* My hands clawed at the canvas of the raft. My free flowing hair twisted up in my fingers. My brain screamed, "Move, Flip over, Push. Do something, Rhi!"

The raft bumped again over more waves and it freed me from the bottom.

When I surfaced, the raft bombed the rapids ahead of me, and I twirled in a free float in my jacket. Leone came from nowhere, swimming upstream toward me.

"There she is," someone onboard said. The guide yelled to kick our feet out in front and just float.

As Leone approached, I involuntarily let out a grateful cry. Tears mixed with the cold water dripping from my hair. After the adrenaline kick, my body quivered like Jello. Air hurried in and out of my lungs without pain. Blood raced through my body. I had survived it again. I reached for Leone. He hugged me to him.

"Here I am," he whispered in my ear.

That was the problem. I nearly killed myself again, and there he came to save the day. Even though my body still quaked, it took on a warm feeling, the kind that left me breathless and wanted those perfect lips to touch mine. His hands on my arm stirred inner coals that threatened to make me lose my mind.

He searched my eyes. We held each other there for a moment. Something magnetic pulled between us and urged us to close the gap, and to feel the warmth of the other's lips as they parted and invited.

My attraction to him left me out of my mind entirely. He, too, seemed to will it. He slid closer to me, then abruptly moved, turned me around, and let the current carry us. He held onto the back of my life jacket and pushed my feet out in front.

We bobbed through the rapids after the raft. The guide pulled his oars through the water holding the raft back for us.

He spun it around to the side I fell off. Before he could tell anyone how to help me back in, Leone had jumped back in and scooped me up in his arms. He hugged me a little while before guiding me back to my perch, a little closer to him.

Stop it! I don't want to need him this badly. I don't want my skin to yearn, and my mind to draw conclusions and my

174

body to will itself at him. Just stop it, Rhi. Sit tall, you are strong. This day will end. Soon. I hope.

"Are you okay?" the guide interrupted my reverie.

Everyone looked at me. *Stupid water. Why did I have to fall out?* I only recently stopped having the drowning dream every night. Now I would probably have that one coupled with the awful feeling of having my face planted against the weight of the raft.

I chanced a glance at Leone. He focused straight over my head with the paddle in his hands, his expression glazed over. I nodded my head.

"Don't worry about the paddle. I lose one each trip. You guys on the left will have to work a little harder," amusement laced through the guide's voice. "Row, row, row..." he commanded.

Leone leaned forward and whispered in my ear, "Sit close, so I can grab you if needed."

His breath on my wet skin made me shiver with excitement. Even though my stubborn mind told me to move away from him, I feared going under the raft again. I wanted to avoid the sinking feeling that took me right back to my worst nightmare of drowning. Through the morning, we hit more rapids. I would bump backwards into Leone. He absorbed the impact, always ready for it. He never skipped a beat with the paddle. A couple of times he pulled his legs in around my hips to lock me in place. Although I tried to not allow it, I felt reassured and safe.

We beached for lunch at a spot that had a restroom. I walked off by myself to use it. I needed the time.

As I approached, a familiar figure strode out from behind the outhouse. He had red hair and dark glasses. I jumped back a step. I recognized him as the same man from the side of the river. I noticed he wore a button-up, cotton shirt with the top, three buttons open. I could clearly see the designs in his two necklaces.

A red stone glinted in the sunlight. I had seen the two necklaces somewhere. The mall. I remembered seeing them at the mall, worn in the same fashion—this must be the same man from the mall.

The man hadn't done anything to me, but my mind screamed that old term my mom used to say when I had been small, "stranger danger". What a moment to flake out and go juvenile. A large group of people were at this beach. What could a stranger do with so many others around? If I screamed, they would see him. Yet the tension surrounding me sent sensations prickling along my skin and might as well have been lightening about to strike. I shook my head to clear my mind. I decided my nerves had no right to go overboard. I kept on my path for the restroom.

As I passed him, I smiled and then looked down, not wanting to engage in conversation. He paused for a second and I could feel his eyes on me as I strode confidently toward the restroom. Then I heard pounding feet running toward me from the direction of the beach. Leone grabbed my arm and half dragged me to the restroom, glaring malevolently at the man.

The man raised his hands in the air to say, 'No harm done, just looking.' Then he turned and moved away up the road. He glanced over his shoulder at me. I spied Lauriel, who had also sped up the hill toward us. Had I missed something big? I shrugged my arm to make Leone let go of me. I didn't want him to touch me. It made my body do things my mind needed me to avoid.

Why had Leone and Lauriel come to my rescue? I needed to know, although I had to admit I felt better. My frayed nerves calmed as soon as I knew Leone had arrived at my side.

Leone let me go and apologized. I meandered toward the bathroom, irritated at him rescuing me again. Second time today. How would I beat this if he kept touching me and being close? Lauriel took his place, walking behind me.

I went inside and focused on the whole situation. What would have happened had they not been there? That guy had leered at me in the mall with a smile that creeped me out, one of those hunches you get, like women's intuition telling you that something is just not right. Mom always told me to listen to that inner voice. Well, look where that got me. In a raft, rescued by Mr. Can't-Seem-To-Live-Without-You touching me and turning me to mush inside again.

I believed my intuition to be broken for the most part. This moment, for instance. Geeze, Rhi. What if this guy had been an axe murderer? What would you do? Talk him to death? Out-wit him with your slightly blonde humor? Yet, out of all the people there, why Leone and Lauriel? Why had no one else noticed the guy?

As I mentally whipped myself for not taking things more seriously, I opened the door and saw Lauriel standing outside the bathroom.

"What is going on?" I asked Lauriel, as I walked toward her.

She did not answer; she just attached herself to me all the way back to the group.

The rest of the trip Lauriel sat statuesque. She paddled and paused when needing to. Her eyes ventured to the bank of the river. She glanced at Leone frequently. They seemed to be having an entire conversation with their intense glances back and forth. Unease fluttered in my gut, threatening to cause issues for me later in the day. I desired to go home and curl up in my blankets at that very moment. Leone laid a hand on my shoulder as if to calm me. If that had been his intention, it had the opposite effect. Now my body ached to lean back into him. I needed my body to have no feelings about him and to remain numb. I did not want to live in chaos.

Finally, we returned to school. Lauriel made small talk and accompanied me to my final class of the day. Homework from the other classes awaited me. I scanned over the items so I would know what to grab from my locker.

When the bell rang, Dante surprised me at the door of the classroom.

"What are you doing here?" I asked.

"I'm here," he paused, "setting up for a back-to-school night. They asked for assistance from last year's football team. I said I would help." He grinned awkwardly at me.

I thought his excuse sounded off the wall. I stepped into the rush of people and headed toward my locker.

"How did rafting go?" His voice indicated that he had no intention of leaving me alone.

I didn't answer.

When we stopped at my locker, he continued in a joking tone, "Did you fall out or otherwise cause a commotion?"

My body slouched and I peaked at him from the corner of my eye. Such a nice feeling to know I could be entertainment for some people. He chuckled at me and then hung around scanning the halls. I twisted the combination lock. He moved back and forth from foot to foot. What could he be nervous about? Our conversation had stagnated. I looked around as well, thinking it was weird that he still stood there. Lauriel bounced through the hallway, dancing between people. She obviously had her cheesy disposition back. Dante and Lauriel glanced at each other and then Dante tapped me on the shoulder and waved good-bye.

"Are you ready?" Lauriel asked.

Something about this situation gnawed at my mind. I had to speak up.

I turned toward Lauriel with my hand on my hip. "What exactly is going on here?"

"Nothing. Why do you ask?"

Really, I guess I am just stupid. My mind reeled over the
implication of Lauriel's lying to me. I thought she had grown
to be a good friend. I turned and stomped toward the door of
the school. She followed so close to me I could smell her fruity
perfume. The ride home remained quiet except for the radio. I
think Carlee knew to just drive in silence. Once home, I
murmured a lame good-by and scrambled into my house. I did
my homework, helped out with the dishes, and went to bed
early.

That night I dreamt again of drowning at the lake and
Leone's strong arms pulling me to the dock. For the first time
in a long while, I remembered the sting of my lips after he had
resuscitated me. I felt the desperation of his body as it labored
to bring me back to life.

The feeling in my lips never left as I dressed for school. My
mood left me even gloomier than the evening before.

At school, Leone rested in his familiar seat in the back
corner of the class. We had a direct view of each other with
one empty desk between us—forced to sit closer because
someone had taken the window seat.

I avoided looking at him. I put my hands in my lap and
fidgeted with my fingers. I could tell his eyes were on me. I
looked up when someone ran into class after the bell and filled
the empty seat. We made eye contact as the student sat down.
Leone leaned forward in his desk to stare at me around the
girl.

I jerked my head around to see the front of the class. I sat
far enough back in my seat to block Leone's view of me. I
could feel my lips tingling. I touched them lightly,
remembering my dream. I recalled the look in his eyes from
yesterday as we bobbed in the water. The only two people in
the whole world. He had almost kissed me—I knew it. I closed
my eyes to keep back that I-could-cry feeling.

The girl in the seat between us suddenly rose and walked to the front of the class. It threatened to sink me. *Don't look at him. Don't even think about it, Rhi.* I turned my body and looked out the window. When the girl returned to her seat, I opened my notebook to take notes.

My lips still tingled. I gazed down at my paper and closed my eyes. I touched my lips with my fingertips. I allowed my mind to drift back to the dream for a moment, remembering the shock. When the teacher addressed the class, I glanced at Leone. I was jerked from my private moment by his smile. I glared my annoyance at him—that he seemed to know what my mind had replayed.

Math devoured any sanity I had left. Leone could observe me the entire time. I couldn't hide. The most torture came from him helping the gorgeous creature sitting right behind me with her math. He used his soft and courteous, debonair voice that had entranced me so much. Her giggling responses to him affected me like Ipecac, not to mention his excited and hearty laughter in response.

Even worse, the tingling in my lips intensified. They were alive with the feel of him breathing life into me the day on the dock. The sensation would not leave me alone. I leaned my head down and rubbed them, trying to create a different sensation. I pinched them a few times hoping the pain would change everything.

I excused myself from class to use the restroom. I meandered down the hall to the bathroom and wasted as much time as possible. When I came out, Leone stood waiting for me. I tried to move by him, but he put his hand up on a locker and blocked me from passing.

I stopped and lowered my head. *Don't look up, Rhi. Those eyes will ensnare you. Just... do something else.*

I caught a glimpse of his chest. I could see the details in the weave of the fabric in his shirt. My feet seemed frozen to the ground. I focused on his neck, the muscles tight, creating a hollow dip above the joint in his collar bone. I imagined what it would feel like to run my lips along those strong muscles.

I couldn't feel my arms or legs. The air felt still and warm. Too warm. I shuddered as I breathed in. My hands grew clammy.

Don't look at him.

My legs were weak and started to wobble. I could smell him. *Don't look into his eyes.* My stomach did flips.

"Have you watched 'Hiding Places' on your DVD yet?"

There I stood, gazing into his eyes again. Did he say something to me? It took me a minute to process everything.

I stammered, "Oh, n... no. I haven't." My last words forced themselves out. I lowered my eyes to his belt, trying to grasp the conversation, then raised them to meet his in defiance. I knew I was trapped, and even worse, I liked it.

Stupid me. Argh!

I ducked under his arm and raced around the corner back to class.

I slouched in my chair with my head on my arm. Writing my math problems out, I focused so I wouldn't be required to look around. Leone had come back to class and began helping the girl behind me again. I closed my eyes. Why couldn't I just make my mind up to be done with this mess and stick to it?

When the bell rang I fled from the room.

I believed my stomach had turned itself inside out—I could not fathom eating at lunch. Lauriel sat with Leone and his crew. Carlee noticed my funk and edged close to me and never asked any questions.

The remainder of my classes might as well have been one of those silent movies. I didn't hear anything my teachers said.

The final bell ended a miserable torture that had begun nine hours before.

In the staggered day classes the following day, I managed to stay away from Leone, although he made sure to look at me enough to make me uncomfortable.

The next morning I arrived early to history class and claimed the desk next to the door. It made for a fast escape. When Leone walked in, I kept my head down, searching my book for nothing, but acting as though it consumed my every thought. I looked at his pants' legs as they stopped in front of me. I saw his hand tap his leg. He turned and walked past me.

I heard the desk behind me slide across the floor a little, indicating he had chosen to sit behind me.

Really? Cut me a break.

I poured all of my effort into watching the teacher. I made a point to notice every letter he wrote on the board and every paper he touched. It helped me to focus on something other than the heavenly smell wafting from the seat behind me.

Halfway through class Leone excused himself to use the restroom. On his way out he passed close to my desk. I saw his finger tug at the paper on the edge of my desk. In turn, it fell to the floor.

He bent down and grabbed it before I could.

He spun to give the sheet to me and brought his face close to mine. His eyes locked on mine. "Here is your paper. You have some homework tonight," he directed in a soft, stern voice. Then he disappeared out the door.

Tears stung my dry eyes. I shook my head to get it under control. I clenched my fists. I knew I could not take anymore. I walked to the history teacher's desk and told him I felt very ill. He excused me to go to the nurse's office. I grabbed my books and left.

I lay down until lunch when the nurse insisted I try to eat something. In the lunchroom, Lauriel shared a table with Leone again. I sat next to Carlee. She talked to people around us, but stayed close by.

"Are you doing okay today, Rhi?" Carlee asked quietly.

"I think so." I paused. "Just not feeling good today."

"I hope you feel better tomorrow. I really wanted to have you stay the night."

I trudged through the rest of my classes, trying to hide in my small bubble, wishing I had on a disguise of an unnoticeable person.

I plodded to the car by myself. Carlee stood there. We waited for Lauriel. When she finally showed up, she proclaimed that she had waited frantically for me at my locker.

I mumbled an apology.

When we pulled into my driveway, Lauriel got out with me.

"Rhi and I have some homework to finish up," she insisted.

"Okay," Carlee said, looking at me and shrugged her shoulders. "Call me later, Rhi."

Confused, I led Lauriel into the house. My parents weren't home yet.

"Where is the DVD, Rhi?"

"The DVD?" I asked her. She had never even talked about Leone when we were around, let alone any of his crazy beliefs. The safe feeling I'd had about Lauriel ran through my emotional shredder. I slumped down on the couch.

"In my room on my dresser." Before I could protest, she sped to my room.

Leone caused this. I could not focus in my classes. I felt heart sick. I swooned when I had to be next to him. I lost my appetite. I longed for him. *What is happening to me? Have I lost all control over myself?* I hated him for it. He was just strange. He manifested a friend in his sister whom I had believed I could trust. I swayed back and forth with my arms crossed, lightly running my finger across my lips.

I hadn't realized Lauriel made it back down to the living room until I heard the television turn on. She paused and looked at me. I stared aimlessly at the wall.

"Rhi."

I looked up at her. She raised the DVD to show me.

She put it in the DVD player. She flipped through some chapters and clicked on the options. She entered the code and Leone appeared on the screen again. From the look of it, it had been filmed in the same location as the first section I had watched.

"The directions you are about to hear are important. The clearing you are searching for is in a remote spot. Secluded from everyone."

I glanced at Lauriel with my eyebrow raised. She pointed toward the television screen, despite implying I was a child being punished.

"Go straight up the hill. You will cross two game trails. On the third one, take a right and follow it up and over the top of the mountain side. It will descend into some rocks and almost disappear. Keep an eye out for it. It will drop you down the other side quickly. At the bottom is a river. You must jump in and swim with the current downstream. There will be an old bridge there, go under it. There are rocks on the left side, get out after the rocks. There will be a map under the larger rock; you will have to tip it to get it out. Follow the directions from there. Hurry and try not to rub up against anything!"

Then the screen went blank.

"Okay, Rhi. Remember, three game trails, to the right, go over, down, swim, bridge, rock, map and don't brush up against anything." Lauriel recounted the steps for me.

"Now that I finally watched it, could you be so kind as to tell me what is going on?" I stood my ground. I had reached my limit on garbage for the day.

"No. I think we are good now. Leone is leaving you alone—I asked him to do that. He is just determined to make sure you are safe. You are quite welcome to ignore him, but I will not let you ignore me. Now, let's get your homework done. Shall we?"

Was I coming or going? This tornado needed to stop spinning so Dorothy could find her red slippers and tap them together for a swift return to reality.

Lauriel's behavior made me want to push her away. I didn't need people messing with my mind.

She settled at the kitchen table with her books. I chose to stand at the counter. I did my best to ignore her, until she crumbled up a page of paper and tossed it at me, hitting me in the head. I frowned at her. She tossed another one and I dodged.

"Lighten up," she urged.

"Easy for you to say," I countered.

"Game of pool then? The loser has to be nice to the winner the rest of the night."

I understood the stakes. We really had no reason to play— I already knew she would beat me soundly. I couldn't come close to her ability. *Fine. If she insisted on harassing me for a while, then so be it.* My studies seemed farthest away from my mind, even with the books open in front of me.

While we played, Lauriel talked about some of the weird things she noticed about someone in one of her classes. I knew of the person, and when she did an imitation of him it made me laugh. By the time the game had finished, I didn't want to snap her head off as much. I did think it prudent to start hanging out more with Carlee though. She, at least, did not impose extremely strange sanctions on me.

185

We finished our homework. I went into the living room and started to watch a movie. Lauriel joined me.

We were watching one when my Mom came home. Soon after that Leone swung into the driveway to pick up Lauriel.

Friday, thank goodness. I had to survive one more day, then I could rest for the weekend.

On the way to school, Carlee officially asked me to stay the night at her house—her mom had okayed the plans. I texted my mom from the red phone Leone had given me. Lauriel insisted that it stay with me the last week. I had to admit, I understood the convenience of it. Mom responded that I could stay. We were planning to go right after school. Carlee invited Lauriel as well, although I would've been happy knowing I would have a night with just Carlee.

Leone didn't show for his classes. I thought that turn of events would make it easier. Instead, I found myself watching the door to see if he would show up late.

In English, sitting beside Lauriel, we took turns reading out loud.

I glanced out the window and noticed a red car at the road. The man with red hair leaned against the door, staring into the window of the classroom. In fact, staring at me.

Why me? How could he tell me apart from others? He stood far enough away from the window I had to squint to see any details. The posture, the grin, the necklaces. Yes, the same man from the rafting trip and the mall. Lauriel heard me gasp and followed my gaze out the window.

She studied me through her wide eyes. I remembered the directions to the hiding place. Had this been the reason they prompted me to watch the DVD? My stomach gurgled.

This could not be real. I peered out the window again. He stood there staring, unmoving. He seemed to be smiling.

Lauriel glanced at the clock. She looked at me.

She mouthed, "The hiding place."

Pain, like being kicked in the stomach, caused me to put my hand on my gut. I thought I would be sick at any moment. Light-headed—did someone turn up the temperature in the room? A stranger had ogled me three times now. It didn't seem like an earth-shattering event. A little creepy. *Rhi... come on, that's a lot creepy.* His eyes always seemed amused. I trembled like a small animal trapped by the talons of a raptor. The Ghiovanies seemed to know the danger before I did. How was it possible, and who did I trust?

"I need to call my mom," I whispered.

She looked horrified at me. "No, Rhi! Stick to the plan of going to Carlee's. I will tell her something to help cover—I'll leave a note or something. We do not want your parents getting hurt."

My parents? I choked down a sob. My existence flipped around me. Why couldn't everything just be the same?

The bell rang. I scanned the yard out the window. He was gone and so was the car.

Lauriel grabbed my arm. I was sure she didn't mean to be so rough. She rushed us through the crowd in the hallway. I couldn't see where we were going. Dazed and confused, I followed her feet as she swerved around people. I glanced behind me, paranoid the red-head would be there, like a psychotic killer in a horror movie.

Lauriel stopped. I scanned the crowd ahead of her and then back behind me.

Dante materialized through the milling people. Where had he come from?

Lauriel's intensity slammed into me as she stated, "It's time."

And we were on the move again.

We caught Carlee as she paused on her way into the cafeteria. I didn't hear what Lauriel told her, but Carlee looked at me and nodded. While they were talking, I peered over my shoulder and spotted red hair.

He dodged people at the far end of the hall from us, but
headed in our direction. I grabbed Laurel's arm.

She gazed down the hall and pushed me in front of her,
away from him. Dante stayed behind.

Instead of going to the front of the school, we dashed
around to the back, at least Lauriel did, as she towed me. We
rushed into the forest that rimmed the track.

I spotted Leone tapping his foot, obviously waiting for us.

"Take her jacket and clothes," he ordered Lauriel.

"What?!" I asked. He nodded at me.

"Trade clothes with Lauriel, please. And fast." He turned
his back to me.

I felt a rush of panic—everything appeared wrong, like a
refugee having to flee and give up her belongings. My books
were left behind on a table in the school hallway, the only
evidence that I had been there that day. I didn't even know if I
would make it back to use them. Had I shown up this morning
and walked onto the set of a Stephen King movie?

But the red-haired man looked just as real as any other, I
could not deny it. A few tears blurred my vision and I wiped at
them with my shirt as I pulled it overhead.

"There," Lauriel soothed. She kissed my cheek and slipped
out of the forest back to the school.

Leone thought I had finished, but Lauriel was much faster.
I still pulled at her pants, trying to get them on, when he
turned around.

"Sorry." He twisted so that his backside faced me once
again.

I finished and announced, "Done..." I started to say
something else, but the words caught in my throat as Leone
reached to grab me. He stopped short when he noted the tears
smeared down my chin. He raised his hand to caress my face,
then seemed to read my soul in my eyes.

"Rhi, I will sacrifice myself for you," he promised as he traced a fresh teardrop back up my cheek with his finger. He bent down quickly and kissed my cheek, still wet with salt.

In one fluid motion he picked me up. He peered into my eyes as he carried me.

Formerly his gaze brought me peace, but now dark, twisted feelings mixed in. No relaxing, no swooning, just darkened hopes.

His truck sat on an old, dirt road through the trees. He opened the door and pushed me in.

We sat in silence for a little while. My mind drew a blank. What had happened today? From where did this red-haired man come? Why did he seem to focus only on me?

When we were a great distance from the school, Leone started to talk. "The plan is to stop by your house. You have five minutes to get what you need. Then we have to hide you until we can stop him. We don't know who he is. He seems to be interested in you. I need to make sure you are safe, as well as your parents. If you aren't there, your parents should be fine. Lauriel is using your clothing to keep him focused around the school for a time. We aren't sure how long it will keep him there."

"My parents, Leone? I don't understand any of this. Please don't let anything happen to my parents." My desperation returned more fiercely than the first time I ran into Dante, after he had hunted on the mountain.

"Rhiannon, please understand. We only thought him a nuisance, happenstance, in the wrong place at the wrong time. I should have listened to myself. We did not and still do not know, if it's you he's after. It seems he has a one track mind. I'm not going to take any more chances."

"But my parents," I pleaded to hear him say they would be safe.

He didn't respond until we reached the house.

"Touch as little as possible." He opened the door for me, grabbing things that I reached out for before I could. Every time he reacted to my attempting to grab anything, I wanted to scream.

"Leone, if I am in this much danger, then who will keep my parents safe? You have to promise me. They are all I have."

Leone's eyes narrowed and he frowned at me.

"Sorry, Rhi. I overlooked your natural need." He ran his hand through his hair.

"My family will constantly watch your parents, at work, at home, everywhere. If this guy realizes you haven't been here, then he will most likely leave them alone. I understand your need to make sure and I respect it. I will make it so."

Knowing my parents would be safe helped to ease my mind a little. I packed my essentials and we left.

He drove us to his house next.

I went into the kitchen. Leone disappeared toward his room.

His mom stood there, along with four others whom I did not recognize.

"Hello, Rhi," Nohi said. "There is no time for introductions." She referred to the three younger kids and one beautiful, blonde woman.

The blonde stood with her arms crossed and appraised me from head to toe. She did not smile. In fact, she did not hide the snarl on her lips or the raised eyebrow. I felt I was not welcome in her presence.

"Here is some food." Nohi shoved a bag at me. "We will be keeping track of things here. You follow the instructions." She hugged me and shoved me toward the back door.

"But why?" I felt like a mouse in a maze, without direction or explanation.

"Why?" The blonde's tone was incredulous and she cocked her head to the side and emphasized her crossed arms. "Are you kidding?" she asked.

"Enough," Leone's firm voice sounded from behind me. I spun around to see him staring her down.

"You will assist Lauriel at the school," he commanded her. She glared at Leone for a moment and raced to the front door. When it slammed, the house shook.

I knew for sure I did not want to cross her in the future.

"Nohi, do you mind tracking down Rhi's mom and keeping an eye on her?" He patted Nohi on the shoulder.

"Not at all," she responded.

"I will ask Dante to find her dad and do the same," he explained.

"Where are you going?" I needed to know.

"I'm thinking that he will try and show up at your house. It's logical."

I shivered.

Leone pulled me toward the door to the back of the house.

Dante waited by the tree line. He motioned me toward the forest. Seeing him there, beckoning me to go into the forest, forced me to stop short.

My vision of him, in a very scary form, happened in the hills above here.

I had to focus on the Dante that stood before me and tell myself he would not hurt me. My feet still didn't want to move.

Leone hugged me.

"Rhi," he pleaded, "stick to the plan, please. I beg of you. I am coming right behind you, as soon as we find him."

He pushed away from me and grabbed both bags.

What if I never see my parents again? If I stepped into that forest, it could be the last time for everything.

Dante took a few steps into the forest and extended a hand in my direction.

Leone grabbed my hand and pulled me. My rooted feet did not move freely. They seemed laden with concrete. My mind became a tangle of thoughts, screaming for me to run away. Dante got closer to me as Leone pulled.

"Run, Rhi." My brain shrieked. I pulled back a little and Leone stopped to look at me.

I shook my head "no" and tried to pull my hand back. Salty tears betrayed me, hot and stinging, as they found their way down my cheeks. I didn't care that I appeared weak.

He didn't let go. He came to stand in front of me, dropped my bags, and reached for my other hand. Tingling sensations raced up my arms. Inside my fears grew lighter. A peace formed from somewhere deep.

"Rhi, I swear on everything I have ever held sacred. You are the most important thing to me. I do not have the ability to know who this is that stalks you, or what he is capable of. I just know that I have to act. Dante has vowed to protect you with his being, as have I."

"Please, Rhi," Dante begged, "I promise."

I looked at him and then back to Leone.

I took a deep breath and let a shaky exhale trickle past my lips before saying, "See you soon?" I searched Leone's black eyes.

"Yes," Leone assured me.

Dante and I started into the forest. I glanced back at Leone who watched us go. His fists were clenched. When I peeked back again, he had gone.

We trudged up the mountain, heading to the north. He led me as far as the game trail that I needed to take.

"Run from here until you get to the river," he ordered. "Do not stop and do not look back. When you reach the note, replace the rock. Be careful. Hide from anyone that might see you. You will not be alone for long."

I nodded my head. I felt as if my bowels would loosen at any moment. I needed to keep moving and my queasy stomach would have to wait. Death might be down this hill. I had no idea what to expect.

He motioned for me to go. I ran. I glanced back in time to see him following me, wiping his sweater along the trail to cover where my feet hit. Odd. Why would he do that? I let the question slip from my mind as my feet struggled to stay on the path.

The game trail did just what Leone said it would do. After topping the mountain it dropped almost straight down the other side. Loose rock bounced down the trail in front of me. I slid and gyrated from side to side. The water ran below me.

The trail leveled out and followed the river. The flow slowed as it spread to a thirty-foot-wide expanse. I imagined it would bottle neck below this point and pick up incredible speed, just like the rapids I fell into on our raft trip.

I stood and stared at the misleadingly calm water. Under it, the rocks and the undertows waited. I heard gurgling and slurping from somewhere in the middle as the current twirled into a funnel that disappeared for a few seconds. It reappeared in the original spot, like a trap door spider waiting to consume the fresh water and any unlucky voyager that may have chosen to ride, sucking them down to the inky, dark depths.

My stomach gurgled. My palms were sweating. If water spirits existed, it seemed that they had a desire to trap me down there with them. *Why do I tempt fate? Why on earth had Leone chosen to force me back into the water?*

I looked at the bank as it flowed around the bend. The game trail ended here. Instead, enormous, sharp rocks jetted up from the earth, and I did not think anything would be able to maneuver through them. A very large, overgrown thicket stretched from the water's edge and appeared to run farther than my eyes could see.

I could go back. I scrutinized the trail I had just come down. Steep.

The image of Dante wiping the trail down with his shirt flashed in my mind. What had been the purpose?

"Don't touch anything," Leone's words crept into my mind from the video. *But why? What exactly is at stake here? Why do I need to jump through these insane hoops?*

"Red hair and a devious smile. That's why," I answered my own question in a shaky voice. Leone said he didn't know the person, but it seemed his interest lay in me. My back muscles spasmed, reminding me I needed to relax.

I spied the life jacket in the bushes and slipped it on. I fastened the straps.

Watertight bags, I noted for the first time. Planned out. The whole escape had been planned to the last details.

I waded into the water up to my knees. The tingling in my legs felt like tiny fingers attempting to grab me. *Come on, Rhi. Water spirits don't exist. Like the tooth fairy.*

I backed out of the water, clutching the bags. My shoes squished with the water. I shivered in my wet pants. This whole event was totally absurd.

No. This had to be some bizarre joke.

Where are the cameras? I searched the terrain for a movie crew—it looked far too treacherous for any kind of candid camera event.

I gasped. My breath became quick and choppy. I felt excruciatingly hot, as if I were standing outside in the blazing summer with a parka on, even though my calf muscles were chilled from the drenched leggings. I felt tears trickling. Panic tightened its grip on me like a tourniquet to a mortal wound.

"I can't do it." My voice sounded distant and small—not the powerful pep talk I had intended to give myself. "I could just stay here." I rocked from side to side. I knew I would drown this time if I went into the water. *No one here. Just me.* I had nearly drowned two times now. I shook my head, reaffirming I didn't need to go in. I plunked down on a rock and wrestled with my thoughts.

I rolled the days events around, telling myself it had all been a joke and I could go home now. Something inside knew better. I knew better because my thoughts did not command my muscles to stand and climb the hill back to my house.

Loud crashing from above jerked me from my trance. It sounded as if a huge tree branch lost the battle with gravity, or perhaps something bigger blasted down the hill toward me. *Could it be an elk?* I strained to see back up the path, in the direction the sound had come. I stopped breathing and listened.

Too quiet. Even the insects had quieted their alien music.

No more thought necessary, I splashed into the water and plunged into the deep. The current swept me.

I turned myself to observe the trail. Watching until it disappeared from sight. Nothing.

Now, at the mercy of the water, I bobbed. The water didn't like me. I grabbed onto the bags, fearing my life depended on it. I kept my feet down stream.

"Point feet down stream," my mantra spilled out through my husky voice over and over.

I could hear a faint gurgling sound ahead of me. I cried out. Rapids. Inevitable and unwelcomed. I searched the banks and found nowhere to get out. The sound grew louder. I kicked my feet, the effect turning me in a circle.

I could see the spray shooting in the air. The rock must be huge here.

I screamed, I would not make it through this.

I rolled onto my belly and kicked toward the bushes at the water's edge. The current's will was stronger and launched me straight into the rapid shoot made by the water careening between two boulders. My head dunked under the water.

Flip over, feet down. Roll, Rhi, roll.

I kicked and flailed, my bags hitting me, until I once again viewed sky and river in front of me through a screen of water that drenched my eyelashes and hair.

Then I could see spray and more rocks. I became a pinball bouncing from obstacle to obstacle. The river had control.

Past the rapids, the water slowed again. I wiped my face. My body trembled.

I clung to the bags, brightened with the realization that I had come through it. Scary, but I did it. I breathed in.

Yes. I'd made it. I'd done it myself without drowning. I didn't want to. I had been forced into it, but I made it just the same.

I made it, but did not plan to do it again. I would walk.

I would float until I spied rapids again, then I would get out and hike around them.

I stayed closer to the bank to allow me to get out quickly.

As the curve in the river straightened once again, the bridge came into view.

"Thank you. Yes," I congratulated myself.

I stayed with the current as it flowed under the wooden overpass, then kicked to the side where I saw larger rocks.

I climbed out and looked for a rock that might be the one that held the map I needed. I pushed around, some would not budge and others had nothing under them. I dropped one on my fingers. I swayed back alternating between grabbing and shaking my hand.

I reached down again and pushed a few more rocks, nothing. I threw some behind me and heard them splash.

A breeze picked up and rustled the leaves clinging to the trees. The hair on my neck stood. I hunched down by the rocks and surveyed the surroundings. Perhaps I had made too much noise. I couldn't see anything. My nerves were on overtime.

Maybe I should be more concerned with Leone and his family. The thought occurred to me that I had been trusting their odd behavior and not paying attention to the screaming

196

of my mind telling me to avoid and get away from them. Well, I couldn't say that exactly, my body seemed to only desire Leone, and even my mind betrayed me at times. Okay, a lot of the time. But logically, I needed to be on guard. I might have already gone too far into their diabolic scheme.

I finally pushed hard on one of the rocks, and it gave way. A note sat under it inside a clear bag.

"Rhi, turn and go through the water. You will be able to cross downstream where the water runs shallow. Walk between the bushes at the other edge and up the rocky cliff. You will not be able to see it right away, but there is a cave. I have left a flashlight next to the opening so you can see in. I will be there soon. Do not make a fire until I arrive." Weird way to tell me about a cave. *Why hadn't he just told me about the cave in the stupid video?*

Did I want to follow the directions anymore? It's a cave for heaven's sake. And a dark one at that from the sound of it. Maybe he had decided to kill me there. Slash me up into tiny bits and leave me for the coyotes. Would they ever find me?

I shoved the note in my pocket, staring downstream in the direction the note said to go.

No. I don't want to play big-bad-wolf anymore. I do not remember signing up to play the part of Little Red Riding Hood. Maybe I should just take the road out.

I heard something then. I looked back toward the bridge. The red-haired man stood there, glaring at me. My chest hurt. Had my heart had stopped beating?

His eyes glowed red, unlike any I had seen, except for the evil man in my dreams. My body went cold. I stepped back from him and fell on the rocks. I dropped one of my bags. I turned to run up the bank, away from the water.

He blocked my escape. I moved back to the other side. He followed my movement. Then he growled, deep and throaty. I cowered to my wavering knees. I had been wrong. I knew inside myself that this man meant me harm. Leone must have been right. Maybe they were in it together. My head shook, my hands clutched the bag to my chest.

"Your friends thought they could outsmart me." An evil grin curled his lips. "Doesn't surprise me really. They didn't know that I have hiked these mountains. I know the trails. I drove these roads until they spit me out miles from anywhere."

He hopped down the rocks to stand by me. I sank away from him, the bag my only security. He brushed my wet hair away from my face and neck. "I'm really just curious about you," he advised. "I wonder why you have your own coven protecting you."

"What?" I avoided looking into his eyes. What on earth is a coven?

"A coven," he spat it out like the word left a bad taste in his mouth. I shrank from him as he came closer. "You don't know, do you? Interesting. What game is it then? You smell like every other human I have ever met."

Game? Human? He smells me as a category filed under human? I looked at him with my mouth open.

"Maybe a little more delicious than the others, but why you? I was created to watch you. I needed to find you and capture you, but I am not going to hurt you. Oh no, that is for him to do…" He tipped his head up and to the side, scanning the sky. He put his fingers to his chin and remained silent for a second. I sneaked backward on my knees a few inches.

"Crazy, don't you think?" He flicked my shoulder with his hand. I flinched and swayed away from him. "We take so many lives. Why would this one matter?"

Then he moved closer, forcing me to sit down on my buttocks. I pushed with my feet until I could no longer move backward. He grabbed me then.

"Don't you know?" He lifted me up and glared into my eyes. His fingers dug in, my bones were mere putty within his grip. A scowl crept over my face. I did not want to cry out. Burning red from under his lashes bore into me, he lifted me above him. I struggled to get away. He dropped me and shook his head. I noticed the tension in his body ebbed a little when he had stopped.

Sounds echoed from the mountain I'd descended up the river from us. He glanced over his shoulder and then looked back at me. For several seconds he paused—then he grabbed me and flipped me over his shoulder. My gut landed hard on top of his granite shoulder and I exhaled so hard I could not scream. Saliva dripped from my mouth. Blood rushed to my face, making it fiery. I felt the veins on my neck bloat under my fingers. They ached with the pressure.

After a few seconds I gasped for air.

He raced with me. The continual jarring made it impossible for me to get more than a groan from my lips.

Help followed behind me. It had to be. That must be the reason he ran. We traveled up the road a distance, fast enough that I could not focus on the blur of the scenery as it sped by. The jostling loosened my bag from my grip and it tumbled to the dirt. I perched on his back to stop the constant punching of my stomach, now cramping and threatening to expel any contents.

I began hitting him. His back felt like a brick wall. I emitted a yell as I used all my energy in hitting him and flailing my legs. All the while, I kept an arm as a prop on his back, which allowed me to breathe.

He jumped, knocking my arm loose, and I landed on his shoulder, knocking my wind out again.

He sprinted down the embankment and scuttled into the water.

I gasped for air as we entered the swirling torrent.

It seemed he decided to use the same tactic that I had used earlier, at Leone's instruction. He used the water to get away, making me float in front of him.

We stayed in the water a long time. I, at least, had someone holding my head out of the water this time. Yet, fear still screamed in my head that rapids were ahead and the thoughts of drowning left me numb. I could not decide what would be worse, drowning again or the thought of what this man wanted to do with me.

"Help me," I screamed as loud as I could, hoping anyone following would have a chance to hear me.

I knew he would shut me up—he had hold of my life jacket and pulled me close enough to clamp his hand over my mouth and nose.

I could not breathe. I fought with his hand, trying to rip it from my face. It easily overpowered me and he pulled me back to his chest.

"I wouldn't do that if I were you. I could rip your head clean off your neck right now."

The tone in his voice told me he would follow through. I swatted at his hand, trying to indicate I needed breathe. I kicked the surface of the water.

"I will let you breathe again if you promise not to yell."

I shook my head.

"You promise? I could dunk you under this water and you will not come back up alive." I tried to look at him. *Is he serious? He would drown me. No. Not that. Not the cold, heavy water in the lungs again.* He pushed me away from him but kept his hand to my face. He twisted a hand full of my hair in his other hand so that I had to face him.

He must have seen the terror in my expression and smirked at me.

He slowly pulled his fingers away from my nose. I inhaled as deeply as I could.

"You promised," he warned. "I'm not nice to people who don't keep their promises."

As he removed his hand from my mouth, I straightened in the water. He had let go of me. I gulped air in through my mouth and rubbed where he had pulled my hair.

I turned from him and faced down stream. No sense in trying to swim away. I didn't want to drown at his hands.

He grabbed my hair again, using it as a rudder to guide me in front of him.

My only chance would be to stay alive long enough for Leone's group to find me. They had to find me, or I didn't expect to make it back alive.

As we went through some rapids, he dipped my head underwater. I came up spewing, just as another wave washed over me. I grabbed at my captor's arm to try and get him to release me. He would not—I knew I needed to hold my breath when the next one came.

Finally, he pulled me out of the water far downstream from where we had been, and on the other side of the river. Trees and bushes were thick at the water line—then they gave way to steep cliffs that rose above us. He put me on his back and told me to hold on. He started to climb the face of the cliff. After a few seconds, I let loose of him and began to slide down his back.

I gazed down and realized he had climbed faster than I thought. We were already level with the tops of the trees. The ground far below would have broken my body in the fall. I stopped sliding and held onto his waist for dear life.

He grabbed me by one arm and pulled me up his back to where I could hang onto his throat. I clung there, willing myself not to look down.

Halfway up he stopped on a ledge. He dropped me onto it. The angle sloped forward. Dirt and small rock shards made it slick enough that I couldn't stop myself from gliding forward. He stopped me with a hand on my stomach and pushed me backward until my back rested against the rock wall. My knees were bent, my hands were planted at my sides, fingers digging into the dirty stone I rested on. The soles of my feet dug into the edge of the rock ledge, helping to keep me in the same spot.

"Sit still and you won't slide." His lips were pursed and his eyes narrow slits as he examined me. "I could crush every bone in your pretty little body. I can do things you would never dream of with my physical strength, if you try and defy me, to escape me. Understand?"

I whimpered and concentrated on the river far below, peeking through the tops of the trees.

"Do you think they will find you here? Do you think they care enough to search all night for you?" He waited for me to respond.

I gulped air through the fear of being so high above the ground, perched on a small ledge like a daredevil.

I relaxed my muscles and began to slip again. I clawed at the rock beneath me, trying to push myself back.

"They will find you. Don't worry. They are good trackers. Here is my warning to you, little rabbit. Do not leave yourself unnoticed, anywhere. I will be watching. I do not care what my creator wants. He forgot I move about of my own free will. But know this, if I find this game interesting enough, I might take you for my own."

He ran a finger down my cheek. I gawked at him—hoping my expression displayed the disgust I felt at his touch, but thought only fear might have registered.

He leaned down. I pushed myself backward, smacking my head into the rocks. He traced his tongue across the path his finger had taken.

I moaned and closed my eyes. I didn't dare move my hands or feet.

"Very tasty. Traces of salt, you're marinating." He chuckled, then disappeared. From the sound of the rocks, he went up.

I scarcely breathed. Every time my lungs expanded, it would push my back away from the rock far enough that my position on the cliff became threatened.

I spent time screaming. Nothing came of it. It required me to grip with my feet, fill my lungs, and force it from my chest as quickly as possible. I then had a few moments of scrambling to get situated again before completely losing my grip. My position, shifting on the precipice, so unnerved me that I chose to sit in silence until I could hear something or someone.

I watched the sun start to go down. The colors turned to reds and oranges, painting the tops of the trees and the mountains. It didn't take long before shadows surrounded me, and the level of sunlight receded to the top of the cliff above me.

I thought I would definitely be rescued. He left me alone after all. Why had he chosen me in the first place? He said something about being created. I remembered that. Maybe he had grown up as one of those coo-coos that thought God spoke to him and gave him one job to complete. Maybe he had a vendetta against klutzy, young, blonde females. I could not figure out what would drive someone to do something like this.

For hours I sat there, holding on, trying not to slip forward with the natural slope of the rock. The muscles in my back, arms, and legs had grown weak with the continuous straining to hold onto my precarious perch. The wet clothing, slightly warmed from my body temperature, now started to feel like the cold water in which I had recently been submerged. My body tired, and my mind numbed—I wanted only to sleep and have this nightmare disappear into calming dreams. But now, as the sun disappeared, tears of defeat met with the dampness of my shirt, confirming my place in some kind of hell.

I cried out loud. With complete dark around me, I didn't think I could hold myself together, let alone stay on the ledge. There came no response. Still alone.

My grip hardened on the rocks, as sobs loosened inside me. Desperate. *How long will it take for my ability to cling to dissipate? Should I just let go and get it over with? How hard will it be to fall to my death? How long would it take to hit the bottom and not have to remember?* I imagined the inviting release of all my muscles. The rushing of the wind along my face would feel refreshing. If I waited until full dark, I would not even see the ground coming. I could imagine myself bungee jumping until the end. It wouldn't be so bad.

Another sob broke from my throat. It would be bad. It would be the worst, and I knew I could never do it.

By the time I had no more tears to give, exhaustion hit me. The sun had gone. The chill crept into my skin and settled into my heart. Dark. Not even the moon had risen into the sky. I began to shiver. As my already tired muscles quivered, I could feel my pants moving over the grains of sand under me like ball bearings in oil.

My damp clothes feeling like ice cubes, and the cool of the night, coupled with my inability to move my limbs freely, made it unbearable. My body convulsed with shivers—my teeth chattered, sounding like a woodpecker in my head. With the blackness around me, it became hard to discern when my eye lids grew heavy enough to close. I would catch myself as my head bobbed to the side and the ledge seemed to move from under me. The rock giant had decided I'd overstayed my welcome. I jolted myself awake more than once.

Talk to yourself. Keep yourself awake, Rhi.

The only comfort that came to mind was a prayer from my childhood. "If I shall die before I wake, I pray the Lord my soul to take." I paused. The irony of the words made me laugh which caused me to slip a little. "Geeze, Rhi. Could we choose something a little more up beat here? Do you think?" I reprimanded myself as I resettled on the rock.

"Okay. So where to go from here? Uhhh." I needed to find some mental place where I could challenge my brain enough to remain awake. "The rocks. Yes. The rocks I am sitting on are old. Very, very old. Probably jutting up through the earth from some plate tectonic things that crashed into each other millions of years ago." I paused and thought about what I had just said.

"That sounded so intelligent. Maybe I should take a class on geology some time."

"No actually, I do not think I would be interested enough to take a full semester of geology."

"Well, then maybe we can just rent a DVD about the rise of mountains." I auditioned different voices as I conversed with myself.

"Yes, Rhi, I think we could do that. Like the one we watched in history class. Remember, it talked about how the earthquake caused the culture on the island place... Where was it again?"

"I can't remember."

"Oh, anyhow, it changed their culture. They believed it had been their gods' doing. It had such a profound effect that the society is still changed from it."

"Yes, profound. I know something else profound. Like my life. My life had been normal. Completely teenager. Pulled this way and that, wanting to be unnoticed, but loved by those close to me. Free to be me. Yes, free. That is what I miss most. Not stuck to a cliff. Not locked in the gaze of blue eyes. Not seeing him everywhere I am. Not aware of him in class with every breath I take. Not smelling him and having that weird serenity surround me like I'm in church, for gosh sakes. How about when he touches me?

I fell silent again. I knew that intensity.

"Not making my body swoon under his touch. I swear my loins have a mind of their own when he does that. And the dreams. When I am fully unconscious, it would be nice to not dream of him."

"My normal life. Slipped away. Can I go back to it... if I survive this cliff?"

I thought about Leone. I had done a good job of waking up my mind. Alert now, my senses piqued. My body tingled imagining his touch. My breathing intensified as I remembered when we were in the water and he had leaned in to kiss me. I knew I desired it as much as my entire body needed it, even though my mind put the brakes on. If I had known tonight would be my last night, I might have indulged myself with those perfect lips. I would not have regretted it. At least I would die knowing what a true kiss felt like.

I heard a faint call. I straightened my back and gripped with my fingers.

Had I heard that? A human voice or coyote? Coyotes were not a danger this high up. I held my breath to listen.

I heard it again. I could not distinguish enough to know what the sound was.

I mustered a small sound from my throat. If it were a wild animal, it would probably be scared away from here.

I waited through a long pause that seemed like eternity.

I heard it again, a little closer. "Rhiannon!"

"Here!" I yelled. The effort loosened me from where I sat. I pressed back to my spot.

Closer now, "Rhiannon?"

"The cliff!" I yelled a little softer, trying with all my might to be loud, yet remain still. "The cliff," I said, barely audible.

Was my mind toying with me now? I might be asleep for all I knew. I clawed at my leg. No, I definitely felt it on my icy skin. Had I been found? Maybe the weird guy is messing with me. I cringed at the thought. I did not want to see him again.

I heard something in the water far below. It sounded as if the current tried to push its way through an object, just to be redirected around it. I heard the forward movement as whatever it was came closer. My heartbeat echoed in my ears. I strained to make sense of the world below me, willing my eyes to see through the dark, or my ears to catch any clue that could work in my favor at that moment.

Silence.

"Rhi? Say something again." The voice came from below me. I knew the voice.

"Up here. Help me. Please…"

I heard rocks again. The scraping sound grew closer, approaching from the ground up the side of the cliff. Louder.

"I'm here." And he was. Leone pulled me up and hugged me tightly. It seemed we would fall. I could feel his muscled arms surrounding me. As I kneeled on the rock, I reached to hold the wall, assuring myself if his grip loosened, I would have one for myself. I grabbed his outstretched arm instead.

"Rhiannon. Can you hold on to me?"

"Yes, I think." His smell had been sent by heaven. Life saving. Alive.

He pulled me over to him. I clung to him with my legs around his waist. My head leaned on his shoulder. He started to go back down the rocks. I tried to hold still so as not to lopside his load at all and cause us both to fall.

I slowly felt around his waist for any sort of ropes. I could not find one. That guy who had brought me here had scaled the wall without one as well. I tried not to think about how they did it. Instead, I would delude myself by believing that they both must have tons of experience with rock climbing.

Such feats could only be performed by a few people, those daredevils that do extreme sports. They clamber up and down sheer cliff faces with only hands and feet. However, those daredevils achieved this without the added body to carry. I would not have believed this could have possibly been successfully performed at all. Yet there I was, clinging for the second time, to someone untethered and moving with fluid motion vertically on a rock wall.

How can this be? I do not see how this can be achievable. We should be falling.

I gripped tighter.

Red eyes, white eyes, black eyes, strange behavior, messages of fettered love, dreams, dreams, and more dreams. Now the unbelievable. I could feel him under me and surrounding me. Fatigue allowed the darkness to penetrate the outer regions of my mind. Deeply I knew I needed answers to the many vagaries that I had witnessed and could no longer pass off as my own issues or my mind playing games with me.

For now, I was too tired and too concerned about getting down the mountain to mention my uneasiness. I felt we would slip at any moment. I only allowed myself to take shallow breaths even though my body yearned to gasp and cry. *Have to hold it together for just a little while longer.*

His smell surrounded me. That clean, woody lavender helped to soothe the ache in me. It created an unfathomable calming in my soul. My body succumbed to my weakness and went limp.

When we reached the ground he sat down—his hands clung to me, wrapping around my back, rocking back and forth, comforting me as he would a precious child.

I could feel the skin of his neck sliding against mine as my tears drenched us. My muscles quivered, they released the tension of holding on. My back began to throb from the position I had been in for the entire afternoon and evening.

My eyes drooped as he rocked me. My sobbing reduced to a panting.

"How…" escaped my lips. The rest of my question slipped back into my mind, as the silent haze of sleep blanketed my thoughts.

Somehow we made it across the water. My eyes opened again when I heard him yelling to the search party. Soon they were surrounding us. I could only hear voices in the dark. I knew Lauriel's, Dante's, and Nohi's, but there were others that I didn't recognize. I heard Leone explaining as he walked with me.

And I remembered being carried. I felt safe.

When I woke, I was in a beautiful bathroom with a huge tub, my sore body being lowered into the warm, bubbly water. I focused on Lauriel's red hair pulled back into my baseball cap she wore. She began washing my hands and helped file down the edges of my nails where they had broken on the rocks on the edge of the cliff.

"Thank you," my voice sounded groggy even to me.

"Just let me help you," she beseeched as she smiled at me.

She washed my legs and studied the gashes I had there. I glanced down at my shins. I did not remember getting cut. She moved to my arms, softly cleaning the deep purple bruises forming on my arms where the man had clenched them. She washed my hair with the shower nozzle and put some conditioner in it. After rinsing my hair, she held up a towel.

"Are you awake enough to stand?"

"Yes, thank you." She averted her eyes as I clambered to my feet. My muscles still ached from holding one position so long on the cliff's edge. In the mirror, I noticed the puffy skin around my eyes from crying. My eyes felt as if they had been ground by sand paper.

I wrapped myself in the towel, as she passed me a tee shirt and some boxers.

"They are Leone's," she apologized. "I will give you my clothes tomorrow—yours are ruined." She turned from me as I slipped the tee shirt over my head and then proceeded to dry my legs before slipping on the boxers. My body stung with each movement.

She handed me a soft, fluffy robe. I put it on and used the towel to wrap up my hair. She motioned for me to sit on the vanity chair.

I looked around. This must be her mom's bathroom. It matched the kitchen, mimicking her Italian taste. A knock at the door broke the silence.

"Come in," Lauriel said.

Leone opened the door. He held a mug in front of him.

"You look very tired," he addressed my reflection in the mirror.

"I ache," I responded. He nodded that he understood.

Lauriel bandaged my fingers and the palms of my hands, which looked like raw hamburger from being gouged by the rocks.

"What about my parents?" The thought popped into my head.

Lauriel patted my shoulder and faced my reflection. "They are fine. Dante has scouted the area around your house. There have not been any fresh scents around your house."

"Scents? I don't understand any of this." I informed Leone's reflection in the mirror. I quickly glanced at myself and noticed my raised eyebrows and wide eyes. I could not help but think that I looked like a lost, scared child.

"Do you feel like you can stay up for a little while longer?" Leone asked.

"Yes." *As long as I can understand what's going on.* I gawked at myself. I felt like pieces of me had blown away and were scattered everywhere, like pieces of a crystal dropped from a high place. I needed to put them back together—I needed my reflection back.

"Then I think perhaps tonight I need to tell you a story." He handed me the mug of hot chocolate. I sipped the rich liquid which soothed my insides. Leone picked up the hairbrush, and after taking the towel from my head, began delicately brushing out the ends of my hair.

I stared unabashedly at his reflection in the mirror, entranced.

As Leone softly, lovingly, stroked my hair with the brush, his voice broke the spell. "Rome used to be the highest society in the Mediterranean. Eventually, the power shifted to peoples of Germanic decent. This transition marked the beginning of the Middle Ages."

What on earth did the Middle Ages have to do with me here today? My expression reflected confusion, but I remained silent to allow him the benefit of the doubt.

"It became the seat for the Roman Catholic Church. In April of 799, the newly appointed Pope Leo III led the traditional procession from the Latern to the church. Two of the previous Pope's noble followers attacked the procession and dealt the new pope a life-threatening wound. The Pope fled, but soon returned with an army from the King of Franks and French Bishops. The King declared a judicial trial to decide if Leo would remain Pope or if the deposers' had reason to overthrow the church's leader."

"Leone, I need to understand things that happened today," I stated firmly and did not sway from looking at him.

He nodded at me, blinking his eyes. He focused back to my hair and started to tell his story again. I decided he must have some point to make. "This trial, however, ended up being only a part of a well-thought-out chain of events that, ultimately, surprised the world. The Pope was declared legitimate, and the culprits subsequently exiled. But the uproar was not enough. Pope Leo III crowned the King of the Franks as the Holy Roman Emperor." He paused and looked at my reflection again. "The first Holy Roman Emperor."

I had always thought that the Holy Roman Emperor always existed as a title. I guess I never gave it much thought.

"This single act divided the empire in two," he continued. "Constantinople, in modern day Turkey, and the great Charlemagne and his conquered lands from the ocean of modern day France to the Western Territories above Constantinople. His influence remained vast and great."

I knew it meant the empire had been huge before the split, wrapping around most of the Mediterranean Sea.

I noticed that Leone's eyes had glazed over. He had stopped brushing my hair. He reflected and continued his story. "Charlemagne stood six-foot-three, not so uncommon today. In his time, however, he towered over the shorter-statured people. He commanded attention due to his heavy build, sturdiness, and considerable stature. He had a round head, large and lively eyes, and a slightly larger nose than usual. His neck was thick and short. He had white hair in his older age, but remained attractive. His disposition was always bright and cheerful. All this made him appear a gentle giant."

My expression grew quizzical. He spoke of the king as though he were there with him and knew him intimately. I almost laughed out loud at the idea.

I fiddled with the robe and took another sip from the cup.

The inconsequential action brought Leone back to the real world, and he began to work his way up my head to my scalp with the brush. I closed my eyes, enjoying the sensations.

He continued. "You would probably know his name as Charles the Great." My eyes popped opened in recognition. He glanced at me in the mirror. He nodded, seeming to acknowledge that I knew the name. "Charlemagne had twenty children over the course of his life with the ten known wives or concubines that he kept." My eyes widened in the mirror at that knowledge. Twenty children, why on earth would someone want that many?

"The first son borne to him he named Peppin. He had been borne a hunchback. Despite his deformity, King Charles loved him. He doted on him. The knights in court favored him. He grew up positioned to take over the throne for his father."

I tilted my head to one side so he could brush and again closed my eyes. His fingers tickled my ear as they scooped the hair from around it.

"It would inevitably not last. King Charles grew tired of his woman and found a wife. She birthed a son. As he aged, the queen demanded that her son be the future king. Even though Charles knew Peppin to be intelligent, he feared what the people would think about following a physically deformed leader. In the end, Charles agreed."

Leone inhaled a deep breath and sighed before he began again. "Charles formally disinherited Peppin, a young man by their standards, and had the Pope baptize his son Carloman. At his baptism, he inherited the name Peppin, a name passed down from the kings before him."

I shifted again, moving my head to the other side to allow Leone's delicate hands to work. His fingers left tingling ripples along my skin where they touched.

"Peppin, the first, had been allowed to remain at court, and Charles continued to give the boy preference over his younger brothers. Peppin also remained a popular friend of discontented nobles. After a few years, several of them played upon Peppin's dislike for his brothers and convinced the deformed prince to play the figurehead in their rebellion. The conspirators planned to kill Charles, his wife Hildegarde, and his two sons by her. Peppin the Hunchback would then be set upon the throne as a more sympathetic and more easily manipulated king."

Leone held the brush tightly in his hand. When I opened my eyes, I met his in the mirror. His face appeared to be godlike and carved out of stone.

"The day of the assassination, Peppin pretended to be ill in order to meet with the plotters. The scheme nearly succeeded, but a knight stumbled upon the plan and swiftly stopped the action. All that had plotted against Charles were charged with high treason and sentenced to execution. Charles could not bear to have his first born son's fate match that of his nobles. He had Peppin placed in a monastery instead."

Leone fell silent for a time. He looked down at my shining hair and said, "I'm finished. Would you like to go sit in the living room, or would you rather go up to my couch?"

"I would be ok on your couch." I knew I should make another choice considering how drawn to him I had become, and considering he had saved me—again. I already struggled to keep the victim mentality from controlling me.

Through my foggy mind, I listened to Leone's story. I wondered why he had chosen that one, but did not mind too much. I wanted answers, but was relieved that I had finally stopped quaking in my skin.

We meandered through the front hall, and his mom rushed over to me. She gave me the biggest hug and kissed my forehead. She stepped back, still holding my arms and examining me.

I winced when she grabbed me where deep bruises existed from my earlier escapade. She released me.

I rubbed the sore spots.

"Oh, hon, are you okay? I did not mean to hurt you." She looked from me to Leone.

Lauriel approached from behind Nohi. "She has some deep purple on her arms, probably from being banged around so much," she explained to Nohi.

"I think they are from where he grabbed me," I choked as the words came out. The memory raced to the surface, unwanted. I closed my eyes and turned my head away, fighting the tears that threatened. Leone wrapped his burly arm delicately around my shoulder and pulled me to him.

"I think Rhi just needs to relax for a while." I could hear his chest vibrate with his words. It helped me to overcome the desire to cry.

"Can I get her some pain reliever or something?" Nohi's voice trailed behind her. It seemed she had already moved toward her bathroom.

"Yes," his voice soothed me, "that would be very helpful, I think."

I heard her feet on the stone floor of the entry way again and felt Leone's body move toward her as he accepted the pain reliever.

He guided me. I opened my eyes and watched the floor.

As we entered the hall to Leone's rooms, I noticed the light on. This time, the hall appeared alive with rich, dark wood and books along the right. A table at the far end featured a carved wooden box spotlighted by a lamp. A dark blue ribbon accentuated its delicate features. I thought for a moment. Had I had seen the beautiful box before? I could not remember.

On the top floor, Leone led me to the extremely deep couch.

"Here, take this," he commanded as he handed me a white pill and glass of water. "It will help your pain and help you to fall asleep."

I eased down on the edge of the couch and swallowed the pill. I placed the half empty glass on the carpet at my feet.

He pulled blankets from the armoire and laid one out, folded it in half length wise. It reminded me of a small sleeping bag. I climbed into it. The couch wrapped around me, sinking me into its softness. Leone climbed in beside me and laid my head in his lap.

"Do you feel like resting now?" he asked. Only a faint light glowed from a lamp he'd turned on before shutting off the main light. My body relaxed into the most comfortable position, and I didn't want to move. It seemed my limbs had already slipped off to sleep. My mind, however, still bounced from the thoughts of jagged rocks, to aches, to scrapes, and then to the sun setting on my desperation for soothing. All camouflaged by red hair and angry eyes.

"Can you just continue talking to me?" I pleaded. "Your voice is helping me keep my thoughts on something else." He ran his fingers through my hair lightly.

"Please let me know if you want me to stop," he offered and then continued the story. "Things would be very different if Peppin had been executed. That particular monastery had secrets and those secrets made the occupants powerful. They used the church to hide their evil. The King himself did not know the extent of their abilities. The alliance proved to be in the King's favor, but the hidden agenda had been theirs. By tying their power to the King's rule, they could live in the shelter of his protection, knowing he would always turn a blind eye."

I moved my head a little on his leg. He scooped a handful of my hair and ran his fingers through it. "The King believed he had found favor with God. In fact, in his mind the favor he aspired to came through that very monastery. He called only on their superior grace when he went to war. He would actually take them with him—they were brazen enough to be among the first in battle. They insisted on it. Those wars were always won, though the King never understood quite why."

Leone quieted for a moment.

He whispered, "Are you asleep yet?"

I shook my head. "No. Not yet."

"Constantinople had a queen. She had been in rule when the Pope made that ill-fated decision to crown our King as the first Holy Roman Emperor, stating that he had divine appointment to do so. By the Pope's creating this position, the power went from God, to the Pope, and then directly to the Emperor. But the Pope had several reasons for these actions. By designing a divine appointment, he took the power away from the throne of Constantinople. He, in essence, dethroned the queen and commandeered rule from all her progeny. He created a division in the country."

Leone played with my hair, twisting strands around in his fingers.

"King Charles understood the game well. He requested her hand in marriage repeatedly. He would have effectively gained the lands that she occupied. His kingdom would have expanded to Egypt."

How could one man control an area so large? My mind tried to imagine the way it would have worked, but Leone continued.

"Her constituents became angered with her simply because she took too long to respond. They had their reasons, but they replaced her on the throne. Of course, that ended King Charles affections."

Leone paused a second then asked me, "Have you ever heard the saying, 'Hell hath no fury as a woman scorned'?"

"Yes."

"Well, King Charles could never have guessed what chain of events he allowed to be set in motion by her dethroning. She had been kept abreast of the dealings with Peppin and which monastery he had been sent to. He had been easy for her to access. She preyed upon his soft soul and kind heart. He had never been approached by a woman before, and she held more control over him than any other being. He became her puppet and a means to destroy the King, or so she thought."

I tried to imagine what it would be like to be sent away from the family with whom you grew up, to live with monks. That life meant changing daily life, praying every minute, eating only what is offered, and austerity versus the pampered life of the court. All in a split second—Peppin would have learned a new way of life.

"There were things, unnatural... moving against her plans. Peppin had begun the process of becoming a full member of the monastery. He had, in effect, sworn to die for the forever life and preservation of the monastery. I do not believe he could have known what the monks meant by that.

"Over the course of the courtship with the queen, she talked him into the overthrow of the Holy Roman Emperor. As the first borne son, he truly had been next in line for the throne. She moved herself into position to help him rule his rightful people."

I raised an eyebrow at that. It seemed like an ages old soap opera. Who was sleeping with whom, and who liked whom, and who back-stabbed whom... Crazy to think about things like that happening in real life, so long ago.

"One day when she visited, she found Peppin had taken ill. He thrashed about on his floor in pain, color gone from his face. She thought he had been poisoned. He promised her that had not been the case. For days she came back to see him, and his condition never improved.

"Then on the last day when she arrived, his sickness fled. The only reminder of his illness was his extreme paleness, and red lips and eyes. He had just recovered from the worst of diseases. But what she did not know was he was no longer human."

He paused, and I turned my head to the ceiling. *No longer human? Did I misunderstand him? Did he mean that he had made decisions that were so bad he could no longer be viewed as civilized?*

"Not human?" I inquired.

"No," he continued without explanation. "He planned at that moment to make her his forever partner. She knew something had happened to him, too late. He had one of the other monastery inhabitants there to assist with her transformation. He himself would have killed her in his new formed hunger for blood."

Hunger for blood? What had the queen done to him? "Leone, why did he want her blood? Had she done something, shared something that made him think she could no longer be trusted?"

"Not 'thirsty to see her dead', but 'thirsty' as in he wanted to drink her blood."

"Drink it? What?" My mind reeled. "Cannibals?" I spat. The thought made me want to throw up.

"Not exactly. Let me tell you more and see if you can follow." His voice softened.

I remembered the red-haired sick-o telling me my tears had been like a marinade for him. I shivered thinking he wanted to eat me. I shook my head, trying to get the vision from my head.

"Are you okay, or have I spoken too much?" Leone rubbed my back.

"Just had a bad visual. I need you to keep talking—your voice helps."

"Are you sure, Rhi? I don't have to go on," he assured me.

"I promise I will let you know when I need to stop."

"All right then.

"At the moment the knight and his battalion barged through the front of the monastery, they found the queen screaming as she fought the monk from her body. He had bitten her repeatedly down her neck. She wailed in apparent agony. Peppin's eyes were wild and hate-filled. He lurched for the nobles, ready to tear them apart. The fighting started. The leader of the nobles had an idea about what might have been happening, and reached the queen whom Peppin had tried to defend. In one motion, he killed the queen to release her from her pain.

"Peppin flew into a rage over the love of his life. He ripped through the nobles with inhuman strength. They were literally torn to pieces. He grabbed the knight by the throat and raised him from the ground."

I gasped. Leone patted my shoulder. I tried to understand what strength it took to rip a person to pieces. I had remembered being told, as I floated in the water being held by my hair, that my attacker could rip my head from my shoulders with little effort. At that time, I believed the statement showed the level of anger I had elicited from him, not a matter-of-fact statement. I wondered now how someone could physically do something like that.

"Ripped apart, as in flesh with a knife or something?" My voice trembled at the memory.

"Unfortunately, no. He used his hands. You must understand, he was no longer human." He tried to calm me. "I think I should stop."

"No, please. I will definitely not sleep now. Please, finish to the end of the story, so I can have a resolution in my mind over it."

Leone paused for a moment before he continued. "Peppin told him, 'I will not be so kind as to release you from life. I condemn you to eternal Hell for what you have done.' He bit the noble on the arm and dropped him to the floor."

Bit on the arm. Big deal. I hardly thought being bitten matched the severity of the troops being ripped to pieces. "What happened to the knight? Did he only have a bite mark? What happened to the King? What happened to the monastery?"

Leone chuckled. I really did not understand why my questions were so funny.

"The King had been saved—in fact, he fathered more children, including three future kings." He paused as if contemplating how to proceed. "The monastery, full of very clever beings, had been cleaned up. All the bodies were taken to a field and spread out to make it look as if a massacre had occurred. The monastery continues on today."

I gasped, "Still today?" *How could it still be in existence? Surely it had evolved a different set of rules and fallen under control of different people. It happened so long ago, the building itself must be in ruin.*

His fingers traced circles in my back. When he spoke, his voice sounded hollow. "Yes, still today. My reason for telling you this is the danger. Danger that has to do with that monastery."

That monastery is threatening me? Or a threat to me? Huh? How could a monastery, from eons ago, be remotely interested, in tiny, little Idaho? Let alone in an average nobody like me?

"Sorry," I finally said. "I just do not understand how I could be in trouble with a monastery. Lots of people don't go to church and do much more horrible things than I do. How could I be in trouble?" I felt the defensiveness I had had with him when he first brought me into this room. I sat up.

"I have vowed to protect you. You must allow me to do that," his eyes and voice beseeched me.

A chill settled in my soul. Thoughts accosted my brain. *People being ripped apart and eaten? I am in danger from an old stone building somewhere. How is this possible?*

I remembered looking into the deadly, angry, red eyes of my captor earlier and knew it to be true. *But how? Dreams. Red eyes in my dreams.*

I knew I would lose myself.

"I don't understand." I began to weep again. I had always been independent, and now found that I had to have help to survive. "How can I be in danger from things that are set in the past? I mean, even saying the year feels foreign to me… 800. What… how… I do not…"

I could not get the words to come out in a comprehendible form.

"This is all so much for you to take in. If I show you something, will you not panic?"

"I won't," I promised and realized that it had been a lie the moment I said it. I felt panic rush through my veins at that very moment. The men with the big, white, straight jackets were probably already on high alert, just awaiting a phone call.

He got up and turned off the light.

He whispered from across the room. "Ok, just look over toward me."

I turned to face the direction from where he had spoken. Darkness.

As I searched for anything to focus on, a faint glow developed where the voice had been. Something moved toward me. It seemed to have stolen the light from the moon's glow, but with the quick movement and the lack of moon outside, it could not have been. It came toward me steadily and did not disappear into a shadow. I crawled closer to the edge of the couch.

My eyes began to discern the shape of hands. Both hands. They had a glow to them. They methodically unbuttoned his shirt. The warm glow was stronger on the bare skin beneath his shirt. His neck, too, faint... and his face. I could see. But his torso brightest of all. He emitted enough radiance that I could make out the details of his skin.

"Leone?" This could not be happening. This could not be real. "Leone, what is going on?" I sat back on the couch a little.

"Rhi. This is me."

I moaned and wanted to run. Not another freak. Please. "No one does this... thing... this glow-y... thing," my voice raised in pitch. I began to cry and rock back and forth. Had I come to this moment, after the horrifying encounter on the cliff, just to be killed here in a secluded room?

"Rhi, please." Agony rimmed his tinny voice. "Have I once hurt you? Have I even made any motion toward you in any way that made you think I could possibly hurt you?"

I wrestled with his question.

"Once, when I first saw you on the beach below my house."

I heard him exhale. "Yes, you are correct. I had been so long without you, my need for you so great. I couldn't contain myself for that split moment. My desire almost overwhelmed me."

I found myself surprised by his admission.

He continued, "Rhi, since that moment, which I wish to forever take back, what have I done?"

I couldn't avoid it. Through my sniffles, I mumbled my defeat, "Saved me... repeatedly."

He chuckled, "I will never hurt you. This..." I saw one of his glowing hands motion toward his body, "looks unacceptable, I understand. You have no idea how many times I've dreamed of being normal again—of being released of this body."

I heard the edges of despair in the trill of his words. His sincerity settled my nerves enough to look at him.

Amazing and new. It reminded me of lightning bugs. I needed to touch it. What would it feel like to run my fingers over that skin?

"But why? Why is it that your skin does this?" I thought about us being in the nuclear age, and how big companies dumped their life-altering garbage in rivers and streams. "Is it from fall out?" I gasped.

He laughed. "I wish it were that simple. You're funny, Rhiannon."

I didn't think I was being funny. I simply tried to understand it. He actually stood in front of me, glowing. What normal world did that fit into?

I clung to the edge of the couch. I wanted to touch him. I paused for a minute, staring. I reached out.

I drew my hand back, not knowing if he would object to my touching him. He stepped closer.

The second my fingers touched him, he brightened. The intensity made me squint. He breathed out with his eyes closed, as if welcoming the sensation. Electricity coursed up my arm as well, almost magical. My fingers caressed his skin. The intensity of light grew, rippling out from where I touched.

I withdrew my hand. He dropped the sides of his shirt.

"Rhi, I may be a monster, but I will never hurt you. I cannot live away from you. You see what you do to me. I will let you go on with your life, but I have to be close. You will not even know that I am there. I swore it—to protect you. And that is why I am here. Nothing more."

Nothing more... It sounded like a death sentence for me. I had so many questions. A part of me feared the unknown and the answers that might come. This was unheard of, yet right in front of me. He had saved me today at the point when I visualized my own death. I strangely found more comfort in my confusion.

I grabbed his hand to pull him to me. He stood there, his bare skin close to my face. I rested my cheek to his stomach. Never before had I been close like this to anyone, but the intimacy between us felt normal. It gave me more peace than I had ever known. Like my first dream, I remembered his adoring eyes. So happy, safe, and loved.

I closed my eyes and turned my head. I kissed his stomach. His luminosity grew again, piercing through the darkened veil of my eye lids.

He pulled me up to stand in front of him. Instead of kissing me, he just hugged me. I knew in that moment that my dreams had been right. My body had been telling me all along. I wanted to kiss him.

He held me close, breathing heavy into my ear.

"Rhi, I cannot," were his only words to me. "I want you to watch the DVD. It will explain more. I'm sure you have tons of questions. I wouldn't blame you if you wanted never to see me again. I will understand and respect your decision. Please do not tell anyone about me. I think I need to leave you tonight."

What? Leave me? No way! Not with freak boy on the loose. Not with the humming in my body. No way. I reached for him as he turned to go.

"No, Leone, please don't go. Please. Just stay." My voice trembled. He had it wrong. The feeling of peace with him washed away the uncontrollable fear. How had I misunderstood that for so long? I didn't want to lose it now.

I clutched his hand, and we crawled back onto the couch. I pulled the covers over me. He buttoned his shirt again and lay behind me, cradling me in his arms. I finally felt at home. The settling inside me mimicked the way my dream felt. I could rest peacefully forever in his arms, a safety shield around me, blocking me from even my own deep, dark thoughts.

I asked him to tell me more about the story. He said the rest would wait for another time and told me I needed to sleep.

224

"What about you?"

"I don't need much. I will be fine."

"You have a lot to share."

"Indeed. You have no idea," he agreed.

I relaxed, listening to sounds of his room, of him. He traced the edge of my face until I fell asleep.

11

Remembering

I knew something followed behind me. I felt like prey. The hair on my neck responded. My feet pounded the uneven ground.

I knew it broke custom for women to run. It denounced my elegance and made me improper—therefore, if I had been caught, I would be looked down upon by society. I loved to run. I would run whenever I broke free from the town.

I knew how to gain speed and race. I grabbed the bottom of my full skirt and petticoat and dashed as though my existence depended on it. And it did.

I could see the moat around the castle wall. So close, I noticed the ripples on the water lapping against the embankment beneath the towering stone.

The bridge. I just needed to cross it for safety. I headed dead center toward it.

I left that morning to search for him. Gone for days now, word had come about the massacre of his men. Terror ripped my heart in two, even though nothing of him had been found. We were different than most couples. We were best friends. Our world, I discovered, was becoming complete. I could not wait to tell him. Then came the deadly news.

I'd left early that morning, finding paths and trails. I looked in our favorite meeting places and at the pond where we would swim, away from the eyes of people. I searched in desperation until the sun burned high in the sky. It beat down on me as I reclined on a rock to rest. Gasping for air and tracing the different places in my mind that I might still look for him, I held my head in my hands. I had to find him. My life would be a waste if he never came home. I had to know. Where had he gone?

I heard something behind me.

I jumped up and spun around.

A black figure with red hair and a huge lump on his back lunged toward me.

Peppin. I knew those facial features and his familiar hunched back. Although, I never really noticed his hunch after the first few times we had talked. I found him to be a kind person.

This was not the same Peppin at all. His eyes burned like the sun into my face. He growled. Not a human growl, it came out low and guttural like a warning before the strike of a wild animal.

Human? Animal? Peppin? But how? Death stared at me.

His hand reached out before I had a chance to step backward. It closed around my neck, lifting me from the ground. The grip, vice-like, stopped my breathing. I grabbed his arm to try and pull myself up and release the pressure on my throat. My feet kicked, trying to find anything to stand on. He looked like the worst of all nightmares possibly born to the human mind. The most horrifying of faces, I knew my imagination could not have come up with it.

I tried to plead with him, but no sound could squeeze out. I thought my eyes would burst from their sockets from the pressure in my head.

He planned to kill me. I was looking into the eyes of the ultimate predator, menacing and inhuman. I'd been trapped like an unsuspecting varmint. I must be in Hell, nothing like this existed on earth. How had this creature taken a form that resembled the king's son?

Fear lanced through my core. *My baby. Our baby. How stupid of me!* Quite possibly my last connection to him, and I had thrown both of our lives away to search for him.

The monster's face twisted as he restrained himself from this murderous act.

After a pause, a sinister smile played across his lips. His laughter thick and deep.

"What a great thing we have here!" He turned me from side to side, ogling my body. "I could never have imagined. Rhinata, can it be true? Two hearts beat in this body of yours?"

He knew my name. It had to be Peppin in some hell-bound form. My mouth opened to scream. Forever silent in his vice-like hold my words remained unacknowledged.

No. No. No. How could he know that? Not my baby.

Smiling. He seemed amused at his knowledge. *Would he let me live? Please, let me go.* Leone. He had been friends with Leone.

My feet attempted a new pattern of kicking the air—my hands clawed at his arm.

"Aw, yes. I see it is true. How delicate a situation for me. Let's see. How to lure him in?" He dropped me back to the ground. My footing uneven, I slipped to the ground in a pile of trembling flesh. I rolled to my side, holding my throat, gulping in air. I kept my eyes focused on him. My mouth worked open and closed—I moved my tongue out and down. My windpipe felt crushed. As uncomfortable as it felt, I breathed and that meant I still lived.

"Leone, I'm searching for Leone." My voice sounded odd.

"Of course, you are." He flipped the back of his hand toward me dismissing the obvious.

I scrambled backward, crablike along the ground to escape him. Keeping up with me seemed little issue for him. I noticed his feet did not even touch the ground. *Ungodly! I do not want to be here with him—this creature that I had taken pity on.*

He had his finger on his chin, tapping it, looking deep in thought. "Yes, very good. Tit for tat, I think." His eyes turned back to me. "It is really nothing against you. I remember our kiss well. I want you to know, Rhinata, you did indeed break my heart at first, eyes only for Leone. I think I had fallen head over heels in love with you."

He pulled his hands to his chest and looked up to the heavens, an expression of mock peace forming.

"Child's love," he spat, throwing his hands down, beside himself.

He had loved me? Oh not so good, Rhinata. Something in me understood why I had lingering worries over being slighted by him in our friendship. I finally understood why he'd isolated himself.

Peppin broke through my thoughts and glared into me. "Except for the spawn of him growing in you, I might have made your death quick and painless. But now, see...I must make him watch."

What? He planned to kill me, no matter what. But Leone still lived. Where? "What have you done with him?" I yelled. Tears traced lines down my cheeks.

"Oh, poor innocent Rhinata. Sheltered life that you have led. He has been a very bad boy."

"No!" I screamed. He lived. I had to find him. If only I could get to him. He did not know about the baby.

"And two for the price of one. How sweet!" he chided.

"Don't tell him. Just kill me if that is your plan. Spare him of that detail." If he planned to kill me, it would be best to have the baby remain secret.

"Oh, what is this? He does not know, does he?" His laughter boomed. "Oh, this is too great! You selfish little girl.

You never told him about his child. Do not worry—the knowledge will make it even more exciting." Peppin rubbed his hands together, enlivened at the gift he had just received. "He will be ignited into the chase like nothing matters except to save you... and his precious unborn child."

Save me? No. I did not want to be the bait that would trap him. I wanted to find him. He had probably been hurt by this demon creature. Was his life draining from him? Had he been dealt a mortal wound? Or was he held captive somewhere? Is that why he could not return?

"Where is he?" I demanded.

"I am sorry for your loss. It is simply your great love's fault. He is to blame really. He is a murderer and the price must be repaid." He tilted his head toward me and raised an eyebrow. He brought his hands together in front of his heart in a prayerful gesture and levitated close to me.

"Now is your time to flee. I wager you this, beautiful woman..." His hand swept through my hair, "if you can reach the castle by the time I get you, I will let you live—today." His wide smile revealed unusually white teeth.

I froze to the spot. Did I miss something? Did he just tell me to go?

"Run!" he commanded.

I turned and scrambled through the leaves under me, trying to distance myself from him and gain my footing. I dashed into the closest trees to block me from his view.

"Run, run, run...!" his voice followed me.

Trees blurred past me. I felt the pounding of my pulse in my neck. My dress caught on bushes and branches. I could hear tearing, but I never faltered. If I arrived naked and crossed that bridge, it would be worth it to know I would see my Leone again.

I sprinted through the afternoon. When my limbs grew tired, I imagined Peppin's breath on my neck. It elicited a new burst of energy each time, pushing me closer to my freedom.

Not until I saw the castle did I feel the sensation of being followed.

My feet throbbed from the rocks and uneven ground. Tears that streaked through the dirt on my face and dried long ago, held my skin tight. My hair washed wildly over my face, a mess with leaves and sticks.

I knew I had a chance—the bridge, so close I could make out the details of the stone and mortar.

A swishing sound surrounded me. Black enveloped me. Pressure on my back, like something had jumped on me. Then hands wrapped themselves around my chin and the back of my head. Robes in my face, I could see the woven pattern. I tried to scream, but my lips had been forced shut with the hand gripping my jaw. As I became lifted from the ground by my head, my feet searched for anything solid, still running. The hand under my jaw let loose, and in a split second the skin under my left ear burned with the sensation of a dozen ice picks gouging through my flesh. Searing pain shot through my neck and coursed through my head. *Was I on fire?* As my feet met with the ground again, I caught sight of blood spurting from my neck onto my clothes and the road, propelled with every beat of my heart.

I knew at that moment, my life would be short. It did not hurt as badly as I might have imagined. My forward motion, unhindered through all the action, left me on a course with the stone handrail of the bridge. I had only a moment to reach up before crashing into it.

"No! Rhinata!" His voice floated to me in a dreamlike fog. All was finally good. I only wished to see him one last time before darkness found me.

My forward motion did not stop when I hit. I slid into the stone, hitting it low—my upper body flipped over the edge. I managed with one hand to grasp the stone as my body became airborne. My weight descended upon my fingers with stunning force. I reached with the other hand and clawed for a grip.

232

My vision had already started to slip from me. I just wanted to stare into his eyes one last time. *Hold on, Rhinata.* There he was. Like a gift. Looking down into my eyes. Peace. His hand reached down and grabbed the apron of my dress. My hands slipped from their perch. I fell.

The apron held.

Our eyes locked onto each other. My neck no longer stung, but I could feel the trickling of blood dripping down my skin. I noticed the apron, close to my face now, drenched in the red, sticky mess. I knew I only had moments. What a blessing to have the pain gone. It must have been the run. My body must have given up on feeling anything after overexerting itself.

My apron started to rip. The sound echoing in my head—bouncing around in the haze that had once held so much information. My eye lids tried to close on me. I focused on keeping them open, to take in Leone, until their weight became unbearable.

"Rhinata! A baby?"

Were those tears thick within his voice? I squinted to try and focus. I could not see any falling down upon me.

He raised me toward him slowly, perhaps to keep the apron from ripping more. He used only one hand, not even struggling with my weight.

He finally reached out with his other arm and pulled me to him.

"Rhinata." His face full of pain as he looked at my neck.

Then he seemed to growl through clenched teeth. "I am not strong enough," he whispered.

"I love you, Leone." *Did I actually say the words or did I just think them?*

A deep-throated groan came from him. His face twisted as he tried to control himself.

"My baby…our baby! I will avenge you. I will save you." I saw a shimmer in his eyes. Hope? Or determination?

I lay in his lap, gazing up into his face. In one fluid motion, I watched him slice his arm and dark red, thick blood oozed from the wound. He held his arm to my lips.

"Please, Rhi, just swallow. That is all you need to do. Just swallow. I will find you again."

Blood oozed in my mouth. It felt thick and congealed on my tongue and burned there. Not a metallic taste as I expected. Instead it clotted there, like a bitter poison. I pushed air out of my lungs, trying to repel it. I felt drops hit my cheek as it sprayed. Most of it still pooled in my mouth. I was too weak.

I could hear him pleading with me to swallow.

I finally did—ripping at my throat all the way down.

Leone slumped—his shoulders sagged. He let his head drop down toward me.

I heard the deep menacing voice of Peppin screaming words of disbelief and disapproval from somewhere behind Leone. I didn't want him to be the last thing I saw. I gazed only into Leone's eyes.

Leone bowed over me, convulsing, grieving without tears.

"Memor meus diligo eternus! Memor meus diligo eternus!" He repeated the sweet words to my ears as we rocked. The words made perfect sense to me. "Remember my love everlasting." He kept repeating those Latin words. I let the rummy sensation wash over me. I closed my eyes, staying entranced.

My insides stormed like lightning, bright and hot. I had never felt my soul before. What thoughts could describe that strange and creeping feeling that grew in the pit of my being? It pulled my memories in. It ripped at my voice, my heart, my laughter, my sorrow, and all my pain. Every ounce of being that made up the subtle and the obvious aspects of me bundled tightly in my core. A cocoon ready to burst.

Leone continued to chant.

I grew faintly aware of the heart beating in my womb. The sound grew louder, thundering with each thump, echoing into

234

the chasm. A new tear escaped my eye. The heartbeat slowed. I focused on it, yearning desperately to remember it. I wanted that memory to be wrapped up along with the others in my soul. I wanted always to have the knowledge of a life inside me. Small flutterings tickled in my abdomen. Those moments I wanted to believe were the baby's movements, but I could not be sure. I wanted to lock those away with me. I wanted so badly to know what our baby looked like and smelled like. Did it resemble my Leone? Had it been a boy or a girl? Those were answers that I would never have.

I released. I floated away. No pain, only the anguished sounds of the pleading and sobbing Leone.

Screaming ripped from my lips as I bolted upright on the couch. Tears gushed down my cheeks. Sobs gripped me so hard my body convulsed.

Leone pulled me tight to him.

"I'm here," he reassured me in the dark.

Where was I? I felt around me. Soft cushions? I reached for my neck. Skin still intact. I felt the soft blankets at my waist. Pieces of reality crept back in like a trickster who had stolen my sanity and had decided to return it in fragments.

Leone held me close and brushed my hair from my face.

Sobs uncontrollably retched themselves from somewhere deep. I splayed my hands on my belly. There had been a life in here. I could still imagine the tiny fluttering. *A baby. Our baby.* My body began to tremble. I couldn't stop crying.

Leone leapt off the couch and turned on the light. He returned to my side.

"Rhi, are you hurt?" He sat down next to me. He looked at my hands on my stomach then made eye contact with me. I couldn't form any words. How could I explain? I cried for the loss of a child I never knew, so long gone. My life. My baby. What had it looked like? How would it feel to nuzzle my nose into its baby soft neck and kiss it? I would never know. All of it gone, lost in time. The memory of a child assigned itself to a special place in my heart, and indeed, to everything I ever would do from that moment on. How could I explain what I felt when I couldn't even tell myself?

Leone wrapped me in his arms, facing me. My sobbing slowed to the rhythm of his rocking. He held my cheeks in each hand, then pushed me away to look into my throbbing eyes.

He didn't need to say anything. I buried myself back into his arms. After some time, I thought I could speak without my voice failing. I leaned back and peered at him.

"It had been me. I remembered. It was so real. How can that be? A baby! Our baby?" He closed his eyes tight. He inhaled quickly and held it. The edges of his mouth dipped down as he slowly exhaled. When he opened his eyes, his brows furrowed. The expression reminded me of my mother's, in the hospital waiting room when the chaplain told us we needed to pray for Dad.

Leone's expression brought new tears from me. I knew he understood.

He pulled me to him and held me tighter, rocking me again.

He began singing low lyrics I didn't understand. I wiped the back of my hand across my nose. He produced a hanky and wiped my tears, then handed it to me.

When I finally stopped bawling, he whispered in my hair, "I am so sorry. I am so sorry."

We cuddled there, and I had moments of crying and then no feeling at all. The conflicting emotions ebbed and flowed like waves in a tide of memories. Each time they crashed into the shore, new beliefs formed. I had lived before. I had memories, not dreams. They just found their way home through my slumber.

"I remember," I said flatly. "Smells... thoughts in my head, I remembered what I ate and where my belongings were.

It didn't seem like a dream. I *knew* my mind, and I *knew* the places I went. Leone, I knew our baby." Tears started again, not as hard. "I felt our baby! How can it be that I know that feeling inside me, so intimately, when I have never experienced it in my life?"

"Rhiannon. Of all the memories to find, you have reconnected with the hardest one. I cannot tell you how horrible it is to have you remember it. I wish I could take that one from you and not have you relive it."

He hugged me tighter.

After a time, he turned the DVD back on. "This might help a little bit. But we don't have to watch." He considered for a moment. "Please be honest. If this is too much for you, I will shut it off."

The main menu of the DVD had many items. He moved the cursor through them. There were so many it filled the television screen. He scrolled down. He selected a title a few from the bottom. The title said, "The First Time". He entered a code that unlocked the screen.

"I hadn't expected this memory to be the first one to hit you. So many are good. This is one of the worst." He set the remote down next to him, as if worried he might need to grab it.

Leone on screen began.

"My love," his tone was tender, "if you are watching this, then you have remembered the most devastating experience in my existence. I relive this more than you know. The pain has not lessened over the years. It is bitter in my soul."

I hugged the Leone in my arms tighter. The TV Leone paused.

"I uncovered the plot to assassinate the Royal Family by the first born son. Some of the nobles from court plotted against the King. At the time, Peppin the hunchback, the King's firstborn son, lived in the monastery. His plot had unfolded from that location."

I adjusted my position a little where I lay.

"My troops and I camped in a field that night. While they slept, I kept watch. A peasant came during the night to warn me. The things he said were strange. He told me of the feedings that happened at the hands of the beings in the monastery. He told me he waited for the day when any help would come."

I snuggled closer to the firm body sitting with me. He wrapped his arm around my shoulder a little tighter.

"The peasant's account meshed with the stories told by Romans who observed that as soon as the occupants of the monastery had arrived in Rome with the great King Charlemagne, people went missing. No one dared to run away or make any statement against the monastery. They knew they would be hunted down and silenced for good. I had pondered the peasant's tale.

Those strange and unbelievable things were still in my mind when we broke the door down the next day."

The story Leone had told me earlier slipped back into my mind.

"My mind reeled as I saw the dethroned Queen of Constantinople crumbling to the floor, bitten about her neck and arms. The fire burning in the fire place cast a red glow about her billowing dress as it wrapped itself around her. Her scream etched itself forever into my mind even as I raced forward.

The unearthly beings that stood there with red eyes growled their warnings at us. All that the peasant had said seemed true about the beings who lived there."

I bolted upright on the couch. I tore my eyes from the television to glance at Leone. I knew red eyes—in my dreams. I knew red eyes from the man who had kidnapped me. They haunted me.

"The story you told me…"

"Yes." He sat up along side me, pausing the DVD.

"You were the knight?"

"Indeed. That responsibility had become my undoing and that of all the troops on that night. If I had believed the story from the peasant, I might have stayed clear. Then again, I had been young and eager to prove my worth to the King."

I wedged back between his arm and his body, thinking about how that moment could have changed everything, even the moment we shared right then on the couch.

Leone started the video again.

"The troops immediately jumped to my aid. I sneaked to the back of them and circled around. I drew my sword and rammed it through the queen's heart, hoping to cure her agony, not fully realizing that Peppin's plan had been to keep the queen for eternity. I misjudged.

Peppin, the meek and weak, had transformed. The body that had once left him a little helpless as a person, now possessed strength beyond comprehension.

In moments he had ripped through my troops, thrashing their bodies to pieces. Before I could react, his engorged hand wrapped around my neck and lifted me from the ground."

Instinctively, my hand clutched my neck. I remembered that pain from my dream.

"He had become crazy with rage, his eyes burned into me. 'I will kill you slowly,' he had told me. 'I will make you see pain like no other for killing my love.'

And in that moment I understood. I would die at the hands of a man that I had once fostered and cared for deeply, because of the family situation he had been born into.

But then he must have changed his mind because he sputtered to me, 'I will watch you die. Die to a life of eternal Hell. Forever thirsting for the blood of those you hold dear.' He laughed at his idea of revenge, then bit into my arm and feasted on my blood. He left me drained, but not entirely dead. The pain stabbed me immediately and with great intensity. I realized the pain the queen had been going though."

I shuddered with the knowledge. Leone and I had shared that experience. Both of us bound by the same inferno caused by the one called Peppin. I replayed my experience through the memory in the burning streets of Atlanta. I remembered how the poison spread down my neck and across my chest. Leone, sitting beside me, rubbed my back, while the on-screen Leone recounted his pain.

"He threw me from the monastery. Dazed and agonizing, I struggled away. I found a fallen tree and spent what must have been days moaning and wailing, as my body died and transformed to this life. Finally, when most of the pain had left me, he found me. Having discovered you, he teased me. He explained his intention to kill you—to take from me what I had taken from him. But he had a change of heart, and in turn, changed his mind.

We had both been new to the experience, but he had been transformed days before me. Those days had enabled him to become familiar with the thirst for blood and his heightened senses.

He said he had found you out looking for me. He'd wanted to kill you then and there and bring your body to me, but he heard the second heart beating within you. You had divulged that I didn't know about the

baby. He thought of a way to torture me with the
knowledge."

I twisted toward Leone. He blurred in my vision as my
eyes filled with tears. I shook my head to protest the fact that
Peppin had used our unborn child against Leone in such a
cruel way.

"He bartered your life by telling you to run toward
home, and if you reached the gates of the castle, he
would let you live one more night." The Leone on the
screen paused with sorrow etched on his face. "You
were the pawn. His game piece. I had become his
enemy."

I collapsed back into Leone's chest and momentarily let the
silent tears wet his shirt. Then I returned my attention to the
television with my eyes wide, trying to see above the pools in
my eyes.

"I faltered trying to move and keep my balance. He
knew the first days of transformation were a struggle.
Every sound from near and far was driven to my very
core. Every smell, every creature's heartbeat, every
scintilla of sensory input, my new ability absorbed and
struggled to identify. In knowing this, his game had
been great. I had but to reach you first to save your life
and that of our child's. He disappeared."

I gripped Leone's clothing in my fists. Breathing heavily—
tears streamed down my face. I didn't think I could relive that
dream through Leone's eyes. My mind already swirled with
that remembrance. The pain there on the screen too intense. I
knew the pit of my being as it folded in on itself, before I let go
the first time. I remember his face above me, screaming and
crying. I remember from ages past. I remember the child in my
womb, its heart beating rhythmically, yet slower and softer, as
it too slipped away from me. That was all the memory of it I
had.

His gift of knowledge—his explanation of watching me slip would end up torturing me. I imagined that deep down he wished to have died right there beside me. How had he endured? Here he sat today—centuries removed, yet still beside me. And me, struggling to believe myself strong enough to have made it through the same events he had.

He touched my face with his hand. I couldn't tear my eyes from the television. I could feel him watching me. "My speed was uncontrollable to me. The trees moved by so fast, and the crystal clarity of my vision took all of my focus. I crashed into many trees, breaking them in two—bushes and shrubs shredded with my passing, but made my footing uneven. The sounds around me were deafening. I could hear a thousand heartbeats from the animals. Pattering and racing, all of them inundating my ears. The echoes of trees bouncing from others, the breaking of branches, and the ultimate crash bellowed in my piqued mind. They echoed through the cavern that had once been occupied with human thoughts and needs. They overrode everything. I clasped my hands on my ears trying to block them out. I fell from the reeling."

How had he made it? I could not understand the ability to hear everything around me, down to the tiniest of sounds. It would probably drive me insane.

"But I had to keep going. I had to reach you."

The voice paused.

"When I saw you in the clearing, he had already grabbed you. Which you obviously now remember. I will not tell you what my eyes witnessed; it will be my burden." The voice on the TV became soft and sullen.

I released my grip on Leone's shirt. As relieved as I had been that he did not divulge the pain from his point of view, I could not help but imagine it. He had watched as Peppin ripped my throat. He must have seen my blood pulsing from

242

by body as I had. I bet he would have broken through the stone itself to get to me. I lay in his lap, staring into those eyes, not knowing at all what he had gone through. I, selfishly, had only wanted to see him once more before I died. He could not follow me. He had been robbed of the joy I had been able to feel over the knowledge of our child growing inside me. He only knew the pain from the loss of it. He would have to carry on.

And here he sat, right beside me, after so long. His love for me must be beyond anything I could comprehend.

He drew me closer to him.

The TV voice continued.

"I pulled you over the stone and rested you in my arms. I watched your life slip from me. Peppin enjoyed the spectacle. I had too many emotions running through me. Powerfully, my new life required me to eat. Your blood invited me. It smelled sweeter than anything I could ever remember. He counted on that. He wanted me to be the one to kill you. His ultimate malevolence played to its fullest in front of him. I struggled with my sudden animalistic need. I heard that extra heartbeat. Sweet and tiny. I could feel it under my hand."

I adjusted my foot under me. Leone loosened his hold on me.

"That precious being tore me back from my fight with frenzy, to focus on you. Then I remembered something odd the peasant had told me. I thought it strange and had discounted it. When a human soul intertwines with the congealing blood of a newly formed..." the TV Leone paused and skipped over whatever word he should have used, "...what I had become...then your soul would never find heaven. It would come back to the earth, always returning. I needed you so desperately in that moment."

The voice on the screen seemed to plead.

"My mind was my last weakness. I should have let you go. But without a moment's thought, I gouged into my arm and dripped my disgusting inhuman blood into your mouth. I begged you to swallow."

After a pause he said, "You finally did."

I gasped, recalling the thick, congealing substance. It had been bitter and vile. It had burned as I forced myself to swallow it. Then the swirling had started deep inside me.

"Peppin had been off in the distance enjoying his game. When he realized what I had done, it was too late to stop it. He raged. By the time he approached us lying in the dirt, your blood had smeared all over me. Your life and the life of our baby slowly left me there alone. He had succeeded in destroying everything I needed to live and even took my ability to end my own life. He had the sweetest of revenge."

The man I loved on the screen paused and looked down, off screen. I rubbed Leone's stomach under my hand for comfort.

The voice began again.

"Peppin hit me from behind and then fled. I sprawled out over the top of you. I recollected you in my arms and held you.

In the dark, I mourned. Someone happened upon us and hurried into the town. Soon, the townspeople surrounded me—your body taken from me. In the rush, I withdrew from the crowd and disappeared into the forest. I was hungry. For you and for food. I killed rabbits and small animals, but they never filled me. I killed a deer the next day, and my thirst did not feel as overpowering. I thought I would chance going back into the village.

"I returned to our house. The instant I walked in, I knew I could never return. Your scent flooded me. It

was everywhere. It seemed to cling to the very walls. I
changed from my clothes, washed, grabbed a few
things that you used and left.
I attended your funeral. My spirit screamed."
How could he have carried on that whole time? I didn't
know if I possessed such fortitude to continue on, had I been
faced with the same situation.
"The King himself attended with his family, to honor
my loss. He talked about understanding. He wanted
counsel with me, as to the reasons behind the murders
in the field and what happened to you, my wife. I
could only nod."
Wife. The feel of it rolled around in my mind. I had no
recollection of a wedding. I didn't know if I wanted to recall it,
to be a wife and have the responsibilities that came with it. I
didn't know what that meant. I did not know how to enter
into that thinking.
"I walked in front of the mourning procession. Your
father stumbled through the street, devastated behind
me. Your mother matched his grieving. They drove me
heartsick, understanding their loss. I stayed long after
everyone had left. I kissed your sweet face once more,
then helped to carefully bury you. I did not want the
grave diggers to touch you or to throw dirt onto you
without care. They thought I had gone insane. I was."
My grave? I had a grave? Chills raced down my back. I
trembled imagining. Dark, deep, dirt. Lots of crushing dirt.
Cold, airless, and lonely grave. I still lay in that hole,
somewhere on the other side of the world.
My mind spun trying to fit together the concept of being
alive now, in this moment, with the knowledge that I had been
dead and buried multiple times.
"I cannot tell you how long I sprawled beside your
newly mounded resting place. My anguish consumed
me. When I did leave, I spent months in the forests. I

did not experience cold or hot. I hunted because the hunger never left. I avoided people. I had no intention of killing. The only bit of hope I had was in the words of the peasant. I prayed he had been correct. I went north in search of information. Very little could be found and even then I had to specially request it. I had to use the position I held in court and my good name. I could only hope. That hope began to grow like a separate life force in me. I headed to the area now called France where the monks from the monastery had originated. I uncovered more information, but I still had no proof as to whether or not it had been accurate. I could not know if you would ever come back."

The screen faded to blue.

I lay my head in Leone's lap. He traced the lines of my face. He pulled my hair back and brushed it with his fingers.

So much to consider—overwhelming. So many parts of me had been dormant for so long. *Who else had I been in far off times? Did I enjoy the same things then as now? Did I act the same? How does it work? How can it work? It defies logic. Yet, here I am faced with the horrifying truth.*

Will the real teenage girl locked in time please stand up? Oh wait, Rhiannon... not so fast. Let's choose someone else and just watch it unfold.

"Are you okay?" I could see Leone's empathy etched in the softness of his eyes.

"So much." The enormity of it made me want to wake up from this horrible nightmare I found myself in.

"Rhiannon, are you afraid of me?"

I clambered up and gazed into his tranquil blue eyes.

"No, Leone. For the first time, I understand my own feelings about you. They are older than I am." I paused when I said the words. It seemed strange that I had been fighting so hard against them.

I continued, "Am I still in danger?"

"Grave," he whispered solemnly. "Peppin sees you as a game. One that returns for his sport. He likes to torture me— he never sees my debt as paid. He sends spies off and on to check and see if you have arrived yet. The two of us are tied together. He created me, after all. I'm different from him— from most. My purity in spirit when my transformation occurred became visible on my body. I glow," he simply stated. "It dims incredibly when you are between lives. I can look completely human. It is when you arrive that my glow returns again. In that respect, by my creating you, I am tied to you physically. It is when we are the closest, when our lips touch, that my light is electrifying. It becomes a beacon to him. He's drawn to it. Then his games start."

I noticed that Leone's eyes drooped at the corners and lacked their normal shine. I imagined they emulated his anxiety.

"I fear that when I touched your lips at the dock, when I willed life back into you, that it might have started the game already."

His eyes venerated as did his words. "I have to be around you when you arrive. For hundreds of years I wait to see you, hear you, and smell you again. For me the time is unbearable. Vos es meus tantum votum." He closed his eyes. "You are my only desire."

He looked so vulnerable and desperate. I swung my leg over his lap and put my hands on both sides of his face. So beautiful and dear to me. Somehow in some altered universe, I was still his wife. I paused to think on the implications of souls being married for centuries. He opened his eyes. They seemed to burn with longing.

I could no longer resist. I kissed his forehead, his eyes, his cheek, and moved closer to his lips. His skin burned bright around me.

In an instant, he spun me off him and cradled me on the couch. One arm tucked under my head and the other held my body. He lay on top of me, holding his weight off with his arm and his leg. My pulse began to race. His lips were so close to mine, I could feel the beginning tingles.

"We cannot do this." His desire shined in his eyes. He struggled to keep his lips from touching mine. His breath came in fast, short wisps dancing across my face. "It is not worth the consequence. I do not require you to love me back. I only require knowing you are alive and safe." He rested his head on my beating heart.

"Oh, my own private heaven." He lay there. "It sounds so different to me than anyone else's. It always beats the same. When I'm alone and you're nowhere close, I replay this sound. It comforts me."

I listened to him. My heart raced. I burned to have him. *Simmer down, Rhi. Simmer down. Reel it in. Can anything be worse than this feeling of desire?* Even when I lay there, consumed in flames, I knew there was. I knew my own death over and over.

I thought about that. How desperately agonizing. A tear escaped my eye. After so long, I finally understood. Life and love were one. It does not matter, the little things that annoy or cause us to be judged. Existing slips away too easily to deny all the beauty there is in being. He was the love of my lives. We could not love physically, but the comprehension that I had found my soul mate, the caring, the compassion, and for so long a time, meant I had found home. I did not have to move to find it. I only had to live, at some point, in some far off place. It would always be there.

Leone straightened himself and lowered his face to mine.

I realized as I studied his eyes and as my blood began to stir again, that his admonition would be very hard to obey. My body contained an age-old memory of him like an amputee who still felt her leg.

"Where does Peppin stay?" I changed the subject.

"He and his type are still in the monastery. They have built a few of them now, located around the world. They move regularly and let a few generations pass to make sure the people do not suspect. He has created more monsters over the years. He hopes they will do his bidding. Even though the body goes through a transformation, the mind remains and so does their will. He has limited control over what he creates."

Leone positioned me beside him. He continued, "He is obsessed with you. I think he has come to enjoy you as well. Though, I believe, his enjoyment is more entertainment. He has spent time with you before."

"What do you mean?"

"He found you first once. He acted human. He courted you—he wooed you. His desire had been to have me find the two of you in love. Instead, he grew angered that his ruse hadn't worked. You found fault in him and wanted nothing to do with him."

My stomach grew queasy. *Peppin had courted me?* I relished the fact that it had not been a memory I chose to recall yet. Just thinking about how he looked—the red eyes, the bald head, the white skin—made me ill to think I could ever be close to him.

My body didn't want to move. Every last drop of energy had drained from it, even though most of it came from being mentally drained. My skull seemingly tipped open and pressure-washed of all the fuzzy uncertainty. Leaving only the naked truth for me to deal with. I definitely didn't have enough years in this body to remember a feeling of holding a child in my womb.

"Leone, for the record," I hesitated. "What are you?"

"Don't you know by now?"

"I...I think so," I stumbled.

He grasped my chin so that my eyes would meet his. "Tell me, please."

"I believe that you are inhuman. I believe you can do things that I could never dream of. But the way you look, the way you act, and the way you... love does not fit into my mind at all with anything that can be inhuman."

I squeezed his arm and continued. "The way the stranger acted and the things that he could do. His powerful strength. And from what you have told me about Peppin and the way he behaved in my memory, I can easily see that he is evil. That fits closer to the ideas I hold in my mind. I can easily call him a vampire."

I watched Leone as he slowly shook his head in agreement. "And that is the curse that he gave to me. Eternal life, thirst for blood, super human strength, no warmth, extreme eye sight, ultimate hearing, no need to sleep even when you desire to never wake, a memory that won't fade, the game of keeping the love of my life from me, and the extremely overwhelming desire to spend the rest of eternity with you and only you."

He halted his explanation as if to ponder his next words, then continued, "My life, I lead differently from his kind. That's why I glow. It is a combination of the purity in spirit that is a blessing from God in my life and my choice to never take a human life for food."

I winced. "Never?"

"Never."

He shifted his eyes momentarily toward the blue screen on the television, then back at me. "I have never consumed human flesh or blood. I saw it as the one thing Peppin would not take from me. My choice to act humanely. It has driven him mad. I have had the unfortunate predicament of tasting it on occasion, however. It is really a supernatural hunger that takes over. I can only describe it as a fury, like piranhas finding a feast. It would only take minutes for me to completely kill someone. I do not know how I refrained from it on those occasions. I have many years of practice now."

"Amazing." The thought of piranhas frenzied eating gave me chills. "So how do you... fill yourself?. How do you overcome the need to eat?"

"Really, because I decided never to eat this way, it has been easy to avoid. I hunt in the mountains. I find wild animals. When I have to look human in social situations, I will eat meat that has hardly been cooked. I don't enjoy chewing, but I do it. My choice is to do the best I can with the circumstances I have been given."

"It must be hard to try and fit in all the time in a world that's changing around you."

"It's not as hard as you would think. Really, fitting in has mostly stayed the same over the centuries. It is society's wants and desires that change."

"Centuries," I repeated the word. "Centuries... what have you seen with your eyes? What places have you visited? I have so much to ask you!"

He quietly chuckled at my burst of enthusiasm. "So much. Probably too much. I guess I have become an exceptionally accurate historian." He pointed to the books that were on the floor. "I decided some time ago to write accurate stories of history. Some authors get the idea they knew what happened in the past because of artifacts and letters. I grew tired of reading interpretations, so I wrote the truth."

My eyes widened. "Really?"

"Yes. It's a peculiarly funny twist. I have been writing now for a very long time. Under different names, of course. Every now and then, my work comes back to me, like this year in our history class."

"The author on the book." My mouth hung open. When I spoke it was with a slight chuckle. "I noticed the name sounded similar to yours."

He nodded gratefully at me. "It feels good to know that I can give a small gift and teach children accurate history."

"Leone, that is unbelievable."

"I suppose it is a bit of a tribute to you. My way of keeping you alive for me. And it pays well." He motioned to the house around us.

"You paid for the house?"

"Mostly. I've had many more years of investing than anyone else."

That made sense—it was just beyond my realm of comprehension.

"Why have you never turned me into a vampire? Why have you never kept me for eternity?"

His face revealed the pain the topic caused him.

"I took an oath. One that I, to this day, believe to the depths of whatever soul still remains in me. I would never change you without your knowledge and approval, and without you being completely aware of all the sacrifices you would be making for the rest of your human time on earth— and then eternity. If I were given the choice now, I would not choose this life. It has never been easy. But if I did not have conviction in my beliefs, then I would not stand for anything worthwhile. When I beheld you pregnant with our child and I heard both of you... both of your hearts beating, it was the most precious gift. Something had been completed inside of me. You were never given the chance to have that completeness. I will never take away that experience from you. You need to have your human life." The emotion in his voice told me more than his words could.

I reached out and touched him. We were silent for a while.

"But wouldn't my being changed alter his game? Wouldn't he give up?"

"I have thought about that countless times. I used to think it would. I believed it fully. I, on other occasions of your life, have pushed you too quickly and ultimately lost out. I have had to learn patience. I'm still not sure this time—events are happening so quickly and it scares me. I'm trying to be careful. That is why we made this DVD. The family decided it would be better than confronting you all at once. This way, we could explain it on your terms as your memories came back." He continued with his original thought. "I believe that now, after so many different connections with you, Peppin would still try to destroy you and me, even if you were inhuman with me. Ultimately, my family and I have talked about this time with you. We are in agreement that we need to help you understand as quickly as possible, and only with your wishes and a clear and present danger will I transform you."

My mind hadn't been prepared to hear that in my lifetime, right now, he had already thought about making me a vampire. I sat up and looked at him.

"There is selfishness in me," he admitted looking humbled. "It kills me each time I lose you. I wait for centuries sometimes, before you come back to me. In those moments when I relive the loss, I think I could bare you loathing me, just to have you. But I know it would not work. I would never change you without your approval." His expression grew taut. "You have no idea what it is like to hold you while your earthly life slips away. It is something I have done many times. But I know what it is like to live every day and never sleep, never rest, and always hide."

I stroked his face. I understood why he had a desire to keep me from that fate.

"I do not want to push too much onto you right now. We need to watch more of the DVD, but now you need to rest. Some of it we have now already talked about." He turned off the television.

We lay on the huge couch, his body cool against mine. I wrapped up in the blankets to keep me warm. He lay next to me for the rest of the night.

I finally slept.

12

New Direction

As the morning brightened, my stomach growled.

"You need to eat something," Leone advised. "It must be an entire day since you last ate."

"I am rather hungry."

I still had his tee shirt and boxers on. I didn't want to change yet. I slipped into the robe again and we strolled, hand in hand, down to the kitchen. My eyes seemed swollen and skewed my vision.

Everyone was, of course, awake and settled around the kitchen in chairs.

All vampires. The thought of it seemed surreal.

Nothing bubbled, or steamed, or fried on the stove. No cereal boxes or toast and butter and jam proclaimed the breakfast hour. Not one morsel of food lay out anywhere. It seemed obvious to me now.

Everyone's attention had been focused on each other before we entered the kitchen. I heard laughing and grumbling. As we walked in voices grew quiet. Lauriel jumped up and left for her bathroom the moment she saw me. Nohi reached out and drew me in. I looked like a wreck, if the expression on her face was any indication.

"Rhi, I feel horrible that yesterday happened at all," she commiserated and then kissed my cheek.

Several smaller kids around the table jumped down and skipped to Leone. He made no mention of young ones in the house.

The force of them colliding with him would have sent me flying. He didn't budge. He nimbly picked up a curly, blonde-haired girl. She looked to be about three years old. She wiggled and latched onto his neck. She wore a frilly, light pink outfit adorned with white lace. Her leggings and shoes matched. She was absolutely adorable.

Lauriel rushed back in and started dabbing a light blue gel around my eyes. "I have to say, that is one thing I don't miss!" Referring to my swollen eyes, talking more to everyone else than to me. It soothed the irritated feeling where she dabbed it.

"Thank you," I said. "They must be bad."

She looked at me, trying to find something to say that would help me feel better but then gave up. "Like a nightmare." Shooting me a lopsided smile, she hugged me and flited away.

Leone tilted his head toward the preschooler in his arms. "This is Naomi. She is still very new to this life. She had been changed and left alone. A new changeling must have transformed her, because he left her alive—barely, but alive. She is a great love." He hugged her to him. "She is truly her age, sweet and adorable." I reached over to stroke the back of her hair.

She growled an inhuman sound, and her eyes flashed completely white. She bared her teeth and lunged toward me. Leone pulled her back.

"She is also very dangerous to you. She has to be taught self- control. Her natural desire now is basic, and therefore, off limits to you." He spoke right to me. I stepped back, nodding.

She was beautiful, light rose cheeks, red lips, long, blonde curls, and a sweet, round face. She would be angelic, accept for her white, menacing eyes. I imagined her more dangerous than anyone in the room. She would draw people in with the cute and adorable innocence—the perfect hunter, luring her prey to her. I was frighteningly impressed by her, spellbound at her complexity.

"This is Toby." Leone pointed out a handsome young boy about five years old. He wore denim pants and a black tee shirt. I imagined him to be of Spanish-descent.

"This is Kharma." He motioned toward a brown-haired, brown-eyed girl who appeared to be eight. She had dressed smartly in a long sleeved, button-up shirt with black slacks and high heels. She looked like she'd played dress up with a fashion designer.

"And this is Melia." Leone indicated toward the last child. She had thick, red hair and green eyes. Probably nine, she stood taller than Kharma and had lost a lot of her baby fat.

They all awaited my response. I said, "Hello." Then, almost as a reaction, they rushed to me. Considering how Naomi had snarled, I jumped backward into the door frame. They all hugged me in an instant and peered at me with adoration. There was nothing menacing in their behavior. None of their eyes glowed white with hunger, like Naomi's. I felt safe. I hugged them back.

Toby spoke first, "Rhiannon, it is a great pleasure to meet you. We have heard so much about you. What would you like for breakfast? Melia, Kharma, and I would like to make it for you." His voice still had a child-like quality to it, but his words were phrased perfectly and eloquently. His mannerisms and his politeness threw me off—they seemed to age him. I glanced toward Leone.

"He was changed fifty years ago."

I placed my hand to my lips. To be stuck in a child's body, I could not imagine.

Leone continued, "Melia and Kharma were friends in life. Kharma changed first and then, well, as a new changeling, she changed Melia. Naomi is the only real child here. That is why we are so careful with her right now. Dante discovered her in Boise only a few weeks ago. He knew she needed help." I looked toward Dante. He beamed with pride at Naomi, much like a father would.

"My gosh," I blurted out. "So there are more of you? Close by?"

"Really, we have been the only ones in the area for a time," Dante explained. "There has been no manifesting activity or masticating in this region for twenty years. We think your admirer, as he seems, is probably the culprit of Naomi's change." He pointed toward Naomi.

"The question is, who is he, why had he been created, and by whom?" Angelina spoke in even tones as she twirled her blonde locks around her fingertips.

Dante clarified, "It seems pretty obvious from the news reports that he himself is new. He kills randomly and dangerously close to populated places. One group of people heard screaming close to them, down an alley. A body was discovered still warm to the touch. Unfortunately, he does not complete his work, in the case of our Naomi."

"So, there could be more like her?" I inquired, fearful for myself and for all people in close proximity. I imagined loved ones being killed by others they trusted. The beloved family member, newly converted, might be unable to stop their uncontrollable hunger.

"Don't worry, my classy dame." Lauriel danced toward me from the other side of the room. Her red hair bounced in short waves, accented by the lights overhead. "We are not going to be letting *you* out of our site!"

"The obligation seems to be ours," Angelina said sarcastically.

Everyone ignored her tone.

Lauriel dragged me to the table. I glanced at Leone. He lowered Naomi to the floor. As I sat down, she pranced over to me and extended her arms toward me. I flinched. She persisted and struggled to climb into my lap. I didn't reach out to help her in case she bit me.

The robe on my leg slid out from under her and caused her to tumble to the floor. She hit her head with a large wooden thud. No one moved or spoke. I was horrified that I had just dropped a child, even one as dangerous as Naomi. I instinctively reached out to help her. She did not cry, as I would have expected. Instead, she presented me with an irritated glare. She seized my outstretched arms before I could get my wits about me and rescind my offer. She climbed quickly into my lap.

Before anyone could assess the safety of the idea, she turned her head to my arm with her mouth open. Angelina, from her chair next to me, whipped her hand under Naomi to block the bite.

"No, Naomi. Rhiannon is the only one who would get very hurt from your biting."

She glowered at Angelina with big doe eyes. Just to be defiant and stubborn, she quickly twisted her head to my other arm and attempted the same thing. Lauriel's hand flew there in an instant.

She scolded, "Naomi, do you like Rhiannon?"

Naomi nodded her head, curls bouncing.

"Ok, then, no biting Rhiannon. She will get very sick. Do you remember your owies?"

"Owies," Naomi whimpered. The memory must have been horrifying for her.

"Yes. Those owies you will give to Rhiannon."

Naomi's eyes widened and she looked up at Lauriel with a captivated expression. The pain must have been forever etched on her poor little mind.

"No!" she said forcefully. "No to Rennannon!"

259

"That's right, Naomi," Nohi agreed. "If you bite Rhiannon, you will not get to play with her."

She bestowed the most adorable, angry face on Nohi and lunged toward me like a ton of bricks, knocking the wind from me. She bear-hugged me as if to say, 'No one is taking Rhiannon away.'

Everyone laughed at that, including me. A bruise would surely form where she had hit me with her head, but I didn't mind. I cuddled with her. She popped two fingers in her mouth and sucked on them. With her other hand, she twirled her hair.

The kids with the grown up minds were cooking for me in the kitchen.

Leone faced me. "Rhiannon, we need to talk in detail about yesterday. I know you have been through so much, the kidnapping, the cliff, and the memory coming back. But I think it best, with all of us here, so you will not have to repeat anything."

Gasps emitted from others at the table.

"Your memories? Which one?" Nohi's concern emanated in her tone.

Leone's face hardened when he answered for me, "Our baby."

I wilted as the words pierced me.

Here I sat—a teenager in body and experience, with memories that spanned centuries. Children in the kitchen had lived longer than I had, and they cooked my breakfast as we discussed the child I lost. The thought made my head spin.

Nohi hurried over to me and placed her hand on my shoulder. "The hardest memory, dear. I am so sorry!" Her voice sounded like she would cry if her eyes would let her.

"Momma," Naomi put her wet fingers to my cheek.

"No," I whispered, barely audible, to Naomi in a kid-like manner. "Rhiannon did not get to be." A strange sadness intensified inside me. I distinctly remembered the feeling and would never forget the sensation of my baby's existence. A tear betrayed me to everyone.

I wiped it away as soon as I felt it touch my cheek, trying not to make a big deal. I stood, lifting Naomi with me and toddled around the end of the table. More tears welling up, threatening to overrun. I didn't want to make a blubbering idiot of myself in front of everyone.

"Sorry," I murmured, "please excuse me." I passed Naomi to Nohi and blindly escaped from the room. I bounded toward Nohi's room, the only bathroom that I knew. I felt weird going in there without permission. I hesitated in the front entry way, not sure what to do.

Leone joined me and held me as I cried until I had no more to give. Then he led me into the bathroom to wash up.

When we returned to the kitchen, my breakfast waited on the table. My stomach gurgled in anticipation of the food. My mouth salivated as I surveyed the eggs and pancakes. The bacon smelled delicious. I picked up my fork and chose a combination of bacon and eggs for my first bite.

The conversation centered around me. I didn't like being the focus of their attention. They should be enjoying their day, not harping on the events of Rhi.

"He obviously knew our entire plan," Dante said. "He beat us to her and knew right where to go."

I swallowed my mouthful. They had set up an entire plan to rescue me. They had devoted time to my safety. I looked around the table at the intensity of their faces. They were all very serious about their endeavor.

A few details that the red-haired devil himself divulged during my capture would answer some of their wonderings. Through a mouthful of pancake I shared, "He told me he grew up around here. He knew these mountains inside and out." My mind drifted back to the conversation at the water. He had grabbed me there and left the bruises. I rubbed my arm.

"From here, huh?" Dante mused. Then he turned to the others. "I told you. I bet it was that accident down out of Boise. Where they found that devoted dog next to the wrecked truck." He clasped his hands together. "It just sounded too odd to be anything else. The door ripped from its hinges and the feedings in Boise. It all makes perfect sense."

I just listened. I'd taken another bite of my food as he spoke, but it grew tasteless in my mouth. I swallowed it without enjoyment. I didn't want to die at that angry man's hands, but I am just one human. It appeared he had killed more that they had not been able to help. I did not want to relive yesterday, but others had died before me.

"What else did he say, Rhi?" Leone asked.

"He said he was curious about me. He wanted to know why I had a cov... cov... umm...a group of you protecting me."

"A coven?" Dante grumbled, "I hate that term, it makes us seem akin to a gathering of witches."

I shuffled in my seat and thought about what he said.

"Yes, I think that is the word he used, but I had no clue what he meant at the time." I definitely did not see the connection to pointed hats and broom sticks.

"He said he was curious, huh?" Lauriel wondered.

"He also told me he would be watching me. If he found me interesting he would capture me again. He said he didn't intend to kill me." I didn't care—the realization a shock to my mind. How could my emotions have become so shut off?

They all grew quiet.

"Did he say why he would not kill you?" Melia pressed for more information.

"No, he just mentioned a 'he' that had ordered him to capture me. And he mentioned a 'he' that had ordered him to do things. He made up his mind, however, and there would be nothing 'he' could do about it because of his own free will."

"Peppin!" Leone hissed. "His game has begun." His voice boomed. His eyes flashed red.

I dropped my fork onto my plate and clutched my chest. I gaped at Leone. Angelina and Lauriel must have heard my heart rush because they both turned at the same time to stare at me. I did not want to be the game. Not in this life. Not in any life.

"No!" I croaked, my hunger replaced with a sudden urge to lose the contents I had stuffed myself with.

Leone tried to wave the last comment from the air, sorry to have caused me angst. He bent down beside me and placed his cool hand against my cheek. "Rhi, what else did he say? Did he mention Peppin at all? Is he close?"

"No. He didn't say anything else. Only that he, my captor, would be watching me. He would be deciding if he wanted to keep me himself."

Leone jumped up and growled again. Lauriel's hand rested on his shoulder, patting him.

"We need to have a plan of action," Kharma directed.

"I agree." Dante scowled.

The idea of everyone putting themselves in danger over me made me worry. Had no one thought about the end? Everyone rushed about making sure I felt secure and safe, but what of the innocent people that had no idea their lives would soon end, and for what cause? So some deranged lunatic could keep an eye on me? My hands clenched in anger and I pushed them into my leg until I could feel my knuckles.

"Why don't you let him have me? I wouldn't want all of you to be hurt or your future to be ruined. Think of all the people that have already died because of me."

They all stared at me, except for Angelina. She seemed to have thought of that already.

Another nagging question played with my mind. "How many have died because of this same kind of situation throughout all of my lives?" The idea left my mouth and too late I realized that I was not ready for the answer.

"Possibly hundreds," Angelina spoke in a cool, even tone, as she pirouetted to face me. Her eyes bore into me.

I scooted back in the chair. *Hundreds?* Heaviness settled on my chest, he reaper himself pushed all of his weight onto me. I might as well have carried his scythe with me from life to life.

"I have to go!" I stood up from the table.

"No, Rhiannon!" I should have known Leone would not agree.

"It is not so easy," Dante pleaded.

"I remember you," Melia recalled in her childish voice. "The last time you were with Leone, I remember you. I felt so heart-broken when we lost you that time. You have come back to us again. I do not want you to go." The sincerity in her face conveyed the depth of her sorrow.

How could she have such strong feelings about me? I had just met her. I grasped my head hoping to control my thoughts. This all confused me greatly. I didn't think that others had remembered me like Leone had. I was at a loss for words.

"The truth is, Rhi," Dante continued, "no matter what you look like, you have been a part of our family, before most of us were even in the family." I struggled to understand that. My head spun with all of my thoughts. I plopped back down and placed my elbows on the table on either side of my plate, pressing my temples between the palms of my hands. So much death—children, adults, people with loved ones. How many lives had I disrupted just by existing?

"We wait for you. We move where Leone feels a strong connection. He is usually correct," Lauriel said.

"We believed in Leone from the beginning and trust in the kind of being he is. We followed his lifestyle. We took an oath with him to protect you... even when he said we did not need to." Toby offered the explanation in his high-pitched voice.

"There are only three of us who have not done so. I have never met you before, but in just the time you have been here, I have seen our family come to life. They are so in love with you and so glad to see you. How could I not pledge for your safety?"

Everyone fell quiet. I could guess that Naomi had been one of the other three, and I thought the last one to be Angelina. She seemed to disapprove of me somewhat. I didn't look up to gain confirmation in her expression.

"Thank you, Toby," Leone said. He returned to my side, stroking my hair. It felt right to have him beside me.

"It seems one choice is easy," Angelina sounded indignant, confirming my assessment of her feelings as correct. "Just change her already, Leone."

Voices erupted around me. Everyone held an opinion. Most of them were in favor of letting me make the choice. Angelina stood her ground as the only one wanting 'my drama', as she put it, done with once and for all.

My drama? I'm new to all this. I can understand from her perspective how annoying it must be to move and hide and have me appear and reappear. But I am not a dramaseeker, in fact, I stay away from those that thrive on it. Yet, here I am, discovering I'm the Queen Mother of Drama. No one else has ever been able to stretch it out this long. Maybe I should get a Daytime Emmy Award for Best and Longest Running Soap Opera.

Leone leaned over me toward Angelina, talking about his code and how worthless life is without something like it. She disagreed. Others gave examples of Leone's chivalrous nature, including a story of how he saved her.

I stood and exited the room.

The voices behind me cut short. My leaving ended the conversation.

I strode to the front door and barely had my hand on the knob when everyone surrounded me. I jumped back, my hand twisting the knob. I had to get used to the suddenness of their movements. I quickly surveyed their faces. Leone's foot prevented me from opening the door wide enough to get through.

"I need some fresh air," I informed him. Fresh mountain air. I wished I were back at the coast. I needed to lose myself in the tide, to let the crashing waves wash all of this away. I just needed to have nothing in my mind for a while.

"Sorry," he conceded and held the door for me to go out on the patio. I wandered to the left where I had seen the beautiful furniture. He followed.

When I glanced behind me, I noticed that everyone else stayed in the house. There were no more loud voices, just murmuring.

"Leone, I have to go home." I sank into a beautiful wrought iron chair. The deep cushion engulfed me. "My parents are going to be worried if I don't show up."

"You're right. I didn't think of that this morning. I'm sorry."

"How am I going to be able to hold myself together?" I worried aloud. I knew that my parents would know something was wrong. Mom could read me like an open book. I felt pretty sure that as soon as I told her "I was kidnapped by a vampire last night" she would think I had gone bananas. "This is a lot to take a hold of in one day. I feel weak and old all of the sudden."

He contemplated me as I concentrated on the forest. I avoided looking directly at him.

"There is really nothing I can do to save myself. I just want to make sure my parents are safe." I cast a firm look at him. "I don't know if they are the same parents I've always had, but I love them more than anything. They raised me in the only life I truly know."

"Of course, Rhiannon..." He nodded his assurance, eyes black in the sunlight. "Can you introduce me to your parents today as your boyfriend? I'm not saying that I want us to date or force anything like that onto you, but it would make being at your house much easier."

I giggled at that, in spite of my anesthetized mood. I had awakened this morning to find out I had been married to this man for hundreds of years, with few memories to go with it and now he asked to give the appearance we were dating. No strings attached.

"What, pray tell, do you find so amusing?" He smiled at me.

"This whole thing. My existence... my repeated existence," I emphasized the last part, leaning forward in my chair. "Leone, in the matter of... what, a few hours now, I discovered I have been married, carried a child, been murdered I don't know how many times, and have been responsible for the deaths of hundreds of innocent people." My hand flew to my forehead as I pushed myself back into my chair.

"I'm sorry to have all of this hit you this morning," he sighed in a quiet voice.

I closed my eyes and laid my head on the back of the cushion. I knew the way my words had spat from me, they sounded angry. Was I angry? I didn't choose this. It would be much simpler to just be the old Rhi, the one in this body, not the others. Angelina obviously harbored some strong opinions about me. The worst part about that was I didn't blame her. In fact, if I were in her shoes, I probably would be acting similarly.

I shook my head as it rested on the chair, contemplating the negativities of this predicament.

It wouldn't have been so bad if my parents were not in danger and if I didn't have the sick and disgusted feeling of being responsible in an absolutely unconscious way for the lives of so many. My mind tried to visualize the people. *Their faces. What had their names been? How did their families find them? Did they find them or were they lost forever?* Questions that will never be answered. I could not pull images from my mind of the lost. I could not even dignify their deaths with a memory—it reinforced the irrelevance of their existence, my taking them early from the world had created. They had not been blessed with time—time to do wonderful things for others and create a greater and richer world for those around them.

I began to cry. My birth caused the dominos to fall. A long line of the dead streamed out behind me. All were a burden for me to carry, and one of them, my child.

I rocked back and forth and sobbed into my hands. The gauze wrapped around my wounded hands soaked up the moisture.

Leone reached around me and held my shoulders.

"Hey. What can I do to help you?"

I could not speak—the flood gates from hundreds of years opened.

Leone moved to the front of me and perched on the coffee table.

He pulled my hands from my face. I did not want to look at him, so I leaned forward until my head rested on his shoulder.

He rubbed my back.

I concentrated on the green grass that extended down the side of the yard. My tears ceased, and what remained of any happiness and joy evaporated with them. Only emptiness remained, filled with resentment and hate over my existence.

Leone pulled away after some time and gazed into my eyes.

"I don't like what I see there." He pointed to me. "I have seen that glazed look in your eyes before, and I know what it means."

I felt as if I was about to be scolded for doing something wrong. I focused my gaze downward and started to unwind the gauze on my hands.

"You listen to me," he commanded.

Yup, I was correct. He began his lecture. "None of this is your fault. Not one thing."

He paused. I didn't have anything to say, he knew exactly where my mind had gone to.

"Rhi?" He must have wanted a response. *What does he want me to say? 'I feel great! Everything is good! I just learned, indirectly, I murdered hundreds of people.'*

"Rhi." His voice sounded much firmer than before. "If you have to blame anyone, put it on me. I told you I forced you to drink my blood. I try to find you every time to stop this from happening."

I pondered the palms of my hands. The cuts, still red and irritated, would heal. I focused on the loose skin, peeled back in spots. That would heal.

"Yes, Leone, but how many more people will die because of me?"

He sat back. His mouth appeared to form words, but nothing came out.

"So, that's it," he finally concluded. "The people." He bowed his head, and his hands trembled on mine.

"I feel your empathy." His statement fell flat. *Feel my what... my feelings? No, you don't.* I rolled my eyes. *How could anyone know my feelings?*

"It is another sinister twist to Peppin's game, but it is not mine or yours. He kills wherever he is. He does not think twice. He does not care who it is. If he wants them eliminated or if it is mere convenience, he will kill them. He is worthless."

I studied him. He didn't look away from his palms.

When he did glance up, I recognized the years of torment in his eyes. His lids quivered to hold back his emotions.

"It is not your burden to carry, Rhi," he whispered to me. "If there is blame to be had, put it on my shoulders. Hate me for it, Rhi. Hate me, not you. I am the reason you come back. I am the reason you relive this pain, over and over." His lips trembled.

I sat there, unsure. As his hands rested on mine, my skin tingled. I knew why.

"Leone, I need to go home. I need to sleep, if I can. I feel drained, so drained. I'm afraid my brain has shriveled up. Please drive me?"

He nodded and stood up. As we left the porch, I held his hand. When we entered the house, I followed behind him and noted the slouching of his shoulders. His head hung low.

After I changed into an outfit Lauriel gave me, Leone drove me home.

We did not speak on the way.

He let me off down the drive-way, in case my parents happened to be watching for me. They still thought I had stayed with Carlee.

"I will be around." He pointed to the area around my house. "Out here. You and your parents will be safe." Then he turned around and drove back across the bridge that crossed the stream below our house. I watched him turn at the place where Dante had been fishing, and the first place I felt Leone's arms wrap around me. He hid the truck well in the bushes as I dragged myself to the house.

Mom and Dad were unpacking more boxes in the family room.

"Hi." I heard Dad's voice.

"Hello," I greeted, reminding myself to sound chipper.

"Did you have fun last night?" Mom probed lightly.

"Yes. We just hung out," I mustered. I didn't want to officially lie to them. Technically, I hung out on a cliff for most of my evening. Still, I knew I had lied and that made me want to crawl into a shell. I wished I could spill all of my anxiety to my parents, and have them tell me everything would be just fine and they would make sure no one hurt me again.

I shuffled to my room and collapsed on my bed. I gazed out the window. My thoughts completely washed away.

13
Life Continues

Leone never left me alone from that morning on. He sat in my room as I slept and watched me from a distance when I needed time with my parents. We were trying to make sure my parents didn't get the impression that Leone was smothering me. I felt quite different about him. I would rather spend every waking moment looking into those enchanting eyes. Carlee and I hadn't really done much with each other since the previous Friday. So much had taken place, it almost seemed like we had grown apart. None of it had been anything she did or failed to do. There had been no way to involve her in the situation. Life had simply changed.

Returning to school the following week had also been different. Classes proceeded, homework assignments came and went.

"I have to say," Leone spoke to me during that first week back, "it's so much nicer with you accepting the fact that you love me, instead of acting like you didn't even know me."

I punched him. He had been right, though. I'd been silly to think I had control over it.

I spent the afternoons keeping my mind occupied with studies and Leone. Lauriel even spent time with us. I somehow felt older. I mysteriously knew more than most of the people that surrounded me. I had become more settled than most of my friends, and it seemed to distance us. Carlee and I still took turns driving to school. I couldn't help noticing how our conversations were lacking. Lauriel always sat in the back as a passenger.

By the end of the month, my constant fear of my stalker ebbed. Leone's family remained intense and determined to keep an eye on me at all times.

I wanted to do some things in town. I hated being cooped up in my house all the time. Leone didn't like the idea. I decided we were going to the movies with Carlee and Kyle, whom were now dating and carrying on like love birds. Bob and John tagged along with us. Some of the other kids from school came, too. It felt good to get out. Bob still seemed to be indifferent to Leone's and my relationship. Throughout the movie Leone traced my ear with his fingertip, sending chills down my body.

Our math teacher kept his promise. He moved the classroom around. I ended up partnering with Amy, the girl that had sat next to Leone and still showed signs of her infatuation for him. I had to endure her batting eyes and hair flinging in his direction. The weeks sped by.

It turned out that I helped Amy through some of the tougher ideas in math. It amazed me to discover I had some things in common with her. Things I would never have guessed. She constantly worried about what other people thought of her. I did too, but my issue focused more on the fact they might be thinking about me at all. I didn't feel the need to change anything about me to fit into what others wanted.

She also liked some of the same music as me. So that gave us some general topics to discuss if we had a moment of awkward silence, which usually came after she flaunted herself to Leone. She struck me as a generally good person, although I picked up on some sadness that I couldn't figure out. Some emptiness about her she attempted to fill with curt opinions of others, and a facade that would make her more enjoyable if she would only drop it.

With fall, the weather grew chilly and the leaves changed in the trees. Snow would be falling before we knew it. I was told there would be enough to coat the ground here for most of the winter. I could hardly imagine it as the fields currently had large machines clearing harvests.

My worry about my problem stalker started again—strange things began to happen. Farm animals ended up missing around the valley. Mysteriously, the investigation never found any traces of animal kills. It was the only thing that made me realize my danger could still be present. There were no explanations for the disappearances. It seemed that they just gave up trying to find any clues. Of course, I had no way of knowing if they really had anything to do with my stalker, but it kept him fresh on my mind—paranoid enough to keep me watching over my shoulder, letting others go before me around corners, and staying close to groups of people. If there were noises that seemed out of the ordinary, I jumped. I felt relief when my parents would both return home from work, knowing for sure they were unharmed.

My dreams were as real as ever. Of course, my ability to understand helped with the intensity of them. I had new ones occasionally and so many questions. Leone answered a few, but never quenched my appetite for knowledge.

He told me that we had time to go through the details once our stalker disappeared for good.

I began to notice a piqued interest in how they hovered around me. Leone's family constantly combed the area looking for signs of him. When I confronted Leone about it, he passed it off as nothing. I only discovered the truth when I overheard Dante and Leone discussing the situation in quieted tones.

Dante had picked up my captor's scent once again, around the school and my house.

I shivered with the knowledge. I decided to stick closer to them, even more so than before.

Friday night came and Lauriel invited me to spend the night with her. My parents were very skeptical. I explained that his mom would be there, and all the guys had planned on an overnight hunting trip into the mountains. I didn't lie, even though the incident did not require any guns for them. After deliberating over the details, my parents agreed.

We drove up to the house. Nohi kissed me as I walked in. She held my hand and patted it. Everyone surrounded me, talking to me with excitement. All but Angelina. She stayed in the kitchen with her boots on, waiting for everyone to exit out the back with her.

Leone scooped me up and spun me around, kissing my chin. He placed me down on the ground again.

"I will be back early tomorrow. I hope you will still be here." He smiled down at me.

"I plan to be." I touched his cheek with my hand. Being in love with him came as easy as breathing.

After the group left, I walked through the house. I looked again at some of the antiques that were in the front entryway. I didn't want to touch any—I knew how old they were. Knowing now what I did not know the first time I touched them. I wondered where they came from.

Lauriel walked in behind me.

"Can you tell me where these things were collected?" I asked.

She looked at me with her eyes wide. "Ya, I think."

"This." I pointed to the brown and white, etched, bone box on the large, round table.

"That is from the Middle Ages. Around Greece, I believe," she stammered and fidgeted with her hands.

"I remember that it's old. I was more interested in who it originally belonged to." I smiled at her.

She seemed relieved. "Oh. You know, it is nice to have you remembering. I forget sometimes that I don't need to be vague with you anymore." She laughed and tapped me on the arm, then pointed at the box. "This belonged to Nohi. She had actually been 'buried' with it."

I gasped. "She was buried?"

"Yes. It was really the only logical way to let her family go through grieving then moving on. It was her choice entirely. I can't imagine being buried alive," she said. Creepy, crawly worms seemed to wiggle through me as I pondered.

"How did she get out of it?" I asked.

"Leone and Dante dug me up late that night," Nohi explained, walking into the room. She put her arm around my shoulder. "It was an awful experience, the whole thing. I watched my family as they grew old and passed away. Unbearable." She sighed and looked at the box. "We deliberated on the issue and decided we would never encourage another to be buried alive. My body might have changed, but my mind had definitely remained human." A weak smile teased the edges of her lips.

I tried to imagine the horror she'd gone through, hearing dirt pilling up on her casket. Not to mention the pain of watching her family pass away as she never aged.

"What made you decide to change?" I asked.

"I donated a lot of my time to the sick and needy. I decided to not be one of the noble women that flaunted my latest fashion or snubbed my nose at the lower class people. I watched how hard they worked. I worked in affiliation with the church, assisting the poor. Leone had been there as part of the donation effort, always helping. I thought him to be very kind—and very lonely for his age. I never knew why he helped so much and never looked at the ladies in court. He was so handsome. He turned many an eye." She smiled at me. "My family and I fled the city when the bubonic plague hit. After the initial round had cut through the Italian countryside, my family returned to our manor. We had a lot of cleanup to do. Many dead were littering the roadways, others dying where they lay. In that time, there were so many dead, no one cleaned up the bodies."

I had an idea of how that looked from my dream.

She continued, "Somehow, I contracted the disease. I took ill in no time. As soon as I figured it out I ran from my house, leaving only a note. My husband was devastated. He never remarried—it might have made it easier for me."

Her eyes had glazed over as she spoke. She looked down at her hands then continued, "Leone found me in the woods. He told me I was kind, and the world would be a better place if someone like me could continue to exist. He explained he could help me overcome the sickness. I told him yes and... he changed me." She rolled up her sleeve to show me the old scar on the front of her arm. "Vampires can become different if they drink tainted blood, so he apologized that he did nothing but bite me."

"Different?"

"Yes, disfigured actually. It is how diseases of humans act on the body of the vampire," she explained to me. "I don't understand the process completely, but it takes less time to transform if most of the body's blood is drained first. Of course, I later found out he never did that anyway. True to his word, that man. He has never killed a human by drinking their blood."

She turned then and opened the glass case that held the pyxides. She grabbed the can shaped container from the top shelf with the light blue and dark blue fleur-de-lis pattern surrounding it. The vessel fit in one hand. She passed it to me.

"This belonged to you," she said.

I stepped back and inhaled deeply. "Me?"

"Yes." A twinkle lit her eyes. "Leone bought it for you when you were first married. He bought for himself from the same vendor. They look similar." She pointed to the one left on the shelf with the light blue pattern, the "IHS" flag in the decoration. "He said you loved dark blue, so he tied it with a dark blue ribbon to hang from your waist."

I looked at it. *I owned this. My hands touched this before, when it had been new. I used it daily. In a life I shared with Leone, both of us young and innocent.* I opened the lid. Inside were some old, odd-looking, circular, metal pieces. A face, of sorts, raised on each, reminding me of the profile on the American nickel, except the head resembled a bald man with olive leaves crowned atop. The coins were cool and heavy. They were as large as silver dollars, but not perfectly round and crudely made compared to modern day coins. The words engraved were in a foreign language.

"That is money from 800 AD. The money you carried at the time of your death," she explained.

I wanted to drop them. *Cursed? Could they hurt me?* "Silly, Rhi." I chided myself. Still, staring at them, I couldn't help but imagine what I had intended to buy and why. *Do they look the same in my hand now, as they would have back then? They don't feel powerful and wealthy to me—they feel ancient and lost.*

It felt surreal to be talking about my death in an age so long passed I could not fathom. *How does this work? How many other people have reconnected with themselves like this from somewhere in the past?*

I fumbled to put them back and shoved the pyxide toward Nohi. I wiped my hand on my pants, hoping to remove death from me. My mouth remained agape as I watched her put it back on the shelf.

"This belonged to Leone as well." Lauriel pointed to the Cuir Bouilli, the leather document container with the three chambers. "It still holds documents intended for the Pope himself. They were important, but never made it." Nohi and Lauriel exchanged glances.

Unbelievable. The Pope? My jaw must have flung open like a trap door, again.

Lauriel laughed at me. "These are also his." She pointed to the paintings around the room. "Originals actually. He has, over time, been asked to sell them. But they remind him of you, and no amount of money is worth losing them."

I studied the paintings along the wall and found myself walking into his hallway, running my hand down the books. Lauriel turned the light switch on and the lamp glowed. I pulled out one of the books. A history book. I snickered and put it back. I should have guessed the topic.

I glanced down all of the books to the table in the corner. I noticed the wooden box with the dark blue ribbon. I walked toward it, curious, when Nohi called from the other room.

"Do you ladies want to paint toes and fingers, and watch sappy movies?"

Lauriel dashed out of the room.

I knew I wanted to join them, but I also wanted to look at more of the things they had collected. What items had my hands touched over the centuries? Which ones had been in my possession or changed any of the moments that had been part of another life?

I looked at Lauriel. She appeared anxious to start our evening—looking toward the kitchen and back to me as she hovered in the doorway.

I glanced around at the books in this corridor. I decided I would wait to investigate the only item that piqued my curiosity in the room. I made a note to look at the wooden box sitting on the table, then turned and walked toward the kitchen. I'd never had a pampering night.

We watched old movies and painted our toenails. Nohi made me dinner and popcorn. I told her not to worry about it and that I would be fine, but she explained she has always loved to cook and now had an excuse to do just that.

I was the first, and the only, to fall asleep.

Next morning, the hunters returned home.

Naomi ran about excitedly, bouncing off the walls. Dante beamed with pride. "She brought her first deer down, all by herself," he said.

Naomi clapped for herself, smiling at everyone.

"Great job, Naomi," Nohi said.

Leone paced behind Dante and Naomi. Tobi stood close to him, watching. Leone's fingers were on his lips, and he stared at the floor, his other arm crossed his chest. He moved to Lauriel and pulled her aside. He whispered to her.

She jumped back. Her pupils dilating, she reached her hand to his shoulder. She said something to him, then put her hand over her mouth when he responded by nodding his head in a "yes" motion.

I eased closer to them and heard Lauriel say, "He was here?" as she pointed to the ground.

Leone nodded to her again.

Who is she talking about? A chill slithered up my back. I didn't want to know the answer, yet knew I could not deny it.

"Yes, he just watched from what we could tell," Leone continued in a whispered tone.

When he met my gaze, he rushed to my side. He reached out his hand.

I shook my head 'no' at him. I definitely did not want to have another meeting with my stalker. I finally felt safe enough to enjoy myself. Would I be cheated out of my freedom, and locked back inside my worries and fears?

"Rhi, we need to be very careful. I will not allow anything to happen to you!" He stated it expecting I would argue with him. I had no intention of bickering. I just knew stalker-boy had already managed to get close to me with all of Leone's family watching out for me. I knew Leone would do everything he could to protect me. But how could any of us be more careful than we were being now? Aside from using the restroom, no one allowed me to leave their side.

The news led me back into my black mood. My normally cheery disposition drained, and a zombie-like personality reappeared. I knew if I noticed my mood transformation, it had probably become unbearable to everyone else.

Lauriel took me home. I wanted to be with my parents more than anything. Once my nightmare-to-be had decided to make his presence known, I wanted to hover at home until I had to leave for school on Monday morning. Leone promised me my parents would have someone watching them continually. Wherever they would be going during their work days, one of the Ghiovanies would not be far behind.

That Monday, Amy and I were to complete our math lab. Both of us were required to work on it for a completed score. She didn't show up for school. In two days, we would be dismissed for Thanksgiving break. The assignment counted for a large portion of our grades. I grew angry with her as I sat in class—the time slowly ticking away. I looked to the door, hoping she would slip in late. I knew the teacher would call on our group because our assignment hadn't shown up on his desk. I crossed my arms and sat back in my chair.

Just as I feared, the teacher called me up front. I explained that my partner wasn't in school and she had the assignment. He screwed up his face in a "heard that before" grimace and told me we would get a lowered grade for being late. I nodded as I exhaled and turned to go sit down.

I needed to keep my grade up in class. I worked hard on my grades, not that I bragged about them. I wanted options after high school, not flipping hamburgers for the rest of my life.

I didn't know Amy's number. I wished to myself that she'd chosen to show up and turn in our work before the holiday.

I dropped Carlee off after school that day. Lauriel walked into my house with me. Leone and she would take turns keeping me after school so my parents didn't get the impression we were addicted to each other in some warped obsession. At least, not in the way they would think.

I placed my books down on the kitchen counter. I saw the note. It hadn't been there when I finished the class earlier in the day. Wedged in the tight pages of my history book sat a pale piece of paper with writing bleeding through it. I had no idea what to expect. *Did Leone write me a note? What did he want now?*

I opened it.

'Amy is alive.'

What? I took a quick breath. I didn't recognize the writing. I jerked my head up to where Lauriel sat to see if she'd noticed. She was thumbing through her book. *Is this a joke?* This had to be somebody's sick humor. Even as I asked myself, my hands began to tremble. I reread the words.

'Amy is alive, but only for a short while. It is you I want. If you divulge this letter to anyone, you have sealed her fate.

Be wary. Do not tell a soul of this letter. You must come alone and leave no trail.

You are the only one that can save her. When you can break away, you will find your next instruction located behind the shed at your home, under an old milk container.

281

Stick to the directions. If you are followed, your parents will be next.'

My parents? I stared at the words on the page. *My parents.* For the first time, the danger to them slapped me in the face.

The fear of losing one of them had started with my father's near fatal accident. I had already faced the idea of living without a parent. I knew full well that I did not want to relive anything like that. I shook my head 'no' and felt my eyes sting as they threatened to fill up.

I folded the paper, realizing I needed to keep myself in check. I turned to the sink and grabbed a glass. I started the water running and acted like I needed to get a drink as I blinked repeatedly, trying to make the tears go away.

He had Amy, and my parents were now in direct danger. I couldn't get the thought to leave me. I sipped some of the water and put the glass down.

I glanced at Lauriel. She continued to flip through her book. She seemed unaware. I needed to think. My thoughts scattered.

What would I do if my parents... I needed to not think about it. I know his strength. He climbed that cliff with me. He'd threatened to drown me. I thought about his red eyes. I shuddered and let my lids slip closed. *What can I do? Amy must be horrified.*

"Everything alright?" Lauriel asked.

"Ya, I just had a moment of remembering the cliff."

The way Lauriel looked at me, I knew I needed to explain some of the anxiety I felt. It had probably imprinted itself into my face.

"I have a headache." I reached for my forehead.

She stood up from the table. "I'll get you something."

As she walked toward the bathroom, she asked, "Is it in the medicine cabinet?"

I nodded.

I tucked the note back in my book.

Lauriel turned the corner to the kitchen with a bottle in her hand.

"Are you sure you're okay?" She tipped the bottle and shook out two white pills. "I can hear your heart booming like thunder."

Darn it. I hate how my bodily functions gave me away to the Ghiovanies.

"Yes." I racked my brain for an explanation that would assist me. "I'm frustrated that my math assignment is going to be late."

"Huh," she said, rocking back on her foot with her arms crossed. I couldn't tell if she believed me or just wanted more explanation.

I closed my eyes and focused on my thoughts. *What are my options? I could turn the note in. It will be easy for me. The police can save her. Right? That's the right thing to do in the movies, but movies deal with mortals.*

My stalker will know. I thought about his strong grip, how he lifted me off the ground in his hands. I reached up and ran my fingers on my upper arm without thinking about it. *He doesn't sleep. He will be watching my every move. This is beyond anything a human can do to save her. They'll mess up, thinking they are dealing with a man. They'll surely underestimate him. He will kill Amy.*

I stood still. I could not even feel the air around me. I felt myself sway. *Kill her. I can't let it happen.* My eyes threatened to betray me again. I felt ashamed of my human ability to cry when emotions got the best of me. I grabbed the counter and turned toward the sink before opening my eyes. I pushed the handle up and scooped a large amount of water in my hands and plunged my face into it.

I felt Lauriel's hand on my back at the same moment the chill touched my skin. I welcomed the sensation. I wiped my eyes as I released the handful. I scooped up another and repeated my action.

Lauriel handed me a towel.

"What's up, Rhi?" Her voice light and airy.

"Just overwhelmed I guess." It wasn't exactly a lie.

She patted my back.

I had my face buried in the towel. "What if he gets my parents?"

I started to cry.

Argh! Stupid tears! I cried into the towel for a moment. Lauriel wrapped her arm around my shoulder.

"We'll not let that happen." She tried to assure me. "No way."

I lowered my towel and wiped my eyes. I nodded at her.

She walked back to the table and flashed me an uneasy smile as she sat down.

But I knew, I knew they had already missed his tactics. I knew he had already counted coup against them. *Maybe if they surprised him... Leone's family might be able to locate him. They can trace his scent, surround him, and rescue her.*

Lauriel looked back at her book.

I opened mine to the note, concealing it from Lauriel.

'If you are followed, your parents will be next.'

My options dissolved in my mind. My knees grew weak. I studied the pen marks. I noticed where the force of the writing had gouged the paper. The letters themselves seemed rounded and bulging with anger. *What if the Ghiovanies failed again?*

If I gave myself, he would leave my parents alone. He would set Amy free.

> It is you I want. If you divulge this letter to anyone,
> you have sealed her fate.

I decided on my plan. In order to save the people I loved, I needed to sacrifice myself. My stomach felt it had bottomed out. An empty pit inside threatened to engulf me. *Is this how becoming nothing feels?* I swallowed and straightened on shaking legs. I knew what I had to do, and I would do it to the best of my ability.

The worst thing that could happen would be my death. I watched as my quaking hands closed the book with the note inside.

I know now that my life will repeat again if anything happens. I swallowed though my throat felt like the Sahara.

Amy didn't have that luxury. If he killed her, that was it.

My parents would be destined to the same fate.

No, just me, I am the only one that needs to die. Leone will have to go through the hard task of finding me again, then helping me remember. He will never forgive himself for losing me this time.

My heart broke just thinking about Leone crying over my body the first time. I remembered his words as he explained, burying me with great care and not letting the undertakers throw dirt on my body.

The prostrate stance I had taken melted. My body slumped down until I lay on the counter top with my head on my hands.

The fact was a lot of people would be devastated by my sacrifice.

Maybe I have time to think about it. Yet, I knew the problem with "thinking about it". When it was something as large as this, it doesn't really sort itself out, it just prolongs the inevitable.

I drug myself from the kitchen without looking at Lauriel. I plopped on the couch and pulled my feet in. I hugged my knees and sank into the cushions.

My mind rattled like a rusty cage. Nothing connected into a delineated answer that would solve everything. Every thought concluded with pain for someone, and they all had long term effects. Amy's kidnapping would change everyone's lives, no matter what path I chose. He left it to me to bear the weight of the decision.

Lauriel sat down on the couch and put her hand on my foot. She sat in silence with me.

Leone sat in my room that night, running his finger along the side of my face.

I hoarded every second of his touch. I had reconciled with myself as I sat with my parents at dinner. I would not allow physical harm to come to anyone because of me. I figured it to be the worst of all the evils I had to choose from. They would only have to live with the emotional pain of my loss. It will grow easier as time passes, just like losing Grandma two years ago.

I would allow this last memory of his touch to be what I focus on in the coming days. I did not want to imagine what horrors I would encounter. I needed to focus only on making myself available and rescuing Amy.

Even as I lay there, trying to grow a hero inside myself, feeding her courage and big words, fear and doubt plagued me.

Will I turn out to be a coward in the critical moment? Will I succumb to the terror my human mind could not fathom? In the final hour, will I betray myself as the simple, selfish creature I have always denied myself being? Could I possibly choose to let Amy die just so my eyes can rest upon Leone's again? Is it conceivable that, that person exists inside me? I shuddered at the thought. *Who is the real Rhiannon?*

I felt Leone lean forward. His lips, soft and dewy, kissed my forehead.

I can tell him. I need to talk to someone. I feel like I'm going to explode, the words could burst from me at any moment. Just to have someone else's opinion on the matter could help me settle something in my mind.

I turned my head on my pillow toward him.

I looked at his blue sweater, then to his eyes. I noticed the sweater accented the deeper blue around his iris. I could not steal my gaze back, as incredible as they were.

"Penny for those thoughts," he whispered to me.

My thoughts. I closed my eyes and turned my head back to the pillow.

"I'm going to give myself up. I am going to save Amy. She is being held captive by a maniac and she has no idea what she is up against. I really want to talk with you about my choices..." *No.* Not even a treasured penny from Leone could rip them from me. The words died on my lips as I thought about the faces he would make, and how he would jump off my bed, storming about in an effort to assert himself as the one who would stop this unacceptable event.

I knew the situation would then escalate into a vampire tracking party that would get Amy killed, only because my mouth was too weak to conceal the truth.

No. I need to be firm in my resolve to sacrifice myself.

"Just tired and thinking about my parents," I told him.

I had no idea how long I had to save Amy. I figured I should follow the direction on the note. I knew she'd been gone for days now. The last time I'd seen her was the week before. We'd worked on our math.

I had no idea how I would sneak away from Leone or his family. I would have to keep myself aware of any opportunity to slip off by myself.

The next morning it was my turn to drive us to school. Leone sneaked out my window and waited for me like normal. He walked around the house to make sure all would be safe. Lauriel would be driving his truck to meet us this morning like so many times before. He would run and meet her up the road where they would strategically switch places, acting as if he'd been the driver all the way from his house. He would then park his truck in my driveway and let me drive us all to school.

I heard his truck down the road and looked out the window. He blew me a kiss and ran into the trees on his way to the road to meet it.

I wished he wouldn't disappear from my sight. A longing crept into my heart. I knew what I needed to try and do today, and I missed him already. I thought for a second that I should have allowed him to carry this burden for me, like he had done so many times before.

I exhaled and walked out to my car. As I climbed in, I glanced down and noticed another note folded and wedged around the bottom of the steering wheel, same color as the last one. I pushed myself back into my seat, trying to ignore it.

I sucked in a breath and looked around. Leone did not seem at all on edge this morning before he dashed into the trees, as if he'd picked up on a scent.

Is he still in my car? I gulped. I didn't want to turn around. My body felt like mush. I closed my eyes tight. I breathed in and out then turned to peer into the backseat. *Nothing.* I eased back into my seat.

My hands shook. I fumbled for the note. It felt icy in my hands.

I unfolded it as I heard the gears in Leone's car kick in. I assumed he had climbed in behind the wheel as it started toward my house. It still seemed faint enough that I figured I had a few seconds to read it.

> The time is now. Go behind your garage. Your first
> instruction is on a paper under the large milk
> container.

I looked out the passenger side window—Leone's truck was not in view.

I raced to the back of the garage, opposite the house. Three large milk containers lined the back wall, among old boards and disintegrating boxes. I pushed the first one aside, nothing. Shoot, I knew Leone would panic if he noticed I wasn't in my car. The second one held the note. I grabbed it, noticing my white plume of breath lingering on the air. I needed to hurry.

The groan of the engine indicated its incline to the top of the driveway. Would he see me walking from behind the garage?

I shoved the notes in my pocket as I ran back around the front of the garage. I knew I had to read it, but I couldn't risk Leone seeing it in my hand. How much time did I have before it would be too late for Amy?

I saw the grill rise above the edge of the road, and I could see his face in the driver's seat. He scowled at me, eyes squinting, lips pursed.

He parked and jumped out, walking straight toward me. I kept the course to my car and looked down at the ground. I knew I'd been discovered, deviating from our plan.

"What were you doing?" he asserted. When I looked up, he was scanning the area.

"I thought I heard a kitten behind the garage." I was a horrible liar. The way the words blurted out I knew this was no exception. *Hold your ground, Rhi. Although... if he gets the information out of me, I will no longer have to take responsibility for it.* The idea made the sickened feeling in my bowels lighten.

"A kitten," he spat, arching an eye brow and crossing his arms.

"Ya, it disappeared when I went to look. I must have scared it." I knew I couldn't hold his gaze with that lame excuse. I jerked toward Lauriel to break the conversation. "Ready?"

Leone grabbed my arm. I looked into his eyes inadvertently. The very thing I needed to avoid.

"Rhiannon, my love."

I pleaded in my head, Oh please don't make me melt right now. I want to cry in your arms and have you tell me everything is just fine. Please let me be cold and firm. I have to keep going.

He looked at me. His head tilted to the side, his eyes steely enough to pierce through me. A slight smile played at the corner of his mouth. He said nothing, just continued to look into my eyes. The silence told me he knew I'd lied to him. I felt like a child. I broke eye contact and looked at his shirt.

I turned and jumped in the driver's seat.

Lauriel had been standing and watching the exchange between Leone and me. She focused on Leone, knowing he would tell her what had happened.

Without a word, Leone climbed in the back behind the driver's seat. I found it odd, because he always sat in front with me when I drove.

Lauriel must have found the situation different as well, she shrugged her arms before opening the passenger door.

As she sat down, I realized I wouldn't have to interact with Leone in the front seat. I could make it to Carlee's house and then to school without answering his questioning eyes. I felt relief over that simple fact, until I glanced in the rearview mirror.

Leone's pupils had grown big. I gulped. They were transitioning to black as the sun's rays began their first brightening of the sky. I knew he intended to continue this conversation.

"Lauriel." He spoke, not taking his eyes from me. I looked down as I put my car in drive and started turning toward the driveway from the parking place, much faster than normal.

She grabbed the window with her hand to steady herself as rocks sprayed from under my tires.

She made a screwed up face as she looked at me, then to Leone.

"It seems our dearest, Rhi, decided to chase kittens this morning." He continued.

She looked back at me.

"Where were you looking for them again?" His tone indignant as he prodded for the answer he knew was bogus.

I rolled my eyes. "Behind the garage."

"Rhi." Lauriel exhaled.

"Exactly." Leone matched her emotion. "It seems that she thinks she can just walk around and fend for herself."

I turned onto the main road.

I hate being the weak link. I felt my jaw tighten. I pushed my foot down on the pedal. The car raced over the loose gravel. I just needed to get to Carlee's house. I knew they wouldn't talk about this in front of her.

"I know you are well aware of the danger." He continued to focus on my eyes in the mirror.

He just won't stop.

"Yes, I know the danger. I feel the danger. It follows me to the bathroom now." I referred to the privacy I no longer had. "Danger is in my dreams, and at my dinner table, and at my desk at school, and in my car as I drive." To emphasize my frustration, I swerved the steering wheel, sending the car into a fishtail.

My other hand flew to the wheel as I tried to correct my error. Lauriel's hand grabbed the wheel, as she directed the tires, she down shifted with her other hand. The engine growled its dislike as the RPM shot up on the gauge.

I pulled my foot off the pedal, pitching forward as the speed promptly decelerated. The car quit skidding sideways, and I put my foot on the brake.

Out of all of us in the car, I would have been the only one injured if it ended in an accident. My heart rate rolled like a drum solo at a rock concert, and sitting there motionless, I could hear my breath rapidly matching my heart's tempo .

I looked at Lauriel. She had sucked in her lower lip as she pulled her hand to my shoulder. The look in her eye told me she wanted to ask questions about my mental state.

I thought to myself. Don't go there, please.

I looked at Leone through the rearview mirror. His face had grown even sterner, a look I didn't think possible. He said nothing.

Praying he would remain silent until we picked up Carlee, I pulled my foot off the brake and eased it onto the gas pedal. I didn't want another reckless episode in the car.

We drove in silence to Carlee's house.

Carlee bubbled on about the four hour phone call with Heath the night before. She hit the high points, which I honestly could not remember as soon as she said them. She kept repeating that he told her he loved her. Now her world, as she put it, was perfect. She just knew every day from now on would be a fairy-book romance. I found myself thinking how great for her to be living more than I ever would. To be enjoying a love in her heart and beaming over it. Actually she oozed it. It made me sick. Such a contrast to the way my day would go. I would ultimately end up in the worst place my mind could imagine.

I glanced from time to time in my rearview mirror. Leone seemed to be made of stone. His expression never changed, except for the sunglasses he had slipped on for the sake of Carlee. I finally gave up and flipped the mirror to where I could not see him.

Everyone grouped together in the cafeteria. At first I wondered why they all stood so close together, crammed in, standing room only. I realized I hadn't noticed the chill in the air that morning. I supposed I was numb to it.

"Isn't that right, Rhi?" Carlee tried to get my agreement.

I looked at her, trying to remember the conversation that I was obviously supposed to have a part in.

"Rhiannon, come on, you haven't forgotten, have you?" She rolled her eyes at me with a smile on her face.

"I, uh." I tried to recollect any tidbit from our dramatic one-sided dialogue that would clue me in.

She waved a hand at me and started talking to the four ladies that walked up to us. I had trouble focusing on other chat as well.

I have to read the note. It might as well have been burning my pocket, as focused as I was on it. My hand itched to dig it out right there. I didn't know how long he would give me before he did something to Amy.

"I'm going to use the restroom," I whispered to Lauriel.

I made it into the stall, pulled the note from my pocket, and unrolled it before I heard the door. I smelled fruity perfume and knew she had, unsurprisingly, followed me.

'Your next note will be attached to a sunken rope at the dock where you almost drowned. Funny story, though Amy did not know too many of the details. The rope is red.'

My hands dropped to my side as I stared at the blue stall door. I hadn't gone back to that dock on purpose. Why had he chosen that dock? I had to admit, it fit into the anomalous events that I believed he desired to make me face that day. I stared up at the ceiling. *I want to be invisible and nonexistent. I don't know if I can do it.* I sank down onto the toilet seat and began to rock back and forth. It seemed my horror had just started, either I would let my acquaintance die or I would offer myself up.

Somehow, between third and fourth periods, I escaped.

I overheard a conversation as I stood at my locker. Someone had just lost a close cousin to a car accident. She talked about how everyone talked about her relative at her funeral, making everyone cry. Her mother had stood up and explained that her daughter would have wanted everyone to remember her as a caring, loving person and not to cry for her.

Those words stabbed me. I visualized Amy's funeral. People crying, parents devastated, all because I had been a coward.

Lauriel turned long enough for me to slip into the disorder of students in the hall.

Before I could talk myself out of it, I raced to the exit. I felt in my pocket, thankful I slipped my keys into it instead of my locker that morning.

What am I doing?

I just needed to get to my car. I kept looking over my shoulder, sure I would be caught by Leone. *If I can just drive away, I will be able to sort out the details of my plan. Do I have a plan?*

I knew as soon as Leone noticed I disappeared, he would be hot on my heels.

I drove as fast as I could. I skidded along the back roads, looking over my shoulder. I'd been so focused on watching my tail, I hadn't realized I had driven all the way to the dock at the lake, next to my house.

I stopped the car when I saw the water. I didn't intend to make it all the way here. I wanted to stop and think. I trembled at the sight of the dock. The morning mist rose from the water, the sun burning through it. The view looked more ominous that I remembered.

I slowly edged my car forward and put it in park close to the dock.

As soon as I stepped out, I searched the bushes and trees. At any moment, I knew the awful man with angry, red eyes would jump out. I coaxed my feet, willing them to step onto the dock. I needed to hurry, but my body did not want to move.

My mind flashed to the darkness under the water. My eyes shot to the tree stump sticking out of the water. My hands reached for my chest. *Can I go through with it?* I heard my blood pulsing in my ears. I swallowed, trying to relieve myself of the familiar bile taste in my throat and the memory of the burning in my lungs.

Still not sure if I would complete what I had now started, I knew for sure I wanted to leave this place. I scanned the edges of the dock. I couldn't see a rope. I would have to walk on the dock. I looked up at the sky and shuffled from foot to foot attempting to gain my courage.

I looked down at my blue sneaker and watched as I lifted it, taking the first step onto the dock. With each step, it got easier.

I stayed to the middle. Hoping the rope would come into view. I scanned for anything red. He made me walk to the very end of the dock.

"I hate you," I spat at him, hoping he was not in the area to hear me.

I kneeled down, back from the edge so as not to fall in. I leaned forward and grabbed the rope and began pulling it up. It seemed long. I looked around again to make sure no one snuck out of the woods. Still alone, I focused on retrieving it.

The anchor didn't seem very heavy. When I finally reached the end, I could see a shoe tied to it, filled with sand. The note, in a watertight bag, had been tied to one of the shoe laces. I struggled to untie the shoe from the red rope. Sand flipped all over me and the dock, and wedged itself under my fingernails. The fish- smelling water doused my pants.

I ran back to the car.

My breaths rapidly puffed my cheeks.

I dropped the shoe and the note as I tried to separate the two. Sand dropped onto the seat and the console.

"Dang it."

I ripped the plastic bag and threw the shoe onto the passenger floorboard.

I decided I needed to get moving before Leone caught up with me. I knew it would be best to avoid the roads I would normally be traveling. I turned onto the main road, away from my house and town. It ran around the southern end of the reservoir, adding an hour at least, to my drive, if the note told me to go somewhere in Donnelly.

As I drove the washboard road, I unfolded the paper with one hand.

> 'Do you want to see her? Don't get caught.
> I left you a memento, her shoe. Something to remember her by incase you decide to turn around and run.
> Think on this. You know what I am capable of. You know I am unstoppable. Make your choice and make it wise. I will not stop with Amy. I will get you. It is only a matter of when, and how many lives you choose to play with.'

I gulped. I knew, too well, that hundreds of lives had been lost over the years because of me. I looked up to the road and corrected my trajectory before I careened into the culvert. *He will not stop until he has me. I cannot let him harm anyone.* I read on.

> 'Your next note will be at the Donnelly gas station.
> Look for it at the end of the patio, tucked under the edge, closest to the road.'

I gave myself too much time to think as I made the long loop around the lake. I easily talked myself out of being the hero. I had enough notes now that I could turn them over to the police. The police would track it from the gas station. They would find Amy. She would be alright.

I thought about my unsuspecting and innocent parents. What a disaster I have them in. They would be next.

I hit the steering wheel with my hand.

No more people, Rhi!

When I arrived at the gas station, the same one I first saw Leone in earlier in the summer, I looked around.

A large white SUV sat at the gas pumps. The guy leaned on his truck with his hand and watched me as I approached the building. Another car waited at the other pump, the owner still sat inside. People in a group were talking as they walked toward the front door. Early morning travelers no doubt, getting coffee, gas, or snacks for the long stretch of road. I felt as obvious as a clown at a funeral, my intensions so unlike everyone else's. Surely they would notice me kneeling at the end of the patio, searching under it. I did it anyway.

Some, indeed, looked my way. Most went back to what they were doing. A couple of them decided I acted weird enough to warrant a stare.

Wrappers, empty soda cans, and loose change resided in the dark space. It didn't seem anyone ever cleaned. I pulled out a few pieces of wadded up paper. They were unlined and white, not like the faint yellow paper used with the other notes. When I selected one that looked folded, not crinkled, I opened it. The same arcing letters and deeply gouged paper affirmed the correct match before I even read it. I raced to my car.

I drove down the road a bit and pulled over, trying to get away from the curious looks.

Studying the note, it seemed to be taking me away from Donnelly.

I had to follow directions, marking off 3.5 miles on my odometer then turning left. As I approached, I could see an old dirt road. Old enough that it didn't have a green sign with a name, like most of the others. *Where is he directing me?*

The note instructed me to drive twenty-six miles on this road. I had to travel it slow, the rhythmic upheavals in the road made every loose object in the car bounce. It sounded like noise, no rhyme or reason. It complemented the chaos in my mind, screaming at me to turn back.

I glanced behind me and noticed the dust billowing across the road. No breeze swept it away. It effectively cloaked me from the main road, until I disappeared into the tree line at the base of the mountain.

My next instruction had me turning north on a road that paralleled the base of the mountain. As unmarked and uninhabited as the roads were, I hoped my choices were correct. I needed to drive fifty miles in this direction.

The mountains were beautiful, but I did not want to notice it. It threatened to find a place inside me that would allow me to find peace. The only thing I could harmonize with, at that moment, was something ugly and dark.

As I climbed higher, the view back across the valley became clearer over the tops of the trees. Just as the road I traveled started to descend toward the base of the mountain again, my directions made me turn right. The new road was a switchback that climbed steeper, back in the direction I had just driven. From the looks of it, the road hadn't been repaired in a long time. My car slid to the downward side of the hill more than once. My knuckles grew white as I clung tighter to the wheel.

I slowed even more, creeping only enough to move me forward, the tires growling for a grip on the pebbled dirt.

I stopped breathing over the huge gully that cut itself deep into the road bed, from water running down the side of the mountain. It appeared large enough to me that my entire car could fit in it. As the front of my car dipped into it, one side at a time, it seemed my vehicle would tip and begin its roll to the bottom of the hill.

I screamed and threw my foot on the brake. The frame of the car groaned, an ominous sound, as it came to rest haphazardly on both sides of the uneven crevasse. I moaned with my uneven breathing as I tried to gain composure. Although my heavy machine slid slightly to the side, it seemed to be settled at the moment. I did not want to back up or turn the wheels the wrong direction. The precarious position told me I rested on a thin line between successfully getting out of the pickle I found myself in and high-centering the rig— ultimately tipping down the hill.

298

I reached for the gear shift and slid it into high. I quickly let my foot off the brake and applied enough gas to keep me in the same spot. I could see more dirt over the driver's side hood and knew I needed to drive that side of the car up it. My traction would have to hold.

I had been in the cab with Dad on roads like this, of course he was driving. As he completed the assent, I would panic to myself, thinking the dirt would slap my side of the vehicle first when we spun. He would always seem to know what my sharp intake of breath meant, because he would laugh at me and tell me roads like this always looks worse in the cab. I prayed this new situation would be the same.

The engine groaned, trying to pull the weight up the incline. When the tires spun out, the car jolted, sending waves of white hot dread down every limb. The view out the passenger side window indicated the slope on the other side of the car had been too steep to grow grasses and trees. The only things visible were the tops of the trees rooted to the ground far below, and the valley and mountains in the distance.

I focused straight ahead. I could not go in reverse.

"Please, hold, come on, hold," I pleaded with the traction. "Don't fail me. Let's go now."

The car inched slowly upward, tipping sideways evermore. My body trembled so hard I feared my joints would fly apart.

It slipped a few more times before my automobile successfully breached the top of the washed out road. I drove until I reached the top of the mountain, ready to descend the other side.

I jumped out and ambled around, trying to shake off my rubbery muscles. I quickly looked back the way I had come and shook my head. It didn't look so bad from here, but I knew better. I looked across the other side of the hill. It seemed to be a slower decent, and I hoped it would be easier to travel. I doubted I would be able to successfully make my way back on this road.

The sun shifted to the other half of the sky when I started to descend the other side of the mountain. I drove a while longer before the note instructed me to park my car in an abandoned, overgrown campsite.

The air had a definite nip to it, but the sun—and my nervous disposition—kept me warm.

For the next leg of the journey, the note told me to walk the path. I left the comfort of my car. Out the windshield to the thick forest, I could see the walking path originate from the campsite and drop down the hill between the trees.

What if I run into wild animals or hurt myself? I have nothing with me. I searched my car for anything I could take to protect myself. I grabbed my phone and turned it off. I figured I could hide it until I knew my final destination. Other than my phone, I had nothing in the car.

I opened the glove compartment. Tucked along side the road map and insurance document lay a small flashlight that my dad stashed for emergencies. *I love you, dad.* The thought of him made me want to cry. I remembered back to one of the many occasions when he told me he believed in me, and that I could do anything. I knew a situation like this would never have crossed his mind. Would he be proud of me for trying to save Amy? I looked out the window again as I pondered.

He would probably find some way to rectify my decision, that's how much he loved me. I gripped the flashlight tighter and decided I'd better make myself get out of the car before I talked myself into driving off. I touched the keys still hanging in the ignition. *Do I need them?*

I decided to leave them. If someone happened upon the car they would be suspicious if the keys were left in the ignition. I hoped they would assume someone walked into the forest and did not come back.

The trail had become slightly overgrown with vegetation. I traveled it, looking for the clearing the instructions talked about. I walked deeper and deeper into the dense, never-ending thicket—up and down hills. I thought my hike would never end.

I broke into the clearing at dusk.

I noticed a large, black blindfold hanging in a tree. The message instructed me to wait until dark, then put it on and sit and wait. He would not come until I did everything he asked. I read the passage as I walked. The moment I stepped into the meadow the gravity of the situation hit me. I peered into the darkened shadows of the undergrowth. *Is he watching me now? I am alone. I followed the instructions.* I stood perfectly alone in the rough field. Come full dark, I would not need the blindfold—I would be engulfed in isolation.

I trembled. *What on earth am I doing here? Do I have enough time to retrace my steps?* He has to be close, probably closer than I am to my car.

I imagined the shadows creeping toward me I envisioned the sounds that would come alive and besiege me. I turned and sprinted to the path I had just been on. I raced, hoping to get to my car before I lost all daylight.

I could hear Amy's voice, from some hidden resource in my mind. The way she trilled her words as she told me the name of her favorite song—my favorite song. She liked some of the same things as me. She could be me. How would I like to be in her position? I was the only one who knew how to get to her.

My feet stopped as I headed down the path that would lead me to my car. I longed to be inside it with my doors locked and the warmth pumping from my heater. I took a few steps in the direction of that comfort.

"I am Amy's only hope."

I bent from my waist and placed my hands on my knees. Absentmindedly, I watched a stink bug meandering along the path. I stood, closing my eyes in frustration at the decision I knew I had to make. I turned back in the direction of the deserted, dark meadow.

I trudged slowly back toward it, my feet felt weighted in cement. Amy was important, more important than my fear of facing this event. I knew if the worst thing imaginable happened, I would live again. I would focus on that thought, for Amy.

When I made it to the clearing again, I walked around it. It had grown darker, but I could still see green plants all around. Stink brush smelling like a skunk, yarrow plants, and different species of wild flowers—including lupine, were all starting to wilt with the cold. The thick pine trees surrounding the clearing smelled alive and sharp.

I realized I hadn't seen any wild animals at all throughout the day.

I sat on the rock in the middle of the clearing—thankful I wore my blue jeans. They would help to keep me warm. I rested there for the remainder of daylight. My thoughts were on Amy. Then my family and Leone. I could imagine their frenzy at that moment as they searched for me.

As dark enveloped me, I turned on the flashlight. Something scurried through the brush to my right, small and fast. Crickets started their repetitious droning. Something rustled the tree tops. I stood with my flashlight and shined it upward. I couldn't see anything. I moved the beam to the tree in front of me and edged toward it. I studied the shadows to make sure nothing moved. I grabbed the blindfold and raced back to the stump.

14

Self Sacrifice

Darkness had surrounded me for what seemed an eternity. My flashlight batteries drained. I tapped it, futilely trying to elicit any light from it. Every sound seemed to rush toward me. I found myself jerking left and right, or spinning completely around, expecting to see something unwelcomed ready to attack me, whether it be a bear or a mountain lion or my stalker. After a time, I closed my eyes, realizing it didn't matter if I my eyes were open or not, the ebony vacuum that surrounded me had long ago taken my sight. I fought back tears that would feel so good to release. I'd gotten myself into this, and there was no use crying. Anyway, it would be over soon.

I tucked my flashlight into my pocket. My entire body shook, whether from the bitter cold or my terror of the darkness. With quaking fingers, I fumbled to place the blindfold over my eyes. There would be no way to see light through it, even if there were any.

The full force of my decision weighed on me. How ludicrous for me to actually be wasting time here, awaiting my captor, as if begging him to take me away from my home and my family—my sanity. At barely 18 years old, I had the full responsibility to save Amy's life. I knew if I had gone to the police, they wouldn't have believed the story of the redhead's cunning, strength, and inability to die. They might have believed the note, but the search would ensue in an incredibly wrong direction. It would end in Amy's death.

I took a deep, shuddering breath.

Leone would be devastated. He proclaimed that we made it through my remembering my previous lives' memories faster than ever before. He believed this time things would work out differently.

"Now look at me, alone in the dark, actually waiting to find out when my number will be up." My voice sounded out of place with the ambient noise of the wild.

Leone will be angry with himself. Lauriel, too, would feel betrayed. After all, I sneaked away from her in the hallway.

I guessed my sneaking paid off. Even though I wished to hear Leone's voice right then, screaming for me to answer him through the blackness, nothing reached me.

I listened to the night again. The same sounds repeated—snuffling, swishing, occasional growls, and muted squeaks. It must have been the animals that called this meadow home. The repetition comforted me.

Goose bumps prickled up and down my body. I rubbed my arms and pulled my legs closer to keep warm. I knew it would be cold enough to see my breath. I wished that I'd grabbed my winter coat from my locker before I left school.

My chest tightened. So much darkness surrounding me, it finally slithered like snakes into my hope. the ebony cocoon Designs spiraled in my closed eyes, shooting colors through my vision as I tried to focus on something. The twirling threatened to pull me down into it. I tried to see it, but it seemed to shift, evading me. I needed light. I wanted to see.

Maybe I could turn on my flashlight again. The note had been specific, though. 'I will come when there is absolute darkness and no movement.'

New sounds, scratching and chattering, poked at the edges of my imagination. I tuned into every little sound. I knew some of them were imagined, as intent on hearing as I was. It was probably nothing.

I pulled my feet in closer and hugged my knees.

I sniffled as silent tears wet the blindfold.

My parents would never recover. They would blame themselves and second guess their decision to move.

The news about this incident would resonate nationally, "In a small Idaho town, two teenage girls were taken from their families."

There would be speculation. Were the disappearances connected? Further digging would reveal that we sat next to each other for a time in math class, the only proof that we'd known each other. The abduction would baffle authorities. They would have no idea what they were tracking. I wondered if my stalker would let them find our bodies. Maybe I would beg for that, for my parents' sake.

I rocked on the stump, rubbing my hands together. I needed to concentrate on other things. My body had to maintain against the dark dangers of the night. I didn't know if I could stand anymore. More tears from their resting place. I sniffled and rested my nose on my pants.

I hit my leg with my balled up fist. "Stupid, Rhi. This has to be the dumbest thing you have ever done in all of your lives."

I noticed stillness for the first time. The sounds had stopped. The rustling in the trees and bushes had ceased.

No change in the air around me, no new scent, nothing I could hear. I felt a breath on the nape of my neck. I craned my neck away from it, the hair stood on end. I strained to hear. Nothing.

Yet, something stood behind me. I could sense it. I held my lungs still. I could feel breath again on my neck. I stopped my scream before it could announce my horror to the world, causing my body to quake. I did not know what had crept up so close to me. If it were a wild beast, would it attack when provoked? I felt it again. New goose bumps matched my shaking. I felt my insides releasing, I could puked. I knew for sure he loomed behind me.

A shudder escaped my lips, revealing my cowardice. Tears cascaded from their dam and soaked into the blindfold.

Breath, again on my neck. I could not have been more helpless at that moment if my ankle were stuck in a bear trap. My legs twitched, willing me to run. In the pit of my stomach, a sickness grew. I thought for sure my bowels would loosen, or that I would throw up, just like when I had food poisoning years ago. This time pure anxiety knotted my insides. The stress, stretched tight like a rubber band, threatened to snap— sending pieces of me flying in every direction. The feeling spread through my body, leaving me weak and drained.

I sensed movement without any sound. The skin on the nape of my neck quivered as the pungent warmth of his exhaled air flitted across my cheek. On instinct, I moved my head away slightly. I needed to stand my ground as much as possible. I could not let him know how much fear permeated my being.

Movement again, I heard the brittle grass crunching as weight compressed it into the ground. Bitter air brushed my other cheek. I was prey—and I was in way over my head.

Without a hint of what was to come, my hand was jerked behind my back. My shoulder wrenched, and my unbalanced body threatened to topple off my wooden perch. Then, so quickly, my hand joined the other arm, was coiled backward, and the two were shackled together behind me. The position made them ache. I pulled against the cold metallic cuffs, but they dug deep into the bones of my hands.

A blow caused my body to jerk sideways. I was unable to catch myself. The fall was inevitable. I dropped from the stump, flailing my legs to try to catch myself. I pushed my left shoulder out to lessen the impact on my head. I hit, then rolled onto my side. My shoulder throbbed, but I managed to cushion most of the impact.

Not able to see anything, I pulled my legs up and shoved off the ground with my elbow, hoping I would attain a sitting position. Instead, he pushed me back until I lay on my bound arms and hands. In an instant his weight covered me, crushing the wind from my lungs. My arms felt they would disconnect from my body.

I yelped, arching my back upward to relieve the pain in my hands. My abdomen pushed up into his. I wanted away from him. Even through clothing, this closeness disgusted me. He smelled warm and musty—repulsing me. I hated the feeling in my gut.

"Get off me," I hissed.

Breath on my chin tickled the fine hairs.

"You are very hard to get to, Rhiannon," he punctuated each syllable of my name slowly, savoring the sound. "Leone keeps you well guarded these days. I bided my time, studying you. I know your routine inside and out. Fascinating."

I squirmed, intending to get out from under him. My arms screamed in anguish as the metal cut deeper into the skin—my knuckles grating over the gravel. His weight pushed my shoulders into the ground. I squeezed my eyes tight and bit my lip.

I felt his tongue trace my jaw line, wet and slimy, imitating a garden slug's track. It left a trail of freezing air.

I cried out and dug my feet into the ground to push away from him. I thrashed my head and body, trying to make it hard for him to do anything else.

He chuckled deep and long. Then he stood. The piercing pain in my arms calmed to a dull ache. I rolled to the side and wiggled my hands.

Hard arms grabbed me around my waist. He flipped me over to my belly and hoisted me off the ground. He flung me over his shoulder, like a dead animal— I could hear his pants' legs brushing together near my ears as he moved. Occasional branches scratched at his jeans. Every once in a while, one would hit my face. Then we stopped.

I heard a vehicle door open, and he pushed and prodded me as he stuffed me inside. Then we were driving.

"Where is Amy?" I demanded, controlling my tone.

No reply.

"Where is Amy?" My voice squeaked as it grew louder.

I heard and sensed the acceleration of the vehicle. When we rounded the first corner, I braced myself so as not to tumble to the floor.

"Is Amy still alive?" I needed to know.

The car spun, and the seat slid from under me. My feet hit the door as I bounced, then landed on the floor. Still no response. He slowed down a bit—the motor cut back.

I lay sprawling on the floor. My stomach rested on the hump between the two floorboards of the back seat—my knees wedged into the base of the door. My face was pressed to the carpet that reeked of vomit. I could hear rocks bump the undercarriage of the vehicle. I wiggled to ascertain how I could right myself.

I pulled my knees under me, then braced myself on the seat with my forehead. The blindfold slid off one eye. I catapulted my body onto the seat again and sprawled with my chest toward the back of the seat. I strained to see anything out the window through the darkness. Only the faint glow from the dash-lights outlined the seat above me.

The drive droned on. I fell asleep at some point.

When I awoke, sunlight had diminished the shadows.

I peeked out the window. Where was I? Could I see anything that would tell me my location? Trees, tons of treetops, the sun highlighted their upper branches.

No, nothing was familiar. Nothing but trees—not even a discernable rocky out-crop disrupted the landscape to give me guidance.

The car slowed. I sneakily glimpsed over my shoulder and spied my captor, red-haired and with fury ablaze in his eyes. I could tell through the slits that his eyes were red, his scowl menacing.

He reached his hand into the back seat and jerked the blindfold down over my eyes.

We drove a small distance farther and then stopped. He yanked me from the rig. Although I could feel the warmth of sunlight, the crisp air brought chills to my skin after the heat in the car.

"Even if he tracks your scent as far as the road, it will end there for a while. After I put you in the car, it will be hard to smell." He seemed very proud of himself.

"Take my blindfold off!" I demanded. Where were we?

"Oh, no, my dear. I do not think so—not yet. You will have no idea where you are when we reach where we are going. This next trick I learned from him. It is a very fitting twist really."

He uncuffed one of my hands and slipped something on me. A life jacket. I gasped. With the air temperature outside, he could not possibly send me down stream in the water.

He cuffed my hands together again. I pulled back, shaking my head.

"Please don't cuff me," I pleaded. "I have to be able to move in the water."

He laughed at me. "No, we are not going in the water. We are going on the water." My panic ebbed a little.

He grasped me roughly and dropped me onto a hard metal seat. My feet rested at odd angles that allowed me to imagine the shape of the bottom of the boat.

In seconds I jolted, as the boat seemed to tilt out from under me. I jerked to the side as a fast current caught us. I heard oars moving, thudding hollow against the metal. So we were in a row boat, not a motor boat. The current seemed strong. Waves slapped the side. I didn't think I would be able to stay dry. If we capsized, I would need to paddle in the freezing water, and my hands were bound. Another shock of panic surged through my veins.

"Untie me," I demanded. "This is dangerous. I will die in the water."

The water sloshed on the side of the boat, spraying my face and neck. I shook to get it off. The boat tossed from side to side with the strong current—I used my feet to keep myself upright. I continually corrected my balance by pushing harder on one foot than the other, as the motion of the boat repeatedly shifted.

Then thud, we hit something. I screamed as forward motion ceased, stopped much like a last minute decision to slam on the breaks instead of running a yellow light. My body soared forward, but I caught myself with my feet. The boat began to rotate. I heard the oars and felt a reverse pull as the boat turned and pointed the bow behind me downstream.

The sudden reverse knocked me backward into the cold aluminum bottom of the boat. A little puddle of wet seeped into my jeans and shirt, spreading the cold like tentacles up my hip. My skin felt frozen in ice crystals. My legs, propped on the bench, locked me in place on my side. The space I had fallen into was so small I couldn't pull my knees to me. I lay on one arm, with my head bobbing to the swell of the current. Although he seemed to navigate the water better with the boat pointed in this direction, my head kept hitting the hull. I hoped we wouldn't bash into anything again.

My shivering increased to a teeth chattering level that echoed in my skull.

I felt a long pull that pushed the boat to the right, and then sand rubbed the hull under my head. The oars thudded in the bottom of the boat. I heard his boot knock against the bench I had sat on, and its groan as it took all of his weight. His clothes rustled over the top of me as he jumped out of the boat. As he lifted the bow up, the water receded from under my pants. I felt myself moving, boat and all, farther onto the sand. He seized my aching, cold body and situated me on the ground. Then the familiar sound again of sand scraping on aluminum accosted my hearing.

Did he really push the boat back into the water? "Wait!" I pleaded, "Not the boat!"

I heard the hollow thudding as it hit rocks on its way down stream. *Yes. He had done it alright.*

"The boat," I fumed aloud and wanted so badly to hit him. I reached out with my bound hands, not sure exactly where he stood. "Why did you do that? I can't survive that cold water," My voice stammered.

"Do not worry, you won't need it. When the first snow falls, which will be soon, there will be no trace of you."

I gulped. *No trace as in... no bones, flesh, mind?* Did I want to know the answer to that?

"Where is Amy!" My trembling voice matched my knocking knees.

He did not answer again. Could that mean he had already taken care of her?

I closed my mouth—my body convulsed uncontrollably even though I wished to appear strong. Fear had become my only reality. *I would die, isolated and alone, and probably soon.* Right when I thought my legs were going to buckle under me, he grabbed me and flipped me over his shoulder.

The trail was uphill. His rock-hard shoulder jutted into my gut. I had to take deep breaths and hold them in order to breathe. Each of his strides was like being punched in the stomach. I forced myself to focus on sounds and smells around me.

A waterfall chattered to my right. It sounded small, just a trickle. Then the only sensation for a while was the cold air. I imagined my breath to be noticeable. The temperature could be below zero.

He jumped up on something big and back down. The force knocked the wind, like a lancing flame, out of me. I started kicking to get my breath. He seemed to notice and stopped. He put my feet down on the ground. I struggled for breath—my head felt fuzzy. It took a moment for me to force air into my lungs. It rushed in all at once—forcing me to bent over and gasp a few times.

"I will be sure to jump easier next time." I didn't know if he intended his statement as a lame form of apology or not. Why would he care anyway? He meant to kill me—why not suffocation? Not that I wanted it. Maybe he had some torture in mind. I banished that thought and focused on my feet. He allowed me crouch for a moment while I gained my breath.

I detected that the ground under my feet seemed spongy, as if covered with a moss blanket. I slipped my foot intentionally around, trying to act unstable. There weren't any larger plants here. I stood up and spread my legs wide which he must have interpreted as a gesture for him to carry me again—I blindly analyzed the area, like Braille with my feet. The second before he picked me up again, my foot discovered an abrupt edge, between a ridge of the roots of small bushes and the trodden mossy trail. I hoped I was correct. That was the only evidence I had that might mean we were traveling on a game trail. In that same instance, I was hoisted again over his shoulder.

I heard no sounds for several minutes except the rhythm of our movement, and felt constant burning in my lungs, as I continued to breathe through the jarring of my gut.

I tilted my head when the roar of a larger waterfall materialized to my left.

I stored the information, just in case. I would not be defeated easily by him—he would have to fight to kill me. I needed to make sure Amy still lived. If a chance arose to escape, we would do it together. If Amy was already dead, I would need to find the courage to save myself.

A little farther up the trail he stopped. He rotated toward the direction we had just come, then sidled a few steps. I sensed walls enclosing me—the sound of feet shuffling bounced back at me in quick repetition. After a few steps, he lowered me from his shoulders and maneuvered me forward—forcing me to sit.

The cushion below me felt like a nest of sticks and leaves, dry and hard. Although we were sheltered, the temperature changed very little from the outside. Father Winter hiked with us and decided to stay the night.

I twisted my head from side to side, searching for where he had gone. I heard the snapping sound of wood breaking. Some of it seemed small, other pieces resonated as they were fractured from a large trunk. I heard the sound of someone blowing, like whispered breath aimed at birthday candles. A whooshing followed the unmistakable sound of air being sucked into flames. I yearned to feel the fingers of warmth reach me.

From my right I heard a muffled scream, a panicked realization that someone had arrived.

He crouched by me.

"Talk to her. Let her know she is not alone," he ordered.

"Is it..."

"Yes. I promised she would be alive if you held up your end of the bargain."

I smiled thankfully to myself, in spite of the situation. *She lived.* It meant a great deal at that moment to know I wasn't alone, and that my choice to sacrifice myself had not been in vain. Tears welled up in my eyes.

"Amy?" No answer. I tried again. "Amy. It is Rhiannon, from school. He told me he had you. I'm so glad you're alive!"

"Rhiannon?"

"Yes."

"Are you in on this, too?" She started to cry.

If she'd been able to see me, she would have known I wore a blindfold and had my arms bound.

"No. I'm a hostage just like you. Are you okay?" I hoped to console her.

"I'm starving and thirsty. I haven't eaten in days." She cried uncontrollably for a few moments before she sniffled and gasped for breath. "My body is aching from sitting in the same position. And I've soiled my clothes," she sniffled again, "because he won't let me go to the bathroom anymore."

"What?" I wanted to slap him or hurt him somehow. My outburst set her off again in great peals of crying. I couldn't tell where he was. I tilted my head to listen. I strained to hear over her sobs.

"Excuse me. Captor? Excuse me." No response at first, then he blew into my face, stale and sharp, as he bent down.

He pushed me backward onto the cushion—hands gripping my shoulders. I couldn't move my body backward without my arms, I just toppled over.

"I do not need her anymore. I have what I want now. She is of no importance to me."

My blood chilled. My heart pounded in fear.

"Yes, beat for me." His leg slid between mine and his chest pressed into mine. I wiggled to get free.

"Don't touch me. Leave me alone," I whined inaudible words right before his lips pushed down onto mine. I shook my head to get him to stop. His hands pressed both sides of my face and held me there. He made me kiss him. I went limp. He seemed not to enjoy that and let go.

When his face had withdrawn, I spat his taste out, wanting him far away from me. I was here, yes, but that didn't mean she needed to die.

"Let me help her, please," I begged, hoping to distract him from his current game.

"Why?"

"Because it's me that you want. You captured her to lure me in. You have me now, so let me help her. Please."

He rolled off and sat next to me on the uncomfortable makeshift cushion.

I tried to sit up. I knew he noticed—I rolled onto my knees and pushed off with my forehead. Yet he did not help.

"I beg of you. Please, let me help clean her up and feed her. Do you have food?"

I felt his breath in my face. He spoke slowly. "You are mine. I will not have you running away. You will stay with me until I grow tired of you. I have no need for her, except to sustain me if I choose."

My anger boiled, threatening to explode into a hot stream of tears and vehement words. I could not imagine having come here just to let her die. I bit my tongue, hoping not to enrage him. I needed to plead for kindness.

"She can leave," I stated firmly. Even as I said the words, I tried to imagine Amy making it down the mountain, across a freezing cold river, then walking for days to civilization. I didn't know how she could make it, but I had to try.

She quieted to listen to the conversation we were having. "Does she wear a blindfold like me? Has she ever seen you or where we are?"

"No. Even when she tried to escape, her hands were bound and her blindfold remained over her eyes. I no longer trust her, so there she lies."

315

"I've seen you before. I know what you look like. I can take my blindfold off. Please let me help her. Let me cook something for her. I'll stay with you. I won't leave. Please return her to her home and keep me. If you do this and let her live, I won't fight you. I'll stay. You know this, because I came when you told me you had her. She's the reason I'm here." I gulped down the bile that burned the back of my throat. I prayed Amy didn't object to my plan while the conversation hung in the air like a thick fog. My resolve was fragile, like a house of cards, and the big bad wolf glowered right in front of me ready to blow it all down.

I had to fake it until one of us made it through this alive.

He had proven that he would take whatever he wanted. He could easily kill my family and everyone around me. Amy, at least, would be my legacy—the ultimate gift. If only I could get him to return her home.

I didn't interrupt the silence. The fire snapped and crackled.

A tugging on my blindfold brought a wave of relief to me. He must have considered something I had said. Firelight stabbed at my eyes as they grew accustomed to the intensity of light.

He stooped on the mat in front of me. The mat was long—long enough to lay on for a bed.

The cave ceiling rounded to the floor on all sides. Not perfectly circular, the back wall elongated the area. Smoke twirled from the fire and danced around jagged pieces that extended from the ceiling high overhead. The smoke, I noticed, managed to escape without issue.

Stripes of different colored rock arched like an ancient rainbow from one side to the other. The glow from the fire didn't reach to the edges of the cave and created eerie images, like miniature creatures lurking along the base of the walls.

Behind me, the cave entrance was the only indentation in the rock room. However, I couldn't see out, the opening hidden around a corner.

I looked to my right and saw Amy lying on a mat similar to mine. She seemed to be curled in a ball.

I looked back at him. "Can you release my arms?"

Hesitation swept across his face.

I steeled my voice and asserted, "We both know you are faster than I am and inhumanly strong. You could snap my neck in a blink of an eye." Amy cried out at that statement. I kept my eyes on his. Even though I trembled at the power he exuded, I did not back down.

He relented and uncuffed my arms. I rubbed feeling back into them, but they ached worse with each movement. I could only imagine how horrible Amy's felt.

I examined the cave, searching for anything I could use to collect water and possibly use to cook over the fire.

I picked up a plastic water bottle discarded in the corner.

I glowered at our captor. "What do you want me to call you?"

He gaped back without blinking.

I had no desire to defend my position or argue. I could think of some names I would like to call him, but chose to keep my words in check. I simply said, "Captor, I need you to fill this with water from the stream." I extended my hand with the water bottle.

He glanced at it, then back at me. I knew he understood, so I assumed we were locked in a silent power struggle. Much to my disadvantage, with my shaking hand, I dropped the bottle.

Stupid body! It is hard to exist as a force to be reckoned with when your extremities won't even stick up for you. I reached down and snagged the bottle from the ground. I stood straight, with my head high—not wanting to give the impression that my bottle fumble had befuddled me at all. I had, in fact, not been left short in the determination and tenacity categories.

A faint smile played on his lips as he crossed the floor. He grabbed it from my hand.

He angled slightly as he walked away. Over his shoulder he uttered, "Sam." He walked toward the mouth of the cave and turned back. "Do not leave." His brown eyes seared into me.

I ignored him and kept searching through the discarded items in the corner. He must have brought a backpack with him that I didn't see. Luckily, discarded trash yielded a black plastic bowl.

When Sam returned, I created a make shift tripod high over the fire and tied the filled water bottle to it. I kept the bottle moving to keep it from melting while the water heated. I had heard somewhere that it worked. I'd never tried it before and prayed it succeeded. I needed to get warm water for Amy. Soon enough the water was tepid.

While I cleaned Amy, Sam stayed on the other side of the cave. He hunched with his back to us while I worked. Vampire politeness, I assumed.

Amy's body was a mess—quite different from her perfect hair and makeup at school. I felt horribly sorry for her—this wasn't her fault. Her situation was fully my responsibility. She had been abducted simply because of her proximity to me in class.

Her skin was blistered where her urine had pooled.

She cried out as I gently washed her. Each sob pierced my heart a little deeper and reminded me that I made the right decision. She didn't deserve to suffer like this.

Sam required that her arms remain cuffed. He acquiesced enough, due to my constant battering, to allow me to use my cuffs on one of her arms while hers remained on the other. Both were attached to the bed for the sake of cleaning her. She screamed as I rotated her into a flat position, her muscles had become so cramped.

I removed my top shirt and shredded it to make rags for cleaning. Even though I had been able to wash out her underwear and let them dry next to the fire, I didn't know if I would be able to clean her pants.

The air in the cave grew colder as the fire burned low. I could see my breath. I knew Amy had to be freezing in her t-shirt and wet skin. I built up the fire with more wood.

Our beds needed to be moved closer to the fire for us to stay warm. The air, peppered with snow—an unwelcomed visitor, would arrive soon. Sam would have to make a run for town. We needed clothes and containers. He could survive without any of those items—Amy and I were a different story. I did a 'humf' with my exhale as I imagined the way the conversation would go.

"Sam. I have Amy cleaned up, but I need things, toilet paper, towels, sweats, socks, coats, blankets, pots, or a frying pan, drinking cups, a knife, toothbrushes, and a hairbrush, and water and food." I demanded it. I had no intention of negotiating.

"I am not leaving to get anything."

"Let me put it to you this way…" I had nothing to lose. "It's going to snow, and very soon by the feel of the air. We are both freezing." He looked over his shoulder at me. "I have no way to clean Amy's clothes right now. We'll both freeze to death here. The fire can't stay hot enough to keep us consistently warm. I'm not asking for much. I'm asking for things so we can survive."

He turned back, contemplating the opening of the cave. He stood and ripped off his long sleeve shirt and tossed it at me. "Put that on her for now."

"I need the key again." I reminded him.

He moved toward me, the muscles in his chest rippling with each step. They were very defined, the strength in his body unmistakable. I shuddered at the power visible there. He leaned over with his face next to mine. I expected him to say something.

He reached into his pocket and pulled out the key and handed it to me. His eyes deliberately avoided the mat with Amy behind me.

"I'll find you if you leave. You'll wish you were dead." Then he disappeared through the opening of the cave.

He left me the key. I caressed it. This was power. This was a test.

I allowed myself to smile. I clutched it in my hand and looked at where Sam had just exited. We could escape. I bit my lip, trying to hold back the laugh I felt tickling my ribs. I leaped in the air as I turned to look back at Amy.

My elation evaporated as I took measure of her body. She was skin and bones. She appeared fragile and weak. Her skin oozed around her wounds. I doubted she would make a good travel companion.

Argh! The prime opportunity to run. I could see us now, me almost carrying her straight down a slick game trail to a river. Ice cold water. I would have to do the swimming. We would both drown. Actually, Sam would find us before then and we would both be dinner. Or dinner and desert, whatever he tells himself while he is 'eating'. A shiver twisted down my spine. It took me a moment to get over the sickened sensation in the pit of my stomach.

Indeed, we would not make it far. I sighed and felt the dread sneaking up on me again like a hangman's noose.

I tossed my running away idea and uncuffed one of her arms. I helped her to sit up and removed her blindfold. I figured it would be okay with Sam gone.

"I'm only letting you see while he's not here."

She hugged me and started to cry.

"Amy, we have to be good. Okay?" She nodded, still hugging me. "We both have to be very calm and obey him. I think he is going to take you home—let's not blow it."

I straightened her and undid her other arm. I handed her the shirt, and she put it on. Its length fell to her legs as she tried to stand up.

I helped her. I could tell her body had grown extremely stiff from lying in one position on her bed for so long.

I handed her dried and warmed underwear. She stumbled as she put them back on.

She limped around the cave, leaning against the wall for balance. The fire emitted a little light still.

I took off my shoes and socks. "Amy, here, put these on. They will help your feet stay warm." I thought about the red shoe that he had taken from her. Her feet probably had frost bite by now.

She walked shakily over to my mat and sat to put them on. I would have given her more of my clothes, but I wore only a shirt and pants myself.

"Amy, I'm going to step out and go to the bathroom. I'm just going to the mouth of the cave."

Her eyes widened, reminding me of a deer in the head lights.

"I'm coming with you!" I imagined she had to be more afraid than I at that moment. At least I knew what we were up against. Although, I couldn't be sure it would be more of a comfort knowing. No, in this instance, I believed ignorance had to be bliss.

"Okay. Maybe we can grab some fresh branches for your bed." Realization hit. "And my phone! We will use my phone."

I dug into my pocket. Empty. Where had my phone gone? Panicked, I searched around my bedding and around Amy's. The corner where all the garbage had been thrown did not reveal the red shiny life-line either. After a time, I admitted temporary defeat.

We walked slowly to the mouth of the cave. Our breath whitened in the frigid air. The crispness of the day popped out large goose bumps on our uncovered skin—although the sun burned bright into my eyes, it withheld even a fraction of its warmth. I took in everything as quickly as I could. A path ran right in front of the cave. It rose from the left, down a slight hill that disappeared around rocks, to the right of the cave. It climbed higher until it disappeared. Straight across from the mouth of the cave another hill jutted up abruptly. It loomed as tall as the trees around it, obstructing my view of anything beyond it. I could hear a faint water fall, dinky from the sounds of it. Of course, it could have frozen over with the first snow.

I peered to the right again. The ground spread out flat in front of the cave, providing area to find branches and a make shift restroom. I tiptoed to the edge of the rock wall, carefully, in my bare feet. I ducked behind some dormant bushes and used the restroom.

I couldn't believe I misplaced my phone. The worst possible scenario I imagined was Sam getting it, I would never get it back. I needed to locate it. Maybe as I took apart Amy's bed, I would find it in the branches.

On our return to the cave, I collected anything that might be soft for Amy's bed. She helped as much as she could. Even though she winced as she bent down, she didn't complain. We gathered moss and small twigs to build a new, and perhaps more comfortable, bed for her. After several trips, our collection was adequate.

Back in the cave, we tossed her old bed into the flames. I did not find the phone. In the back of my mind I worried that Sam already had it.

We began assembling her new bed while the fire completely consumed her old one. It took a while to build, but surprisingly it actually supported her.

I had constructed it closer to the fire for warmth—it meant we would have to be careful with any loose embers.

As I started to push my bed closer to the fire, Amy laid back down on her bed and fell asleep. She curled on her side with her hands tucked under her cheek, a position the cuffs would not have allowed. I could only imagine her exhaustion level, but her overall demeanor seemed a little more peaceful.

I continued working. I added logs to the fire as needed.

I bent down, fixing the last part of my bedding when I felt a presence behind me.

I spun around quickly.

Sam towered over me, glaring toward where Amy slept.

In a whisper he hissed, "Where are her blindfold and cuffs?" Anger edged his voice, and his eyes were black. I knew that I needed to calm him.

I put a hand softly but firmly on his chest and in as unruffled a tone as I could muster, said, "I will put them back on now. She needed to move and use the restroom." I pointed to the beds, now closer to the fire. "We needed warmth, so we moved our beds. Really, having her help made the work easier."

Sam continued to glare at me.

I strode over and grabbed Amy's blindfold from the floor. I glance to the side of the fire pit as I reached down and spied the red phone propped next to the stones, hidden from Sam's view. Thank God. My heart skipped a beat.

With new focus I snuck closer to her. I needed to return her to her captive state before I could rescue the phone. I placed the blindfold over her face with my hand in front of her eyes on top of the blindfold. She startled, just as I thought she would, and attempted to sit up.

"It's just me," I let her know. She relaxed a little. "I need to put your blindfold and cuffs back on now." She leaned over and allowed me to tie the blindfold.

I tossed a pleading pout at Sam. "Can she please keep her hands free?" I held up one of her wrists and showed him the red area where the cuffs had removed skin.

He angered again, glaring hotly at me, then Amy. His body seemed to puff up—his hands clenched and released. I could see the veins popping out on his neck. I knew the answer. I put the cuff on one if Amy's wrists. She exhaled in defeat.

I needed to keep him on the other side of the fire. I needed to get that cell.

Before I could cuff her other arm, Sam threw a bag at me. I caught it before it smacked into my head. He almost knocked me off my feet.

Almost greedily, I rummaged in the bag and pulled out a pair of sweats from the top. My chance.

"Could you please turn around?" I felt a bit of euphoria over knowing my plan would work. Sam shook his head and turned his back to us. I jumped to toward the phone. In one fluid motion, I stuffed it in my pocket and spun to face Amy. I felt like dancing at my small and successful deception. I guided her feet through the sweat's leg holes and steadied her as she stood. She pulled them up and then sat down. I patted her leg hoping it translated the hope I suddenly felt.

Sam turned back to the fire and applied more logs.

I searched through the bag until I found a sweater. I helped her pull it over her head, holding the blindfold securely in place. She wiggled out of Sam's shirt and fed it through the neck hole of the sweater, all the while making sure she remained completely covered. I wadded up Sam's shirt and hurled it heartily at him. I wished for the ability to throw a mean, fast curveball, but the shirt unwound in the air and fluttered about like an injured bird. It did little but fall at his feet. Strike one... bummer!

I placed Amy's handcuffs back on.

I found socks and a blanket in the bag as well. He brought only one pair of everything. Nothing for me to wear? Or are these items for me to wear when Amy no longer needs them?

Reality slammed me into the direness of our situation. The phone triumph dwindled. Why hadn't he taken her with him when he went for the bag of goods?

At that moment, I loathed him with such severity it tasted like venom in my throat. With gritted teeth and through slitted eyes, I faced him. I glared and repeatedly pointed my finger in the direction of the bag. I communicated silently for Amy's sake.

I glanced down at her sitting on the bed, then back to Sam. He ran fingers through his hair and looked down. He still held his shirt in his hands, so the motion rippled his muscles across his abdomen. He moved fluidly, and reminded me of a lion prowling, his sinewy physique horrifying, yet inspiring awe with every step. The most proficient predator, I knew Amy and I could die in a second.

"I'm taking her back tomorrow," he said in low tones, as he turned to face the cave entrance.

I had been wrong. I sent up a silent prayer of gratitude. I relaxed my shoulders and dropped down beside Amy.

"Thank you. Thank you very much," I blurted as Amy started to cry, leaning into me.

"I get to go home?" she whimpered. "I get to go home."

"Yes, Amy. Tomorrow." The words sounded like a death sentence to me. Warm tears cascaded down my cheeks, matching hers. I finally guaranteed her survival, but felt very unsure of what the next few days would hold for me. After a few moments of rocking back and forth, I rose and walked to Sam.

He did not turn as I neared him.

"Please tell me you'll make sure she lives all the way home. I've kept my word. Please don't let anything happen to her."

Without acknowledging my request, he strode out of the cave. I followed him.

As he approached the mouth of the cave, I noticed snow falling. White wisps blew around the mouth, driven by a cold breeze. The view seemed out of place and disjointed. The first snow always brought me out of the house to marvel at the sky. Somehow, viewing it on a high mountain without any promise of escape, reminded me of death—cold, solitary, and stark.

"It's snowing," absentminded words dropped from my mouth. I knew it would be cold in the night. I mentally catalogued the amount of wood we had.

"Can I gather wood? We're going to run out."

Sam turned to look at me.

"I did not think of that. Yes, but you have to stay close. Do not try to leave. I did not expect to see you when I returned. I would have tracked you and found you. I might have chosen to kill you. I was shocked to see you still here."

My blood ran cold. I ignored the statement about my death.

"I promised," were the only words I could muster.

I returned to the other bag he brought and checked its contents. It held a blue coat which I gratefully donned.

I didn't glance at him as I stepped past into the cold air.

I studied my surroundings as I chose the path to the right, past the rocks that I used for a restroom earlier. My breath caught.

The path descended from here into a valley enclosing a deep blue lake. From somewhere at the bottom of the lake, I could hear a waterfall. I wondered if it could have been the waterfall I remembered as he carried me to the cave.

A thick line of pine trees stood on the other side of the lake. Snow trailed down the mountain above the lake. I could still see the smooth rocks that extended from behind the trees and ran to the top of the light grey peaks. The rocks ascended so steeply that hardly any vegetation grew there. My eyes scanned the lake again. A small island located to one side hosted a solitary, live tree. I understood that tree and could not tear my eyes from it. Like me, it stood freezing, alone, and against all odds, defiant to the harsh world around it.

Few sounds resonated from the forest. Creatures had taken shelter from the cold. I could smell the wonderful, crisp pine and musty scent of the forest floor. Some of the beautiful white, purple, and yellow flowers were still colorful, frozen by the oncoming winter.

I bent down to pick up wood and twigs. I didn't want to freeze out here.

"You know I'll have to cuff you tomorrow to make sure you stay. I can only imagine that Amy had a lot to do with your reason for not leaving today." The voice came from behind me.

"You will do what you have to, I'm sure."

"Rhiannon, if you are not here when I return, I will kill her." He retreated a few steps from me.

A warning. Either way, I knew my fate. Just let Amy live. I paused there to scan the beautiful landscape in front of me. My last view of a peaceful scene? I felt insignificant compared to the snowy world around me.

The path in front of me sloped at a steep angle. Loose dirt and rocks had piled up on most of the path. Even though fresh snow fell onto the path, no footprints showed any comings and goings. I doubted Sam had carried me from this direction. If I chose to escape, the steep hillside would not be easy to travel. My scent would give me away. My only chance would be a head start. I, of course, would wait to make sure Amy made it home safely.

I picked up more wood and then carried my armload into the cave. I dropped it at the fire and returned to get another armful. I noticed Amy had lain out on her bed and fallen asleep. Back out, I observed Sam near the mouth of the cave with a rabbit in his hand. I feigned disinterest and went to find more wood. Even though my stomach grumbled in its empty state, the rabbit didn't sound appetizing. I deliberately stepped to the left of the cave to look for tracks. I found what I was looking for. In the soft soil, there were many prints. He had come and gone enough to trample the soil. As the weather set in, the ground froze them in place. I knew we came this direction, past a waterfall on the left and one on the right. I faintly thought about the phone in my pocket. I didn't dare turn it on with him around—it would make a sound, and he would rage. I would have to be careful.

I collected wood until the pile reached high in the cave. I didn't want to run out of fuel. We had to keep warm.

I covered Amy with the blanket and finished cataloging items in the last bag.

I now had a frying pan, toilet paper, a towel, a coat, a blanket, a drinking cup, a knife, a toothbrush, and a hairbrush. I brushed my hair. It felt good—something normal to do. Then I brushed my teeth.

"I need to get some water so I can boil it," I asserted to Sam. He nodded and followed me out. I opted to go left this time down the path toward what I thought I remembered to be a waterfall.

"Pretty soon you will be able to melt snow," he gibed from behind me.

I translated that as, "Don't get used to long walks like this." I didn't intend to stay long enough for anything to become habit. We walked in silence. Trees were thick. The path I followed was a game trail. It seemed to continue on downhill into the trees. I stopped at the waterfall. It made a bellowing sound, but misled my expectations. The amount of water flowing down the rocks had been little more than a trickle which plummeted loudly into the pool below. I wedged the frying pan between larger rocks to fill it.

I turned to go back to the cave. Sam stepped in front of me.

"I will bring you some food tomorrow." He seemed to be making sure I knew my freedom was his to give and take. The conversation didn't need to exist. I didn't care and slipped passed him.

Sam hadn't forced me to kiss him again. When he came close I smelled him, my stomach churned and my skin crawled. I hoped that he would keep his distance.

He cooked the rabbit over the flames. Amy woke for a little while, and I helped her eat. She went back to sleep.

I lay close to her to share the blanket. My feet were at her back, my head at her feet and, surprisingly, I slept.

I woke in the morning to my hands being bound with rope, behind my back and tied to my feet. I wondered where he had hidden the rope, but it served its purpose well. I couldn't move. So much for me getting to my phone while he took her back to town.

I craned my neck to watch him carry Amy, with the coat on, toward the mouth of the cave. Her loud screams echoed and like arrows pierced my conscience.

I yelled to her. "Amy! You are going home. Stay calm. Leave your blindfold on! Please, Amy, do what you're told and you will be home tonight!"

She quieted to a whimper as he carried her from the cave. I heard him snap at her to be quiet. Silence descended upon me.

I lay there with the fire burning close, the blanket haphazardly covering me. The fire crackled above the faint sound of large wet flakes hitting the ground outside.

Holiday weekends were nearing. I always spent them with my family, who by now were surely devastated and anything but festive. My family and friends would have renewed hope that I was still alive as soon as Amy could tell them of our captor.

Then dread set in as I wondered if he would have to move us? Would they be searching everywhere in the mountains

329

when they found out we were in a cave? Had she seen enough
when we walked out to tell them about the large lake? Would
they be able to identify the region from her description when
they talked to her?

My arms already ached in this hogtied position.

I closed my eyes to soak in the warmth from the fire. I
must have fallen asleep again because when I woke up, the fire
had died down. The flames barely reached above the wood—
just embers.

I looked toward the pile of logs. It seemed to be a mile
away from me in my bindings. I wiggled a little to see how
much I could move. Sticks dug into my arm and leg, which
resolved that. I would not be going anywhere. It would get
very cold in here, very fast.

Bound as he left me, I spent the day in the same position.
My mind devised all the escape plans it could. Each one ended
in disfavor. I grew angrier, fighting against my ties. This would
be the perfect time to leave. Amy would soon be free, and that
freedom sealed my fate.

How could anyone fight a vampire with a one-track mind?

He wanted me. If it came down to it, my best defense
would be to take myself out of the picture. Peppin would have
lost, Sam would have lost, and my Leone would lose again.
That thought held me. How could I make Leone go through
my death again?

I wondered what my next life might be like. I often
recognize glimpses now of past lives—ball gowns, Puritan hats,
hard work, castles, burning cities, war, battleships, and some
dark and indiscernible images. I guessed I might be living one
of the memories that future Rhi's would have as nightmares.
What ending would it be? I gulped, not wanting to think about
any details associated with my death.

What path would my soul choose the next time? Knowing
now that I would be back, made my death seem easier. It's just
a matter of pain and letting go. That said, my very human

heart nearly burst when I considered my parents pain at losing their only child. What agony...

I could accept the change. I haven't really given it much thought. Perhaps in the back of my mind, the idea hung there as an unlikely option, but it wasn't a choice I had to face yet. I contemplated that option openly now. I could be with Leone and never have to leave him. I could still be with my parents, but would they understand? How would I tell them? How would I explain their growing old while I remained young? How could I continue living after their deaths and the deaths of everyone I knew and loved for eternity?

I had a life to live still. Could I exist like Leone, Lauriel, Dante, and Angelina? Would the thirst for blood make it impossible? Naomi seemed to have control over it, and she was young. She has never bitten me.

The truth bubbled to the surface on my scattered thoughts. I did not want to die. I had a passion for living, for learning, and I understood people had to hurt to grow. I didn't want to die. The realization caused me to feel weak. All of the triumphant thoughts of cheating death faded, and cowardice remained.

Tears of fear and loss poured from my eyes, soaking my hair and my shirt. I wept until I was numb inside.

15

Better Times

I looked up into the face of love. He smiled at me, holding an apple for me to eat.

I had no desire to talk at that moment. There seemed to be a deep hole inside me as if someone had ripped out my heart. I did not know if my stomach growled, but I reached my hand out to him. It was a child's hand—dirt clung to the skin and was packed under the nails. I held the apple and stared at it.

I looked from my hand to the woman close to us. She wept without tears. She appeared disoriented and weak. She hunched forward over a white and brown engraved box.

I knew I didn't need to eat the apple. My stomach might as well have been made of stone. I walked to where she sat, and extended my hand with the apple. She looked at me through her veil of invisible tears. Her eyes burned red—entirely red.

I remained calm. I held out my hand with the apple. She started to shake and a low grumble came from her throat. Her lips parted. A chill ran down my spine.

Firm hands grabbed me around my waist and lifted me off the ground. I spun in the air and away from her.

The other man in the room rushed to her side, murmuring to her in low tones.

"She is going to be fine, Rhi. She is going to be fine." The man that held me whispered in my ear. We entered a dark hallway.

The scene changed.

When I walked from the shadow of what I thought had been a hallway, it transformed into a street filled with people. I wore new, clean clothes. I ambled, hand-in-hand with someone. I glanced up and admired her beautiful face smiling down at me from under a deeply hooded robe. The same woman I had held the apple for. Her eyes were dark this time. A faint happiness played inside me when I beheld her.

I gawked at the crowd. People chatted in the sunlight, roaming from one vendor's cart to another. Fresh fruit and grain stands, poultry and meats drew the crowd. This city was alive. Women paraded in long peasant dresses, and the men wore long-sleeved shirts and crudely made pants. Hay spilled from piles along the walls of houses, in-between the vendors. We strolled through the crowd. We looked for someone in particular on this day.

She grasped my hand tighter, and a faint gasp came from her lips. She halted. I followed her gaze. A beautiful dark-haired girl about my age purchased an item from a fruit vendor. The little girl seemed unhappy—no smile gleamed in her young eyes. The hand I held began to tremble.

She took one step toward the child. Her free hand covered her lips.

The vendor yelled some angry words to the child, causing her to stagger away in fear.

The woman next to me dropped my arm and moved a few steps forward, before being stopped by one of the men behind us.

"Nohi, we cannot interfere. They have to live as though you died." He hugged her for support, understanding how difficult it was to watch her daughter struggling with her life, alone, without her mother.

"I don't know if I'm strong enough for this, Dante. I cannot bear to watch. She is so sad without me."

"Your only other choice is to move away and let them live," his voice remained assuring and soft. "How can you explain to them that you are raised from your grave? They would fear you and never understand."

"I can change them," she blurted out.

"You could. There is nothing stopping you." He patted her shoulder. "Nohi, do you really want them to live the way you do? Do you want them to know the constant hunger? Do you want them to never sleep? Do you want them to worry about eternity?"

The young girl disappeared around the corner.

Nohi, struggling with the emotions, hurried away from us. We followed her to a side street, away from the busy traders' row.

I felt a deep sadness for her. I ran to catch up, and wrapped my fingers around her hand, pulling her to a stop.

"I love you, Nohi," I uttered, gleaming up into her tortured face.

She bent down and hugged me. We walked on together.

We entered the church where we found Leone handing out donations to the families who jostled in line. Survivors of the plague, they were accustomed to coming to the church everyday for assistance. He and others scooped cups full of flour, eggs, and any other food that they had.

He turned when he saw us and gave me a large embrace. When he saw the look on Nohi's face, he held her.

"I'm sorry," he whispered. The chance meetings with her family must have occurred a lot.

She squeezed him, then sauntered to a bench along the wall. I crawled up next to her, wanting badly to comfort her. I understood about losing those held dear. A few years previously my parents died in the plague, but I still missed them terribly. Nohi had been the one to die in her family, but her loss appeared harder to live with.

"Nohi." I braved a conversation with her.

"Yes, Rhi?" she encouraged me.

"I know I could never replace her, but to me, you are my mom."

A weak smile curved from the corners of her mouth, and she kissed my cheek.

"Rhi, you have taught me so much about life. Of course you are a daughter of mine. I want you to remember, no matter what happens, you must always fight to the end. Keep going until there is nothing else to give. It is life, and sometimes it makes you earn your way."

I had no way of understanding what those words meant.

16
Time in the Cave

I awoke freezing cold. Nohi's words ringing in my mind, "You must always fight to the end. Keep going until there is nothing else to give."

I understood those words now. I watched embers in the fire, glowing faintly. The cave had become wrapped in ebony silk. My body shivered to keep warm and the blanket barely covered me. I wiggled my arm to get the blanket up my body, but this action had the opposite effect as more of my arm became exposed.

I brought my knees toward my face and grabbed the blanket in my teeth. I pulled toward my head. The blanket moved from my waist area, beginning to expose my feet. Pulling at the middle of the it had the effect of folding it in half over my body.

Finally, I rolled into a ball with the rope stretched taut, intent on reaching the end of the blanket, now down past my knees. I barely gripped the cloth with my mouth and finally pulled the top of its fuzzy warmth up around my neck. The added layer seemed to help a little. It was the lumpy, loose bed that let the cold seep in from below me.

I listened to the cave. No sounds. I struggled to be sure—Sam moved without a sound. I wondered when he would return. Previously, I hoped he would stay away for a long time, but now, as cold as my body had become and as dark as the cave had grown, I knew I would need the fire. With my arms and legs bound, moving to the wood pile would be impossible. My body ached from lying in the same position. My bladder past full reminded me how Amy could no longer deny that necessity.

Leone's face flashed through my mind—so beautiful inside and out. I visualized him handing out food to the starving people. Ironic that he fed the starving, while he, himself, had not consumed solid food in hundreds of years. I missed him. I tried to recreate his smile in my mind, with the dimple that I loved. I replayed his touch on my skin and the thrill it sent through me. I doubted I would see him again—in this life. My heart sank. How powerful was a love that someone would chase it through the centuries?

I hadn't been able to kiss him because of the brightness it created. Peppin would know Leone had broken my defenses, and the final hunt would start. I never fully touched his perfect, supple lips to mine. The aftermath would not be worth it. I closed my eyes and imagined how my lips would feel. Remembering the shocking sensation they had after he had given me mouth-to-mouth resuscitation, the one that lasted days, I imagined it would consume my entire body to fulfill that desire. If I saw him again, he could not stop me. If I was destined to die, I wanted that for myself.

I just had to see Leone again. He lived vividly in my memories—his adoring eyes shared his love for me, and his loving touch caressed me even here. I knew the passion that we shared. I crept back to some of those great feelings that were locked in the layers of my soul. How could one person feel such a strong connection to another? It possessed my entire being. I could not find words to describe it.

Then, in the midst of my beautiful feelings of profound
love, I was forced to return to the ugliness of my situation. I
heard a rustling behind me. My body stiffened. I stopped
breathing to hear every, slight sound. Could it be a wild
animal? Or Sam?

The answer came as wood thudded into the fire.

"Please, undo my bindings," I insisted, through forced
politeness. "I'm freezing and in pain."

Without a word he came over to me and pulled back the
blanket. As he fumbled through the knots, I agonized with the
movement in my arms and then my legs. Barely able to stand, I
shuffled toward the cave entrance.

Sam was there in an instant, grabbing my arms hard.

I glared at his eyes, redder now by the faint glow from the
stirred coals.

"I have to use the restroom," I pronounced each word
with purposeful annoyance.

He nodded, turned, and grabbed the toilet paper from the
bag. His eyes bore into me as I snatched it from his grasp and
moved toward the opening.

The accounts of him from the television news reports were
definitely wrong. He must have snow-balled all the people in
his life into believing he had been a good, kind-hearted person.
I didn't think him capable of having anything resembling a
redeemable quality.

The air outside might as well have been dry ice induced. I
knew my skin would peel away at any moment as it curled
with the effects of frostbite. About a foot of snow had fallen,
and I wore only my shirt and pants. I couldn't decide if my feet
felt as if they had touched the hot coals of a fire or been frozen
in huge ice blocks. Each step pierced with excruciating stabs of
pain.

The feeble sun left the sky dark and ominous for the night.
The snow reflected enough ambient light that I could discern
between darker and lighter shadows. The white world that

surrounded the cave would only get deeper as the winter continued.

The swirling flakes drove the chill into my bones like a jack-hammer. If my bladder had not ached so badly, I would have chosen to wait.

I dashed to my place next to the rocks. When I had finished, I scurried to the cave entrance. Sam waited just inside and handed my shoes back to me that Amy had worn. He followed behind me into the cave.

The fire danced a welcome. I met it with outstretched arms and stretched the soreness from my aching body in its warm embrace. I waltzed with the flames, warming front first and then back. I ignored Sam.

He brought the coat to me that Amy had worn. As I seized it I noticed blood smeared down one of the arm sleeves.

I shoved it toward him.

"Why is there blood?" Rage bubbled in my veins, hot and uncontained.

He avoided the question by veering away and picking up the pack he had brought in.

Sliding closer to him, I demanded. "Did you kill her?" I scowled at the coat. Blood that had frozen to the sleeve began to liquefy next to the fire. How could he? My stupid eyes gave into the wrong emotion again and filled up with liquid cowardice. I blinked them back in disdain. She had been so frail, but she could have lived—it would have been so easy. Why did he have to kill her?

"After me keeping my promise, after me not trying to flee you, and enduring all of your abhorring treatment, you killed her anyway?" I flung my arms up and yelled a long, bellowing scream that embodied all of the dormant emotions I had stuffed down but allowed to simmer. Now I spewed them all out. When the last of my rage had been spent, I steadied my gaze at him. "You're evil."

He flipped around so quickly that my only response was to
pull the coat into my chest. My feet moved backward as his
face came within an inch of mine.

His mouth snarled like a wild animal. The hair on my neck
stood on end. His eyes went white. My heart pounded loudly.
Too loudly, I felt sure. I pulled the coat up under my chin.

He grabbed me and slammed me to the rocky ground. My
arms were pinned under his chest. Sam's growling grew in my
ears, sending ripples of terror down to my core. I knew he
would end this quickly.

"No, no, no!" I begged, trying to block his mouth from
landing anywhere on my body. He would have me consumed
in minutes.

Tears were the only thing that came from me, like a dam
bursting. I thought of Amy. Had she been this scared, or had
he done it in a way that she couldn't see it coming?

His hands flung the coat to the side and grabbed my arms,
pinning them to the stone above my head. I gasped, as I
sprawled out like hide staked to the ground for drying. I could
not protect myself.

He poised above me, ready to land on me. For a second my
life balanced on a precipice. If he regained control, I might live.
A devious smile curled his lips. Triumph over his prey? He
slowly lowered his head to mine.

His inhuman growling, though quieter, was still audible to
me. My shallow breaths came fast as I tried to hold onto any
sense of sanity. He drove his leg in between mine, forcing them
apart. His body loomed over me. His eyes were regaining a
semblance of color. Not his normal color, but not white.

He closed them tight and arched his chin to the ceiling. He
shook his head, fighting for some kind of control.

When he looked back at me, his eyes burned crimson. He
smiled eerily at me again. My entire being edged with
premonition. *Get away.* My feet kicked. Even though his desire
to eat had obviously passed, knew what red eyes meant. His

eyes were the boding color of Peppin's before he killed me. *Get away, Rhi!*

I cried out, "No!" and tried to move from under this animal. I remembered the pain as Peppin had drained my life from me. Thrashing and bucking under his weight, I fought to free my hands and move my body. I tired quickly. He laughed at my futile attempts.

He bent down and licked my jaw.

My eyes were wild, darting around the cave, searching for anything I could grab. My limbs, like concrete, could not move under his strength. I resigned myself to stare at the ceiling and wonder how to stop this.

He grabbed both wrists in one of his large hands. He ran his other hand down my cheek. His smell made my stomach turn, and his touch made my skin recoil. I tried to pull myself away from his advancing hand to no avail. I remained stuck to the rock beneath, like a moth tacked in a display case. I feared this cave would be my tomb. For a moment, a profound grayness weighed on my soul.

A fear-filled moan escaped my mouth as I tried to move away from his hand, tracing my neck.

His mouth hovered over my ear. "I bet Leone has not caressed your lovely body yet, has he?"

I shut my eyes tight and turned as far away from his face as I could, smashing my cheek into my arm. His breath reeked of blood. I shuddered at the thought of smelling Amy on him.

"That's what I thought," he mused. "So you are fresh." His light-hearted voice made my throat spasm. My stomach threatened to spew any remaining contents all over him. I wished for it to happen, but it wouldn't.

"You are mine." He sounded so sure of himself.

He dug into my hip and clutched forcefully at my waist. Pain coursed through my side as he tightened his grip. I yelped in pain.

He automatically released some of the grip. He traced his finger tips up my shirt and along my belly. I closed my eyes tight. I whimpered as I shook my head no.

My mind screamed, Leave me alone. Don't touch me with your filthy hands. Your cruel, sadistic, calculating, revolting hands." Anxiety pounded in my brain. *Don't move your hand up. Please. Please, Lord, stop him. I don't want this.*

He leaned into my ear again. "Imagine me." His sickening words were loathsome to my ears. "You will feel me. You will come to know me. I will be all around you, and my poison will fill your blood. And, eventually, you will be mine."

I understood that to mean he would use my body and then kill me. *My body is only flesh, bone, and blood. Those are the things he is talking about taking. I will never give him my mind. My soul is already spoken for.*

"You will never have all of me!" I leveled my voice to speak and dared him with my eyes.

He laughed and moved off of me, withdrawing his hand from my shirt. "There are things that you will have no choice in giving."

"What?" I challenged courageously, even as I slid away. "My body?" I continued, scampering backward along the ground toward the fire. "My bones, my blood?" When I bumped into the hearth of rocks, I squatted and glared at him. "You will *never* have my mind, and you will *never* have my soul."

He jumped at me, but I didn't move, holding my ground. A strand of hair stuck to my lashes. I glared through slitted, angry eyes—my teeth clamped so tightly that my head shook with the force. *Bring it on. Better to end it now and quickly, than to endure your touch again.*

"All of you!" he demanded.

I said nothing and continued to glare at him.

His burning red eyes lashed into me. At any second, he could snap and crush me with his powerful body. I remained resolute in my decision to meet my fate rather than let him have any part of me. My side stung from his forceful advancement.

He leaped to his feet and spun until his back was to me. He flexed his fists and pulled them out to the side. Even through his shirt I could see the muscles bulging. He roared loudly, the horrifying sound bouncing off the cave walls. I covered my ears to stop it but the sound reverberated in my bones. He raised his arms over his head as if beseeching some deity and released the last of the fury.

He slowly pirouetted until he faced me. "If you will not give me all of you, then Leone will never have you either."

Small consolation. I tilted my head to the side. I knew my soul would come back to be with Leone. I trusted that Sam had no knowledge of it.

"It would be of no consequence." My voice remained flat. "My soul is locked to forever repeat life. If you kill me, I will return. So get on with it," I dared, refusing to allow him any power over me.

He deliberated for a moment—his eyes focused on the floor. "I was created to watch you, capture you, and not hurt you. I am to report back to 'him' when everything is ready." He turned to me, expressionless.

Ready? I shuddered as I realized Peppin had to be close. He waited for everything to be ready again to destroy me. I know my death's at his hands. I took in the measure of Sam. *Yes, I think I would rather pursue my death through a different source. One unlike the floating abomination. My own game. Sam thinks he is the only one with free will. If I upped the stakes and let Sam kill me, Peppin would have his fun spoiled.* A smile played across my face.

Sam took so long thinking on 'Peppin-theater' and how he had become caught up in it, I thought he would understand and change his mind about me. He walked toward me. His next words made me understand that I had misjudged.

344

"You are the game." He laughed harshly at his realization. "I'm just the game piece." He spoke as if confused, but resigned to his role in my demise.

"You." He pointed at me as I hunched, ready to run, next to the fire. "You," he reiterated loudly, "are the thing that twists the plans and deters the logic? Simple, frail creature!" He grabbed a strand of my hair. "I could crush you in a second. Not so much a sport. You are easily captured, easily swayed, weak, vulnerable, easily killable, and consumable."

I flinched at his last word, my courage abating.

He narrowed his eyes. "Why?"

I did not answer.

"Why?!" His voiced boomed and he crouched to face me.

I just stared at him. To tell him the story would give him more power over me. Those things, so long ago, still ached deep inside like a fresh wound. I coddled the memory and did not want to share it with anyone accept Leone.

I looked away, wishing he were here to help me.

He clutched my throat, forcing me to meet his gaze.

"Tell me!"

His angry, bloody eyes infused fear in me. I speculated what kind of a human being he had been. My mind conjured up a red-headed bully as a child. One who had grown into a foul-mouthed, rude, obnoxious man, a man who purposefully fought others and exploited women.

"What were you like as a human?" I spat the cold words at him.

His next motion came so quickly that I barely had time to close my eyes. His fist appeared out of nowhere and simultaneously a sharp pain slashed. My body hurtled sideways, then blackness.

When the cave came back into focus, a man at the fire with clenched fists and tense demeanor rocked slightly on his heels.

I closed my eyes against the pain that lanced through my skull like no other I had ever felt. I pulled my leaded arms up and touched my face. Above my right temple a huge aching bulge protruded. I winced and moaned. I tried to open my eyes again to check the stranger, but a spasm of pain shot pinpoints of light through my eyes and into my brain. I felt a stirring in my gut. My thoughts seemed fuzzy. Nothing really connected, disjointed notions whizzed like bullets through hazy consciousness. *Where was I? Who was the man?* Something sticky plastered my head. Wet and thick, it stuck to my fingers. I pulled my hand down and confirmed. Blood. Dark red.

Then the memory of Sam coursed back in. *How could I still be alive?* He might have consumed me and had it over with. Had he satiated his need with Amy? The thought of Amy's terror sent shocks of grief through my senses. What had he been like to her? I felt the warm saltwater trickle down my cheek.

Sam spied me and left in an instant, but returned just as quickly. A baggy rustled and seconds later a cold pack rested on the lump on my temple. I winced with the sudden cold, then wrestled the bag of snow from him and rolled over on my left side. I perched the pack on my temple unfettered, to clarify my intent to accept no help.

Turned away from him, I could allow my emotions to remain hidden. The loathing and contempt I felt for him fully consumed me, but grief caused my psyche to ponder Amy. *I am so sorry. I hope you felt no pain.* I speculated that she had. I suspected her death mirrored the memory of my own at the teeth of Peppin in Atlanta.

Sam stood by my bed. I couldn't be sure if he watched me or not. I didn't care much. I just wanted the pain to go away. The pressure in my head felt like a vice had been placed there and someone continued to turn the crank. I yearned for release from the internal throb. *It would be so much easier to let him end it now. I could easily slip away from the pain.*

I curled into a ball, concentrating on counting numbers with my eyes closed. I tried maintaining the count to the rhythm of my heartbeats, instead, they matched the pulsing I tried so hard to ignore.

I shifted in and out of consciousness. I glimpsed the light changing through the cave entrance from day to night. Visions of very little light, then full dark, and brightness again repeating, kaleidoscoping together.

My stomach growled. I rolled over again to face the fire, which revealed Sam stoically seated on the cold ground staring at me with not a flicker of emotion in his eyes.

Coldhearted demon. Stare at me. Go ahead. Wonder what it's like to be hit and treated like this? I thought about that for a moment. *No. He probably enjoyed every minute and thinks he has the right.*

He reached behind him into the rocks and grabbed a metal plate.

An ear of corn browned by the fire, some type of meat, and an apple rimmed the plate. The corn looked so good, I greedily snatched it from the plate. Ravenously, I devoured the food without sitting up.

"I heard your stomach while you were sleeping," he provided.

I just looked at him. *Wish you could hear my thoughts, Creep.*

"Your head looks a little better."

My answer remained locked in my mind. *Are you trying to feel guilty now? Way too late for that. Kidnapping me, Amy, intruding on my body, hitting me. I will be made a saint, indeed, if I'm ever able to find forgiveness for you.*

Before I could appropriately deal with the situation, my stomach revolted. I had barely rolled forward before I vomited onto the ground. Electric-like currents shot through my head as I bent there. My stomach deceived me and would not allow me to eat. And I thought it couldn't get any worse.

Sam's arm wrapped around my shoulders and laid me back onto my bed. I let the plate slide to the floor—the metallic clamor echoed through my fog.

He grabbed a drink of water for me.

"This will heal." He placed the cold pack back on my forehead before cleaning up the mess with leaves from my bedding.

He remained quiet and kept his distance from me while I slipped into sleep.

The nights and the days blended together. The pain in my head remained fierce. I wanted some medication to take away the pain, but we had none. Sam had been unwilling to leave me and get some.

"I have to use the restroom." I realized I smelled like urine and it disgusted me. I must have gone on myself while unconscious. I had to clean up the crusty, filthy feeling. "Please help me to walk out of the cave." As much as I did not want his help, I feared falling and reinjuring my head. I couldn't imagine any more pain.

Sam crossed the cave and helped me to stand. He supported one arm as I stumbled to the mouth of the cave. Once there, he led me through the deep snow. At least another foot had fallen since my last outing.

I guided myself along the rocks and said, "I'm good now— you can go away." But he stayed, averting his eyes while I took care of business.

The sunlight pierced my eyes. A break in the clouds and the reflection on the snow threatened to blind me. Squinting did not help.

I cleaned myself with fresh snow. I stepped carefully back along the rocks toward the mouth of the cave. Nearly there, I tripped My body fell into the snow. Without the coat, snow immediately saturated my shirt both inside and out. My pants were already snow packed and my skin frozen. Ironically, the chill felt like a burn. It was strangely welcome, giving me a respite from the constant ache in my head.

Before I knew it, Sam scooped me up from the snow.

He carried me back to the bedding. He had heated a cup of water.

I sipped it. I could feel it warming me from the top of my raw throat all the way down. The sensation soothed.

I lay down again and rested, waiting for the spinning to stop.

When I awoke again, the sun was up. How many days had passed since he hit me?

Sam was focused on the fire.

"Sam, is your intention to kill me? If so, now would be a great time to do it. Thanks to you, the pain in my head is so great it would be a welcomed relief." My body felt hollow and weak. Sam remained quiet, but his posture changed. He seemed defensive. He returned his stare into the fire.

"Why are you the target?"

I hadn't expected to have this question posed to me. It was my turn to remain aloof. I squinted at his backside. After a long silent pause, Sam shifted again to question me.

"Why are you hunted?" he restated his inquiry.

I understood that this would not be the last time he asked, so I carefully considered my answer.

"I am bound, much like you, to live eternally," I stated, hoping to satisfy his curiosity without going into detail. "I have the blessing of not remembering each time I return. I am truly a babe learning everything again, acquiring memories through the same steps each and every time, to learn to live like every other human."

"Repeating?" he questioned.

"Yes." I exhaled loudly, deciding how much to share. "It seems that my first birth occurred around 780 AD. I'm not sure on that, as I've not asked specifics on my first life, so I'm uncertain. Possibly, I was in my twenties when I first died."

Sam seemed too confused to say anything. I hoped I didn't have to explain any more, but his questioning look made clear that the conversation would continue.

"You and I are tied in a way to the same creature," I shared. I thought I recognized understanding in Sam's expression.

"Do you remember the name of your master?" I asked. Master did not seem like the correct term for Peppin.

"No."

"What did he look like?" I probed.

"I remember black robes, red eyes, and a bald head. His skin seemed whiter than the snow."

"Yes." I closed my eyes, hoping to fend off the image. "I know him, too."

"Do you now." Sam responded, more a statement than a question. He had figured as much.

"Yes. He is Peppin. He is my constant threat. His sport is to find me and kill me." My headache grew to be more like explosions with every pulse beat—and my pulse sped up just thinking about the dreams where I relived Peppin killing me. I lay back down on my bed and curled my legs up.

"He did something to me that caused me to forget everything." Sam grimaced. "Not until you asked me the other day about my human life did any glimpses of it start to filter through my anger and desire for blood." He quieted abruptly and walked closer to my bed. Though I had closed my eyes against the pain in my head, I could tell he moved close enough to sit on my bed when he continued talking.

"I need to know what happened to cause you to be his 'sport.' He took my life from me and reprogrammed me to find you. I cannot tell you how strong his command is on my mind.

350

It consumed me entirely. Why would that be? I was not allowed to kill you. I needed to find a way to let him know about you... every detail. Somehow, there had been no question as to why. It simply became the most important thing."

Stupid hobby, killing me. I lay on this bed of sticks, trying to hold myself together. *Really?* I did not feel like a prize. Sam had been right about that. *Frail. How could that be any fun? I just learned about it and I am already sick of it. How could Peppin keep it up for centuries?*

"Peppin has been a monk all these years. He lived in a monastery around 800 AD. He transformed there." I continued to lay with closed eyes. How much did I want to tell? I chose to disclose only the basic story. I would not share any details about the baby.

"Peppin." Sam repeated the name.

"Yes, Peppin. A hunchback."

"Oh, I remember!" Sam uttered.

I explained how Peppin had toyed with me, then sent me running for my life back to the castle just to rip my throat out in front of Leone. "He had hoped Leone would finish me off with his new thirst for blood. Instead, Leone, desperate to find a way to save me, forced me to drink new changeling blood. It locked my soul to earth. I'm destined to repeat life, forever."

Sam's shoulders sank, and he hunched deeper onto the bed.

"I was created for a game spanning centuries?" Sam barked out the incredulous realization.

We were silent. A few tears escaped my eyes. I felt the bedding shift as Sam stood. No sound followed, but I felt my spirit quiet, as though I remained alone in the cave. Sam must have gone.

I awoke to my stomach cramping again and threw up the water I had swallowed. I wondered if the head injury would allow me to live. Considering such a fate might be a new twist to my many deaths, I would almost welcome it. I chuckled to myself, although faintly, considering the strain it took. I loved the irony of it—two vampires ready to kill me, but in the end, a caved-in skull and a freezing cave might be the impetus for my demise. How romantic. It will be nice to let my own body make its final decision. I wondered if I had even grown old in any of my previous lives.

When I awoke, light still filtered into the cave, and the fire burned bright and hot. I must not have slept for very long.

I rolled over slowly to peer through clenched lids at my surroundings. The pain seemed even greater.

I raised my hand to my head, blood had crusted around the edges where it had dried, but the center remained spongy and swollen where a membrane had formed to lock out the air. The ice pack had mostly melted.

I decided to get more snow for the bag, and to melt some snow, and clean myself and my clothes. I slowly righted myself, trying to keep the room from swaying. I paused in a sitting position for the wave of nausea to dissipate.

I did want to live. With Sam not here, I weighed my chances of survival out of the cave and down the hill in feet of freezing snow.

I considered where the last conversation with him had left me. Did he still plan to keep me and kill me?

My life had twisted in so many directions, and though I intently loved Leone, I still did not understand the desires and the passionate nature of vampires. At what point did vampire desire overcome logic?

Leone seemed to have it under control, but he had centuries of practice. Even with that experience, I had seen the flash of white eyes, hungry for my blood.

I raised myself very slowly. The rocks under my feet seemed at odds with each other. With each step, they seemed to move out from under me. My body had grown so weak that

I couldn't keep my balance and felt all of my trust had been thrust upon noodles to hold me up.

I checked my pants' pocket and found my phone still there, turned off. It took me a long time to reach the entrance to the cave. I crept along, holding the wall for support. As I emerged, the sunlight stabbed like a sword into my brain and intensified the throbbing in my head.

I could make out the details of rocks to my left, past the opening of the cave. The top of the rock was bare of snow.

I rested there. I hoped my eyes would adjust to the light so I could once again identify my surroundings and figure out an escape plan.

I climbed onto the skinny rock, barely fitting with my knees pulled into my chest. The day felt much warmer than the previous ones with just enough warmth to tease. I assumed the winter still had a lot to give.

I dumped the water from the baggie and stuffed handfuls of snow into it. I tied off the top and placed the bag on my wound.

I closed my eyes. The chill in the air felt bearable with the sun beating down on my body. I had to turn my face away from the direct light to shade my eyes.

I enjoyed the feel of my blood flowing and life returning to my limbs.

I focused on a plan to escape. I did not dare use the phone until I knew Sam had stepped away for sure. I remembered his sense of smell and ability to hear. I thought through the possible characteristics that I didn't know about vampires. There were so many things that could end my escape in a deadly scenario. Could there be a way to poison a vampire? I had heard fleeting stories of tainted blood not killing a vampire, but altering him somehow. Could a vampire become mentally altered? Could a situation arise that would allow me to have an upper hand?

I sat in the same position with my eyes closed long enough that my body ached for me to shift positions. When I moved I tried to open my eyes. To my surprise, the pain didn't feel as great. I kept my eyes narrow and glanced around the area. I could see the hill slanting in front of me to the left. The indent in the snow marked the only trace of a path. Large and small lumps under the white veil indicated either bushes or rocks. This had been the direction I had gone to fill the pan days or weeks before. The same route Sam had brought me in. At the bottom ran the river. I doubted I would be able to make it across alive in the dead of winter.

Thick, white snow cloaked the pine trees—some other time such a sight would elicit "ooh's" and "ah's," but today their load of snow reminded me of the task of survival. Occasionally, large chunks dropped from the burdened branches and cut a slash in the fluff below. The thick tree-line seemed to take the shape of a large valley below the rocky ledge that lined the top of the hill where I sat.

I surveyed the area to the right of the valley, where the crystal blue water formed a small lake. Today, stark white completely covered the vicinity, indicating the lake had frozen over—a faint song from the waterfall at the lake's end hummed through the trees.

Below the lake the valley sloped. Although the details of the rugged terrain were hidden from my view, it seemed to drop quickly, but it might be manageable.

I decided any escape in this terrain would require my injuries to be healed and my strength to return. That meant I shouldn't provoke Sam, to avoid any further injury.

I moved from the rock, and stood, and stretched slowly. My head ached with the movement. The pang stopped me from fully extending my arms overhead.

I looked around the mouth of the cave. Sam perched on top, staring down at me.

I jumped back a step.

He laughed. "Planning an escape?"

"Wondering where you had gone, trying to decide if I had enough time to clean my clothes," I lied.

I took a few steps toward the cave. "I need my privacy. I will let you know when you can come back in." I bent down and packed snow into a big ball. I intended to melt it and wash my clothes.

Sam left me alone, but I played it safe. I wrapped the coat around my waist and zipped it up as far as I could. It made a funny looking skirt. I decided to hide the phone under the edge of Amy's bed while I scrubbed my pants and underwear. I even cleaned my socks. I hated being dirty. The activities took a long time. I had to sit down or work kneeling to regain my strength and keep my stomach from being queasy.

I boiled some water and placed dried meat in it for a broth. While the concoction steeped, I cleaned my clothes.

I sipped broth on Amy's bed as my clothes dried around the fire. I forced myself to keep the warm liquid down. I needed it to clear my fuzzy mind and give myself strength. Although my stomach moaned in protest, my body started to perk a little from the nutrition of the soup.

I felt well enough to tear apart my bed and burn it piece by piece. I decided to use Amy's, because it had not been soiled, and the extra moss and leaves we had packed into it would keep me warmer.

By the time I finished burning my bed, my clothes had dried, stiff and warm. I had scrubbed and boiled the smell out of them. They felt much nicer.

I checked the opening of the cave—no Sam. I reached under Amy's bed and sneaked my phone out and crammed it into my pocket.

I left the coat on the bed and sauntered out with just the sweater on.

Sam had disappeared, although he would be keeping an eye on me. My plan was not to make a complete escape, but to turn on the phone and try and call Leone. I slowly meandered away from the cave. Sam would seize me in an instant if he believed I was escaping from the cave. I ambled to the left, down the path that he had brought me on. Sam did not come for me.

My injuries would hobble any run, but I solidified a less physical plan.

I walked as far as the first waterfall. I crept up to the edge of it and bent down. I scanned the area around me and pulled the phone from my pocket. I hoped the sound of the waterfall would muffle the phone's activation sounds. I simultaneously dipped my hair in the water, cradled the phone against my stomach and turned the phone on. Fear zipped through me as the chime sounded louder than expected. I pushed it into my gut to muffle it.

Just in case Sam watched me, I left the phone cradled in the fold of the sweater and dipped the side of my blood crusted head in the water. I gritted my teeth to bear the sting of the freezing water as it touched my scalp for the first time.

I worked my fingers into it and moaned as a sensation as sharp as knife points stabbed into my wound. I gingerly fingered around the outside of the scab, freeing as much dried blood as possible. I couldn't stay long with my head in the water—the cold too intense. I pulled my head back and waited for the dripping to ease from my hair and for the ice needles to stop poking into my scalp. I slid the phone into the sweater pocket and stood. Through the increased dizziness, I remembered to wring out my hair.

I searched for Sam again. I had been gone for at least ten minutes, and he still did not appear.

I had to push it a little. I walked down the path farther, toward where I thought the second waterfall had been. Still no Sam.

I pushed on the side of the phone, hoping I hit the volume key, effectively silencing it.

I wondered if I should make a call or text first. Texting would be quieter, but would it work this deep in the woods?

If time allowed for only one or the other, the right choice was crucial. I chose to text first and then to call. I needed to be sure one message made it to the other end. Texting would make less noise. And that meant if Sam was close, he would not hear me talking. I knew I could send it, then I could call. I could leave a voice message if no one answered.

I rounded another cliff on the left that would give me a little privacy—just in case.

What would I say? I knew I pushed my luck on time. It would have to be short.

"Highway toward South out of town, left, down river, cross river, high mountain, waterfalls, in the cave."

Those were the most important highlights I could give him, and the only ones I knew for sure about my whereabouts. I hoped these words narrowed the search for me—hopefully it would all fit into one text.

I pretended to rest against the cliff, waiting to see if Sam would materialize out of the woods. I dug the phone out, opened it, and started to text.

I shook like a sapling in the wind. I dropped the phone and it flipped closed. *Shoot! I was half way done.*

I snatched it again. In my hurry, words were misspelled. Leone would have to figure them out. I clicked send. My heart pounded—each beat hammering behind my eyes, causing my vision to blur. I tucked the phone back into my pocket.

I expected an impending blow to knock me from my perch. Nothing came. No Sam.

Did I dare try to call? I could not be sure the text made it from here to there.

I drew in a few deep breaths, inspected my surroundings, and pulled the phone out. I scrolled to Leone's name, connected and I heard a ring. Leone's frantic voice answered. "Rhiannon! Where are you?"

"Leone." Uncontrollable emotion to washed over me. My throat choked, threatening tears. *Not now, darn it!* "Leone. The mountains..."

Sam stood beside me, glaring. He ripped the phone from my hands.

I could hear Leone pleading for me to continue.

So close. I prayed the text message had been successful. I trembled at the look in Sam's eyes, assuring that I sealed my fate.

Sam laughed into the phone as he put it up to his ear. "Poor Leone. Amazing creature, this Rhiannon." His red eyes never wavered from me. "Now, of course, she is in trouble with me. We had a deal, and well, good luck finding her." The call disconnected as he crushed the phone in one hand.

My legs trembled. He yanked my arm and flung me toward the path. For what seemed an eternity, my feet danced through the air, futilely kicking to make contact with the ground. For a moment I was weightless—when my feet hit, I tumbled to the ground.

"I let you wander down. I thought about stopping you. I noticed you wash your hair. I turned to find some food for you, and then you were gone." He heaved me onto my feet and shoved me hard up the trail toward the cave. My brain bounced around off my skull. "You should never have crossed me."

I could hear the frozen tips of my hair swishing on the coat with each step as I walked—trying to focus on the uneven ground. My distorted vision made it look magnified. My feet still stumbled from lack of balance.

"Your luck is not so good." He steadied me on the walk into the cave. He supported my other shoulder with his free hand, further helping me to balance.

I bit my tongue so as not to resist his help, but I didn't want him to touch me—my skin crawled wherever his hand rested.

When I reached my bed, I flumped down and curled into a ball, again exhausted. My head throbbed from the simple walk and my fear of Sam.

His clothes were wet, probably from being in the snow. He took off his damp shirt, spread it out on the rocks next to the fire and squatted to face me.

"This situation has me thinking," Sam stated as he pulled at his chin. "Peppin longs to kill you. Leone wants to be with you. Am I correct?" Sam eyed me expectantly, but I did not answer. "I will take your silence as confirmation."

The fire burned lower and cast shadows across his face, and deepened the definition in his muscular torso. The small animal he had killed for me lay in a heap next to the stone hearth.

"The one thing neither of them figured on was me. You see, in creating me, poor Peppin thought he had a weak mind to control. You asked about my being human. Well, I remember in life having been very intelligent. I downplayed it around my friends and family to fit in. In truth, I understood what people were thinking. I could beat them to the answer they were seeking. I also understood the scientific world around me, generally without studying it." He registered my confusion and offered explanation.

"For instance...," he expanded, "when my mother broke her arm on a hike, far away from anyone or any dwelling. I, as a child, instinctively knew what to do. No one could explain it, not even me after people found out what I did. By everyone else's account, it was a phenomenal feat. My mother's bone had broken through the flesh. I simply went to work, set the bone, sealed off the wound, bound it with cloth, and made a splint with wood."

My queasy stomach churned with the thoughts of her arm, but Sam continued on.

"All the while, she screamed in agony. But I knew... I could see all the veins and blood flow, and minute fragments of the bone reflected in my mind. I knew exactly how to manipulate the arm to produce the correct effect. All of that, a doctor would have relied on an x-ray for." He bent closer as if to gauge my response, then back to continue his story.

"Previously, I had thought myself normal," he admitted frankly. "That incident was the first time I realized that my mind existed as an anomaly. Because I was a child, adults passed off my actions as a fluke. I knew better. I had used my brain in a most unique way to save my mother's life, and I was well aware of every step of the procedure."

His lips sneered as he leaned toward me again. I sank back onto the wooden platform.

"From then on, I practiced my ability. I touched living things and could imagine their internal structures. My mind visualized diagrams that were not in the medical books yet— muscles that were not mapped, veins that hadn't been charted. I had almost completed nursing school when Peppin found me."

I jerked my head to face him. "Can you even imagine the heightened ability my transformation gave me?"

He gloated, arms raised toward the cave ceiling, as if addressing a large and adoring audience.

I wondered where he ventured with his conversation. *Could he have an intensified aptitude for kidnapping teenage girls? For creating inhuman acts? For murder?*

He whisked more logs onto the fire.

He studied my face. "I touched your wound." He pointed to the large lump on my head. "I can see all the correct things working together to heal it. Your upset stomach will eventually go away, although you might feel weak for days."

360

I harrumphed, the intended communication being, 'Whatever, and thanks for your part in it, jerk.'

He smiled at that. "Peppin misunderstood my talent. I touched him as he changed me. My mind was consumed with such with pain—I remember that now, but tucked under the layer of agony I realized that his tissues and blood were completely different. Nothing flowed in him. It seemed as though his body had frozen into a congealed form."

Great. All I needed to know, gelatinous creatures. I wanted to fall asleep and not wake up.

"His bone deviated from normal also—not the same consistency. It reminded me more of a bird's, porous, seemingly light. It is the same with me now. To change from human to this..." He motioned his hands to his muscular stomach. "It is such a feat of unimaginable proportion, no wonder the pain had surpassed anything that I had ever known. No wonder my mind had blanked out and been rewritten."

I just watched him—wondering if he had decided something regarding my life. I felt I should already know my fate, the way he toyed with me. My head hurt as I tried to focus on anything that would allow me an upper hand.

"No, Peppin misunderstood." Sam nodded to himself and then clamped his hands to his head as if he suffered horrifically. "Imagine the pain."

I didn't need to imagine, I knew. I had experienced the beginnings of it before, from Peppin himself. I slid backward on my bed.

He chuckled, as he approached and kneeled beside me. "The game would stop, you see."

I shook my head, suddenly afraid that I did, indeed, know what he intended. Panic must have been on my face.

"Ah, yes," he said. "I think you do. Really, the change is simple. I would love to actually take the time to analyze the process as it courses through your body, the poison consuming

361

you and changing you. I am most curious to know how it manipulates the bone into a completely different density."

Instinctively, I retreated, crablike, further back on the bed until my fingers touched the cold stone on the other side. I did not want to be a guinea pig. I moved backward and then rolled over to put my hands on the stone behind the bed. I pulled my leg up and dropped one foot to the floor. I tried to lunge away from him. As soon as I started to pull my other foot to me to allow me to stand, he grabbed it and propelled me backward. My body fell to the floor. My hands lessened my fall, sprawling out. I used one leg to leverage myself against twigs, in an attempt to prevent his hauling me back onto the bedding. Only a minor hindrance, however, in a flash he swung his body over the top of me and lay down across my back. My torso and face flattened against the cold stone.

His body covered me with his arms stretching the length of mine. He twined his fingers into mine.

His chest rested on my back. His legs wrapped around mine, I was completely pinned to the ground. This time his body seemed lighter, not crushing me like before. Breathing came easy. That idiosyncrasy must be something else I didn't understand about the vampire body. They had the ability to alter their weight.

The swollen knob on the side of my head faced upward. He brushed his lips along it to my ear and whispered, "Vampire desires run deeper than humans. When one experiences a deep desire, it consumes them. Have you wondered why Leone is so enraptured with you?"

Indeed, I had wondered how time after time, he waited for me.

He continued, "Have you ever wondered why Peppin needs to find you?"

I remained silent, feeling the pain in my head and knowing I could not get out of this position. I could feel his chest rising and falling as he spoke.

"You have become what they need to survive. They cannot help it. You are like food to a human—they *have* to have you to survive. Only their survival is eternity." I wondered at the veracity of his words, but he offered a sensible explanation for both Leone and Peppin's behavior.

My destiny was to repeat. My destiny would always be to die.

"I analyzed you as you sat on the rocks. You moved carefully—you listened and learned about the surroundings. I imagined you were tracing paths across the mountains, getting ready for an escape." He paused long enough to sniff and then kiss the back of my neck. I closed my eyes tight and whimpered, imagining he could sink his teeth in at any moment.

He moved one of his hands, tracing up the entire length of my arm, through my armpit and down the side to my waist. He moved enough to raise my waist from the ground and slid his hand down toward my legs. He rested his body on mine again—his weight a little heavier. I stifled a cry. *No. No. No.*

"I watched you. You are beautiful. If I were human, I would court you the proper way. Our situation, however, is precarious. I do believe I'm just as easily swayed by your allure as Peppin and Leone." He drew up to kiss the center of my back. I squeezed my eyes harder. A tear trickled and dripped from my cheek. Although I refused to imagine what he planned to do with me, my body trembled uncontrollably and more tears silently slipped to the ground.

"Imagine, Rhiannon. Imagine being with me," he persuaded. "I do not want to hurt you. But if I changed you, you would be free. Peppin would lose his sport. You would no longer be hunted. You would no longer have to change lives. You would finally be able to just be."

"I don't want that," my voice wavered, thick and fragile with emotion. "I have parents and a life. I do not want to change."

"I understand that. I would not have chosen this either. But, it's not so bad. Really."

I could feel his tongue lightly circling against my neck. I felt his hand rubbing my inner thigh through my pants.

"It would be painful—there is no way around it. But I will be with you the whole time. I will not leave you. Your skin is so smooth and intoxicating."

My heart withered at the thought of losing the battle with life.

"Please, no," I begged. "I'm not ready for any of this."

He flipped me over on my back. I scrambled to get away while he moved me, but to no avail.

He scooped me into his embrace and kissed me. I could feel his tongue pushing through my mouth. I pushed against his body. He continued as though he didn't notice my attempt to deny him. I finally let him invade without returning his desire. *So, this will be it. I will die being the enjoyment for someone else. But not really die...*

He kissed me gently, trying to caress feelings from me that were not there. I breathed him in and did not like the smell. Hot tears spilled over my temples and into my hair. I vaguely remembered Leone doing similar things that made my body respond in another life. I remembered it so differently.

This body had never done this, and it was as unwilling as my mind. I shuddered with every touch.

His eyes were hungry, but a regular amber color, not white or red. At least feeding did not appear to be his motivation, although I might prefer it. As he looked into my face, I saw his mood change, like a puppy beaten with a newspaper.

He lowered me and looked away. I was so grateful. I sobbed openly and rolled on my side as he moved.

He brushed my hair with his hand and I rolled into a ball next to him.

He kept stroking my hair, staring at me. Something unsettled between us nagged at me—something huge and unfinished as if my sanity hung in the balance. He held all the power.

He stroked my hair again. Something had to happen here, but I lay too weak and overwhelmed to flee. It always seemed to come back to me caving in and giving up.

17

Escape

Sam stood up and walked away. I stayed on the ground unmoving, willing the tension to go away.

I remained still and silent for a while, although the rock under me held no warmth and no comfort. When I slowly slid back on my makeshift bed, I did so as quietly as possible and again curled into a ball. I faced away from Sam. After a time, I heard him busying himself with things.

I had to escape. I saw no other option. I did not want him close to me again. I dared to hope that Leone would be figuring out where Sam hid me. *How can I escape?* I needed a reason to get outside. The only time he ever let me outside was to use the restroom.

The sunlight in the cave gave the indication that it was afternoon. I would definitely be out in the wilderness in the dark if I left now. I had no idea how far the roads were from here. I needed to bide my time and wear all the warm items I had available to me. In order to make it work, I would have to make Sam think I planned to let him change me.

I smelled rich, tangy meat roasting. My stomach groaned with anticipation. I hadn't been able to keep any substantial food down since my injury. I rolled over and sat up on my bed. I reached for my coat and put it on.

Sam watched me.

I stared into the fire until he had finished cooking the food. He passed me the plate. I decided to take small nibbles and let my body digest what it could. I would need strength to have any chance of getting away.

He walked to the entrance of the cave and crouched on his haunches. He could still see me, but I had some peace while trying to eat.

I left my plate next to me. I grabbed my bags and plunked them on my bed. I found my brush and attacked my hair, taking great care around my wound to keep from pulling hard. The tangles were difficult to work out, but with patience my hair smoothed out. I nibbled some more of my food. After I ate as much as my stomach could handle, I used the toothbrush. I tried to give the appearance of readying myself for sleep. While performing my duties, I took inventory. I slid the knife from my plate into my coat pocket. I knew a small knife would do nothing against Sam, but if I were trapped in the woods overnight, it would come in handy.

That had been the only useful thing in my back pack. I stuffed all of the items back, put the plate on the floor, and sipped some of the water from the cup. I would need to sleep in order to keep the small amount of food I ate down.

I also needed to lead Sam on. "Sam, I might need tonight to think about changing. Your argument does have me contemplating the possibilities. I'm tired now." I hoped it would keep him from attacking me while I slept.

He didn't say anything in return. I lay back on the bed and forced my eyes closed. I focused on counting my heartbeats to ease my tension. I tucked the collar of the coat firmly around my neck and pulled my legs up to conserve my warmth.

Thoughts paraded through my mind as I lay there listening to the fire. I knew Leone would be searching hard, I hoped in the correct direction. Tomorrow was the day for truth. I would either survive it, or I wouldn't—no longer waiting for fate.

My stomach churned. I prayed I would be able to keep the food down. As I slipped into sleep, I felt the blanket placed over the top of me. My muscles tensed, every nerve on high alert anticipating any touch or breath upon my skin. Tension eased as time past and nothing happened. I hoped he would leave me alone for the night.

Judging by the light in the cave when I awoke, I had slept through most of the morning.

Time for me to make my move. I spotted Sam moving toward the cave entrance. As I started forward, Sam turned and looked at me.

"I need to use the bushes," I explained.

He nodded and we both left the cave at the same time. I edged along the cave wall to the area I used for my duties.

Sam watched me. When I defiantly made eye contact with him, he turned and followed the path to the left of the cave and disappeared, his back blending into the black shadows of the trees. I knew I had to act fast—this might be my only chance.

I took a few steps and peered in his direction.

I jumped onto the path and cut right toward the large lake. The water flowed downhill from there. My only option would be to follow it down.

I raced down the steep path, picking up more and more speed, like a boulder set free. My feet barely kept up with my downhill momentum—arms flailing and body jarring each time the soles of my shoes squashed through the snow and hit the hard ground. The skin on my face felt detached, like putty drooping after each bounce. A cold breeze blasted freezing breath into my nostrils and lungs.

The path turned to the left and skirted the edge of the lake. I planted my heels in as I slowed to make the turn. As I leaned back, my feet shot out from under me. I landed hard on the frozen ground. My head rolled back with a snap. My eyes clenched as fresh pain lanced through my brain. I finished sliding to a stop on my hands and buttocks.

I jumped back to my feet and scrambled to pick up speed again. I needed to listen for the waterfall—from there, I could follow the stream on down.

My head hurt, throbbing to the pounding of my blood. My heart jammed into my throat, making it hard to swallow. I pumped my arms to propel me forward. A cry escaped my lips from the effort. I squinted one eye trying to keep the head pain away. *Make it. Beat him. You have to keep going.*

The throbbing of my head threatened to make me take heed or become ill again. I had to ignore it.

The path grew steep again, and the descent was filled with loose rocks. I had to go slower. My leg muscles burned as though alcohol had been poured on filleted skin. My knees absorbed most of the impact and felt they would snap. I focused on keeping my balance and not spinning out of control. If I fell, I would get hurt—if I stepped precariously, I could break my leg.

The path bent through trees. Roots from the giants were exposed in places, causing me to strategically place my feet. I could hear a waterfall rumbling ahead of me.

A blood curdling roar sent chills coursing through me.

"No," I pleaded to myself. I needed more time. I had descended far enough below the cave that I couldn't see the hilltop, but I knew he pursued me. No turning back now.

I rushed toward the sound of the waterfall. Water meant I could hide my smell. I hoped the size of the lake reflected a large amount of water cascading down the other side.

The ground rose up in front of me, frosted and white. My feet hit the ground faster than I anticipated, and I had to catch

370

myself on a tree to keep from slipping into the snow. As I swung around the tree trying to stay upright, I chanced a look over my shoulder and saw a blur of color through the trees. He had closed the distance.

I pushed harder. I had to hide in water—my only chance.

The trees gave way to bushes. The mountain seemed to disappear directly in front of me. To my right the water flowed. To the left a mountain loomed at a very steep incline, it formed the top of the valley that held the lake.

I had been so caught up trying to decide on my escape route as I approached the edge of the cliff, I didn't notice Sam bearing down on me.

He grabbed my hair from behind and yanked me back to him. As I jerked to a stop, I tried to pull free from his grasp.

Then I froze at the sight of Leone racing from the snow filled trees below me. *Dreaming? Had my head finally burst? Could it really be him?* I reached out to him.

Sam hissed and clamped my hair tighter, causing me to step back into his embrace.

Leone crouched, ready to spring. Sam led me to the left. Leone peered to where we moved. I could see details of the cliff as we approached. Dark rocks jutted below, among small frozen bushes and dead grass. The spray from the waterfall misted around the trees that lined it, giving an eerie appearance to the vegetation. Icicles formed on the outer branches, which hung low from the weight.

"Stop!" Leone commanded.

Sam said nothing. I looked down at the rocks, twenty feet below me. Sam pushed me away from him, positioning me close to the edge, so close that my left foot slid off the side. Reaching back, I grabbed his arm, hoping to regain footing. I stared at the ground below me. My mouth had opened, but no scream left me. I sharply inhaled and the cold air prickled at my tongue. Leone responded with a forward step.

Sam jerked me back by my hair. "You have been bad, Rhiannon. Now look at what you have done. Leone's here to save you." His breath hissed in my ear. "You have seriously limited my options."

"Leone!" came the scream from below. Leone stiffened in anticipation of Sam's next move.

In one fluid motion, Sam slammed his hand into my right side and pushed me over the edge of the cliff. Instantaneously, with leverage from my precarious grip on Sam's arm, I spun around. I kept myself from flying away from the cliff, but my feet still had no ground under them. I knew if I could grab anything with my hands, I could slow my fall to the rocks below.

I bounced off the rim with my gut, forcing the air from my lungs like a balloon. I managed to grip an exposed root in my left hand from one of the giant trees, but the momentum of my body pulled downward against my precarious hold, and my grip began to slip.

No air to keep me going.

Needed to breath. Needed to hold on.

I glanced down to an incongruent scene—uneven jagged rocks with pillow-soft snow filling in the gaps. Deceptively inviting, but the landing would not be pretty.

Gratefully, I felt Leone's hand wrap around my wrist. His eyes were black in the light of day, and his brow puckered as he gazed down at me.

The bright white from the snow around me started to mingle with the greens. Light and tingly, my body began to float upward.

With a graceful motion, Leone lifted me to the edge above the cliff.

My head swam from lack of air, but as I locked my gaze on his eyes, I couldn't be sure it wasn't just my body's natural response to him. I grabbed for my chest.

Take a breath, Rhi. Come on. Don't pass out now!

Just as the edges of my vision seeped black, my lungs again expanded.

"Rhi," Leone scooped me up and held me as I gulped air into my chest. "My Rhi! I made it." He rocked me.

I reached up and caressed his face. He felt so good under my fingers. Real.

Dante and Angelina stood behind him. Angelina twirled a piece of her blonde hair in her fingers. That, and the way she stood with her hips askew and one arm crossed in front of her, gave the impression that the whole scene bored her.

"Leone, is she alright?" Dante placed his hand on Leone's shoulder.

"She will be." Leone looked up at both of them. "We need to find him."

They all looked at each other.

"Angelina, will you help Rhiannon get down off the hill from here? Dante and I will take chase."

Angelina rolled her eyes and stomped her foot.

She flipped her hand in the air as though trying to shoo little kids away from cookies. "Go," she hissed.

Dante left first. Leone kissed my forehead and gently settled me on a tree root.

"You will be safe. Take it easy." Then he, too, disappeared into the trees.

Angelina stood a moment longer, chomping on her gum, twirling her hair, and staring her black eyes into me. For a moment, they flashed red as her lips, into an evil smile.

I gulped and began shivering.

"What's wrong?" Angelina's mock sympathy was not lost on me as her eyes returned to black.

"I'm just all nerves, that's all."

"Oh, poor, poor Rhi."

I did not have a warm, fuzzy feeling about Angelina.

She stepped over to me, touched the wound on my head and snickered to herself.

"Good work." She smiled down at me. "Better get you home so you can do it all over again." Her words cut. She reached down, yanking me by my arms and threw me onto my feet. I rubbed where her fingers had dug in.

She motioned with her hand which way we were supposed to go, sneering at me.

What on earth did I do to her? It would be better to have never known her. Why did Leone leave me here in her care? I began the descent around the cliff. Precarious footing and my throbbing head made it slow. Angelina showed her frustration by huffing loudly and standing below me with her arms crossed. I assumed that she intended to show her disapproval of my too-slow human limitations.

I didn't care. I needed to take my time, and I didn't feel a need to have her approve of me. I only hoped that she would not decide to kill me. The image of her red eyes stuck fast to my psyche.

"Can you go any faster?" she fussed.

I didn't answer her. I did not even offer her a glance.

"Fine, you know what? There is a game trail just down from here. Take it. It starts to curve up to the other side of the valley, get off and start going down the hill from there. Stay along the water's edge, and I will meet you." Her eyes uncaring when I looked at her.

So this is how it would be. Snotty, beautiful, loathsome creature. 'I wonder why you took the trouble to even come, considering how you really feel.' I hoped my expression indicated my incredulity.

She quipped maliciously, "I actually had hoped to see your body again. Not alive. Well, maybe alive, but barely hanging on. It rips Leone's heart out..." she paused and inspected me up and down, the snarl on her lips contorted her face. She added, "Over you." She threw her head back as if studying something more interesting in the tree tops.

"You!" She pointed to me. "The first few times it killed me to watch him, but now I know what's coming. I thought he could be consoled, but no. Only you. That's it. That's all he wants. That's all he ever wanted." She spat her words, then flipped around and hiked with amazing speed away from me.

I stood there shaking.

She came to see my body die. Isn't that just the pinnacle of friendship? She didn't really care that Leone would relive the torture either? Coldhearted.

I willed my trembling legs to move again.

I pondered Angelina. I wished I could remember some of the memories that we had shared in previous lives that may give me some insight as to what I might have done to offend her.

I maneuvered down the trail on wobbly legs for what seemed like eternity. I rested often to console my throbbing head.

I didn't take the game trail and instead kept to the thicker tree-line just above it to be less conspicuous.

I accessed a place to rest and noticed a lone pine on a natural rise a short distance above the river. I had begun to follow. I decided to rest there.

I picked my way slowly through the snowy ground.

As I approached, I could see a long mound of snow. When I rounded the base of the lone tree, shock shot through me—a familiar blue sock poking from the mound.

I held my breath as I slowly examined the mass. As I analyzed the details, I could see faint colors bleeding through the bleach-white snow atop the form. My eyes discerned intricate details.

Fingers, poking out from their frozen blanket, were dainty, long and thin. I could visualize them having played a piano, but now grasped death with nails cracked and chipped. Skin blue. Cold. Dead.

I choked a sob.

"Do I know this person? No. I can't know this person." I tried to talk myself into believing it was the fate of someone I didn't know as my hands went to my face.

Tears pooled in my eyes, skewing my view. *Could it be Amy?*

I stepped back. *Do I want to know if it's Amy?* A cry escaped me.

Had he really killed her? I saw the blood on the coat. He never did tell me. I realized as I stood there, that I hoped he'd left her alive—that maybe she injured herself and spattered the red onto the jacket.

I had to know.

I stumbled on gelatin legs toward the body.

I reached toward the head, covered in snow. *What will the face look like? Am I ready for it?* I had seen people in caskets before, but they always seemed to be sleeping. They had their natural color about them. I looked back at the hand. Blue.

I need to know. I have to know.

I quickly wiped the snow from part of the face.

Hair, caught in the snow, stuck to my fingertips like cobwebs.

Amy's cold dead eyes peered at me.

I collapsed in a heap in front of her. A low moan resonated deep within and shook my whole being. Sobs broke free. Tears, hot against the cold, cascaded down my cheeks. I rocked back and forth, hugging myself.

I couldn't tear my gaze from her. "Amy, Amy, Amy" I cried, "so sorry Amy. I'm so sorry."

I swore I understood the look in her eyes, frozen in time—horrified. I could barely see her mouth, pursed in an oval. She might have been screaming.

I cried. I imagined myself lying there. I could see Leone in the position I now sat. I replaced this time and this place with so many of my own deaths, and Leone had been there to watch. *Had I lain in a position like this? Had my face found peace or was it locked in torture?*

More tears.

I leaned forward slowly.

I reached to touch her cold face. The skin was frozen, hard and gummy, no longer supple. I tried to close her eyes, but winter secured them.

I jerked my hand back. A new moan emitted from my depths, racking my ribcage.

"I am so sorry, Amy," I whimpered.

My hand swiped away the snow at her neck. I knew instantly that her death had been relatively quick. A gaping hole had been left below her ear.

No bite marks. In fact, no skin remained. Sam had ripped most of her neck out on that side.

I leaned protectively over the top of her. My tears dropped down onto her neck.

She didn't deserve this. All for me. Why? She had been innocent, trying to make her own way. Her only sin to end up sitting next to me in class, a sin in Sam's book anyway. A coincidence she paid for with her life.

I punched my leg with my fist.

I sat back on my feet and rocked with each wave screaming and crying over Amy.

The emotional outburst left me drained. As I regained control of myself, I realized I'd placed my other hand on her shoulder, supporting my weight as I cried.

I sniffled and wiped at my nose.

Tree branches swished from the hill above me. My head jerked up to the tree line, from where the sound seemed to come.

Black robes.

"No." My heart stopped momentarily as shock stabbed my chest.

Black robes, bald head, hunchback, floating, I knew that figure from the depths of my spirit. It filtered through me like old poison, piercing every good thought, every loving feeling until all that remained was the terror of every last moment my being ever endured. All pain, all horror, all death.

My legs rooted to the ground beneath me. I pushed myself backward, sliding down the slight hill.

Red eyes. Curling smile. He reached his hand toward me.

I slid my feet under me and wobbled backward on even ground. I could not tear my eyes from him. He was here, in my world, in my Idaho. All encompassing, the fate of my lives, here and again, I found myself alone. I swiped my tear-soaked cheeks with my sleeve.

"It is proper to say hello when you see someone that you have not seen in a while." His voice sent a chill down my spine. The narrator of my nightmares.

I choked a cry, still retreating away from him. I became faintly aware of the water gurgling behind me.

"Really, Rhi?" He paused, looking down at his hands. He stopped moving toward me. "It is Rhi, isn't it?" His question seemed to amuse him, judging from way he gloated.

"Of course it is—what am I thinking?" He rolled his eyes in mock exasperation before he finally fixed his blood-colored orbs on me. "It puzzles me greatly to this very day, how every time you repeat life, those parents of yours...let's see, how many do they number now?"

Tapping his hand to his chin and counting. "It's so hard to say, but they always give you a name that allows everyone to call you 'Rhi' for short. Funny, little, infinite idiosyncrasy isn't it?" He shook his head and shoulders, imitating a good laugh.

I glanced downhill.

Angelina stood with her arms crossed, watching, not offering any help.

I tilted my head toward her and motioned slightly toward Peppin, hoping to indicate I would appreciate her help.

She just smiled in return.

I should have guessed. She had come to see me die. I clenched my jaw and gripped my fists. I began to scan the area.

The larger river ran behind Angelina. I glimpsed the current as it rushed down stream, disappearing around the bend. The stream behind me, swollen and swift at this location, dumped into the larger river below. I could see the swirling water as they folded together.

Peppin continued his babbling. "It really makes you stop and think. Do you really choose your parents? Your patterns are truly puzzling. Where you appear, when you appear, those are predictions that cannot be made by the wisest of soothsayers. Only Leone has ever been correct." At the mention of Leone's name, my attention focused back at him.

"How strange this time, though." He tapped his chin again. "I felt a faint charge, just a hint of him finding you. Normally, when he touches those lips, the reaction, no matter where I am is like being hit with a bullet. So different this time, I wonder how he hid it from me. No matter. I'm here now, just like every other time." His sick lips curled into a foul smile. "And look at you, your eyes so swollen from your superfluous sniveling. Do you know they are red? Red. We could make them permanently that way. It really becomes you."

I stepped back and evaluated the river. He wouldn't get me without my exhausting every effort to survive.

"Planning for your escape, dear?" Peppin rose a little higher into the air. A large crashing sound came from the forest behind him.

"Don't you worry your pretty little neck. I'm here for a larger fish... this time." His eyes grew wide as he emphasized his words. He spun in the air to face the direction of the sounds.

Large snapping sounds rumbled. Trees ripped and boomed loudly to the ground. I could imagine their massive weight pushing everything in their way as the vegetation beneath exploded.

I cringed, not knowing what to expect. The sounds grew closer and louder.

I stepped toward the water and hugged myself tighter with every blast.

A loud, repeated popping came from the edge of the trees. Close, too close. I froze and stopped breathing to try and listen.

Sam, body turned to the side, checked over his shoulder as his feet skidded in the snow. He held back at the edge of the trees, unaware of what occurred in this clearing ahead of him.

He laughed at whatever pursued him right before another swooshing, scraping, gyrating noise came from another fallen giant. The crash, as the tree hit the ground, sent a cloud of debris, snow, and dirt billowing from the trees into the clearing.

Sam, apparently pleased with himself, started forward again. Fast.

He had descended the hill into the clearing halfway when he realized I was there. In an instant, his eyes fell upon Peppin hovering halfway up the tree between us.

Sam slid to a stop, falling backward and catching himself on his hand.

I checked downhill toward Angelina. Although her position was unchanged, her mouth gaped open and her arms draped at her sides as she stared toward Sam.

Peppin's voice focused on Sam again. "And there he is."

Sam stood up. Lips pumping open and closed like a fish.

Sam must not have known Peppin was there either.

Leone raced to the edge of the forest and stopped short, taking in the scene before him. A growl emanated from him, his white eyes glowing with intensity.

Peppin's focus never left Sam. "Leone, dear friend, so good to see you. Would love to stay and catch up on old times, but I have some business to attend."

As soon as Peppin finished, Sam raced down toward Angelina, then turned up into the thick forest, disappearing into the trees.

Peppin facing Leone, continuing his greeting. "We have some unfinished business. I will be back for it." Then he shot me a glance and bowed, as though he were the most proper of men.

Peppin burst into the forest as Dante zipped beside me from the river above.

"Peppin?" he asked.

My voice could not answer. I simply nodded in agreement.

My legs buckled as Leone ran to me. He supported my weight as he hugged me. I looked down hill toward Angelina. Her eyes were white and she stood glaring at the three of us. Her head tilted forward, hands clenched.

Dante and Leone turned to see her the split second before she tore into the forest following the path Sam and Peppin had taken.

I released and crumpled to the ground, staring after her. Leone sank with me.

Still alive. Peppin could have killed me. Still alive! I knew it wasn't pure luck. Angelina had appeared angry, probably that I'd not been finished off. Now she is chasing Peppin. As much as I hoped her intention would be to plead for my life, considering the conversation we had shared, I knew better.

Leone reached down and collected me. I tucked my head into his neck.

"He killed Amy." I had a laundry list of things to share. Somehow the image of Amy summed it all up.

He hugged me tighter.

"He promised he wouldn't. He said he would take her home." The raw emotion began to bubble to the surface again, cracking my voice. Tears filled my eyes.

"He terrified her, Leone. He tore out her throat. What a horrible way to die," I sobbed. "He... did not even do it... quick, without her knowing."

"Rhi." He patted my back and swayed with me in his arms.

I just pointed over his shoulder.

Dante, at the sight of the fallen tree, inspected the devastation. He shook his head—his shoulders seemed to melt as I watched.

"He did that because of me."

Leone set me down on the ground, and guided my chin with his finger until he could peer into my eyes. "You are not responsible for Peppin or Sam."

I looked down at my dirty hands. "But Amy," I whispered.

"You could not have saved her, Rhi."

I focused on the dirt and ripped cuticles on my fingertips while Leone joined Dante. They conversed in low tones.

I felt unprotected standing in the clearing alone.

I turned to stare in the direction Angelina, Sam, and Peppin had disappeared, half expecting one of them to return for me. I found myself stepping backward toward Leone and Dante.

When they returned to my side, Leone placed a hand on my back. "Let's get you home. I know some parents that would love to see you." Again he scooped me up.

With the intensity of the situation, I'd not focused on the pain in my head. With each of Leone's steps, my head bounced and reminded me of that pain. I winced and tried to hold my head off his shoulder.

We neared the fast-moving water of the main river. After assessing where the water flow spread out and the speed lessened, they walked across. I lay, draped across their four arms, thankfully, observing billowing snow-filled clouds. I heard the swift water's gurgle and churning and perceived them stumbling beneath me every now and then, but we crossed without a drop of cold water on me.

I chose to walk the rest of the way down the steep mountainside because Leone's drenched, cold clothing would have frozen me. It had been slow going with my head pounding fiercely again. Leone used his phone to call out for search and rescue. It took so long for me to descend the rest of the way that they met up with us half way to their rigs. I stopped in my tracks as we broke through the trees and spied their green and yellow coats—civilization, at last.

Had I really made it?

I soaked up the warmth of the blanket they wrapped around me. Tendrils of feeling seeped back into my fingertips. I smiled at the sight of Leone and Dante in their blankets.

After promising the rescuers that I would make it just fine back to the rigs, they allowed me to walk without an immediate check up. Leone and Dante also insisted they were completely fine.

After an hour of hiking, we reached a dirt parking lot, probably an old logging area abandoned for the winter. Snow had drifted, leaving it as deep as three feet in some places. The rescuers loaded Leone and me on the extended seat of the truck and turned on the engine.

Dante followed in Leone's truck.

Leone snuggled close me.

The radio crackled as the team dispatched that I had been rescued. The words filled me. *Rescued.* Relief swept through me like a warm breeze—tears of gratitude slipped into the blanket I used to hide them. *Saved. I will not die today. Is this the first time I had ever escaped Peppin?* I let the question slip from my mind as Leone's fingers began to rub my back. I lay my head in his lap atop a folded blanket.

"Rhiannon!" My mom yelled as she raced to the truck with Dad right behind her.

We crowded through the door into the hospital with me wrapped in Mom's arms—she kissed my hair then alternately pressed her cheek to it. Finally, she stood back and gawked at the wound on the side of my head. Her mouth worked, she wanted to say something—nothing came out. Her eyes glowed from withheld tears. She lowered her eyes to mine and put her hands on my shoulders.

"I'm okay, Mom," I emphasized each word. I noticed that she appeared tired, as I drank in the adoration reflected in her eyes. Kind eyes I didn't think I would ever see again. I hugged her. Dad joined us.

A nurse wheeled in a chair with information that the ER doctor admitted me to the hospital, at least overnight, to take a battery of tests.

Mom and Dad huddled with me in the ER. I was relieved that they had no questions about the circumstances of my disappearance, when the doctor led in a couple of police officers.

They asked a few pointed questions—one of them, if I had been raped. Mom's face paled, ghost-white. Dad clenched his jaw and tightened his fists.

"No," I stated, and both Mom and Dad were washed with relief at the same moment.

The officers obtained Sam's description. I feigned exhaustion and told them I didn't feel like talking any more for the night. I needed to go over things with Leone before revealing anything else. They told me they would come back tomorrow.

After a CAT scan, blood-work, and other poking and prodding, a nurse cleaned and bandaged my head and administered a pain killer.

I awoke, groggy, in my own room.

"You're an angel when you sleep," Leone's voice lulled me from my fog. "You made it. You are one tough woman." He stroked my fingers and kissed my cheek.

One eye had been covered with the bandage for my head wound, so I tilted my head to use the other eye. I smiled at his blue eyes.

Tingling in my stomach, I ached to spend every moment with him. I reached up to touch his face and pled to Leone, silently. *Kiss me, please, Leone. I am alive and want those lips.*

Mom stepped in the door. "Rhi." She ducked back out for a moment and told the nurse I was awake.

Dang. My lips will have to wait. I looked at them for another moment before turning to the door.

Dad came in right behind Mom.

A doctor—different from the night before—arrived and posed medical questions. Where was the pain? Was my vision blurred? And so on. Mom held my leg at the foot of my bed. Dad agonized behind her. Leone hung back by the window, still within eyesight. The doctor poked on my ribs, and I cringed away from his fingers. I'd forgotten my aches and pains were so intense.

"You have bruises all over you, but your head appears to be your worst injury," the doctor confirmed. "How are you feeling? Is there any pain that is worse than any others?"

"My back is sore... and my leg and arm." I pointed to each. Not to mention my head he had just gouged. "Nothing too bad." I attempted cheerfulness in my voice.

"I want to make sure we do a thorough check now that you are awake," the doctor continued. "I'll have the nurse bring some more painkillers as soon as we are done." His reassuring smile faded as he turned back to my body. "Please tell me if there is pain in any of the places I push on."

His fingers moved around my abdomen prodding on different locations to assess any organ damage. He pressed his stethoscope to my chest. "The test results showed no internal swelling. Even with all the outward signs of trauma to head, your skull shows no fracture. Normally, a blow like this one to your skull causes swelling on the brain."

Mom gasped. I figured she probably already guessed at that information.

I glimpsed Leone's anger in the set of his jaw, the twitch of his muscles, and the quick fade of his eyes to white. Panic swept me as I feared someone might see, but he turned away quickly and stared out my window. I scanned the faces around my bed to see if they had noticed. Everyone stayed focused on me.

"We're going to keep you today. We'll look at releasing you tonight or tomorrow. I want some tests done on mobility and memory, and scan the brain again to see activity levels around the injury. I just don't trust head wounds like this. Okay?" He patted my shoulder.

He nodded to my parents. "Do you have any questions for me?"

"What do we need to be watching for?" Dad asked.

"Lethargy, slurred speech, memory problems, dizziness, tiredness, sickness, those will be the longer term signs to watch for…" I looked toward Leone as the doctor finished filling my parents in. Peppin knows I'm here. If I'm going to meet up with him and my fate, then I want the one thing that I have been deprived of in most of my lives.

"Thank you, doctor." Dad shook his hand before he walked out. I looked back at my parents.

My head throbbed from him poking it again.

A nurse came in and gave me a painkiller.

My eyes began to grow sleepy, and the room started to fade. I picked up the faint conversation of Mom and Dad telling me that Lauriel had been the most wonderful gift. She'd taken great care of them. She brought them food and ate with them—I knew she didn't like to eat. She helped keep the house picked up and did their dishes. The way my mom and dad talked about her, I figured she had moved into "adopted daughter" status. The knowledge made me happy.

When I awoke again, Leone looked into my eyes, a small smile on his lips. "I could hear that you were going to wake soon," he whispered to me.

I glanced around my room and noticed we were alone, and the room was dark, except for the unearthly, blue lights from the monitors surrounding me.

"I talked your mom and dad into getting something to eat. They have hardly left your bedside," he explained.

I nodded. "Can you give me my water?"

He stood, reaching for the cup. As he handed it to me, he bent down and kissed my forehead. He remained in that close position to me, making my body tingle for him.

"I want to talk with you about what Dante and I told the officers. You are free to tell them what you need. I would only caution you about details that would explain his abilities as being inhuman." Leone looked down at his hands and avoided my eye contact. "The doctors would question your sanity if you talked about things."

I nodded. We talked about how they found me, and Amy's body. It looked like Amy had been attacked by a wild animal. I didn't like that deception—I felt the truth needed to lie squarely on Sam's shoulders. I knew I had to follow the same story, though. The rest, Leone let me run through with him, so as to take out any inconsistencies that would make my captor seem inhuman.

Leone sat on my bed. I passed him my glass.

I wiggled into a sitting position and leaned toward him.

"When I spent my days in that cave, I ran through memories that I have of you and I. Private ones. Ones that warmed me in places I never thought possible." I reached up to touch him.

He grabbed my hand.

"Rhi…" He began, but I interrupted.

"I realized, Leone, that I could have died—died in another way, not at the hands of Peppin. The pattern would have shifted, or maybe it was part of that pattern all along. I'm sure sometimes events happened that don't involve being a meal."

Leone nodded at my assessment. I made a mental note to ask him about the times that I died that were more natural, but right now, I knew what I needed.

"When things felt desperate or when Sam raged and I feared I could not remain strong, I would remember your body close to me. I would remember your smell and your feel. I could imagine your touch. Those were the things that kept me going." I pulled him toward me until I could feel his breath on my skin.

"Your lips, Leone. I realized I could die without fulfilling my desire to touch your lips." I reached up and traced them with my fingertips. Bright light threatened to rip from his shirt at my touch.

"Peppin," he said.

"He knows." I stated. I moved my face closer to his. The details of his perfect face outlined with his glow. I traced up his cheek and around his hairline. Ripples of light coursed out from my fingertips. I watched them, fascinated by the prospect of me being the only one able to elicit this response from him.

Before I could take another breath, he brought his arm around my back and cradled me. The back of my head rested in his palm. His lips, so soft and moist, slipped across the top of mine. Shivering where they had touched. His radiance grew and I closed my eyes, anticipating the full weight of his lips. I parted mine and tilted my head back.

He kissed my throat and worked his way to my chin.

I moaned in anticipation. How long I had waited for this.

He kissed my cheek, then my nose. He lingered on my eyelids before working his way down the other cheek. It seemed like he paused to taste my skin, as though he might never have it again.

I felt him pull back for a brief second before his hungry lips pressed tightly to mine.

My body filled with a powerful shock. It emanated from us like a sonic boom.

I faintly heard the wires on my machines as they flew about with the pulse. The plastic blinds rattled in the window. The drape in the room slid in its track. I thought my heart would explode with the intensity. My fingers and toes throbbed, every muscle in my body quivered as if one of the wires I was connected to zapped me.

His luminosity filled the room in a wave of brilliance that penetrated through my closed eyes.

The machines, previously unused, began to peal warnings of doom to the nursing staff.

Even as their feet pounded through the hallway toward my door, my body floated to a dreamy, hungry place that my soul had always known. I did not want it to end.

Eternus Series Book Two

Memor

Kimberli Reynolds

The darkness faded.

Rhiannon recognized the woman holding the infant as Queen Hildegard from the dream the night before.

"He is Carloman." The queen's smile radiated at her guest. "We are blessed so soon after the wedding. God is smiling at us. Carloman, the future King. He will be raised to greatness. It is proof of his destiny to be borne at such time as this."

"To be sure." The queen's companion nodded.

"I will make sure that excuse of a boy, Peppin stays away from him. Unperverted and pure, he will be great."

Quickly the scene flashed.

"I'm here again without permission." Peppin cooed at the infant laying in a wooden cradle. "Yes, I must sneak to see you. You are my secret. Inspite of everything, I will teach you all I know, my brother." Baby Carloman giggled and reached for Peppin. Peppin's smile expanded at it seemed his heart would overflow. He picked his brother from the cradle and placed him on his hip so he could look into his face.

"You don't take notice of this hunched back, do you?" His brother gurgled and reached for his shirt.

Peppin's eyes sparkling with life turned to look at the nursemaid as she focused on the hallway. She looked over at Peppin and nodded to him.

"I only have a few minutes little Carloman" He wiggle the boy as his spoke. The big smile on the baby's face caused a pool of drool to form and the edge of his mouth and threatened to spill over as he cooed at the antics of his big brother.

"I will teach you hunting, and fishing and how to fight with swords." Peppin grabbed Carloman around the chest and raised him into the air. Carloman's feet kicked and bucked in delight. The motion elicited a high wail from the boy that forced Peppin to clutch the boy close to him, for fear of someone hearing.

Peppin glanced at the nursemaid again. She frantically waved toward the cradle, indicating her intention to have the child put back.

Peppin gave the boy a kiss on the cheek as he laid him on the soft blankets. Carloman would not release his grip on Peppin's shirt.

Footsteps could be heard, growing louder as they approached the door.

Peppin fumbled with the tiny fingers, trying not to hurt Carloman.

"I must go little brother." Peppin whispered. "If I am found, I will never be able to come back."

As the little fingers slipped from Peppin's cloak, he glanced again at the nursemaid. Her eyes as wide as a goblet, she pointed to the draperies on the opposite wall.

Peppin raced to the tapestry and darted behind it. Before the cloth had even settled into place around him, a voice spoke at the doorway.

"What on earth are you doing here? I can the baby down the hall. Are you not doing your work?" The voice belonged to the Queen and it was rimmed with irritation.

"Yes, mame. I heard footsteps and thought, if it were you, that you may want to be the one to pick him up. He is in such good spirits."

The queen tossed her head into the air and stomped to the crib. She began cooing to her son and picked him up.

She crossed the room dangerously close to Peppin's hiding spot and sat in a chair. If she had been looking as she walked, she would have seen Peppin as the drapes did not completely touch the wall.

Carloman fussed at her and tried to peel himself from her lap.

She kissed the top of his head. "My king. You will be the great ruler. We will get rid of Peppin soon. You will be free to grow up without the influence of such a weak and deformed bastard."

The curtain moved but he queen did not notice, but the nursemaid stared toward it. Her expression pinched as though she fought back tears. From her point of view, she could see enough of Peppin's face, his hand on his mouth as he stared, wide-eyed and the stone floor, to know the words the queen had spoken had cut him deeply.

The nursemaid spun around and began to busy herself with changing the bedding in Carloman's crib.

Peppin stood there as a stone. By the time the nursemaid had finished, the queen was ready to give the baby to her. She kissed him once more and strode to the door. Without turning around and with head held high she scolded, "Don't let that filthy Peppin touch that boy." and then she disappeared.

When the sound of her footsteps disappeared, Peppin slipped from the curtain. He walked toward the nursemaid and his brother, still in her arms. Peppin stood in front of him for a moment. Carloman reached for him. Peppin touched his hand with his finger, looked into his eyes, then glanced at the nursemaid. He dropped his hand away from his brother and started for the door.

"Peppin," the nursemaid called. Peppin disappeared silently into the hall. "he loves you."

 Kimberli has been published in the *IDAhope Anthology* magazine articles including *Idaho Magazine*. She has written multiple children's stories and short stories. *Eternus* is her first in a series of young adult vampire related sagas. Visit her website at http://Eternus.me.

Book 2
Coming soon!

Watch for book 2 to find out if history repeats!

Visit the website to find out more.

www.EternusSeries.com.

Follow the blog from http://eternityseries.wordpress.com/.